6—

THE BELLY OF PARIS

Émile Zola

THE BELLY OF PARIS

Translated from the French by
Ernest Alfred Vizetelly

SUN &
MOON

CLASSICS

70

LOS ANGELES
SUN & MOON PRESS
1996

Sun & Moon Press
A Program of The Contemporary Arts Educational Project, Inc.
a nonprofit corporation
6026 Wilshire Boulevard, Los Angeles, California 90036

This edition first published in paperback in 1996 by Sun & Moon Press
10 9 8 7 6 5 4 3 2 1
FIRST SUN & MOON PRESS EDITION
Revisions to the Vizetelly translation ©1996 Sun & Moon Press
Originally published as *Le Ventre de Paris*, 1873
Biographical material ©1996 by Sun & Moon Press
All rights reserved

This book was made possible, in part, through an operational grant from the
Andrew W. Mellon Foundation and through contributions to
The Contemporary Arts Educational Project, Inc.,
a nonprofit corporation

Cover: *Fruit* (*Display of Passion*), by Gustave Caillebotte
Museum of Fine Arts, Boston
(Fanny P. Mason Fund in memory of Alice Thevin)
Design: Katie Messborn
Typography: Guy Bennett

LIBRARY OF CONGRESS CATALOGING IN PUBLICATION DATA
Zola, Émile [1840–1902]
[*Ventre de Paris*. English]
The Belly of Paris / Émile Zola; Translated from the French by
Ernest Alfred Vizetelly
p. cm — (Sun & Moon Clasics: 70)
ISBN: 1-55713-066-3
1. Paris (France)–Fiction. I. Vizetelly, Ernest Alfred, 1853–1922. II. Title.
PQ2521.V3E5   1995
843'.8–dc20
95-47613
CIP

Printed in the United States of America on acid-free paper.

Chapter 1

AMID THE DEEP SILENCE and solitude prevailing in the avenue several market-gardeners' carts were climbing the slope which led towards Paris, and the fronts of the houses, asleep behind the dim lines of elms on either side of the road, echoed back the rhythmical jolting of the wheels. At the Neuilly bridge a cart full of cabbages and another full of peas had joined the eight wagons of carrots and turnips coming down from Nanterre; and the horses, left to themselves, had continued plodding along with lowered heads, at a regular though lazy pace, which the ascent of the slope now slackened. The sleeping wagoners, wrapped in woollen cloaks, striped black and grey, and grasping the reins slackly in their closed hands, were stretched at full length on their stomachs atop of the piles of vegetables. Every now and then, a gas lamp, following some patch of gloom, would light up the hobnails of a boot, the blue sleeve of a blouse, or the peak of a cap peering out of the huge florescence of vegetables—red bouquets of carrots, white bouquets of turnips, and the overflowing greenery of peas and cabbages.

And all along the road, and along the neighboring roads, in front and behind, the distant rumbling of vehicles told of the presence of similar contingents of the great caravan which was travelling onward through the gloom and deep slumber of that early hour, lulling the dark city to continued repose with its echoes of passing food.

Madame François's horse, Balthazar, an animal that was far too fat, led the van. He was plodding on, half asleep and wagging his ears, when suddenly, on reaching the Rue de Longchamp, he quivered with fear and came to a dead stop. The horses behind, thus unexpectedly checked, ran their heads against the backs of the carts in front of them, and the procession halted amid a clattering of bolts and chains and the oaths of the awakened wagoners. Madame François, who sat in front of her vehicle with her back to a board which kept her vegetables in position, looked down; but, in the dim light thrown to the left by a small square lantern, which illuminated little beyond one of Balthazar's sheeny flanks, she could distinguish nothing.

"Come, old woman, let's get on!" cried one of the men, who had raised himself to a kneeling position amongst his turnips; "It's only some drunken sot."

Madame François, however, had bent forward and on her right hand had caught sight of a black mass, lying almost under the horse's hoofs, and blocking the road.

"You wouldn't have us drive over a man, would you?" said she, jumping to the ground.

It was indeed a man lying at full length upon the road, with his arms stretched out and his face in the dust. He seemed to be remarkably tall, but as withered as a dry branch, and the wonder was that Balthazar had not broken him in half with a blow from his hoof. Madame François thought that he was dead; but on stooping and taking hold of one of his hands, she found that it was quite warm.

"Poor fellow!" she murmured softly.

The wagoners, however, were getting impatient.

"Hurry up, there!" said the man kneeling amongst the turnips, in a hoarse voice. "He's drunk till he can hold no more, the hog! Shove him into the gutter."

Meantime, the man on the road had opened his eyes. He looked at Madame François with a startled air, but did not move. She herself now thought that he must indeed be drunk.

"You mustn't stop here," she said to him, "or you'll get run over and killed. Where were you going?"

"I don't know," replied the man in a faint voice.

Then, with an effort and an anxious expression, he added: "I was going to Paris; I fell down, and don't remember any more."

Madame François could now see him more distinctly, and he was truly a pitiable object, with his ragged black coat and trousers, through the rents in which you could spy his scraggy limbs. Underneath a black cloth cap, which was drawn low over his brows, as though he were afraid of being recognized, could be seen two large brown eyes, gleaming with peculiar softness in his otherwise stern and harassed countenance. It seemed to Madame François that he was in far too famished a condition to have got drunk.

"And what part of Paris were you going to?" she continued.

The man did not reply immediately. This questioning seemed to distress him. He appeared to be thinking the matter over, but at last said hesitatingly, "Over yonder, towards the markets."

He had now, with great difficulty, got on to his feet again and seemed anxious to resume his journey. But Madame François noticed that he tottered and clung for support to one of the shafts of her wagon.

"Are you tired?" she asked him.

"Yes, very tired," he replied.

Then she suddenly assumed a grumpy tone, as though displeased, and, giving him a push, exclaimed: "Look sharp, then, and climb into my cart. You've made us lose a lot of time. I'm going to the markets, and I'll turn you out there with my vegetables."

Then, as the man seemed inclined to refuse her offer, she pushed him up with her stout arms and bundled him down upon the turnips and carrots.

"Come, now, don't give us any more trouble," she cried angrily. "You are quite enough to provoke one, my good fellow. Don't I tell you that I'm going to the markets? Sleep away up there. I'll wake you when we arrive."

She herself then clambered into the cart again and settled herself with her back against the board, grasping the reins of Balthazar, who started off drowsily, swaying his ears once more. The other wagons followed, and the procession resumed its lazy march through the darkness, while the rhythmical jolting of the wheels again awoke the echoes of the sleepy house fronts, and the wagoners, wrapped in their cloaks, dozed off afresh. The one who had called to Madame François growled out as he lay down: "As if we'd nothing better to do than pick up every drunken sot we come across! You're a scorcher, old woman!"

The wagons rumbled on, and the horses picked their own way, with drooping heads. The stranger whom Madame François had befriended was lying on his stomach, with his long legs lost amongst the turnips which filled the back part of the cart, while his face was buried amid the spreading piles of carrot-bunches. With weary, extended arms he clutched hold of his vegetable couch in fear of being thrown to the ground by one of the wagon's jolts, and his eyes were fixed on the two long lines of gas lamps which stretched away in front of him till they mingled with a swarm of other lights in the distance atop of the slope. Far away on the horizon floated a spreading, whitish vapor, showing where Paris slept amidst the luminous haze of all those flamelets.

"I come from Nanterre, and my name's Madame François," said the market-gardener presently. "Since my poor man died I go to the markets every morning myself. It's a hard life, as you may guess. And who are you?"

"My name's Florent, I come from a distance," replied the stranger, with embarrassment. "Please excuse me, but I'm really so tired that it is painful to me to talk."

He was evidently unwilling to say anything more, and so Madame François relapsed into silence and allowed the reins to fall loosely on the back of Balthazar, who went his way like an animal acquainted with every stone of the road.

Meantime, with his eyes still fixed upon the far-spreading glare of Paris, Florent was pondering over the story which he had refused to communicate to Madame François. After making his escape from Cayenne, to which he had been transported for his participation in the resistance to Louis Napoleon's Coup d'Etat, he had wandered about Dutch Guiana for a couple of years, burning to return to France, yet dreading the Imperial police. At last, however, he once more saw before him the beloved and mighty city which he had so keenly regretted and so ardently longed for. He would hide himself there, he told himself, and again lead the quiet, peaceable life that he had lived years ago. The police would never be any the wiser; everyone would imagine, indeed, that he had died over there, across the sea. Then he thought of his arrival at Havre, where he had landed with only some fifteen francs tied up in a corner of his handkerchief. He had been able to pay for a seat in the coach as far as Rouen, but from that point he had been forced to continue his journey on foot, as he had scarcely thirty sous left of his little store. At Vernon his last money had gone for bread. After that he had no clear recollection of anything. He fancied that he could remember having slept for several hours in a ditch and having shown the papers with which he had provided himself to a gendarme; however, he had only a very confused idea of what had happened. He had left Vernon without any breakfast, seized every now and then with hopeless despair and raging pangs which had driven him to munch the leaves of the hedges as he tramped along. A prey to cramp and fright, his body bent, his sight dimmed, and his feet sore, he had continued his weary march, ever drawn onwards in a semi-unconscious state by a vision of Paris, which, far, far away, beyond the horizon, seemed to be summoning him and waiting for him.

When he at length reached Courbevoie, the night was very dark. Paris, looking like a patch of star-spread sky that had fallen upon the black earth, seemed to him to wear a forbidding aspect, as though angry at his return. Then he felt very faint, and his legs almost gave way beneath him as he descended the hill. As he crossed the Neuilly bridge he sustained himself by clinging to the parapet, and bent over and looked at the Seine rolling inky waves between its dense, massy banks. A red lamp on the water seemed to be watching him with a sanguineous eye. And then he had to climb the hill if he would reach Paris on its summit beyond. The Avenue de Neuilly seemed to him interminable. The hundreds of leagues which he had already travelled were as nothing to it. That bit of a road filled him with despair. He would never be able, he thought, to reach the light-crowned summit. The spacious avenue lay before him with its silence and its darkness, its lines of tall trees and low houses, its broad gray footwalks, speckled with the shadows of overhanging branches, and parted occasionally by the gloomy gaps of side-streets. The squat yellow flames of the gas lamps, standing erect at regular intervals, alone imparted a little life to the lonely wilderness. And Florent seemed to make no progress; the avenue appeared to grow ever longer and longer, to be carrying Paris away into the far depths of the night. At last he fancied that the gas lamps, with their single eyes, were running off on either hand, whisking the road away with them; and then, overcome by vertigo, he stumbled and fell on the roadway like a log.

Now he was lying at ease on his couch of greenery, which seemed to him soft as a feather bed. He had slightly raised his head so as to keep his eyes on the luminous haze which was spreading above the dark roofs which he could divine on the horizon. He was nearing his goal, carried along towards it, with nothing to do but to yield to the leisurely jolts of the wagon; and, free from all further fatigue, he now only suffered from hunger. Hunger, indeed, had once more awoke within him with frightful and nearly intolerable pangs. His limbs seemed to have fallen asleep; he was only conscious of the existence of his stomach, horribly cramped and twisted as by a red-hot iron. The fresh odor of the vegetables, amongst which he was lying, affected him so keenly that he almost fainted away. He strained himself against that piled-up mass of food with all his remaining strength, in order to compress his stomach and silence its groans. And the nine other wagons behind him, with their mountains of cabbages and peas, their piles of artichokes, lettuces, celery, and leeks, seemed to him to be slowly overtaking him, as though to bury him while he was thus tortured by hunger beneath an avalanche of food. Presently the procession halted, and there was a sound of deep voices. They had reached the barriers, and the municipal customs officers were examining the wagons. A moment later Florent entered Paris, in a swoon, lying atop of the carrots, with clenched teeth.

"Hallo! you up there!" Madame François called out sharply.

And as the stranger made no attempt to move, she clambered up and shook him. Florent rose to a sitting posture. He had slept and no longer felt the pangs of hunger, but was dizzy and confused.

"You'll help me to unload, won't you?" Madame François said to him, as she made him get down.

He helped her. A stout man with a felt hat on his head and a badge in the top buttonhole of his coat was striking the ground with a stick and grumbling loudly:

"Come, come, now, make haste! You must get on faster than that! Bring the wagon a little more forward. How many yards' standing have you? Four, isn't it?"

Then he gave a ticket to Madame François, who took some money out of a little canvas bag and handed it to him; whereupon he went off to vent his impatience and tap the ground with his stick a little further away. Madame François took hold of Balthazar's bridle and backed him so as to bring the wheels of the wagon close to the footway. Then, having marked out her four yards with some wisps of straw, after removing the back of the cart, she asked Florent to hand her the vegetables bunch by bunch. She arranged them sort by sort on her standing, setting them out artistically, the "tops" forming a band of greenery around each pile; and it was with remarkable rapidity that she completed her show, which, in the gloom of early morning, looked like some piece of symmetrically colored tapestry. When Florent had handed her a huge bunch of parsley, which he had found at the bottom of the cart, she asked him for still another service. "It would be very kind of you," said she, "if you would look after my goods while I put the horse and cart up. I'm only going a couple of yards, to the Golden Compasses, in the Rue Montorgueil."

Florent told her that she might make herself easy. He preferred to remain still, for his hunger had revived since he had begun to move about. He sat down and leaned against a heap of cabbages beside Madame François's stock. He was all right there, he told himself, and would not go further afield, but wait. His head felt empty, and he had no very clear notion as to where he was. At the beginning of September it is quite dark in the early morning. Around him lighted lanterns were flitting or standing stationary in the depths of the gloom. He was sitting on one side of a broad street which he did not recognize; it stretched far away into the blackness of the night. He could make out nothing plainly, excepting the stock of which he had been left in charge. All around him along the market footways rose similar piles of goods. The middle of the roadway was blocked by huge grey tumbrels, and from one end of the street to the other a sound of heavy breathing passed, indicating the presence of horses which the eye could not distinguish.

Shouts and calls, the noise of falling wood, or of iron chains slipping to the ground, the heavy thud of loads of vegetables discharged from the wagons, and the grating of wheels as the carts were backed against the footways, filled the yet sleepy air with a murmur which foretokened a mighty and sonorous awakening, whose near approach could be felt and heard in the throbbing gloom. Glancing over the pile of cabbages behind him, Florent caught sight of a man wrapped like a parcel in his cloak and snoring away with his head upon some baskets of plums. Nearer to him, on his left, he could distinguish a lad, some ten years old, slumbering between two heaps of endive, with an angelic smile on his face. And as yet there seemed to be nothing on that pavement that was really awake except the lanterns waving from invisible arms and flitting and skipping over the sleep of the vegetables and human beings spread out there in heaps pending the dawn. However, what surprised Florent was the sight of some huge pavilions on either side of the street, pavilions with lofty roofs that seemed to expand and soar out of sight amidst a swarm of gleams. In his weakened state of mind he fancied he beheld a series of enormous, symmetrically built palaces, light and airy as crystal, whose fronts sparkled with countless streaks of light filtering through endless Venetian shutters. Gleaming between the slender pillar shafts, these narrow golden bars seemed like ladders of light mounting to the gloomy line of the lower roofs, and then soaring aloft till they reached the jumble of higher ones, thus describing the open framework of immense square halls, where in the yellow flare of the gas lights a multitude of vague, grey, slumbering things was gathered together.

At last Florent turned his head to look about him, distressed at not knowing where he was and filled with vague uneasiness by the sight of that huge and seemingly fragile vision. And now, as he raised his eyes, he caught sight of the luminous dial and the grey massive pile of Saint Eustache's Church. At this he was much astonished. He was close to Saint Eustache, yet all was novel to him.

However, Madame François had come back again and was engaged in a heated discussion with a man who carried a sack over his shoulder and offered to buy her carrots for a sou a bunch.

"Really, now, you are unreasonable, Lacaille!" said she. "You know quite well that you will sell them again to the Parisians at four and five sous the bunch. Don't tell me that you won't! You may have them for two sous the bunch, if you like."

Then, as the man went off, she continued: "Upon my word, I believe some people think that things grow of their own accord! Let him go and find carrots at a sou the bunch elsewhere, tipsy scoundrel that he is! He'll come back again presently, you'll see."

These last remarks were addressed to Florent. And, seating herself by his side, Madame François resumed: "If you've been a long time away from Paris, you perhaps don't know the new markets. They haven't been built for more than five years at the most. That pavilion you see there beside us is the flower and fruit market. The fish and poultry markets are farther away, and over there behind us come the vegetables and the butter and cheese. There are six pavilions on this side, and on the other side, across the road, there are four more, with the meat and the tripe stalls. It's an enormous place, but it's horribly cold in the winter. They talk about pulling down the houses near the corn market to make room for two more pavilions. But perhaps you know all this?"

"No, indeed," replied Florent; "I've been abroad. And what's the name of that big street in front of us?"

"Oh, that's a new street. It's called the Rue du Pont Neuf. It leads from the Seine through here to the Rue Montmartre and the Rue Montorgueil. You would soon have recognized where you were if it had been daylight."

Madame François paused and rose, for she saw a woman bending down to examine her turnips. "Ah, is that you, Mother Chantemesse?" she said in a friendly way.

Florent meanwhile glanced towards the Rue Montorgueil. It was there that a body of police officers had arrested him on the night of December 4. He had been walking along the Boulevard Montmartre at about two o'clock, quietly making his way through the crowd, and smiling at the number of soldiers that the Elysée had sent into the streets to awe the people, when the military suddenly began making a clean sweep of the thoroughfare, shooting folks down at close range during a quarter of an hour. Jostled and knocked to the ground, Florent fell at the corner of the Rue Vivienne and knew nothing further of what happened, for the panic-stricken crowd, in their wild terror of being shot, trampled over his body. Presently, hearing everything quiet, he made an attempt to rise; but across him there lay a young woman in a pink bonnet, whose shawl had slipped aside, allowing her chemisette, pleated in little tucks, to be seen. Two bullets had pierced the upper part of her bosom; and when Florent gently removed the poor creature to free his legs, two streamlets of blood oozed from her wounds on to his hands. Then he sprang up with a sudden bound and rushed madly away, hatless and with his hands still wet with blood. Until evening he wandered about the streets, with his head swimming, always seeing the young woman lying across his legs with her pale face, her blue staring eyes, her distorted lips, and her expression of astonishment at meeting death so suddenly. He was a shy, timid fellow. Although thirty years old he had never dared to stare women in the face; and now, for the rest of his life, he was to have that one fixed in his heart and memory. He felt as though he had lost some loved one of his own.

In the evening, without knowing how he had got there, still dazed and horrified as he was by the terrible scenes of the afternoon, he had found himself at a wine shop in the Rue Montorgueil, where several men were drinking and talking of throwing up barricades. He went away with them, helped them to tear up a few paving stones, and seated himself on the barricade, weary with his long wandering through the streets, and reflecting that he would fight when the soldiers came up. However, he had not even a knife with him, and was still bare-headed. Towards eleven o'clock he dozed off and in his sleep could see the two holes in the dead woman's white chemisette glaring at him like eyes reddened by tears and blood. When he awoke he found himself in the grasp of four police officers, who were pummelling him with their fists. The men who had built the barricade had fled. The police officers treated him with still greater violence, and indeed almost strangled him when they noticed that his hands were stained with blood. It was the blood of the young woman.

Florent raised his eyes to the luminous dial of Saint Eustache with his mind so full of these recollections that he did not notice the position of the pointers. It was, however, nearly four o'clock. The markets were as yet wrapped in sleep. Madame François was still talking to old Madame Chantemesse, both standing and arguing about the price of the turnips, and Florent now called to mind how narrowly he had escaped being shot over there by the wall of Saint Eustache. A detachment of gendarmes had just blown out the brains of five unhappy fellows caught at a barricade in the Rue Grenéta. The five corpses were lying on the footway, at a spot where he thought he could now distinguish a heap of rosy radishes. He himself had escaped being shot merely because the policemen only carried swords. They took him to a neighboring police station and gave the officer in charge a scrap of paper, on which were these words written in pencil: "Taken with blood-stained hands. Very dangerous." Then he had been dragged from station to station till the morning came. The scrap of paper accompanied him wherever he went. He was manacled and guarded as though he were a raving madman. At the station in the Rue de la Lingerie some tipsy soldiers wanted to shoot him; and they had already lighted a lantern with that object when the order arrived for the prisoners to be taken to the depot of the Préfecture of Police. Two days afterwards he found himself in a casemate of the fort of Bicêtre. Ever since then he had been suffering from hunger. He had felt hungry in the casemate, and the pangs of hunger had never since left him. A hundred men were pent in the depths of that cellarlike dungeon, where, scarce able to breathe, they devoured the few mouthfuls of bread that were thrown to them, like so many captive wild beasts.

When Florent was brought before an investigating magistrate, without anyone to defend him, and without any evidence being adduced, he was accused of belonging to a secret society; and when he swore that this was untrue, the magistrate produced the scrap of paper from amongst the documents before him: "Taken with blood-stained hands. Very dangerous." That was quite sufficient. He was condemned to transportation. Six weeks afterwards, one January night, a jailer awoke him and locked him up in a courtyard with more than four hundred other prisoners. An hour later this first detachment started for the pontoons and exile, handcuffed and guarded by a double file of gendarmes with loaded muskets. They crossed the Austerlitz bridge, followed the line of the boulevards, and so reached the terminus of the Western Railway line. It was a joyous carnival night. The windows of the restaurants on the boulevards glittered with lights. At the top of the Rue Vivienne, just at the spot where he always saw the young woman lying dead—that unknown young woman whose image he always bore with him—he now beheld a large carriage in which a party of masked women, with bare shoulders and laughing voices, were venting their impatience at being detained, and expressing their horror of that endless procession of convicts. The whole of the way from Paris to Havre the prisoners never received a mouthful of bread or a drink of water. The officials had forgotten to give them their rations before starting, and it was not till thirty-six hours afterwards, when they had been stowed away in the hold of the frigate *Canada,* that they at last broke their fast.

No, Florent had never again been free from hunger. He recalled all the past to mind, but could not recollect a single hour of satiety. He had become dry and withered; his stomach seemed to have shrunk; his skin clung to his bones. And now that he was back in Paris once more, he found it fat and sleek and flourishing, teeming with food in the midst of the darkness. He had returned to it on a couch of vegetables; he lingered in its midst encompassed by unknown masses of food which continually increased and disquieted him. Had that happy carnival night continued throughout those seven years, then? Once again he saw the glittering windows on the boulevards, the laughing women, the luxurious, greedy city which he had quitted on that far-away January night; and it seemed to him that everything had expanded and increased in harmony with those huge markets, whose gigantic breathing, still heavy from the indigestion of the previous day, he now began to hear.

Old Mother Chantemesse had by this time made up her mind to buy a dozen bunches of turnips. She put them in her apron, which she held closely pressed to her person, thus making herself look even more corpulent than she was; and for some time longer she lingered there, still gossiping in a drawling voice. When at last she went away, Madame François again sat down by the side of Florent.

"Poor old Mother Chantemesse!" she said; "she must be at least seventy-two. I can remember her buying turnips of my father when I was a mere chit. And she hasn't a relation in the world; no one but a young hussy whom she picked up I don't know where and who does nothing but bring her trouble. Still, she manages to live, selling in small quantities and clearing her couple of francs profit a day. For my own part, I'm sure that I could never spend my days on the foot-pavement in this horrid Paris! And she hasn't even any relations here!"

"You have some relations in Paris, I suppose?" she asked presently, seeing that Florent seemed disinclined to talk.

Florent did not appear to hear her. A feeling of distrust came back to him. His head was teeming with old stories of the police, stories of spies prowling about at every street corner, and of women selling the secrets which they managed to worm out of the unhappy fellows they deluded. Madame François was sitting close beside him and certainly looked perfectly straightforward and honest, with her big calm face, above which was bound a black and yellow handkerchief. She seemed about five and thirty years of age, and was somewhat stoutly built, with a certain hardy beauty due to her life in the fresh air. A pair of black eyes, which beamed with kindly tenderness, softened the more masculine characteristics of her person. She certainly was inquisitive, but her curiosity was probably well-meant.

"I've a nephew in Paris," she continued, without seeming

at all offended by Florent's silence. "He's turned out badly though and has enlisted. It's a pleasant thing to have somewhere to go to and stay at, isn't it? I dare say there's a big surprise in store for your relations when they see you. But it's always a pleasure to welcome one of one's own people back again, isn't it?"

She kept her eyes fixed upon him while she spoke, doubtless feeling compassion for his extreme scragginess; fancying, too, that there was a "gentleman" inside those old black rags, and so not daring to slip a piece of silver into his hand. At last, however, she timidly murmured: "All the same, if you should happen just at present to be in want of anything—"

But Florent checked her with uneasy pride. He told her that he had everything he required and had a place to go to. She seemed quite pleased to hear this, and, as though to tranquilize herself concerning him, repeated several times: "Well, well, in that case you've only to wait till daylight."

A large bell at the corner of the fruit market, just over Florent's head, now began to ring. The slow regular peals seemed to dissipate gradually the slumber that yet lingered all around. Carts were still arriving, and the shouts of the wagoners, the cracking of their whips, and the grinding of the paving stones beneath the iron-bound wheels and the horses' shoes sounded with an increasing din. The carts could now only advance by a series of spasmodic jolts and stretched in a long line, one behind another, until they were lost to sight in the distant darkness, from where a confused roar ascended.

Unloading was in progress all along the Rue du Pont Neuf, the vehicles being drawn up close to the edge of the footways, while their teams stood motionless in close order as at a horse fair. Florent felt interested in one enormous tumbrel which was piled up with magnificent cabbages and had only been backed to the curb with the greatest difficulty. Its load towered above a lofty gas lamp whose bright light fell full upon the broad leaves which looked like pieces of dark green velvet, scalloped and goffered. A young peasant girl, some sixteen years old, in a blue linen jacket and cap, had climbed on to the tumbrel, where, buried in the cabbages to her shoulders, she took them one by one and threw them to somebody concealed in the shade below. Every now and then the girl would slip and vanish, overwhelmed by an avalanche of the vegetables, but her rosy nose soon reappeared amidst the teeming greenery, and she broke into a laugh while the cabbages again flew down between Florent and the gas lamp. He counted them mechanically as they fell. When the cart was emptied he felt worried.

The piles of vegetables on the pavement now extended to the verge of the roadway. Between the heaps, the market-gardeners left narrow paths to enable people to pass along. The whole of the wide footway was covered from end to end with dark mounds. As yet, in the sudden dancing gleams of light from the lanterns, you only just spied the luxuriant fullness of the bundles of artichokes, the delicate green of the lettuces, the rosy coral of the carrots, and dull ivory of the turnips. And these gleams of rich color flitted along the heaps, according as the lanterns came and went. The footway was now becoming populated: a crowd of people had awakened and was moving here and there amid the vegetables, stopping at times, and chattering and shouting. In the distance a loud voice could be heard crying, "Endive! who's got endive?" The gates of the pavilion devoted to the sale of ordinary vegetables had just been opened; and the retail dealers who had stalls there, with white caps on their heads, fichus knotted over their black jackets, and skirts pinned up to keep them from getting soiled, now began to secure their stock for the day, depositing their purchases in some huge porters' baskets placed upon the ground. Between the roadway and the pavilion these baskets were to be seen coming and going on all sides, knocking against the crowded heads of the bystanders, who resented the pushing with coarse expressions, while all around was a clamor of voices growing hoarse by prolonged wrangling over a sou or two. Florent was astonished by the calmness which the female market-gardeners, with bandannas and bronzed faces, displayed amidst all this garrulous bargaining of the markets.

Behind him, on the footway of the Rue Rambuteau, fruit was being sold. Hampers and low baskets covered with canvas or straw stood there in long lines, a strong odor of over-ripe mirabelle plums was wafted hither and thither. At last a subdued and gentle voice, which he had heard for some time past, induced him to turn his head, and he saw a charming darksome little woman sitting on the ground and bargaining.

"Come, now, Marcel," said she, "you'll take a hundred sous, won't you?" The man to whom she was speaking was closely wrapped in his cloak and made no reply; however, after a silence of five minutes or more, the young woman returned to the charge.

"Come now, Marcel; a hundred sous for that basket there, and four francs for the other one; that'll make nine francs altogether."

Then came another interval.

"Well, tell me what you will take."

"Ten francs. You know that well enough already; I told you so before. But what have you done with your Jules this morning, La Sarriette?"

The young woman began to laugh as she took a handful of small change out of her pocket.

"Oh," she replied, "Jules is still in bed. He says that men were not intended to work."

She paid for the two baskets and carried them into the

fruit pavilion, which had just been opened. The market buildings still retained their gloom-wrapped aspect of airy fragility, streaked with the thousand lines of light that gleamed from the venetian shutters. People were beginning to pass along the broad covered streets intersecting the pavilions, but the more distant buildings still remained deserted amid the increasing buzz of life on the footways. By Saint Eustache the bakers and wine-sellers were taking down their shutters, and the ruddy shops, with their gaslights flaring, showed like gaps of fire in the gloom in which the gray house fronts were yet steeped. Florent noticed a baker's shop on the left-hand side of the Rue Montorgueil, replete and golden with its last baking, and fancied he could catch the pleasant smell of the hot bread. It was now half-past four.

Madame François by this time had disposed of nearly all her stock. She had only a few bunches of carrots left when Lacaille once more made his appearance with his sack.

"Well," said he, "will you take a sou now?"

"I knew I should see you again," the good woman quietly answered. "You'd better take all I have left. There are seventeen bunches."

"That makes seventeen sous."

"No; thirty-four."

At last they agreed to fix the price at twenty-five sous. Madame François was anxious to be off.

"He'd been keeping his eye upon me all the time," she said to Florent, when Lacaille had gone off with the carrots in his sack. "That old rogue runs things down all over the markets, and he often waits till the last peal of the bell before spending four sous in purchases. Oh, these Paris folk! They'll wrangle and argue for an hour to save half a sou, and then go off and empty their purses at the wine shop."

Whenever Madame François talked of Paris she always spoke in a tone of disdain and referred to the city as though it were some ridiculous, contemptible, far-away place, in which she only condescended to set foot at nighttime.

"There!" she continued, sitting down again, beside Florent, on some vegetables belonging to a neighbor, "I can get away now."

Florent bent his head. He had just committed a theft. When Lacaille went off he had caught sight of a carrot lying on the ground, and having picked it up he was holding it tightly in his right hand. Behind him some bundles of celery and bunches of parsley were diffusing pungent odors which painfully affected him.

"Well, I'm off now!" said Madame François.

However, she felt interested in this stranger, and could divine that he was suffering there on that foot-pavement, from which he had never stirred. She made him fresh offers of assistance, but he again refused them, with a still more bitter show of pride. He even got up and remained standing to prove that he was quite strong again. Then, as Madame François turned her head away, he put the carrot to his mouth. But he had to remove it for a moment, in spite of the terrible longing which he felt to dig his teeth into it; for Madame François turned round again and, looking him full in the face, began to question him with her good-natured womanly curiosity. Florent, to avoid speaking, merely answered by nods and shakes of the head. Then, slowly and gently, he began to eat the carrot.

The worthy woman was at last on the point of going off, when a powerful voice exclaimed close beside her, "Good morning, Madame François."

The speaker was a slim young man, with big bones and a big head. His face was bearded, and he had a very delicate nose and narrow sparkling eyes. He wore on his head a rusty, battered, black felt hat, and was buttoned up in an immense overcoat, which had once been of a soft chestnut hue, but which rain had discolored and streaked with long greenish

stains. Somewhat bent, and quivering with a nervous restlessness which was doubtless habitual with him, he stood
there in a pair of heavy laced shoes, and the shortness of his
trousers allowed a glimpse of his coarse blue hose.

"Good morning, Monsieur Claude," the market-gardener
replied cheerfully. "I expected you, you know, last Monday,
and, as you didn't come, I've taken care of your canvas for
you. I've hung it up on a nail in my room."

"You are really very kind, Madame François. I'll go to
finish that study of mine one of these days. I wasn't able to
go on Monday. Has your big plum tree still got all its leaves?"

"Yes, indeed."

"I wanted to know, because I mean to put it in a corner of
the picture. It will come in nicely by the side of the fowlhouse.
I have been thinking about it all the week. What lovely vegetables there are in the market this morning! I came down
very early, expecting a fine sunrise effect upon all these heaps
of cabbages."

With a wave of the arm he indicated the footway.

"Well, well, I must be off now," said Madame François.
"Good-bye, for the present. We shall meet again soon, I hope,
Monsieur Claude."

However, as she turned to go, she introduced Florent to
the young artist.

"This gentleman, it seems, has just come from a distance,"
said she. "He feels quite lost in your scampish Paris. I dare
say you might be of service to him."

Then she at last took her departure, feeling pleased at
having left the two men together. Claude looked at Florent
with a feeling of interest. That tall, slight, wavy figure seemed
to him original. Madame François's hasty presentation was
in his eyes quite sufficient, and he addressed Florent with
the easy familiarity of a lounger accustomed to all sorts of
chance encounters.

"I'll accompany you," he said; "which way are you going?" Florent felt ill at ease; he was not inclined to unbosom himself so readily. However, ever since his arrival in Paris, a question had been trembling on his lips, and now he ventured to ask it, with the evident fear of receiving an unfavorable reply. "Is the Rue Pirouette still in existence?"

"Oh, yes," answered the artist. "A very curious corner of old Paris is the Rue Pirouette. It twists and turns like a dancing-girl, and the houses bulge out like pot-bellied gluttons. I've made an etching of it that isn't half bad. I'll show it to you when you come to see me. Is it to the Rue Pirouette that you want to go?"

Florent, who felt easier and more cheerful now that he knew the street still existed, declared that he did not want to go there; in fact, he did not want to go anywhere in particular. All his distrust awoke into fresh life at Claude's insistence.

"Oh! never mind," said the artist, "let's go to the Rue Pirouette all the same. It has such a fine color at night time. Come along; it's only a couple of yards away."

Florent felt constrained to follow him, and the two men walked off, side by side, stepping over the hampers and vegetables like a couple of old friends. On the footway of the Rue Rambuteau there were some immense heaps of cauliflowers, symmetrically piled up like so many cannon-balls. The soft white flowers spread out like huge roses in the midst of their thick green leaves, and the piles had something of the appearance of bridal bouquets ranged in a row in colossal flower-stands. Claude stopped in front of them, venting cries of admiration.

Then, on turning into the Rue Pirouette, which was just opposite, he pointed out each house to his companion, and explained his views concerning it. There was only a single gas lamp, burning in a corner. The buildings, which had settled down and swollen, threw their penthouses forward in such a way as to justify Claude's allusion to pot-bellied gluttons, while their gables receded, and on either side they clung to their neighbors for support. Three or four, however, standing in gloomy recesses, appeared to be on the point of toppling forward. The solitary gas lamp illumined one which was snowy with a fresh coat of whitewash, suggesting some flabby, broken-down old dowager, powdered and bedaubed in the hope of appearing young. Then the others stretched away into the darkness, bruised, dented, and cracked, green with the fall of water from their roofs, and displaying such an extraordinary variety of attitudes and tints that Claude could not refrain from laughing as he contemplated them.

Florent, however, came to a stand at the corner of the Rue de Mondétour, in front of the last house but one on the left. Here the three floors, each with two shutterless windows, having little white curtains closely drawn, seemed wrapped in sleep; but, up above, a light could be seen flitting behind the curtains of a tiny gable casement. However, the sight of the shop beneath the penthouse seemed to fill Florent with the deepest emotion. It was kept by a dealer in cooked vegetables and was just being opened. At its far end some metal pans were glittering, while on several earthen ones in the window there was a display of cooked spinach and endive, reduced to a paste and arranged in conical mounds from which customers were served with shovel-like carvers of white metal, only the handles of which were visible. This sight seemed to rivet Florent to the ground with surprise. He evidently could not recognize the place. He read the name of the shopkeeper, Godebœuf, which was painted on a red sign-board up above, and remained quite overcome by consternation. His arms dangling beside him, he began to examine the cooked spinach, with the despairing air of one on whom some supreme misfortune falls.

However, the gable casement was now opened, and a little old woman leaned out of it, and looked first at the sky and then at the markets in the distance.

"Ah, Mademoiselle Saget is an early riser," exclaimed Claude, who had just raised his head. And, turning to his companion, he added: "I once had an aunt living in that house. It's a regular hive of tittle-tattle! Ah, the Méhudins are stirring now, I see. There's a light on the second floor."

Florent would have liked to question his companion, but the latter's long discolored overcoat gave him a disquieting appearance. So without a word Florent followed him, while he went on talking about the Méhudins. These Méhudins were fish-girls, it seemed; the elder one was a magnificent creature, while the younger one, who sold fresh-water fish, reminded Claude of one of Murillo's virgins whenever he saw her standing with her fair face amidst her carps and eels.

From this Claude went on to remark with asperity that Murillo painted like an ignoramus. But all at once he stopped short in the middle of the street.

"Come!" he exclaimed, "tell me where it is that you want to go."

"I don't want to go anywhere just at present," replied Florent in confusion. "Let's go wherever you like."

Just as they were leaving the Rue Pirouette, someone called to Claude from a wine shop at the corner of the street. The young man went in, dragging Florent with him. The shutters had been taken down on one side only, and the gas was still burning in the sleepy atmosphere of the shop. A forgotten napkin and some cards that had been used in the previous evening's play were still lying on the tables; and the fresh breeze that streamed in through the open door-way freshened the close, warm vinous air. The landlord, Monsieur Lebigre, was serving his customers. He wore a sleeved waistcoat, and his fat regular features, fringed by an untidy beard, were still pale with sleep. Standing in front of the counter, groups of men, with heavy, tired eyes, were drinking, coughing, and spitting, while trying to rouse themselves by the aid of white wine and brandy. Among them Florent recognized Lacaille, whose sack now overflowed with various sorts of vegetables. He was taking his third dram with a friend, who was telling him a long story about the purchase of a hamper of potatoes. When he had emptied his glass, he went to chat with Monsieur Lebigre in a little glazed compartment at the end of the room, where the gas had not yet been lighted.

"What will you take?" Claude asked of Florent.

He had on entering grasped the hand of the person who had called out to him. This was a market-porter, a well-built young man of twenty-two at the most. His cheeks and chin were clean-shaven, but he wore a small moustache, and looked a sprightly, strapping fellow with his broad-brimmed hat covered with chalk, and his wool-worked neck-piece, the straps falling from which tightened his short blue blouse. Claude, who called him Alexandre, patted his arms, and asked him when they were going to Charentonneau again. Then they talked about a grand excursion they had made together in a boat on the Marne, when they had eaten a rabbit for supper in the evening.

"Well, what will you take?" Claude again asked Florent.

The latter looked at the counter in great embarrassment. At one end of it some stoneware pots, encircled with brass bands and containing punch and hot wine, were standing over the short blue flames of a gas stove. Florent at last confessed that a glass of something warm would be welcome. Monsieur Lebigre thereupon served them with three glasses of punch. In a basket near the pots were some smoking-hot rolls which had only just arrived. However, as neither of the others took one, Florent likewise refrained, and drank his punch. He felt it slipping down into his empty stomach, like a stream of molten lead. It was Alexandre who paid for the round.

"He's a fine fellow, that Alexandre!" said Claude, when he and Florent found themselves alone again on the footway of the Rue Rambuteau. "He's a very amusing companion to take into the country. He's fond of showing his strength. And then he's so magnificently built! I have seen him stripped. Ah, if I could only get him to pose for me in the nude out in the open air! Well, we'll go and take a turn through the markets now, if you like."

Florent followed, yielding entirely to his new friend's guidance. A bright glow at the far end of the Rue Rambuteau announced the break of day. The far-spreading voice of the markets was becoming more sonorous, and every now and then the peals of a bell ringing in some distant pavilion mingled with the swelling, rising clamor. Claude and Florent entered one of the covered streets between the fish and poultry pavilions. Florent raised his eyes and looked at the lofty vault overhead, the inner timbers of which glistened amidst a black lacework of iron supports. As he turned into the great central thoroughfare he pictured himself in some strange town, with its various districts and suburbs, promenades and streets, squares and cross-roads, all suddenly placed under shelter on a rainy day by the whim of some gigantic power. The deep gloom brooding in the hollows of the roofs multiplied, as it were, the forest of pillars, and infinitely increased the number of the delicate ribs, railed galleries, and transparent shutters. And over the phantom city and far away into the depths of the shade, a teeming, flowering vegetation of luxuriant metal-work, with spindle-shaped stems and twining knotted branches, covered the vast expanse as with the foliage of some ancient forest. Several departments of the markets still slumbered behind their closed iron gates. The butter and poultry pavilions displayed rows of little trellised stalls and long alleys, which lines of gaslights showed to be deserted. The fish market, however, had just been opened, and women were flitting back and forth among the white slabs littered with shadowy hampers and cloths. Among the vegetables and fruit and flowers the noise and bustle were gradually increasing. The whole place was by degrees waking up, from the popular quarter where the cabbages are piled at four o'clock in the morning, to the lazy and wealthy district which only hangs up its pullets and pheasants when the hands of the clock point to eight.

The great covered alleys were now teeming with life. All along the footways on both sides of the road there were still many market-gardeners, with other small growers from the environs of Paris, who displayed baskets containing their "gatherings" of the previous evening—bundles of vegetables and clusters of fruit. While the crowd incessantly paced this way and that, vehicles of different kinds entered the covered ways, where their drivers checked the trot of the bell-jingling horses. Two of these vehicles barred the road; and Florent, in order to pass them, had to press against some dingy sacks, like coal-sacks in appearance, and so numerous and heavy that the axle-trees of the vans bent beneath them. They were quite damp and exhaled a fresh odor of seaweed. From a rent low down in the side of one of them a black stream of big mussels was trickling.

Florent and Claude had now to pause at every step. The fish was arriving, and one after another the drays of the railway companies drove up laden with wooden cages full of the hampers and baskets that had come by train from the sea coast. And to get out of the way of the fish drays, which became more and more numerous and disquieting, the artist and Florent rushed among the wheels of the drays laden with butter and eggs and cheese, huge yellow vehicles bearing colored lanterns, and drawn by four horses. The market-porters carried the cases of eggs, and baskets of cheese and butter, into the auction pavilion, where clerks were making entries in notebooks by the light of the gas.

Claude was quite charmed with all this uproar and forgot everything to gaze at some effect of light, some group of blouses, or the picturesque unloading of a cart. At last they extricated themselves from the crowd, and as they continued on their way along the main artery they presently found themselves amidst an exquisite perfume which seemed to be following them. They were in the cut-flower market. All over the footways, to the right and left, women were seated in front of large rectangular baskets full of bunches of roses, violets, dahlias, and marguerites. At times the clumps darkened and looked like splotches of blood, at others they brightened into silvery grays of the softest tones. A lighted candle, standing near one basket, set amidst the general blackness quite a melody of color—the bright variegations of marguerites, the blood-red crimson of dahlias, the bluey purple of violets, and the warm flesh tints of roses. And nothing could have been sweeter or more suggestive of springtime than this soft breath of perfume encountered on the footway, on emerging from the sharp odors of the fishmarket and the pestilential smell of the butter and the cheese.

Claude and Florent turned round and strolled about, loitering among the flowers. They halted with some curiosity before several women who were selling bunches of fern and bundles of vine-leaves, neatly tied up in packets of five-and-twenty. Then they turned down another covered alley, which was almost deserted, and where their footsteps echoed as though they had been walking through a church. Here they found a little cart, scarcely larger than a wheelbarrow, to which was harnessed a diminutive donkey, who, no doubt, felt bored, for at sight of them he began braying with such prolonged and sonorous force that the vast roofing of the markets fairly trembled. Then the horses began to neigh in reply, there was a sound of pawing and tramping, a distant uproar, which swelled, rolled along, then died away.

Meantime, in the Rue Berger in front of them, Claude and Florent perceived a number of bare, frontless, salesmen's shops, where, by the light of flaring gas-jets, they could distinguish piles of hampers and fruit, enclosed by three dirty walls which were covered with addition sums in pencil. And the two wanderers were still standing there, contemplating this scene, when they noticed a well-dressed woman huddled up in a cab which looked quite lost and forlorn in the block of carts as it stealthily made its way onwards.

"There's Cinderella coming back without her slippers," remarked Claude with a smile.

They began chatting together as they went back towards the markets. Claude whistled as he strolled along with his hands in his pockets and expatiated on his love for this mountain of food which rises every morning in the very center of Paris. He prowled about the footways night after night, dreaming of colossal still-life subjects, paintings of an extraordinary character. He had even started on one, having got his friend Marjolin and that jade Cadine to pose for him; but it was hard work to paint those confounded vegetables and fruit and fish and meat—they were all so beautiful! Florent listened to the artist's enthusiastic talk with a void and hunger-aching stomach. It did not seem to occur to Claude that all those things were intended to be eaten. Their charm for him lay in their color. Suddenly, however, he ceased speaking and, with a gesture that was habitual to him, tightened the long red sash which he wore under his green-stained coat.

And then with a sly expression he resumed:

"Besides, I breakfast here, through my eyes, at any rate, and that's better than getting nothing at all. Sometimes, when I've forgotten to dine on the previous day, I treat myself to a perfect fit of indigestion in the morning by watching the carts arrive here laden with all sorts of good things. On such mornings as those I love my vegetables more than ever. Ah! the exasperating part, the rank injustice of it all, is that those rascally Philistines really eat these things!"

Then he went on to tell Florent of a supper to which a friend had treated him at Baratte's on a day of affluence. They had partaken of oysters, fish, and game. But Baratte's had sadly fallen, and all the carnival life of the old Marché des Innocents was now buried. In its place they had those huge central markets, that colossus of ironwork, that new and wonderful town. Fools might say what they liked; it was the embodiment of the spirit of the times. Florent, however, could not at first make out whether he was condemning the picturesqueness of Baratte's or its good cheer.

But Claude next began to inveigh against romanticism. He preferred his piles of vegetables, he said, to the rags of the middle ages; and he ended by reproaching himself with guilty weakness in making an etching of the Rue Pirouette. All those grimy old places ought to be levelled to the ground, he declared, and modern houses ought to be built in their stead.

"There!" he exclaimed, coming to a halt, "look at the corner of the footway over there! Isn't that a picture ready-made, ever so much more human and natural than all their confounded consumptive daubs?"

Along the covered way women were now selling hot soup and coffee. At one corner of the foot-pavement a large circle of customers clustered round a vendor of cabbage soup. The bright tin caldron, full of broth, was steaming over a little low stove, through the holes of which came the pale glow of the embers. From a napkin-lined basket the woman took some thin slices of bread and dropped them into yellow cups; then with a ladle she filled the cups with the liquid. Around her were saleswomen neatly dressed, market-gardeners in blouses, porters with coats soiled by the loads they had carried, poor ragged vagabonds—in fact, all the early hungry ones of the markets, eating, and scalding their mouths, and drawing back their chins to avoid soiling them with the drippings from their spoons. The delighted artist blinked and sought a point of view so as to get a good *ensemble* of the picture. That cabbage soup, however, exhaled a very strong odor. Florent, for his part, turned his head away, distressed by the sight of the full cups which the customers emptied in silence, glancing around them the while like suspicious animals. As the woman began serving a fresh customer, Claude himself was affected by the odorous steam of the soup, which was wafted full in his face.

He again tightened his sash, half amused and half annoyed. Then resuming his walk, and alluding to the punch paid for by Alexandre, he said to Florent in a low voice:

"It's very odd, but have you ever noticed that although a man can always find somebody to treat him to something to drink, he can never find a soul who will stand him anything to eat?"

The dawn was now rising. The houses on the Boulevard de Sébastopol at the end of the Rue de la Cossonnerie were still black; but above the sharp line of their slate roofs a patch of pale blue sky, circumscribed by the arch-pieces of the covered way, showed like a gleaming half-moon. Claude, who had been bending over some grated openings on a level with the ground, through which a glimpse could be obtained of deep cellars where gaslights glimmered, now glanced up into the air between the lofty pillars, as though scanning the dark roofs which fringed the clear sky. Then he halted again, with his eyes fixed on one of the light iron ladders which connect the superposed market roofs and give access from one to the other. Florent asked him what he was seeking there.

"I'm looking for that scamp of a Marjolin," replied the artist. "He's sure to be in some guttering up there, unless, indeed, he's been spending the night in the poultry cellars. I want him to give me a sitting."

Then he went on to relate how a market saleswoman had found his friend Marjolin one morning in a pile of cabbages, and how Marjolin had grown up in all liberty on the surrounding footways. When an attempt had been made to send him to school he had fallen ill, and it had been necessary to bring him back to the markets. He knew every nook and corner of them and loved them with a filial affection, leading the agile life of a squirrel in that forest of ironwork. He and Cadine, the hussy whom Mother Chantemesse had picked up one night in the old Marché des Innocents, made a pretty couple—he, a splendid foolish fellow, as glowing as a Rubens, with a ruddy down on his skin which attracted the sunlight; and she, slight and sly, with a comical face under her tangle of black curly hair. While talking Claude quickened his steps and soon brought his companion back to Saint Eustache again. Florent, whose legs were once more giving way, dropped upon a bench near the omnibus office. The morning air was freshening. At the far end of the Rue Rambuteau rosy gleams were streaking the milky sky, which higher up was slashed by broad gray rifts. Such was the sweet balsamic scent of this dawn, that Florent for a moment fancied himself in the open country, on the brow of a hill. But behind the bench Claude pointed out to him the many aromatic herbs and bulbs on sale. All along the footway skirting the tripe market there were, so to say, fields of thyme and lavender, garlic and shallots; and round the young plane-trees on the pavement the vendors had twined long branches of laurel, forming trophies of greenery. The strong scent of the laurel leaves prevailed over every other odor.

At present the luminous dial of Saint Eustache was paling as a night-light does when surprised by the dawn. The gas jets in the wine shops in the neighboring streets went out one by one, like stars extinguished by the brightness. And Florent gazed at the vast markets now gradually emerging from the gloom, from the dreamland in which he had beheld them, stretching out their ranges of open palaces. Greenish-grey in hue, they looked more solid now, and even more colossal with their prodigious masting of columns upholding an endless expanse of roofs. They rose up in geometrically shaped masses; and when all the inner lights had been extinguished and the square uniform buildings were steeped in the rising dawn, they seemed typical of some gigantic modern machine, some engine, some caldron for the supply of a whole people, some colossal belly, bolted and riveted, built up of wood and glass and iron, and endowed with all the elegance and power of some mechanical motive appliance working there with flaring furnaces, and wild, bewildering revolutions of wheels.

Claude, however, had enthusiastically sprung onto the bench and stood upon it. He compelled his companion to admire the effect of the dawn rising over the vegetables. There was a perfect sea of these extending between the two clusters of pavilions from Saint Eustache to the Rue des Halles. And in the two open spaces at either end the flood of greenery rose to even greater height and quite submerged the pavements. The dawn appeared slowly, softly grey in hue, and spreading a light water-color tint over everything. These surging piles akin to hurrying waves, this river of verdure rushing along the roadway like an autumn torrent, assumed delicate shadowy tints—tender violet, blush-rose, and green yellow, all the soft, light hues which at sunrise make the sky look like a canopy of shot silk. And by degrees, as the fires of dawn rose higher and higher at the far end of the Rue Rambuteau, the mass of vegetation grew brighter and brighter, emerging more and more distinctly from the bluey gloom that clung to the ground. Salad herbs, cabbage, lettuce, endive, and succory, with rich soil still clinging to their roots, exposed their swelling hearts; bundles of spinach, bundles of sorrel, clusters of artichokes, piles of peas and beans, mounds of romaine, tied round with straws, sounded every note in the whole gamut of greenery, from the sheeny lacquerlike green of the pods to the deep-toned green of the foliage; a continuous gamut with ascending and descending scales which died away in the variegated tones of the heads of celery and bundles of leeks. But the highest and most sonorous notes still came from the patches of bright carrots and snowy turnips, strewn in prodigious quantities all along the markets and lighting them up with the medley of their two colors.

At the crossway in the Rue des Halles cabbages were piled up in mountains; there were white ones, hard and compact as metal balls, curly savoys, whose great leaves made them look like basins of green bronze, and red cabbages, which the dawn seemed to transform into superb masses of bloom with the hue of wine-lees, splotched with dark purple and carmine. At the other side of the markets, at the crossway near Saint Eustache, the end of the Rue Rambuteau was blocked by a barricade of orange-hued pumpkins, sprawling with swelling bellies in two superposed rows. And here and there gleamed the glistening ruddy brown of a hamper of onions, the blood-red crimson of a heap of tomatoes, the quiet yellow of a display of marrows, and the somber violet of the fruit of the eggplant; while numerous fat black radishes still left patches of gloom amidst the quivering brilliance of the general awakening.

Claude clapped his hands at the sight. He declared that those "blackguard vegetables" were wild, mad, sublime! He stoutly maintained that they were not yet dead, but, gathered on the previous evening, waited for the morning sun to bid him good-bye from the flagstones of the market. He could observe their vitality, he declared, see their leaves stir and open as though their roots were yet firmly and warmly embedded in well-manured soil. And here, in the markets, he added, he heard the death-rattle of all the kitchen-gardens of the environs of Paris.

A crowd of white caps, loose black jackets, and blue blouses was swarming in the narrow paths between the various piles. The big baskets of the market-porters passed along slowly, above the heads of the throng. Retail dealers, hawkers, and greengrocers were making their purchases in haste. Corporals and nuns clustered round the mountains of cabbages, and college cooks prowled about inquisitively, on the lookout for good bargains. The unloading was still going on; heavy tumbrels, discharging their contents as though these were so many pavingstones, added more and more waves to the sea of greenery which was now beating against the opposite footways. And from the far end of the Rue du Pont Neuf fresh rows of carts were continually arriving.

"What a fine sight it is!" exclaimed Claude in an ecstasy of enthusiasm.

Florent was suffering keenly. He fancied that all this was some supernatural temptation, and, unwilling to look at the markets any longer, turned towards Saint Eustache, a side view of which he obtained from the spot where he now stood. With its roses, and broad arched windows, its bell-turret, and roofs of slate, it looked as though painted in sepia against the blue of the sky. He fixed his eyes at last on the somber depths of the Rue Montorgueil, where fragments of gaudy signboards showed conspicuously, and on the corner of the Rue Montmartre, where there were balconies gleaming with letters of gold. And when he again glanced at the cross-roads, his gaze was solicited by other signboards, on which such inscriptions as "Druggist and Chemist," "Flour and Grain" appeared in big red and black capital letters upon faded backgrounds. Near these corners, houses with narrow windows were now awakening, setting amidst the newness and airiness of the Rue du Pont Neuf a few of the yellow ancient façades of olden Paris. Standing at the empty windows of the great drapery shop at the corner of the Rue Rambuteau a number of spruce-looking counter-jumpers in their shirt sleeves, with snowy-white wristbands and tight-fitting pantaloons, were "dressing" their goods. Farther away, in the windows of the severe-looking, barrack-like Guillot establishment, biscuits in gilt wrappers and fancy cakes on glass stands were tastefully set out. All the shops were now open; and workmen in white blouses, with tools under their arms, were hurrying along the road.

Claude had not yet got down from the bench. He was standing on tiptoe in order to see the farther down the streets. Suddenly, in the midst of the crowd which he overlooked, he caught sight of a fair head with long wavy locks, followed by a little black one covered with curly tumbled hair.

"Hallo, Marjolin! Hallo, Cadine!" he shouted; and then, as his voice was drowned by the general uproar, he jumped to the ground and started off. But all at once, recollecting that he had left Florent behind him, he hastily came back. "I live at the end of the Impasse des Bourdonnais," he said rapidly. "My name's written in chalk on the door, Claude Lantier. Come and see the etching of the Rue Pirouette."

Then he vanished. He was quite ignorant of Florent's name, and, after favoring him with his views on art, parted from him as he had met him, at the roadside.

Florent was now alone, and at first this pleased him. Ever since Madame François had picked him up in the Avenue de

Neuilly he had been coming and going in a state of pain-fraught somnolence which had quite prevented him from forming any definite ideas of his surroundings. Now at last he was at liberty to do what he liked, and he tried to shake himself free from that intolerable vision of teeming food by which he was pursued. But his head still felt empty and dizzy, and all that he could find within him was a kind of vague fear. The day was now growing quite bright, and he could be distinctly seen. He looked down at his wretched shabby coat and trousers. He buttoned the first, dusted the latter, and strove to make a bit of a toilet, fearing lest those black rags of his should proclaim aloud from where he had come. He was seated in the middle of the bench, by the side of some wandering vagabonds who had settled themselves there while waiting for the sunrise. The neighborhood of the markets is a favorite spot with vagrants in the small hours of the morning. However, two constables, still in night uniform, with cloaks and kepis, paced up and down the footway side by side, their hands resting behind their backs; and every time they passed the bench they glanced at the game which they scented there. Florent felt sure that they recognized him and were consulting together about arresting him. At this thought his anguish of mind became extreme. He felt a wild desire to get up and run away; but he did not dare to do so, and was quite at a loss as to how he might take himself off. The repeated glances of the constables, their cold, deliberate scrutiny caused him the keenest torture. At length he rose from the bench, making a great effort to restrain himself from rushing off as quickly as his long legs could carry him; and succeeded in walking quietly away, though his shoulders quivered in the fear that he felt of suddenly feeling the rough hands of the constables clutching at his collar from behind.

He had now only one thought, one desire, which was to

get away from the markets as quickly as possible. He would wait and make his investigations later on, when the footways should be clear. The three streets which met here—the Rue Montmartre, Rue Montorgueil, and Rue Turbigo—filled him with uneasiness. They were blocked by vehicles of all kinds, and their footways were crowded with vegetables. Florent went straight along as far as the Rue Pierre Lescot, but there the cress and the potato markets seemed to him insuperable obstacles. So he resolved to take the Rue Rambuteau. On reaching the Boulevard de Sébastopol, however, he came across such a block of vans and carts and wagonettes that he turned back and proceeded along the Rue Saint Denis. Then he got among the vegetables once more. Retail dealers had just set up their stalls, formed of planks resting on tall hampers; and the deluge of cabbages and carrots and turnips began all over again. The markets were overflowing. Florent tried to make his escape from this pursuing flood which ever overtook him in his flight. He tried the Rue de la Cossonnerie, the Rue Berger, the Square des Innocents, the Rue de la Ferronnerie, and the Rue des Halles. And at last he came to a standstill, quite discouraged and scared at finding himself unable to escape from the infernal circle of vegetables, which now seemed to dance around him, twining clinging verdure about his legs.

The everlasting stream of carts and horses stretched away as far as the Rue de Rivoli and the Place de l'Hôtel de Ville. Huge vans were carrying away supplies for all the greengrocers and fruiterers of an entire district; *chars-à-bancs* were starting for the suburbs with straining, groaning sides. In the Rue du Pont Neuf Florent got completely bewildered. He stumbled upon a crowd of handcarts, in which numerous hawkers were arranging their purchases. Amongst them he recognized Lacaille, who went off along the Rue Saint Honoré, pushing a barrow of carrots and cauliflowers before him. Florent followed him, in the hope that he would guide him out of the mob. The pavement was now quite slippery, although the weather was dry, and the litter of artichoke stalks, turnip tops, and leaves of all kinds made walking somewhat dangerous. Florent stumbled at almost every step. He lost sight of Lacaille in the Rue Vauvilliers, and on approaching the corn market he again found the streets barricaded with vehicles. Then he made no further attempt to struggle; he was once more in the clutch of the markets, and their stream of life bore him back. Slowly retracing his steps, he presently found himself by Saint Eustache again.

He now heard the loud continuous rumbling of the wagons that were setting out from the markets. Paris was doling out the daily food of its two million inhabitants. These markets were like some huge central organ beating with giant force and sending the blood of life through every vein of the city. The uproar was akin to that of colossal jaws—a mighty sound to which each phase of the provisioning contributed, from the whip-cracking of the larger retail dealers as they started off for the district markets to the dragging pit-a-pat of the old shoes worn by the poor women who hawked their lettuces in baskets from door to door.

Florent turned into a covered way on the left, intersecting the group of four pavilions whose deep silent gloom he had remarked during the night. He hoped that he might there find a refuge, discover some corner in which he could hide himself. But these pavilions were now as busy, as lively as the others. Florent walked on to the end of the street. Drays were driving up at a quick trot, crowding the market with cages full of live poultry and square hampers in which dead birds were stowed in deep layers. On the other side of the way were other drays from which porters were removing freshly killed calves, wrapped in canvas, and laid at full length in baskets, from which only the four bleeding stumps of their legs protruded. There were also whole sheep and sides and quarters of beef. Butchers in long white aprons marked the meat with a stamp, carried it off, weighed it, and hung it up on hooks in the auction room. Florent, with his face close to the grating, stood gazing at the rows of hanging carcasses, at the ruddy sheep and oxen and paler calves, all streaked with yellow fat and sinews, and with bellies yawning open. Then he passed along the sidewalk where the tripe market was held, amid the pallid calves's feet and heads, the rolled tripe neatly packed in boxes, the brains delicately set out in flat baskets, the sanguineous livers, and purplish kidneys. He checked his steps in front of some long two-wheeled carts, covered with round awnings, and containing sides of pork hung on each side of the vehicle over a bed of straw. Seen from the back end, the interiors of the carts looked like recesses of some tabernacle, like some taper-lighted chapel, such was the glow of all the bare flesh they contained. And on the beds of straw were lines of tin cans, full of the blood that had trickled from the pigs. Thereupon Florent was attacked by a sort of rage. The insipid odor of the meat, the pungent smell of the tripe exasperated him. He made his way out of the covered road, preferring to return once more to the footwalk of the Rue du Pont Neuf.

He was enduring perfect agony. The shiver of early morning came upon him; his teeth chattered, and he was afraid of falling to the ground and finding himself unable to rise again. He looked about, but could see no vacant place on any bench. Had he found one he would have dropped asleep there, even at the risk of being awakened by the police. Then, as giddiness nearly blinded him, he leaned for support against a tree, with his eyes closed and his ears ringing. The raw carrot, which he had swallowed almost without chewing, was torturing his stomach, and the glass of punch which he had drunk seemed to have intoxicated him. He was indeed intoxicated with misery, weariness, and hunger. Again he felt a burning fire in the pit of the stomach, to which he every now and then carried his hands, as though he were trying to stop up a hole through which all his life was oozing away. As he stood there he fancied that the foot-pavement rocked beneath him; and thinking that he might perhaps lessen his sufferings by walking, he went straight on through the vegetables again. He lost himself among them. He went along a narrow footway, turned down another, was forced to retrace his steps, bungled in doing so, and once more found himself amidst piles of greenery. Some heaps were so high that people seemed to be walking between walls of bundles and bunches. Only their heads slightly overtopped these ramparts and passed along showing whitely or blackly according to the color of their hats or caps; while the huge swinging baskets, carried aloft on a level with the greenery, looked like wicker boats floating on a stagnant, mossy lake.

Florent stumbled against a thousand obstacles—against porters taking up their burdens and saleswomen disputing in rough tones. He slipped over the thick bed of waste leaves and stumps which covered the footway and was almost suffocated by the powerful odor of crushed verdure. At last he halted in a sort of confused stupor and surrendered to the pushing of some and the insults of others; and then he became a mere waif, a piece of wreckage tossed about on the surface of that surging sea.

He was fast losing all self-respect and would willingly have begged. The recollection of his foolish pride during the night exasperated him. If he had accepted Madame François's charity, if he had not felt such idiotic fear of Claude, he would not now have been stranded there groaning in the midst of those cabbages. And he was especially angry with himself for not having questioned the artist when they were in the Rue Pirouette. Now, alas! he was alone and deserted, liable to die in the streets like a homeless dog.

For the last time he raised his eyes and looked at the

markets. At present they were glittering in the sun. A broad ray was pouring through the covered road from the far end, cleaving the massy pavilions with an arcade of light, while fiery beams rained down upon the far expanse of roofs. The huge iron framework grew less distinct, assumed a bluey hue, became nothing but a shadowy silhouette outlined against the flaming flare of the sunrise. But up above a pane of glass took fire, drops of light trickled down the broad sloping zinc plates to the gutterings; and then, below, a tumultuous city appeared amidst a haze of dancing golden dust. The general awakening had spread, from the first start of the market-gardeners snoring in their cloaks, to the brisk rolling of the food-laden railway drays. And the whole city was opening its iron gates, the footways were humming, the pavilions roaring with life. Shouts and cries of all kinds rent the air; it was as though the strain, which Florent had heard gathering force in the gloom ever since four in the morning, had now attained its fullest volume. To the right and left, on all sides indeed, the sharp cries accompanying the auction sales sounded shrilly like flutes amid the sonorous bass roar of the crowd. It was the fish, the butter, the poultry, and the meat being sold.

The pealing of bells passed through the air, imparting a quiver to the buzzing of the opening markets. Around Florent the sun was setting the vegetables aflame. He no longer perceived any of those soft water-color tints which had predominated in the pale light of early morning. The swelling hearts of the lettuces were now gleaming brightly, the scales of greenery showed forth with wondrous vigor, the carrots glowed blood-red, the turnips shone as if incandescent in the triumphant radiance of the sun.

On Florent's left some wagons were discharging fresh loads of cabbages. He turned his eyes and away in the distance saw carts yet streaming out of the Rue Turbigo. The tide was still rising. He had felt it about his ankles, then on a level with his stomach, and now it was threatening to drown him altogether. Blinded and submerged, his ears buzzing, his stomach overpowered by all that he had seen, he asked for mercy; and wild grief took possession of him at the thought of dying there of starvation in the very heart of glutted Paris, amid the effulgent awakening of her markets. Big hot tears started from his eyes.

Walking on, he had now reached one of the larger alleys. Two women, one short and old, the other tall and withered, passed him, talking together as they made their way towards the pavilions.

"So you've come to do your marketing, Mademoiselle Saget?" said the tall withered woman.

"Well, yes, Madame Lecœur, if you can give it such a name as marketing. I'm a lone woman, you know, and live on next to nothing. I should have liked a small cauliflower, but everything is so dear. How is butter selling today?"

"At thirty-four sous. I have some which is first-rate. Will you come and look at it?"

"Well, I don't know if I shall want any today; I've still a little lard left."

Making a supreme effort, Florent followed these two women. He recollected having heard Claude name the old one—Mademoiselle Saget—when they were in the Rue Pirouette; and he made up his mind to question her when she should have parted from her tall withered acquaintance.

"And how's your niece?" Mademoiselle Saget now asked.

"Oh, La Sarriette does as she likes," Madame Lecœur replied in a bitter tone. "She's chosen to set up for herself and her affairs no longer concern me. When her lovers have beggared her, she needn't come to me for any bread."

"And you were so good to her, too! She ought to do well this year; fruit is yielding big profits. And your brother-in-law, how is he?"

"Oh, he—"

Madame Lecœur bit her lips and seemed disinclined to say anything more.

"Still the same as ever, I suppose?" continued Mademoiselle Saget. "He's a very worthy man. Still, I once heard it said that he spent his money in such a way that—"

"But does anyone know how he spends his money?" interrupted Madame Lecœur, with much asperity. "He's a miserly niggard, a scurvy fellow, that's what I say! Do you know, mademoiselle, he'd see me die of starvation rather than lend me five francs! He knows quite well that there's nothing to be made out of butter this season, any more than out of cheese and eggs; whereas he can sell as much poultry as ever he chooses. But not once, I assure you, not once has he offered to help me. I am too proud, as you know, to accept any assistance from him; still it would have pleased me to have had it offered."

"Ah, by the way, there he is, your brother-in-law!" suddenly exclaimed Mademoiselle Saget, lowering her voice.

The two women turned and gazed at a man who was crossing the road to enter the covered way close by.

"I'm in a hurry," murmured Madame Lecœur. "I left my stall without anyone to look after it; and, besides, I don't want to speak to him."

However, Florent also had mechanically turned round and glanced at the individual referred to. This was a short, squarely-built man, with a cheery look and gray, close-cut brush-like hair. Under each arm he was carrying a fat goose, whose heads hung down and flapped against his legs. And then all at once Florent made a gesture of delight. Forgetting his fatigue, he ran after the man, and, overtaking him, tapped him on the shoulder.

"Gavard!" he exclaimed.

The other raised his head and stared with surprise at Florent's tall black figure, which he did not at first recognize.

Then all at once: "What! is it you?" he cried, as if overcome with amazement. "Is it really you?"

He all but let his geese fall, and seemed unable to master his surprise. On catching sight, however, of his sister-in-law and Mademoiselle Saget, who were watching the meeting at a distance, he began to walk on again.

"Come along; don't let us stop here," he said. "There are too many eyes and tongues about."

When they were in the covered way they began to chat. Florent related how he had gone to the Rue Pirouette, at which Gavard seemed much amused and laughed heartily. Then he told Florent that his brother Quenu had moved from that street and had reopened his pork shop close by, in the Rue Rambuteau, just in front of the markets. And afterwards he was again highly amused to hear that Florent had been wandering about all that morning with Claude Lantier, an odd kind of fish, who, strangely enough, said he, was Madame Quenu's nephew. Thus chatting, Gavard was on the point of taking Florent straight to the pork shop, but, on hearing that he had returned to France with false papers, he suddenly assumed all sorts of solemn and mysterious airs, and insisted upon walking some fifteen paces in front of him, to avoid attracting attention. After passing through the poultry pavilion, where he hung his geese up in his stall, he began to cross the Rue Rambuteau, still followed by Florent; and then, halting in the middle of the road, he glanced significantly towards a large and well-appointed pork shop.

The sun was obliquely enfilading the Rue Rambuteau, lighting up the fronts of the houses, in the midst of which the Rue Pirouette formed a dark gap. At the other end the great pile of Saint Eustache glittered brightly in the sunlight like some huge reliquary. And right through the crowd, from the distant crossway, an army of street-sweepers was advancing in file down the road, the brooms swishing rhythmically, while scavengers provided with forks pitched the collected refuse into tumbrels, which at intervals of a score of paces halted with a noise like the clattering of broken pots. However, all Florent's attention was concentrated on the pork-shop, open and radiant in the rising sun.

It stood very near the corner of the Rue Pirouette and provided quite a feast for the eyes. Its aspect was bright and smiling, touches of brilliant color showing conspicuously amidst all the snowy marble. The signboard, on which the name of QUENU-GRADELLE glittered in fat gilt letters encircled by leaves and branches painted on a soft-hued background, was protected by a sheet of glass. On two panels, one on each side of the shop-front, and both, like the board above, covered with glass, were paintings representing various chubby little cupids playing amidst boars' heads, pork chops, and strings of sausages; and these latter still-life subjects, embellished with scrolls and bows, had been painted in such soft tones that the uncooked pork which they represented had the pinkness of raspberry jam. Within this pleasing framework arose the window display, arranged upon a bed of fine blue-paper shavings. Here and there fern leaves, tastefully disposed, changed the plates which they encircled into bouquets fringed with foliage. There was a wealth of rich, luscious, melting things. Down below, quite close to the window, jars of preserved sausage-meat were interspersed with pots of mustard. Above these were some small, plump, boned hams, golden with their dressings of toasted bread-crumbs, and adorned at the knuckles with green rosettes. Next came the larger dishes, some containing preserved Strasburg tongues, enclosed in bladders colored a bright red and varnished, so that they looked quite sanguineous beside the pale sausages and pigs' feet; then there were black puddings coiled like harmless snakes, healthy-looking chitterlings piled up two by two; Lyon sausages in little silver copes that made them look like choristers; hot pies, with little banner-like tickets stuck in them; big hams, and great glazed joints of veal and pork, whose jelly was as limpid as sugar candy. In the rear were other dishes and earthen pans in which meat, minced and sliced, slumbered beneath lakes of melted fat. And between the various plates and dishes, jars and bottles of sauce, purée, stock and preserved truffles, pans of *foie gras* and boxes of sardines and tuna fish were strewn over the bed of paper shavings. A box of creamy cheeses and one of edible snails, the apertures of whose shells were dressed with butter and parsley, had been placed carelessly at either corner. Finally, from a bar overhead strings of sausages and saveloys of various sizes hung down symmetrically like cords and tassels; while in the rear fragments of intestinal membranes showed like lacework, like some *guipure* of white flesh. And on the highest tier in this sanctuary of gluttony, amid the membranes and between two bouquets of purple gladioli, the window-stand was crowned by a small square aquarium, ornamented with rock-work and containing a couple of goldfish, which were continually swimming round it.

Florent's whole body thrilled at the sight. Then he perceived a woman standing in the sunlight at the door of the shop. With her prosperous, happy look in the midst of all those inviting things she added to the cheery aspect of the place. She was a fine woman and quite blocked the doorway. Still, she was not over-stout, but simply buxom, with the full ripeness of her thirty years. She had only just risen, yet her glossy hair was already brushed smooth and arranged in little flat bands over her temples, giving her an appearance of extreme neatness. She had the fine skin, the pinky-white complexion common to those whose life is spent in an atmosphere of raw meat and fat. There was a touch of gravity about her demeanor, her movements were calm and slow;

what mirth or pleasure she felt she expressed by her eyes, her lips retaining all their seriousness. A collar of starched linen encircled her neck, white sleevelets reached to her elbows, and a white apron fell even over the tips of her shoes, so that you saw but little of her black cashmere dress, which clung tightly to her well-rounded shoulders and swelling bosom. The sun rays poured hotly upon all the whiteness she displayed. However, although her bluish-black hair, her rosy face, and bright sleeves and apron were steeped in the glow of light, she never once blinked, but enjoyed her morning bath of sunshine with blissful tranquillity, her soft eyes smiling the while at the flow and riot of the markets. She had the appearance of a very worthy woman.

"That is your brother's wife, your sister-in-law, Lisa," Gavard said to Florent.

He had saluted her with a slight inclination of the head. Then he darted along the house passage, continuing to take the most minute precautions, and unwilling to let Florent enter the premises through the shop, though there was no one there. It was evident that he felt great pleasure in dabbling in what he considered to be a compromising business.

"Wait here," he said, "while I go to see whether your brother is alone. You can come in when I clap my hands."

Thereupon he opened a door at the end of the passage. But as soon as Florent heard his brother's voice behind it, he sprang inside at a bound. Quenu, who was much attached to him, threw his arms round his neck, and they kissed each other like children.

"Ah! dash it all! Is it really you, my dear fellow?" stammered the pork-butcher. "I never expected to see you again. I felt sure you were dead! Why, only yesterday I was saying to Lisa, 'That poor fellow, Florent!'"

However, he stopped short, and, popping his head into the shop, called out, "Lisa! Lisa!" Then turning towards a little girl who had crept into a corner, he added, "Pauline, go and find your mother."

The little one did not stir, however. She was an extremely fine child, five years of age, with a plump chubby face, bearing a strong resemblance to that of the pork-butcher's wife. In her arms she was holding a huge yellow cat, which had cheerfully surrendered itself to her embrace, with its legs dangling downwards; and she now squeezed it tightly with her little arms, as if she were afraid that the shabby-looking gentleman might rob her of it.

Lisa, however, leisurely made her appearance.

"Here is my brother Florent!" exclaimed Quenu.

Lisa addressed him as "Monsieur," and gave him a kindly welcome. She scanned him quietly from head to foot, without evincing any disagreeable surprise. Merely a faint pout appeared for a moment on her lips. Then, standing by, she began to smile at her husband's demonstrations of affection. Quenu, however, at last recovered his calmness, and noticing Florent's fleshless, poverty-stricken appearance, exclaimed: "Ah! my poor fellow, you haven't improved in your looks since you were gone. For my part, I've grown fat; but what would you have!"

He had indeed grown fat, too fat for his thirty years. He seemed to be bursting through his shirt and apron, through all the snowy-white linen in which he was swathed like a huge doll. With advancing years his clean-shaven face had become elongated, assuming a faint resemblance to the snout of one of those pigs amid whose flesh his hands worked and lived the whole day through. Florent scarcely recognized him. He had now seated himself, and his glance turned from his brother to handsome Lisa and little Pauline. They were all brimful of health, squarely built, sleek, in prime condition; and in their turn they looked at Florent with the uneasy astonishment which corpulent people feel at the sight of a scraggy person. The very cat, whose skin was distended by fat, dilated its yellow eyes and scrutinized him with an air of distrust.

"You'll wait till we have breakfast, won't you?" asked Quenu. "We have it early, at ten o'clock."

A penetrating odor of cookery pervaded the place; and Florent looked back upon the terrible night which he had just spent, his arrival amongst the vegetables, his agony in the midst of the markets, the endless avalanches of food from which he had just escaped. And then in a low tone and with a gentle smile he responded:

"No; I'm really very hungry, you see."

Chapter 2

FLORENT HAD JUST BEGUN to study law in Paris when his mother died. She lived at Le Vigan, in the department of the Gard, and had taken for her second husband one Quenu, a native of Yvetot in Normandy, whom some sub-prefect had transplanted to the south and then forgotten there. He had remained in employment at the sub-prefecture, finding the country charming, the wine good, and the women very amiable. Three years after his marriage he had been carried off by a bad attack of indigestion, leaving as sole legacy to his wife a sturdy boy who resembled him. It was only with very great difficulty that the widow could pay the college fees of Florent, her elder son, the issue of her first marriage. He was a very gentle youth, devoted to his studies, and constantly won the chief prizes at school. It was upon him that his mother lavished all her affection and based all her hopes. Perhaps, in bestowing so much love on this slim pale youth, she was giving evidence of her preference for her first husband, a tender-hearted, caressing Provençal, who had loved her devotedly. Quenu, whose good humor and amiability had at first attracted her, had perhaps displayed too much self-satisfaction, and shown too plainly that he looked upon himself as the main source of happiness. At all events she formed the opinion that her younger son—and in southern families younger sons are still often sacrificed—would never do any good; so she contented herself with sending him to a school kept by a neighboring old maid, where the lad learned nothing but how to idle his time away. The two brothers grew up far apart from each other, as though they were strangers.

When Florent arrived at Le Vigan his mother was already buried. She had insisted upon having her illness concealed from him till the very last moment, for fear of disturbing his studies. Thus he found little Quenu, who was then twelve years old, sitting and sobbing alone on a table in the middle of the kitchen. A furniture dealer, a neighbor, gave him particulars of his mother's last hours. She had reached the end of her resources, had killed herself by the hard work which she had undertaken to earn sufficient money that her elder son might continue his legal studies. To her modest trade in ribbons, the profits of which were but small, she had been obliged to add other occupations, which kept her up very late at night. Her one idea of seeing Florent established as an advocate, holding a good position in the town, had gradually caused her to become hard and miserly, without pity for either herself or others. Little Quenu was allowed to wander about in ragged breeches, and in blouses from which the sleeves were falling away. He never dared to serve himself at table, but waited till he received his allowance of bread from his mother's hands. She gave herself equally thin slices, and it was to the effects of this regimen that she had succumbed, in deep despair at having failed to accomplish her self-allotted task.

This story made a most painful impression upon Florent's tender nature, and his sobs well-nigh choked him. He took his little step-brother in his arms, held him to his breast, and kissed him as though to restore to him the love of which he had unwittingly deprived him. Then he looked at the lad's gaping shoes, torn sleeves, and dirty hands, at all the manifest signs of wretchedness and neglect. And he told him that he would take him away and that they would both live happily together. The next day, when he began to inquire into affairs, he felt afraid that he would not be able to keep sufficient money to pay for the journey back to Paris. However, he was determined to leave Le Vigan at any cost. He was fortunately able to sell the little ribbon business, and this enabled him to discharge his mother's debts, for despite her strictness in money matters she had gradually run up bills. Then, as there was nothing left, his mother's neighbor, the furniture dealer, offered him five hundred francs for her chattels and stock of linen. It was a very good bargain for the dealer, but the young man thanked him with tears in his eyes. He bought his brother some new clothes and took him away that same evening.

On his return to Paris he gave up all thought of continuing to attend the law school and postponed every ambitious project. He obtained a few pupils and established himself with little Quenu in the Rue Royer Collard, at the corner of the Rue Saint Jacques, in a big room which he furnished with two iron bedsteads, a wardrobe, a table, and four chairs. He now had a child to look after, and this assumed paternity was very pleasing to him. During the earlier days he attempted to give the lad some lessons when he returned home in the evening, but Quenu was an unwilling pupil. He was dull of understanding and refused to learn, bursting into tears and regretfully recalling the time when his mother had allowed him to run wild in the streets. Florent thereupon stopped his lessons in despair and to console the lad promised him a holiday of indefinite length. As an excuse for his own weakness he repeated that he had not brought his brother to Paris to distress him. To see him grow up in happiness became his chief desire. He quite worshipped the boy, was charmed with his merry laughter, and felt infinite joy in seeing him about him, healthy and vigorous, and without a care. Florent for his part remained very slim and lean in his threadbare black coat, and his face began to turn yellow amidst all the drudgery and worry of teaching; but Quenu grew up plump and merry, a little dense, indeed, and scarce able to read or write, but endowed with high spirits which nothing could ruffle, and which filled the big gloomy room in the Rue Royer Collard with gaiety.

Years, meantime, passed by. Florent, who had inherited all his mother's spirit of devotion, kept Quenu at home as though he were a big, idle girl. He did not even suffer him to perform any petty domestic duties, but always went to buy the provisions himself, and attended to the cooking and other necessary matters. This kept him, he said, from indulging in his own bad thoughts. He was given to gloominess and fancied that he was disposed to evil. When he returned home in the evening, splashed with mud, and his head bowed by the annoyances to which other people's children had subjected him, his heart melted beneath the embrace of the sturdy lad whom he found spinning his top on the tiled flooring of the big room. Quenu laughed at his brother's clumsiness in making omelettes and at the serious fashion in which he prepared the soup-beef and vegetables. When the lamp was extinguished, and Florent lay in bed, he sometimes gave way to feelings of sadness. He longed to resume his legal studies, and strove to map out his duties in such a way as to secure time to follow the program of the faculty. He succeeded in doing this and was then perfectly happy. But a slight attack of fever, which confined him to his room for a week, made such a hole in his purse, and caused him so much alarm, that he abandoned all idea of completing his studies. The boy was now becoming a big fellow, and Florent took a post as teacher in a school in the Rue de l'Estrapade, at a salary of eighteen hundred francs per annum. This seemed like a fortune to him. By dint of economy he hoped to be able to amass a sum of money which would set Quenu going in the world. When the lad reached his eighteenth year Florent still treated him as though he were a daughter for whom a dowry must be provided.

However, during his brother's brief illness Quenu himself had made certain reflections. One morning he proclaimed his desire to work, saying that he was now old enough to earn his own living. Florent was deeply touched at this. Just opposite, on the other side of the street, lived a working watchmaker whom Quenu, through the curtainless window, could see leaning over a little table, manipulating all sorts of delicate things, and patiently gazing at them through a magnifying glass all day long. The lad was much attracted by the sight and declared that he had a taste for watchmaking. At the end of a fortnight, however, he became restless, and began to cry like a child of ten, complaining that the work was too complicated, and that he would never be able to understand all the silly little things that enter into the construction of a watch.

His next whim was to be a locksmith; but this calling he found too fatiguing. In a couple of years he tried more than ten different trades. Florent opined that he acted rightly, that it was wrong to take up a calling one did not like. However, Quenu's fine eagerness to work for his living strained the resources of the little establishment very seriously. Since he had begun flitting from one workshop to another there had been a constant succession of fresh expenses; money had gone in new clothes, in meals taken away from home, and in payments to new fellow-workmen. Florent's salary of eighteen hundred francs was no longer sufficient, and he was obliged to take a couple of pupils in the evenings. For eight years he had continued to wear the same old coat.

However, the two brothers had made a friend. One side of the house in which they lived overlooked the Rue Saint Jacques, where there was a large poultry roasting establishment kept by a worthy man called Gavard, whose wife was dying from consumption amid an atmosphere redolent of plump fowls. When Florent returned home too late to cook a scrap of meat, he was in the habit of laying out a dozen sous or so on a small portion of turkey or goose at this shop. Such days as these were feast days. Gavard in time grew interested in his tall, scraggy customer, learned his history, and invited Quenu into his shop. Before long the young fellow was constantly to be found there. As soon as his brother left the house he came downstairs and installed himself at the rear of the roasting shop, quite enraptured with the four huge spits which turned with a gentle sound in front of the tall bright flames.

The broad copper bands of the fireplace glistened brightly, the poultry steamed, the fat bubbled melodiously in the dripping-pan, and the spits seemed to talk among themselves and to address kindly words to Quenu, who, with a long ladle, devoutly basted the golden breasts of the fat geese and turkeys. He would stay there for hours, quite crimson in the dancing glow of the flames, and laughing vaguely, with a somewhat stupid expression, at the birds roasting in front of him. Indeed, he did not awake from this kind of trance until the geese and turkeys were unspitted. They were placed on dishes, the spits emerged from their carcasses smoking hot, and a rich gravy flowed from either end and filled the shop with a penetrating odor. Then the lad, who, standing up, had eagerly followed every phase of the dishing, would clap his hands and begin to talk to the birds, telling them that they were very nice and would be eaten up, and that the cats would have nothing but their bones. And he would give a start of delight whenever Gavard handed him a slice of bread, which he forthwith put into the dripping-pan that it might soak and toast there for half-an-hour.

It was in this shop, no doubt, that Quenu's love of cookery took its birth. Later on, when he had tried all sorts of crafts, he returned, as though driven by fate, to the spits and the poultry and the savory gravy which induces one to lick one's fingers. At first he was afraid of vexing his brother, who was a small eater and spoke of good fare with the disdain of a man who is ignorant of it; but afterwards, on seeing that Florent listened to him when he explained the preparation of some very elaborate dish, he confessed his desires and presently found a situation at a large restaurant. From that time forward the life of the two brothers was settled. They continued to live in the room in the Rue Royer Collard, to which they returned every evening; the one glowing and radiant from his hot fire, the other with the depressed countenance of a shabby, impecunious teacher. Florent still wore his old black coat, as he sat absorbed in correcting his pupils' exercises; while Quenu, to put himself more at ease, donned his white apron, cap, and jacket, and, flitting about in front of the stove, amused himself by baking some dainty in the oven. Sometimes they smiled at seeing themselves thus attired, the one all in black, the other all in white. These different garbs, one bright and the other somber, seemed to make the big room half gay and half mournful. Never, however, was there so much harmony in a household marked by such dissimilarity. Though the elder brother grew thinner and thinner, consumed by the ardent temperament which he had inherited from his Provençal father, and the younger one waxed fatter and fatter, like a true son of Normandy, they loved each other in the brotherhood they derived from their mother—a mother who had been all devotion.

They had a relation in Paris, a brother of their mother's, one Gradelle, who was in business as a pork-butcher in the Rue Pirouette, near the central markets. He was a fat, hard-hearted, miserly fellow, and received his nephews as though they were starving paupers the first time they paid him a visit. They seldom went to see him afterwards. On his name day Quenu would take him a bunch of flowers and receive a half-franc piece in return for it. Florent's proud and sensitive nature suffered keenly when Gradelle scrutinized his shabby clothes with the anxious, suspicious glance of a miser apprehending a request for a dinner, or the loan of a five-franc piece. One day, however, it occurred to Florent in all artlessness to ask his uncle to change a hundred-franc note for him, and after this the pork-butcher showed less alarm at sight of the lads, as he called them. Still, their friendship got no further than these infrequent visits.

These years were like a long, sweet, sad dream to Florent. As they passed he tasted to the full all the bitter joys of self-sacrifice. At home, in the big room, life was all love and tenderness; but out in the world, amid the humiliations inflicted on him by his pupils and the rough jostling of the streets, he felt himself yielding to wicked thoughts. His slain ambitions embittered him. It was long before he could bring himself to bow to his fate and accept with equanimity the painful lot of a poor, plain, commonplace man. At last, to guard against the temptations of wickedness, he plunged into ideal goodness and sought refuge in a self-created sphere of absolute truth and justice. It was then that he became a republican, entering into the republican idea even as heartbroken girls enter a convent. And not finding a republic where sufficient peace and kindliness prevailed to lull his troubles to sleep, he created one for himself. He took no pleasure in books. All the blackened paper amid which he lived spoke of evil-smelling classrooms, of pellets of paper chewed by unruly schoolboys, of long, profitless hours of torture. Besides, books only suggested to him a spirit of mutiny and pride, whereas it was of peace and oblivion that he felt most need. To lull and soothe himself with ideal imaginings, to dream that he was perfectly happy, and that all the world would likewise become so, to erect in his brain the republican city in which he would like to have lived, such now became his recreation, the task, again and again renewed, of all his leisure hours. He no longer read any books beyond those which his duties compelled him to peruse; he preferred to tramp along the Rue Saint Jacques as far as the outer boulevards, occasionally going yet a greater distance and returning by the Barrière d'Italie; and all along the road, with his eyes on the Quartier Mouffetard spread out at his feet, he would devise reforms of great moral and humanitarian scope, such as he thought would change that city of suffering into an abode of bliss. During the turmoil of February 1848, when Paris was stained with blood, he became quite heartbroken, and rushed from one to another of the public clubs demanding that the blood which had been shed should find atonement in "the eternal embrace of all republicans throughout the world." He became one of those enthusiastic orators who preached revolution as a new religion, full of gentleness and salvation. The terrible days of December 1851, the days of the Coup d'Etat, were required to wean him from his doctrines of universal love. He was then without arms; allowed himself to be captured like a sheep, and was treated as though he were a wolf. He awoke from his sermon on universal brotherhood to find himself starving on the cold stones of a casemate at Bicêtre.

Quenu, then twenty-two, was distracted with anguish when his brother did not return home. On the following day he went to seek his corpse at the cemetery of Montmartre, where the bodies of those shot down on the boulevards had been laid out in a line and covered with straw, from beneath which only their ghastly heads projected. However, Quenu's courage failed him, he was blinded by his tears, and had to pass twice along the line of corpses before acquiring the certainty that Florent's was not among them. At last, at the end of a long and wretched week, he learned at the Préfecture of Police that his brother was a prisoner. He was not allowed to see him, and when he pressed the matter the police threatened to arrest him also. Then he hastened off to his uncle Gradelle, whom he looked upon as a person of importance, hoping that he might be able to enlist his influence in Florent's behalf. But Gradelle waxed wrathful, declared that Florent deserved his fate, that he ought to have known better than to have mixed himself up with those rascally republicans. And he even added that Florent was destined to turn out badly, that it was written on his face.

Quenu wept copiously and remained there, almost choked by his sobs. His uncle, a little ashamed of his harshness, and feeling that he ought to do something for him, offered to receive him into his house. He wanted an assistant and knew that his nephew was a good cook. Quenu was so much alarmed by the mere thought of going back to live alone in the big room in the Rue Royer Collard, that then and there he accepted Gradelle's offer. That same night he slept in his uncle's house, in a dark hole of a garret just under the roof, where there was scarcely space for him to lie at full length. However, he was less wretched there than he would have been opposite his brother's empty couch.

He succeeded at length in obtaining permission to see Florent; but on his return from Bicêtre he was obliged to take to his bed. For nearly three weeks he lay fever-stricken, in a stupefied, comatose state. Gradelle meantime called down all sorts of maledictions on his republican nephew; and one morning, when he heard of Florent's departure for Cayenne, he went upstairs, tapped Quenu on the hands, awoke him, and bluntly told him the news, thereby bringing about such a reaction that on the following day the young man was up and about again. His grief wore itself out, and his soft flabby flesh seemed to absorb his tears. A month later he laughed again, and then grew vexed and unhappy with himself for having been merry; but his natural lightheartedness soon gained the mastery, and he laughed afresh in unconscious happiness.

He now learned his uncle's business, from which he derived even more enjoyment than from cookery. Gradelle told him, however, that he must not neglect his pots and pans, that it was rare to find a pork-butcher who was also a good cook, and that he had been lucky in serving in a restaurant before coming to the shop. Gradelle, moreover, made full use of his nephew's acquirements, employed him to cook the dinners sent out to certain customers, and placed all the broiling, and the preparation of pork chops garnished with gherkins in his special charge. As the young man was of real service to him, he grew fond of him after his own fashion and would nip his plump arms when he was in a good humor. Gradelle had sold the scanty furniture of the room in the Rue Royer Collard and retained possession of the proceeds—some forty francs or so—in order, said he, to prevent that foolish lad, Quenu, from throwing the money away. After a time, however, he allowed his nephew six francs a month as pocket-money.

Quenu now became quite happy, in spite of the emptiness of his purse and the harshness with which he was occasionally treated. He liked to have life doled out to him; Florent had treated him too much like an indolent girl. Moreover, he had made a friend at his uncle's. Gradelle, when his wife died, had been obliged to engage a girl to attend to the shop and had taken care to choose a healthy and attractive one, knowing that a good-looking girl would set off his viands and help to tempt custom. Among his acquaintances was a widow, living in the Rue Cuvier, near the Jardin des Plantes, whose deceased husband had been postmaster at Plassans, the seat of a sub-prefecture in the south of France.

This lady, who lived in a very modest fashion on a small annuity, had brought with her from Plassans a plump, pretty child, whom she treated as her own daughter. Lisa, as the young one was called, attended upon her with much placidity and serenity of disposition. Somewhat seriously inclined, she looked quite beautiful when she smiled. Indeed, her great charm came from the exquisite manner in which she allowed this infrequent smile of hers to escape her. Her eyes then became most caressing, and her habitual gravity imparted inestimable value to these sudden, seductive flashes. The old lady had often said that one of Lisa's smiles would suffice to lure her to perdition.

When the widow died she left all her savings, amounting to some ten thousand francs, to her adopted daughter. For a week Lisa lived alone in the Rue Cuvier; it was there that Gradelle came in search of her. He had become acquainted with her by often seeing her with her mistress when the latter called on him in the Rue Pirouette; and at the funeral she had struck him as having grown so handsome and sturdy that he had followed the hearse all the way to the cemetery, though he had not intended to do so. As the coffin was being lowered into the grave, he reflected what a splendid girl she would be for the counter of a pork-butcher's shop. He thought the matter over and finally resolved to offer her thirty francs a month, with board and lodging. When he made this proposal to her, Lisa asked for twenty-four hours to consider it. Then she arrived one morning with a little bundle of clothes and her ten thousand francs concealed in the bosom of her dress. A month later the whole place seemed to belong to her; she enslaved Gradelle, Quenu, and even the smallest kitchen-boy. For his part, Quenu would have cut off his fingers to please her. When she happened to smile, he remained rooted to the floor, laughing with delight as he gazed at her.

Lisa was the eldest daughter of the Macquarts of Plassans, and her father was still alive. But she said that he was abroad and never wrote to him. Sometimes she just dropped a hint that her mother, now deceased, had been a hard worker and that she took after her. She worked, indeed, very assiduously. However, she sometimes added that the worthy woman had slaved herself to death in striving to support her family. Then she would speak of the respective duties of husband and wife in such a practical though modest fashion as to enchant Quenu. He assured her that he fully shared her ideas. These were that everyone, man or woman, ought to work for his or her living, that everyone was charged with the duty of achieving personal happiness, that great harm was done by encouraging habits of idleness, and that the presence of so much misery in the world was greatly due to sloth. This theory of hers was a sweeping condemnation of drunkenness, of all the legendary loafing ways of her father Macquart. But, though she did not know it, there was much of Macquart's nature in herself. She was merely a steady, sensible Macquart with a logical desire for comfort, and grasped the truth of the proverb that as you make your bed so you lie on it. To sleep in blissful warmth there is no better plan than to prepare oneself a soft and downy couch; and to the preparation of such a couch she gave all her time and all her thoughts. When no more than six years old she had consented to remain quietly on her chair the whole day through on condition that she should be rewarded with a cake in the evening.

At Gradelle's establishment Lisa went on leading the calm, methodical life which her exquisite smiles illumined. She had not accepted the pork-butcher's offer at random. She reckoned upon finding a guardian in him; with the keen scent of those who are born lucky she perhaps foresaw that the gloomy shop in the Rue Pirouette would bring her the comfortable future she dreamed of—a life of healthy enjoyment and work without fatigue, each hour of which would bring its own reward. She attended to her counter with the quiet earnestness with which she had waited upon the postmaster's widow; and the cleanliness of her aprons soon became proverbial in the neighborhood. Uncle Gradelle was so charmed with this pretty girl that sometimes, as he was stringing his sausages, he would say to Quenu: 'Upon my word, if I weren't turned sixty, I think I should be foolish enough to marry her. A wife like she'd make is worth her weight in gold to a shopkeeper, my lad."

Quenu himself was growing still fonder of her, though he laughed merrily one day when a neighbor accused him of being in love with Lisa. He was not worried with love-sickness. The two were very good friends, however. In the evening they went up to their bedrooms together. Lisa slept in a little chamber adjoining the dark hole which the young man occupied. She had made this room of hers quite bright by hanging it with muslin curtains. The pair would stand together for a moment on the landing, holding their candles in their hands, and chatting as they unlocked their doors. Then, as they closed them, they said in friendly tones:

"Good night, Mademoiselle Lisa."

"Good night, Monsieur Quenu."

As Quenu undressed himself he listened to Lisa making her own preparations. The partition between the two rooms was very thin. "There, she is drawing her curtains now," he would say to himself; "what can she be doing, I wonder, in front of her chest of drawers? Ah! she's sitting down now and taking off her shoes. Now she's blown her candle out. Well, good night. I must get to sleep"; and at times, when he heard her bed creak as she got into it, he would say to himself with a smile, "Dash it all! Mademoiselle Lisa is no feather." This idea seemed to amuse him, and presently he would fall asleep thinking about the hams and salt pork that he had to prepare the next morning.

This state of affairs went on for a year without causing Lisa a single blush or Quenu a moment's embarrassment. When the girl came into the kitchen in the morning at the busiest moment of the day's work, they grasped hands over the dishes of sausage meat. Sometimes she helped him, holding the skins with her plump fingers while he filled them with meat and fat. Sometimes, too, with the tips of their tongues they just tasted the raw sausage meat, to see if it was properly seasoned. She was able to give Quenu some useful hints, for she knew of many favorite southern recipes, with which he experimented with much success. He was often aware that she was standing behind his shoulder, prying into the pans. If he wanted a spoon or a dish, she would hand it to him. The heat of the fire would bring their blood to their skins; still, nothing in the world would have induced the young man to cease stirring the fatty *bouillis* which were thickening over the fire while the girl stood gravely by him, discussing the amount of boiling that was necessary. In the afternoon, when the shop lacked customers, they quietly chatted together for hours at a time. Lisa sat behind the counter, leaning back, and knitting in an easy, regular fashion; while Quenu installed himself on a big oak block, dangling his legs and tapping his heels against the wood. They got on wonderfully well together, discussing all sorts of subjects, generally cookery, and then Uncle Gradelle and the neighbors. Lisa also amused the young man with stories, just as though he were a child. She knew some very pretty ones—some miraculous legends, full of lambs and little angels, which she narrated in a piping voice, with all her wonted seriousness. If a customer happened to come in, she saved herself the trouble of moving by asking Quenu to get the required pot of lard or box of snails. And at eleven o'clock they went

slowly up to bed as on the previous night. As they closed
their doors, they calmly repeated the words:

"Good night, Mademoiselle Lisa."

"Good night, Monsieur Quenu."

One morning Uncle Gradelle was struck dead by apo-
plexy while preparing a galantine. He fell forward, with his
face against the chopping block. Lisa did not lose her self-
possession. She remarked that the dead man could not be
left lying in the middle of the kitchen and had the body
removed into a little back room where Gradelle had slept.
Then she arranged with the assistants what should be said.
It must be given out that the master had died in his bed;
otherwise the whole district would be disgusted, and the
shop would lose its customers. Quenu helped to carry the
dead man away, feeling quite confused, and astonished at
being unable to shed any tears. Presently, however, he and
Lisa cried together. Quenu and his brother Florent were the
sole heirs. The gossips of the neighborhood credited old
Gradelle with the possession of a considerable fortune. However, not a single crown could be discovered. Lisa seemed
very restless and uneasy. Quenu noticed how pensive she
became, how she kept on looking around her from morning
till night, as though she had lost something. At last she decided to have a thorough cleaning of the premises, declaring that people were beginning to talk, that the story of the
old man's death had got about, and that it was necessary
they should make a great show of cleanliness. One afternoon, after remaining in the cellar for a couple of hours,
where she herself had gone to wash the salting tubs, she
came up again, carrying something in her apron. Quenu was
just then cutting up a pig's liver. She waited till he had
finished, talking awhile in an easy, indifferent fashion. But
there was an unusual glitter in her eyes, and she smiled her
most charming smile as she told him that she wanted to

speak to him. She led the way upstairs with seeming difficulty, impeded by what she had in her apron, which was strained almost to bursting.

By the time she reached the third floor she found herself short of breath and for a moment was obliged to lean against the balustrade. Quenu, much astonished, followed her into her bedroom without saying a word. It was the first time she had ever invited him to enter it. She closed the door, and letting go the corners of her apron, which her stiffened fingers could no longer hold up, she allowed a stream of gold and silver coins to flow gently upon her bed. She had discovered Uncle Gradelle's treasure at the bottom of a salting tub. The heap of money made a deep depression in the soft downy bed.

Lisa and Quenu evinced a quiet delight. They sat down on the edge of the bed, Lisa at the head and Quenu at the foot, on either side of the heap of coins, and they counted the money out upon the counterpane, so as to avoid making any noise. There were forty thousand francs in gold and three thousand francs in silver, while in a tin box they found bank-notes to the value of forty-two thousand francs. It took them two hours to count up the treasure. Quenu's hands trembled slightly, and it was Lisa who did most of the work.

They arranged the gold on the pillow in little heaps, leaving the silver in the hollow depression of the counterpane. When they had ascertained the total amount—eighty-five thousand francs, to them an enormous sum—they began to chat. And their conversation naturally turned upon their future, and they spoke of their marriage, although there had never been any previous mention of love between them. But this heap of money seemed to loosen their tongues. They had gradually seated themselves further back on the bed, leaning against the wall, beneath the white muslin curtains; and as they talked together, their hands, playing with the heap of silver between them, met, and remained linked amidst the pile of five-franc pieces. Twilight surprised them still sitting there together. Then, for the first time, Lisa blushed at finding the young man by her side. For a few moments, indeed, although not a thought of evil had come to them, they felt much embarrassed. Then Lisa went to get her own ten thousand francs. Quenu wanted her to put them with his uncle's savings. He mixed the two sums together, saying with a laugh that the money must be married also. Then it was agreed that Lisa should keep the hoard in her chest of drawers. When she had locked it up they both quietly went downstairs. They were now practically husband and wife.

The wedding took place during the following month. The neighbors considered the match a very natural one and in every way suitable. They had vaguely heard the story of the treasure, and Lisa's honesty was the subject of endless eulogy. After all, said the gossips, she might well have kept the money herself and not have spoken a word to Quenu about it; if she had spoken, it was out of pure honesty, for no one had seen her find the hoard. She well deserved, they added, that Quenu should make her his wife. That Quenu, by the way, was a lucky fellow; he wasn't a beauty himself, yet he had secured a beautiful wife, who had disinterred a fortune for him. Some even went so far as to whisper that Lisa was a simpleton for having acted as she had done; but the young woman only smiled when people speaking to her vaguely alluded to all these things. She and her husband lived on as previously, in happy placidity and quiet affection. She still assisted him as before, their hands still met amidst the sausage-meat, she still glanced over his shoulder into the pots and pans, and still nothing but the great fire in the kitchen brought the blood to their cheeks.

However, Lisa was a woman of practical common-sense and speedily saw the folly of allowing eighty-five thousand francs to lie idle in a chest of drawers. Quenu would have willingly stowed them away again at the bottom of the salting-tub until he had gained as much more, when they could have retired from business and have gone to live at Suresnes, a suburb to which both were partial. Lisa, however, had other ambitions. The Rue Pirouette did not accord with her ideas of cleanliness, her craving for fresh air, light, and healthy life. The shop where Uncle Gradelle had accumulated his fortune, sou by sou, was a long, dark place, one of those suspicious-looking pork-butchers' shops of the old quarters of the city, where the well-worn flagstones retain a strong odor of meat in spite of constant washings. Now the young woman longed for one of those bright modern shops, ornamented like a drawing room, and fringing the footway of some broad street with windows of crystalline transparency. She was not actuated by any petty ambition to play the fine lady behind a stylish counter, but clearly realized that commerce in its latest development needed elegant surroundings. Quenu showed much alarm the first time his wife suggested that they ought to move and spend some of their money in decorating a new shop. However, Lisa only shrugged her shoulders and smiled at finding him so timorous.

One evening, when night was falling and the shop had grown dark, Quenu and Lisa overheard a woman of the neighborhood talking to a friend outside their door.

"No, indeed! I've given up dealing with them," said she. "I wouldn't buy a bit of black pudding from them now on any account. They had a dead man in their kitchen, you know."

Quenu wept with vexation. The story of Gradelle's death in the kitchen was clearly getting about; and his nephew began to blush before his customers when he saw them sniffing his wares too closely. So, of his own accord, he spoke to his wife of her proposal to take a new shop. Lisa, without saying anything, had already been looking out for other premises and had found some, admirably situated, only a few yards away, in the Rue Rambuteau. The immediate neighborhood of the central markets, which were being opened just opposite, would triple their business and make their shop known all over Paris.

Quenu allowed himself to be drawn into a lavish expenditure of money; he laid out over thirty thousand francs in marble, glass, and gilding. Lisa spent hours with the workmen, giving her views about the slightest details. When she was at last installed behind the counter, customers arrived in a perfect procession, merely for the sake of examining the shop. The inside walls were lined from top to bottom with white marble. The ceiling was covered with a huge square mirror, framed by a broad gilded cornice, richly ornamented, while from the center hung a crystal chandelier with four branches. And behind the counter, and on the left, and at the far end of the shop were other mirrors, fitted between the marble panels and looking like doors opening into an infinite series of brightly lighted halls, where all sorts of appetizing edibles were displayed. The huge counter on the right hand was considered a very fine piece of work. At intervals along the front were lozenge-shaped panels of pinky marble. The flooring was of tiles, alternately white and pink, with a deep red fretting as border. The whole neighborhood was proud of the shop, and no one again thought of referring to the kitchen in the Rue Pirouette, where a man had died. For quite a month women stopped short on the footway to look at Lisa between the saveloys and bladders in the window. Her white and pink flesh excited as much admiration as the marbles. She seemed to be the soul, the living light, the healthy, sturdy idol of the pork trade; and thenceforth one and all baptized her "Lisa the beauty."

To the right of the shop was the dining room, a neat-looking apartment containing a sideboard, a table, and several cane-seated chairs of light oak. The matting on the floor, the wall paper of a soft yellow tint, the oil-cloth table-cover, colored to imitate oak, gave the room a somewhat cold appearance, which was relieved only by the glitter of a brass hanging-lamp, suspended from the ceiling, and spreading its big shade of transparent porcelain over the table. One of the dining room doors opened into the huge square kitchen, at the end of which was a small paved courtyard, serving for the storage of lumber—tubs, barrels and pans, and all kinds of utensils not in use. To the left of the water tap, alongside the gutter which carried off the greasy water, stood pots of faded flowers, removed from the shop window, and slowly dying.

Business was excellent. Quenu, who had been much alarmed by the initial outlay, now regarded his wife with something like respect and told his friends that she had "a wonderful head." At the end of five years they had nearly eighty thousand francs invested in the State funds. Lisa would say that they were not ambitious, that they had no desire to pile up money too quickly, or else she would have enabled her husband to gain hundreds and thousands of francs by prompting him to embark in the wholesale pig trade. But they were still young and had plenty of time before them; besides, they didn't care about a rough, scrambling business, but preferred to work at their ease, and enjoy life, instead of wearing themselves out with endless anxieties.

"For instance," Lisa would add in her expansive moments, "I have, you know, a cousin in Paris. I never see him, as the two families have fallen out. He has taken the name of Saccard, on account of certain matters which he wants to be forgotten. Well, this cousin of mine, I'm told, makes millions and millions of francs; but he gets no enjoyment out of life. He's always in a state of feverish excitement, always rushing here and there, up to his neck in all sorts of worrying business. Well, it's impossible, isn't it, for such a man to eat his dinner peaceably in the evening? We, at any rate, can take our meals comfortably, and make sure of what we eat, and we are not harassed by worries as he is. The only reason why people should care for money is that money's wanted for one to live. People like comfort; that's natural. But as for making money simply for the sake of making it, and giving yourself far more trouble and anxiety to gain it than you can ever get pleasure from it when it's gained, why, as for me, I'd rather sit still and cross my arms. And besides, I should like to see all those millions of my cousin's. I can't say that I altogether believe in them. I caught sight of him the other day in his carriage. He was quite yellow and looked ever so sly. A man who's making money doesn't have that kind of expression. But it's his business, and not mine. For our part, we prefer to make merely a hundred sous at a time and to get a hundred sous's worth of enjoyment out of them."

The household was undoubtedly thriving. A daughter had been born to the young couple during their first year of wedlock, and all three of them looked blooming. The business went on prosperously, without any laborious fatigue, just as Lisa desired. She had carefully kept free of any possible source of trouble or anxiety, and the days went by in an atmosphere of peaceful, unctuous prosperity. Their home was a nook of sensible happiness—a comfortable manger, so to speak, where father, mother, and daughter could grow sleek and fat. It was only Quenu who occasionally felt sad, through thinking of his brother Florent. Up to the year 1856 he had received letters from him at long intervals. Then no more came, and he had learned from a newspaper that three convicts having attempted to escape from the Ile du Diable, had been drowned before they were able to reach the mainland. He had made inquiries at the Préfecture of Police, but had not learnt anything definite; it seemed probable that his brother was dead. However, he did not lose all hope, though months passed without any tidings. Florent, in the meantime, was wandering about Dutch Guiana, and refrained from writing home as he was ever in hope of being able to return to France. Quenu at last began to mourn for him as one mourns for those whom one has been unable to bid farewell. Lisa had never known Florent, but she spoke very kindly whenever she saw her husband give way to his sorrow; and she evinced no impatience when for the hundredth time or so he began to relate stories of his early days, of his life in the big room in the Rue Royer Collard, the thirty-six trades which he had taken up one after another, and the dainties which he had cooked at the stove, dressed all in white, while Florent was dressed all in black. To such talk as this, indeed, she listened placidly, with a complacency which never wearied.

It was into the midst of all this happiness, ripening after careful culture, that Florent dropped one September morning just as Lisa was taking her morning bath of sunshine, and Quenu, with his eyes still heavy with sleep, was lazily applying his fingers to the congealed fat left in the pans from the previous evening. Florent's arrival caused a great commotion. Gavard advised them to conceal the "outlaw," as he somewhat pompously called Florent. Lisa, who looked pale, and more serious than was her wont, at last took him to the fifth floor, where she gave him the room belonging to the girl who assisted her in the shop. Quenu had cut some slices of bread and ham, but Florent was scarcely able to eat. He was overcome by dizziness and nausea, and went to bed, where he remained for five days in a state of delirium, the outcome of an attack of brain-fever, which fortunately received energetic treatment. When he recovered consciousness he perceived Lisa sitting by his bedside, silently stirring some cooling drink in a cup. As he tried to thank her, she told him that he must keep perfectly quiet and that they could talk together later on. At the end of another three days Florent was on his feet again. Then one morning Quenu went up to tell him that Lisa awaited them in her room on the first floor.

Quenu and his wife there occupied a suite of three rooms and a dressing room. You first passed through an antechamber, containing nothing but chairs, and then a small sitting room, whose furniture, shrouded in white covers, slumbered in the gloom cast by the Venetian shutters, which were always kept closed so as to prevent the light blue of the upholstery from fading. Then came the bedroom, the only one of the three which was really used. It was very comfortably furnished in mahogany. The bed, bulky and drowsy of aspect in the depths of the damp alcove, was really wonderful, with its four mattresses, its four pillows, its layers of blankets, and its corpulent *édredon*. It was evidently a bed intended for slumber. A mirrored wardrobe, a washstand with drawers, a small central table with a worked cover, and several chairs whose seats were protected by squares of lace, gave the room an aspect of plain but substantial middle-class luxury. On the left-hand wall, on either side of the mantelpiece, which was ornamented with some landscape-painted vases mounted on bronze stands and a gilt timepiece on which a figure of Gutenberg, also gilt, stood in an attitude of deep thought, hung portraits in oils of Quenu and Lisa, in ornate oval frames. Quenu had a smiling face, while Lisa wore an air of grave propriety; and both were dressed in black and depicted in flattering fashion, the features idealized, their skins wondrously smooth, their complexions soft and pinky. A carpet, in the Wilton style, with a complicated pattern of roses mingling with stars, concealed the flooring; while in front of the bed was a fluffy mat, made out of long pieces of curly wool, a work of patience at which Lisa herself had toiled while seated behind her counter. But the most striking object of all in the midst of this array of new furniture was a great square, thick-set secrétaire, which had been re-polished in vain, for the cracks and notches in the marble top and the scratches on the old mahogany front, quite black with age, still showed plainly. Lisa had desired to retain this piece of furniture, however, as Uncle Gradelle had used it for more than forty years. It would bring them good luck, she said. Its metal fastenings were truly something terrible, its lock was like that of a prison gate, and it was so heavy that it could scarcely be moved.

When Florent and Quenu entered the room they found Lisa seated at the lowered desk of the secrétaire, writing and jotting down figures in a big, round, and very legible hand. She signed to them not to disturb her, and the two men sat down. Florent looked round the room, and notably at the two portraits, the bed, and the timepiece, with an air of surprise.

"There!" at last exclaimed Lisa, after having carefully verified a whole page of calculations. "Listen to me now; we have an account to render to you, my dear Florent."

It was the first time that she had so addressed him. However, taking up the page of figures, she continued: "Your Uncle Gradelle died without leaving a will. Consequently you and your brother were his sole heirs. We now have to hand your share over to you."

"But I do not ask you for anything!" exclaimed Florent. "I don't wish for anything!"

Quenu had apparently been in ignorance of his wife's intentions. He turned rather pale and looked at her with an expression of displeasure. Of course, he certainly loved his brother dearly; but there was no occasion to hurl his uncle's money at him in this way. There would have been plenty of time to go into the matter later on.

"I know very well, my dear Florent," continued Lisa, "that

you did not come back with the intention of claiming from us what belongs to you; but business is business, you know, and we had better get things settled at once. Your uncle's savings amounted to eighty-five thousand francs. I have therefore put down forty-two thousand five hundred to your credit. See!"

She showed him the figures on the sheet of paper.

"It is unfortunately not so easy to value the shop, plant, stock-in-trade, and goodwill. I have only been able to put down approximate amounts, but I don't think I have underestimated anything. Well, the total valuation which I have made comes to fifteen thousand three hundred and ten francs; your half of which is seven thousand six hundred and fifty-five francs, so that your share amounts, in all, to fifty thousand one hundred and fifty-five francs. Please verify it for yourself, will you ?"

She had called out the figures in a clear, distinct voice, and she now handed the paper to Florent, who was obliged to take it.

"But the old man's business was certainly never worth fifteen thousand francs!" cried Quenu. "Why, I wouldn't have given ten thousand for it!"

He had ended by getting quite angry with his wife. Really, it was absurd to carry honesty to such a point as that! Had Florent said one word about the business? No, indeed, he had declared that he didn't wish for anything.

"The business was worth fifteen thousand three hundred and ten francs," Lisa re-asserted, calmly. "You will agree with me, my dear Florent, that it is quite unnecessary to bring a lawyer into our affairs. It is for us to arrange the division between ourselves, since you have now turned up again. I naturally thought of this as soon as you arrived; and, while you were in bed with the fever, I did my best to draw up this little inventory. It contains, as you see, a fairly complete statement of everything. I have been through our old books and have called up my memory to help me. Read it aloud, and I will give you any additional information you may want."

Florent ended by smiling. He was touched by this easy and, as it were, natural display of probity. Placing the sheet of figures on the young woman's knee, he took hold of her hand and said, "I am very glad, my dear Lisa, to hear that you are prosperous, but I will not take your money. The heritage belongs to you and my brother, who took care of my uncle to the last. I don't require anything, and I don't intend to hamper you in carrying on your business."

Lisa insisted, and even showed some vexation, while Quenu gnawed his thumbs in silence, striving to restrain himself. "Ah!" resumed Florent with a laugh, "if Uncle Gradelle could hear you, I think he'd come back and take the money away again. I was never a favorite of his, you know."

"Well, no," muttered Quenu, no longer able to keep still, "he certainly wasn't over fond of you."

Lisa, however, still pressed the matter. She did not like to have money in her secrétaire that did not belong to her; it would worry her, said she; the thought of it would disturb her peace. So Florent, still in a joking way, proposed to invest his share in the business. Moreover, said he, he did not intend to refuse their help; he would, no doubt, be unable to find employment all at once; and then, too, he would need a complete outfit, for he was scarcely presentable.

"Of course," cried Quenu, "you will board and lodge with us, and we will buy you all that you want. That's understood. You know very well that we are not likely to leave you in the streets, I hope!"

He was quite moved now and even felt a trifle ashamed of the alarm he had experienced at the thought of having to hand over a large amount of money all at once. He began to joke and told his brother that he would undertake to fatten him. Florent gently shook his head; while Lisa folded up the sheet of figures and put it away in a drawer of the secrétaire.

"You are wrong," she said by way of conclusion. "I have done what I was bound to do. Now it shall be as you wish. But, for my part, I should never have had a moment's peace if I had not put things before you. Bad thoughts would quite upset me."

They then began to speak of another matter. It would be necessary to give some reason for Florent's presence, and at the same time avoid exciting the suspicion of the police. He told them that in order to return to France he had availed himself of the papers of a poor fellow who had died in his arms at Surinam from yellow fever. By a singular coincidence this young fellow's Christian name was Florent.

Florent Laquerrière, to give him his name in full, had left but one relation in Paris, a female cousin, and had been informed of her death while in America. Nothing would therefore be easier than for Quenu's stepbrother to pass himself off as the man who had died at Surinam. Lisa offered to take upon herself the part of the female cousin. They then agreed to relate that their cousin Florent had returned from abroad, where he had failed in his attempts to make a fortune, and that they, the Quenu-Gradelles, as they were called in the neighborhood, had received him into their house until he could find suitable employment. When this was all settled, Quenu insisted upon his brother making a thorough inspection of the rooms and would not spare him the examination of a single stool. While they were in the bare-looking chamber containing nothing but chairs, Lisa pushed open a door, and showing Florent a small dressing room, told him that the shop-girl should sleep in it, so that he could retain the bedroom on the fifth floor.

In the evening Florent was arrayed in new clothes from

head to foot. He had insisted upon again having a black coat and black trousers, much against the advice of Quenu, upon whom black had a depressing effect. No further attempts were made to conceal his presence in the house, and Lisa told the story which had been planned to everyone who cared to hear it. From then on Florent spent almost all his time on the premises, lingering on a chair in the kitchen or leaning against the marble-work in the shop. At mealtimes Quenu plied him with food, and evinced considerable vexation when he proved such a small eater and left half the contents of his liberally filled plate untouched. Lisa had resumed her old life, evincing a kindly tolerance of her brother-in-law's presence, even in the morning, when he somewhat interfered with the work. Then she would momentarily forget him and on suddenly perceiving his black form in front of her give a slight start of surprise, followed, however, by one of her sweet smiles, lest he might feel at all hurt. This skinny man's disinterestedness had impressed her, and she regarded him with a feeling akin to respect, mingled with vague fear. Florent for his part only felt that there was great affection around him.

When bedtime came he went upstairs, a little wearied by his lazy day, with the two young men whom Quenu employed as assistants and who slept in attics adjoining his own. Léon, the apprentice, was barely fifteen years of age. He was a slight, gentle-looking lad, addicted to stealing stray slices of ham and bits of sausages. These he would conceal under his pillow, eating them during the night without any bread. Several times at about one o'clock in the morning Florent almost fancied that Léon was giving a supper-party; for he heard low whispering followed by a sound of munching jaws and rustling paper. And then a rippling girlish laugh would break faintly on the deep silence of the sleeping house like the soft trilling of a flageolet.

The other assistant, Auguste Landois, came from Troyes. Bloated with unhealthy fat, he had too large a head and was already bald, although only twenty-eight years of age. As he went upstairs with Florent on the first evening, he told him his story in a confused, garrulous way. He had at first come to Paris merely for the purpose of perfecting himself in the business, intending to return to Troyes, where his cousin, Augustine Landois, was waiting for him, and there setting up for himself as a pork-butcher. He and she had had the same godfather and bore virtually the same Christian name. However, he had grown ambitious; and now hoped to establish himself in business in Paris by the aid of the money left him by his mother, which he had deposited with a notary before leaving Champagne.

Auguste had got so far in his narrative when the fifth floor was reached; however, he still detained Florent, in order to sound the praises of Madame Quenu, who had consented to send for Augustine Landois to replace an assistant who had turned out badly. He himself was now thoroughly acquainted with his part of the business, and his cousin was perfecting herself in shop-management. In a year or eighteen months they would be married, and then they would set up on their own account in some populous corner of Paris, at Plaisance most likely. They were in no great hurry, he added, for the bacon trade was very bad that year. Then he proceeded to tell Florent that he and his cousin had been photographed together at the fair of St. Ouen, and he entered the attic to have another look at the photograph, which Augustine had left on the mantelpiece, in her desire that Madame Quenu's cousin should have a pretty room. Auguste lingered there for a moment, looking quite livid in the dim yellow light of his candle and casting his eyes around the little chamber which was still full of memorials of the young girl. Next, stepping up to the bed, he asked Florent if it was comfortable. His cousin slept below now, said he, and would be better there in the winter, for the attics were very cold. Then at last he went off, leaving Florent alone with the bed and standing in front of the photograph. As shown on the latter Auguste looked like a sort of pale Quenu, and Augustine like an immature Lisa.

Florent, although on friendly terms with the assistants, petted by his brother, and cordially treated by Lisa, presently began to feel very bored. He had tried, but without success, to obtain some pupils; moreover, he purposely avoided the students' quarter for fear of being recognized. Lisa gently suggested to him that he had better try to obtain a situation in some commercial house, where he could take charge of the correspondence and keep the books. She returned to this subject again and again, and at last offered to find a berth for him herself. She was gradually becoming impatient at finding him so often in her way, idle, and not knowing what to do with himself. At first this impatience was merely due to the dislike she felt of people who do nothing but cross their arms and eat, and she had no thought of reproaching him for consuming her substance.

"For my own part," she would say to him, "I could never spend the whole day in dreamy lounging. You can't have any appetite for your meals. You ought to tire yourself."

Gavard, also, was seeking a situation for Florent, but in a very extraordinary and most mysterious fashion. He would have liked to find some employment of a dramatic character, or in which there should be a touch of bitter irony, as was suitable for an outlaw. Gavard was a man who was always in opposition. He had just completed his fiftieth year, and he boasted that he had already passed judgment on four Governments. He still contemptuously shrugged his shoulders at the thought of Charles x, the priests and nobles and other attendant rabble, whom he had helped to sweep away. Louis

Philippe, with his bourgeois following, had been an imbecile, and he would tell how the citizen-king had hoarded his money in a woollen stocking. As for the Republic of '48, that had been a mere farce, the working classes had deceived him; however, he no longer acknowledged that he had applauded the Coup d'Etat, for he now looked upon Napoleon III as his personal enemy, a scoundrel who shut himself up with Morny and others to indulge in gluttonous orgies. He was never weary of holding forth upon this subject. Lowering his voice a little, he would declare that women were brought to the Tuileries in closed carriages every evening, and that he, who was speaking, had one night heard the echoes of the orgies while crossing the Place du Carrousel. It was Gavard's religion to make himself as disagreeable as possible to any existing Government. He would seek to spite it in all sorts of ways and laugh in secret for several months at the pranks he played. To begin with, he voted for candidates who would worry the Ministers at the Corps Législatif. Then, if he could rob the revenue, or baffle the police, and bring about a row of some kind or other, he strove to give the affair as much of an insurrectionary character as possible. He told a great many lies, too; set himself up as being a very dangerous man; talked as though "the satellites of the Tuileries" were well acquainted with him and trembled at the sight of him; and asserted that one half of them must be guillotined, and the other half deported, the next time there was "a flare-up." His violent political creed found food in boastful, bragging talk of this sort, in cock and bull stories demonstrating that mocking need for uproarious comedy which prompts a Parisian shopkeeper to take down his shutters on a day of barricade-fighting to get a good view of the corpses of the slain. When Florent returned from Cayenne, Gavard opined that he had got hold of a splendid chance for some abominable trick, and bestowed much thought upon the question of how he might best vent his spleen on the Emperor and Ministers and everyone in office, down to the very lowest police-constable.

Gavard's manners with Florent were altogether those of a man tasting some forbidden pleasure. He contemplated him with blinking eyes, lowered his voice even when making the most trifling remark, and grasped his hand with all sorts of masonic flummery. He had at last lighted upon something in the way of an adventure; he had a friend who was really compromised, and could, without falsehood, speak of the dangers he incurred. He undoubtedly experienced a secret alarm at the sight of this man who had returned from transportation and whose fleshlessness testified to the long sufferings he had endured; however, this touch of alarm was delightful, for it increased his notion of his own importance, and convinced him that he was really doing something wonderful in treating a dangerous character as a friend. Florent became a sort of sacred being in his eyes: he swore by him alone, and had recourse to his name whenever arguments failed him, and he wanted to crush the Government once and for all.

Gavard had lost his wife in the Rue Saint Jacques some months after the Coup d'Etat; however, he had kept on his roasting-shop till 1856. At that time it was reported that he had made large sums of money by going into partnership with a neighboring grocer who had obtained a contract for supplying dried vegetables to the Crimean expeditionary corps. The truth was, however, that, having sold his shop, he lived on his income for a year without doing anything. He himself did not care to talk about the real origin of his fortune, for to have revealed it would have prevented him from plainly expressing his opinion of the Crimean War, which he referred to as a mere adventurous expedition, "undertaken simply to consolidate the throne and to fill certain persons' pockets." At the end of a year he had grown utterly weary of life in his bachelor quarters. As he was in the habit of visiting the Quenu-Gradelles almost daily, he determined to take up his residence nearer to them and came to live in the Rue de la Cossonnerie. The neighboring markets, with their noisy uproar and endless chatter, quite fascinated him; and he decided to hire a stall in the poultry pavilion, just for the purpose of amusing himself and occupying his idle hours with all the gossip. Thenceforth he lived amidst ceaseless tittle-tattle, acquainted with every little scandal in the neighborhood, his head buzzing with the incessant yelping around him. He blissfully tasted a thousand titillating delights, having at last found his true element, and bathing in it, with the voluptuous pleasure of a carp swimming in the sunshine. Florent would sometimes go to see him at his stall. The afternoons were still very warm. All along the narrow alleys sat women plucking poultry. Rays of light streamed in between the awnings, and in the warm atmosphere, in the golden dust of the sunbeams, feathers fluttered here and there like dancing snowflakes. A trail of coaxing calls and offers followed Florent as he passed along. "Can I sell you a fine duck, monsieur?" "I've some very fine fat chickens here, monsieur; come and see!" "Monsieur! monsieur, do just buy this pair of pigeons!" Deafened and embarrassed he freed himself from the women, who still went on plucking as they fought for possession of him; and the fine down flew about and nearly choked him, like hot smoke reeking with the strong odor of the poultry. At last, in the middle of the alley, near the water taps, he found Gavard ranting away in shirt-sleeves in front of his stall, with his arms crossed over the bib of his blue apron. He reigned there, in a gracious, condescending way, over a group of ten or twelve women. He was the only male dealer in that part of the market. He was so fond of wagging his tongue that he had quarrelled with five or six girls whom he had successively engaged to attend to his stall, and had now made up his mind to sell his goods himself, naively explaining that the silly women spent the whole blessed day in gossiping, and that it was beyond his power to manage them. As someone, however, was still necessary to supply his place whenever he absented himself he took in Marjolin, who was prowling about, after attempting in turn all the petty market callings.

Florent sometimes remained for an hour with Gavard, amazed by his ceaseless flow of chatter, and his calm serenity and assurance amid the crowd of petticoats. He would interrupt one woman, pick a quarrel with another ten stalls away, snatch a customer from a third, and make as much noise himself as his hundred and odd garrulous neighbors, whose incessant clamor kept the iron plates of the pavilion vibrating sonorously like so many gongs.

The poultry-dealer's only relations were a sister-in-law and a niece. When his wife died, her eldest sister, Madame Lecœur, who had become a widow about a year previously, had mourned for her in an exaggerated fashion and gone almost every evening to tender consolation to the bereaved husband. She had doubtless cherished the hope that she might win his affection and fill the yet warm place of the deceased. Gavard, however, abominated lean women; and would, indeed, only stroke such cats and dogs as were very fat; so that Madame Lecœur, who was long and withered, failed in her designs.

With her feelings greatly hurt, furious at the ex-roaster's five-franc pieces eluding her grasp, she nurtured great spite against him. He became the enemy to whom she devoted all her time. When she saw him set up in the markets only a few yards away from the pavilion where she herself sold butter and eggs and cheese, she accused him of doing so simply for the sake of annoying her and bringing her bad luck.

From that moment she began to lament and turned so yellow and melancholy that she indeed ended by losing her customers and getting into difficulties. She had for a long time kept with her the daughter of one of her sisters, a peasant-woman who had sent her the child and then taken no further trouble about it.

This child grew up in the markets. Her surname was Sarriet, and so she soon became generally known as La Sarriette. At sixteen years of age she had developed into such a charming sly-looking creature that gentlemen came to buy cheeses at her aunt's stall simply for the purpose of ogling her. She did not care for the gentlemen, however; with her dark hair, pale face, and eyes glistening like live embers, her sympathies were with the lower ranks of the people. At last she chose as her lover a young man from Ménilmontant who was employed by her aunt as a porter. At twenty she set up in business as a fruit-dealer with the help of some funds procured no one knew how; and from then on Monsieur Jules, as her lover was called, displayed spotless hands, a clean blouse, and a velvet cap; and only came down to the market in the afternoon, in his slippers. They lived together on the third story of a large house in the Rue Vauvilliers, on the ground floor of which was a disreputable café.

Madame Lecœur's acerbity of temper was brought to a pitch by what she called La Sarriette's ingratitude, and she spoke of the girl in the most violent and abusive language. They broke off all communication, the aunt fairly exasperated, and the niece and Monsieur Jules concocting stories about the aunt, which the young man would repeat to the other dealers in the butter pavilion. Gavard found La Sarriette very entertaining and treated her with great indulgence. Whenever they met he would good-naturedly pat her cheeks.

One afternoon, while Florent was sitting in his brother's

shop, tired out with the fruitless pilgrimages he had made during the morning in search of work, Marjolin made his appearance there. This big lad, who had the massiveness and gentleness of a Fleming, was a protege of Lisa's. She would say that there was no evil in him; that he was indeed a little bit stupid, but as strong as a horse, and particularly interesting from the fact that nobody knew anything of his parentage. It was she who had got Gavard to employ him.

Lisa was sitting behind the counter, feeling annoyed by the sight of Florent's muddy boots which were soiling the pink and white tiles of the flooring. Twice already she had risen to scatter sawdust about the shop. However, she smiled at Marjolin as he entered.

"Monsieur Gavard," began the young man, "has sent me to ask—"

But all at once he stopped and glanced round; then in a lower voice he resumed: "He told me to wait till there was no one with you and then to repeat these words, which he made me learn by heart: 'Ask them if there is no danger, and if I can come and talk to them of the matter they know about.'"

"Tell Monsieur Gavard that we are expecting him," replied Lisa, who was quite accustomed to the poultry-dealer's mysterious ways.

Marjolin, however, did not go away; but remained in ecstasy before the handsome mistress of the shop, contemplating her with an expression of fawning humility.

Touched, as it were, by this mute adoration, Lisa spoke to him again.

"Are you comfortable with Monsieur Gavard?" she asked. "He's not an unkind man, and you ought to try to please him."

"Yes, Madame Lisa."

"But you don't behave as you should do, you know. Only yesterday I saw you clambering about the roofs of the market again; and, besides, you are constantly with a lot of disreputable lads and lasses. You ought to remember that you are a man now and begin to think of the future."

"Yes, Madame Lisa."

However, Lisa had to get up to wait upon a lady who came in and wanted a pound of pork chops. She left the counter and went to the block at the far end of the shop. Here, with a long, slender knife, she cut three chops in a loin of pork; and then, raising a small cleaver with her strong hand, dealt three sharp blows which separated the chops from the loin. At each blow she dealt, her black merino dress rose slightly behind her, and the ribs of her stays showed beneath her tightly stretched bodice. She slowly took up the chops and weighed them with an air of gravity, her eyes gleaming and her lips tightly closed.

When the lady had gone, and Lisa perceived Marjolin still full of delight at having seen her deal those three clean, forcible blows with the cleaver, she at once called out to him, "What! haven't you gone yet?"

He then turned to go, but she detained him for a moment longer.

"Now, don't let me see you again with that hussy Cadine," she said. "Oh, it's no use to deny it! I saw you together this morning in the tripe-market, watching men breaking the sheep's heads. I can't understand what attraction a good-looking young fellow like you can find in such a slipshod slattern as Cadine. Now then, go and tell Monsieur Gavard that he had better come at once, while there's no one about."

Marjolin thereupon went off in confusion, without saying a word.

Handsome Lisa remained standing behind her counter, with her head turned slightly in the direction of her markets, and Florent gazed at her in silence, surprised to see her looking so beautiful. He had never looked at her properly before; indeed, he did not know the right way to look at a woman. He now saw her rising above the viands on the counter. In front of her was an array of white china dishes, containing long Arles and Lyon sausages, slices of which had already been cut off, with tongues and pieces of boiled pork; then a pig's head in a mass of jelly; an open pot of preserved sausage-meat, and a large box of sardines disclosing a pool of oil. On the right and left, upon wooden platters, were mounds of French and Italian brawn, a common French ham, of a pinky hue, and a Yorkshire ham, whose deep red lean showed beneath a broad band of fat. There were other dishes too, round ones and oval ones, containing spiced tongue, truffled galantine, and a boar's head stuffed with pistachio nuts; while close to her, in reach of her hand, stood some yellow earthen pans containing larded veal, *pâté de foie gras*, and hare-pie.

As there were no signs of Gavard's coming, she arranged some fore-end bacon upon a little marble shelf at the end of the counter, put the jars of lard and dripping back into their places, wiped the plates of each pair of scales, and saw to the fire of the heater, which was getting low. Then she turned her head again and gazed in silence towards the markets. The smell of all the viands ascended around her, she was enveloped, as it were, by the aroma of truffles. She looked beautifully fresh that afternoon. The whiteness of all the dishes was supplemented by that of her sleevelets and apron, above which appeared her plump neck and rosy cheeks, which recalled the soft tones of the hams and the pallor of all the transparent fat.

As Florent continued to gaze at her he began to feel intimidated, disquieted by her prim, sedate demeanor; and in lieu of openly looking at her he ended by glancing surreptitiously in the mirrors around the shop, in which her back and face and profile could be seen. The mirror on the ceiling, too, reflected the top of her head, with its tightly rolled chignon and the little bands lowered over her temples.

There seemed, indeed, to be a perfect crowd of Lisas, with broad shoulders, powerful arms, and round, full bosoms. At last Florent checked his roving eyes and let them rest on a particularly pleasing side view of the young woman as mirrored between two pieces of pork. From the hooks running along the whole line of mirrors and marbles hung sides of pork and bands of larding fat; and Lisa, with her massive neck, rounded hips, and swelling bosom seen in profile, looked like some waxwork queen in the midst of the dangling fat and meat. However, she bent forward and smiled in a friendly way at the two goldfish which were ever and ever swimming round the aquarium in the window.

Gavard entered the shop. With an air of great importance he went to fetch Quenu from the kitchen. Then he seated himself upon a small marble-topped table, while Florent remained on his chair and Lisa behind the counter; Quenu meantime leaning his back against a side of pork. And thereupon Gavard announced that he had at last found a situation for Florent. They would be vastly amused when they heard what it was, and the Government would be nicely caught.

But all at once he stopped short, for a passing neighbor, Mademoiselle Saget, having seen such a large party gossiping together at the Quenu-Gradelles', had opened the door and entered the shop. Carrying her everlasting black bag on her arm, dressed in a faded gown and a black ribbonless straw hat, which appropriately cast a shadow over her prying white face, she saluted the men with a slight bow and Lisa with a sharp smile.

She was an acquaintance of the family and still lived in the house in the Rue Pirouette where she had resided for the last forty years, probably on a small private income; but of that she never spoke. She had, however, one day talked of Cherbourg, mentioning that she had been born there. Nothing further was ever known of her antecedents. All her conversation was about other people; she could tell the whole story of their daily lives, even to the number of things they sent to be washed each month; and she carried her prying curiosity concerning her neighbors' affairs so far as to listen behind their doors and open their letters. Her tongue was feared from the Rue Saint Denis to the Rue Jean-Jacques Rousseau, and from the Rue Saint Honoré to the Rue Mauconseil. All day long she went ferreting about with her empty bag, pretending that she was marketing, but in reality buying nothing, as her sole purpose was to retail scandal and gossip, and keep herself fully informed of every trifling incident that happened. Indeed, she had turned her brain into an encyclopedia brimful of every possible particular concerning the people of the neighborhood and their homes.

Quenu had always accused her of having spread the story of his Uncle Gradelle's death on the chopping-block, and had borne her a grudge ever since. She was extremely well posted in the history of Uncle Gradelle and the Quenus, and knew them, she would say, by heart. For the last fortnight, however, Florent's arrival had greatly perplexed her, filled her, indeed, with a perfect fever of curiosity. She became quite ill when she discovered any unforeseen gap in her information. And yet she could have sworn that she had seen that tall lanky fellow somewhere or other before.

She remained standing in front of the counter, examining the dishes one after another, and saying in a shrill voice:

"I hardly know what to have. When the afternoon comes I feel quite famished for my dinner, and then, later on, I don't seem able to fancy anything at all. Have you got a cutlet rolled in bread-crumbs left, Madame Quenu?"

Without waiting for a reply, she removed one of the covers of the heater. It was that of the compartment reserved for the chitterlings, sausages, and black-puddings. However, the chafing-dish was quite cold, and there was nothing left but one stray forgotten sausage.

"Look under the other cover, Mademoiselle Saget," said Lisa. "I believe there's a cutlet there."

"No, it doesn't tempt me," muttered the little old woman, poking her nose under the other cover, however, all the same. "I felt rather a fancy for one, but I'm afraid a cutlet would be rather too heavy in the evening. I'd rather have something, too, that I need not warm."

While speaking she had turned towards Florent and looked at him; then she looked at Gavard, who was beating a tattoo with his finger-tips on the marble table. She smiled at them, as though inviting them to continue their conversation.

"Wouldn't a little piece of salt pork suit you?" asked Lisa.

"A piece of salt pork? Yes, that might do."

She then took up the fork with plated handle, which was lying at the edge of the dish, and began to turn all the pieces of pork about, prodding them, lightly tapping the bones to judge of their thickness, and minutely scrutinizing the shreds of pinky meat. And as she turned them over she repeated, "No, no; it doesn't tempt me."

"Well, then, have a sheep's tongue, or a bit of brawn, or a slice of larded veal," suggested Lisa patiently.

Mademoiselle Saget, however, shook her head. She remained there for a few minutes longer, pulling dissatisfied faces over the different dishes; then, seeing that the others were determined to remain silent, and that she would not be able to learn anything, she took herself off.

"No; I felt rather a fancy for a cutlet rolled in breadcrumbs," she said as she left the shop, "but the one you have left is too fat. I must come another time."

Lisa bent forward to watch her through the sausage-skins hanging in the shop front and saw her cross the road and enter the fruit market.

"The old she-goat!" growled Gavard.

Then, as they were now alone again, he began to tell them of the situation he had found for Florent. A friend of his, he said, Monsieur Verlaque, one of the fish market inspectors, was so ill that he was obliged to take a rest; and that very morning the poor man had told him that he should be very glad to find a substitute who would keep the berth open for him in case he should recover.

"Verlaque, you know, won't last another six months," added Gavard, "and Florent will keep the place. It's a splendid idea, isn't it? And it will be such a take-in for the police! The berth is under the Préfecture, you know. What glorious fun to see Florent getting paid by the police, eh?"

He burst into a hearty laugh; the idea struck him as so extremely comical.

"I won't take the place," Florent bluntly replied. "I've sworn I'll never accept anything from the Empire, and I would rather die of starvation than serve under the Préfecture. It is quite out of the question, Gavard, quite so!"

Gavard seemed somewhat put out on hearing this. Quenu had lowered his head, while Lisa, turning round, looked keenly at Florent, her neck swollen, her bosom straining her bodice almost to bursting-point. She was just going to open her mouth when La Sarriette entered the shop, and there was another pause in the conversation.

"Dear me!" exclaimed La Sarriette with her soft laugh, "I'd almost forgotten to get any bacon fat. Please, Madame Quenu, cut me a dozen thin strips—very thin ones, you know; I want them for larding larks. Jules has taken it into his head to eat some larks. Ah! how do you do, uncle?"

She filled the whole shop with her dancing skirts and

smiled brightly at everyone. Her face looked fresh and creamy, and on one side her hair was coming down, loosened by the wind which blew through the markets. Gavard grasped her hands, while she with merry impudence resumed: "I'll bet that you were talking about me just as I came in. Tell me what you were saying, uncle."

However, Lisa now called to her, "Just look and tell me if this is thin enough."

She was cutting the strips of bacon fat with great care on a piece of board in front of her. Then as she wrapped them up she inquired, "Can I give you anything else?"

"Well, yes," replied La Sarriette; "since I'm about it, I think I'll have a pound of lard. I'm awfully fond of fried potatoes; I can make a breakfast off a few potatoes and a bunch of radishes. Yes, I'll have a pound of lard, please, Madame Quenu."

Lisa placed a sheet of stout paper in the pan of the scales. Then she took the lard out of a jar under the shelves with a boxwood spatula, gently adding small quantities to the fatty heap, which began to melt and run slightly. When the plate of the scale fell, she took up the paper, folded it, and rapidly twisted the ends with her fingertips.

"That makes twenty-four sous," she said; "the bacon is thirty sous altogether. There's nothing else you want, is there?"

"No," said La Sarriette, "nothing." She paid her money, still laughing and showing her teeth, and staring the men in the face. Her gray skirt was all awry, and her loosely-fastened red neckerchief allowed a little of her white bosom to appear. Before she went away she stepped up to Gavard again and pretending to threaten him exclaimed: "So you won't tell me what you were talking about as I came in? I could see you laughing from the street. Oh, you sly fellow! Ah! I sha'n't love you any longer!"

Then she left the shop and ran across the road.

"It was Mademoiselle Saget who sent her here," remarked handsome Lisa drily.

Then silence fell again for some moments. Gavard was dismayed at Florent's reception of his proposal. Lisa was the first to speak. "It is wrong of you to refuse the post, Florent," she said in the most friendly tones. "You know how difficult it is to find any employment, and you are not in a position to be over-exacting."

"I have my reasons," Florent replied.

Lisa shrugged her shoulders. "Come, now," said she, "you really can't be serious, I'm sure. I can understand that you are not in love with the Government, but it would be too absurd to let your opinions prevent you from earning your living. And, besides, my dear fellow, the Emperor isn't at all a bad sort of man. You don't suppose, do you, that he knew you were eating moldy bread and tainted meat? He can't be everywhere, you know, and you can see for yourself that he hasn't prevented us here from doing pretty well. You are not at all just; indeed you are not."

Gavard, however, was getting very fidgety. He could not bear to hear people speak well of the Emperor.

"No, no, Madame Quenu," he interrupted; "you are going too far. It is a scoundrelly system altogether."

"Oh, as for you," exclaimed Lisa vivaciously, "you'll never rest until you've got yourself plundered and knocked on the head as the result of all your wild talk. Don't let us discuss politics; you would only make me angry. The question is Florent, isn't it? Well, for my part, I say that he ought to accept this inspectorship. Don't you think so too, Quenu?"

Quenu, who had not yet said a word, was very much put out by his wife's sudden appeal.

"It's a good berth," he replied, without compromising himself.

Then, amidst another interval of awkward silence, Florent resumed: "I beg you, let us drop the subject. My mind is quite made up. I shall wait."

"You will wait!" cried Lisa, losing patience.

Two rosy fires had risen to her cheeks. As she stood there, erect, in her white apron, with rounded, swelling hips, it was with difficulty that she restrained herself from breaking out into bitter words. However, the entrance of another person into the shop arrested her anger. The new arrival was Madame Lecœur.

"Can you let me have half a pound of mixed meats at fifty sous the pound?" she asked.

She at first pretended not to notice her brother-in-law; but presently she just nodded her head to him, without speaking. Then she scrutinized the three men from head to foot, doubtless hoping to divine their secret by the manner in which they waited for her to go. She could see that she was putting them out, and the knowledge of this rendered her yet more sour and angular, as she stood there in her limp skirts, with her long, spider-like arms bent and her knotted fingers clasped beneath her apron. Then, as she coughed slightly, Gavard, whom the silence embarrassed, inquired if she had a cold.

She curtly answered in the negative. Her tightly-stretched skin was of a red-brick color on those parts of her face where her bones protruded, and the dull fire burning in her eyes and scorching their lids testified to some liver complaint nurtured by the querulous jealousy of her disposition. She turned round again towards the counter, and watched each movement made by Lisa as she served her with the distrustful glance of one who is convinced that an attempt will be made to defraud her.

"Don't give me any saveloy," she exclaimed; "I don't like it."

Lisa had taken up a slender knife and was cutting some

thin slices of sausage. She next passed on to the smoked ham and the common ham, cutting delicate slices from each, and bending forward slightly as she did so, with her eyes ever fixed on the knife. Her plump rosy hands, flitting about the viands with light and gentle touches, seemed to have derived suppleness from contact with all the fat.

"You would like some larded veal, wouldn't you?" she asked, bringing a yellow pan towards her.

Madame Lecœur seemed to be thinking the matter over at considerable length; however, she at last said that she would have some. Lisa had now begun to cut into the contents of the pans, from which she removed slices of larded veal and hare *pâté* on the tip of a broad-bladed knife. And she deposited each successive slice on the middle of a sheet of paper placed on the scales.

"Aren't you going to give me some of the boar's head with pistachio nuts?" asked Madame Lecœur in her querulous voice.

Lisa was obliged to add some of the boar's head. But the butter-dealer was getting exacting and asked for two slices of galantine. She was very fond of it. Lisa, who was already irritated, played impatiently with the handles of the knives, and told her that the galantine was truffled, and that she could only include it in an "assortment" at three francs the pound. Madame Lecœur, however, still continued to pry into the dishes, trying to find something else to ask for. When the "assortment" was weighed she made Lisa add some jelly and gherkins to it. The block of jelly, shaped like a Savoy cake, shook on its white china dish beneath the angry violence of Lisa's hand; and as with her fingertips she took a couple of gherkins from a jar behind the heater, she made the vinegar spurt over the sides.

"Twenty-five sous, isn't it?" Madame Lecœur leisurely inquired.

She fully perceived Lisa's covert irritation and greatly enjoyed the sight of it, producing her money as slowly as possible, as though, indeed, her silver had got lost amongst the money in her pocket. And she glanced askance at Gavard, relishing the embarrassed silence which her presence was prolonging, and vowing that she would not go off, since they were hiding some trickery or other from her. However Lisa at last put the parcel in her hands, and she was then obliged to take her departure. She went away without saying a word, but darting a searching glance all round the shop.

"It was that Saget who sent her too!" burst out Lisa, as soon as the old woman was gone. "Is the old wretch going to send the whole market here to try to find out what we talk about? What a prying, malicious set they are! Did anyone ever hear before of crumbed cutlets and "assortments" being bought at five o'clock in the afternoon? But then they'd rack themselves with indigestion rather than not find out! Upon my word, though, if La Saget sends anyone else here, you'll see the reception she'll get. I would bundle her out of the shop, even if she were my own sister!"

The three men remained silent in presence of this explosion of anger. Gavard had gone to lean over the brass rail of the window-front, where, seemingly lost in thought, he began playing with one of the cut-glass balusters detached from its wire fastening. Presently, however, he raised his head. "Well, for my part," he said, "I looked upon it all as an excellent joke."

"Looked upon what as a joke?" asked Lisa, still quivering with indignation.

"The inspectorship."

She raised her hands, gave a last glance at Florent, and then sat down upon the cushioned bench behind the counter and said nothing further. Gavard, however, began to explain his views at length; the drift of his argument being that it was the Government which would look foolish in the matter, since Florent would be taking its money.

"My dear fellow," he said complacently, "those scoundrels all but starved you to death, didn't they? Well, you must make them feed you now. It's a splendid idea; it caught my fancy at once!"

Florent smiled, but still persisted in his refusal. Quenu, in the hope of pleasing his wife, did his best to find some good arguments. Lisa, however, appeared to pay no further attention to them. For the last moment or two she had been looking attentively in the direction of the markets. And all at once she sprang to her feet again, exclaiming, "Ah! it is La Normande that they are sending to play the spy on us now! Well, so much the worse for La Normande; she shall pay for the others!"

A tall female pushed the shop-door open. It was the handsome fish-girl, Louise Méhudin, generally known as La Normande. She was a bold-looking beauty, with a delicate white skin, and was almost as plump as Lisa, but there was more effrontery in her glance, and her bosom heaved with warmer life. She came into the shop with a light swinging step, her gold chain jingling on her apron, her bare hair arranged in the latest style, and a bow at her throat, a lace bow, which made her one of the most coquettish-looking queens of the markets. She brought a vague odor of fish with her, and a herring-scale showed like a tiny patch of mother-of-pearl near the little finger of one of her hands. She and Lisa, having lived in the same house in the Rue Pirouette, were intimate friends, linked by a touch of rivalry which kept each of them busy with thoughts of the other. In the neighborhood people spoke of "the beautiful Norman," just as they spoke of "beautiful Lisa." This brought them into opposition and comparison and compelled each of them to do her utmost to sustain her reputation for beauty. Lisa from her counter could, by stooping a little, perceive the fish-girl amid her salmon and turbot in the pavilion opposite; and each kept a watch upon the other. Beautiful Lisa laced herself more tightly in her stays; and the beautiful Norman replied by placing additional rings on her fingers and additional bows on her shoulders. When they met they were very bland and unctuous and profuse in compliments; but all the while their eyes were furtively glancing from under their lowered lids, in the hope of discovering some flaw. They made a point of always dealing with each other and professed great mutual affection.

"I say," said La Normande, with her smiling air, "it's tomorrow evening that you make your black puddings, isn't it?"

Lisa maintained a cold demeanor. She seldom showed any anger; but when she did it was tenacious and slow to be appeased. "Yes," she replied drily, with the tips of her lips.

"I'm so fond of black puddings, you know, when they come straight out of the pot," resumed La Normande. "I'll come and get some from you tomorrow."

She was conscious of her rival's unfriendly greeting. However, she glanced at Florent, who seemed to interest her; and then, unwilling to go off without having the last word, she was imprudent enough to add: "I bought some black pudding of you the day before yesterday, you know, and it wasn't quite sweet."

"Not quite sweet!" repeated Lisa, very pale, and her lips quivering.

She might, perhaps, have once more restrained herself, for fear of La Normande imagining that she was overcome by envious spite at the sight of the lace bow; but the girl, not content with playing the spy, proceeded to insult her, and that was beyond endurance. So, leaning forward, with her hands clenched on the counter, she exclaimed, in a somewhat hoarse voice: "I say! when you sold me that pair of soles last week, did I come and tell you, before everybody, that they were stinking?"

"Stinking! my soles stinking!" cried the fish dealer, flushing scarlet.

For a moment they remained silent, choking with anger, but glaring fiercely at each other over the array of dishes. All their honeyed friendship had vanished; a word had sufficed to reveal what sharp teeth there were behind their smiling lips.

"You're a vulgar, low creature!" cried the beautiful Norman. "You'll never catch me setting foot in here again, I can tell you!"

"Get along with you, get along with you," exclaimed beautiful Lisa. "I know quite well whom I've got to deal with!"

The fish-girl went off, hurling behind her a coarse expression which left Lisa quivering. The whole scene had passed so quickly that the three men, overcome with amazement, had not had time to interfere. Lisa soon recovered herself and was resuming the conversation, without making any allusion to what had just occurred, when the shop-girl, Augustine, returned from an errand on which she had been sent. Lisa thereupon took Gavard aside, and after telling him to say nothing for the present to Monsieur Verlaque, promised that she would undertake to convince her brother-in-law in a couple of days' time at the utmost. Quenu then returned to his kitchen, while Gavard took Florent off with him. And as they were just going into Monsieur Lebigre's to drink a drop of vermouth together he called his attention to three women standing in the covered way between the fish and poultry pavilions.

"They're cackling together!" he said with an envious air.

The markets were growing empty, and Mademoiselle Saget, Madame Lecœur, and La Sarriette alone lingered on the edge of the footway. The old maid was holding forth.

"As I told you before, Madame Lecœur," said she, "they've always got your brother-in-law in their shop. You saw him there yourself just now, didn't you?"

"Oh yes, indeed! He was sitting on a table and seemed quite at home."

"Well, for my part," interrupted La Sarriette, "I heard nothing wrong; and I can't understand why you're making such a fuss."

Mademoiselle Saget shrugged her shoulders. "Ah, you're very innocent yet, my dear," she said. "Can't you see why the Quenus are always attracting Monsieur Gavard to their place? Well, I'll wager that he'll leave all he has to their little Pauline."

"You believe that, do you?" cried Madame Lecœur, white with rage. Then, in a mournful voice, as though she had just received some heavy blow, she continued: "I am alone in the world and have no one to take my part; he is quite at liberty to do as he pleases. His niece sides with him too— you heard her just now. She has quite forgotten all that she cost me and wouldn't stir a hand to help me."

"Indeed, aunt," exclaimed La Sarriette, "you are quite wrong there! It's you who've never had anything but unkind words for me."

They became reconciled on the spot and kissed one another. The niece promised that she would play no more pranks, and the aunt swore by all she held most sacred that she looked upon La Sarriette as her own daughter. Then Mademoiselle Saget advised them as to the steps they ought to take to prevent Gavard from squandering his money. And they all agreed that the Quenu-Gradelles were very disreputable folks and required close watching.

"I don't know what they're up to just now," said the old maid, "but there's something suspicious going on, I'm sure. What's your opinion, now, of that fellow Florent, that cousin of Madame Quenu's?"

The three women drew more closely together and lowered their voices.

"You remember," said Madame Lecœur, "that we saw him one morning with his boots all split, and his clothes covered with dust, looking just like a thief who's been up to some roguery. That fellow quite frightens me."

"Well, he's certainly very thin," said La Sarriette, "but he isn't ugly."

Mademoiselle Saget was reflecting, and she expressed her thoughts aloud. "I've been trying to find out something about him for the last fortnight, but I can make nothing of it. Monsieur Gavard certainly knows him. I must have met him myself somewhere before, but I can't remember where."

She was still ransacking her memory when La Normande swept up to them like a whirlwind. She had just left the pork-shop.

"That big booby Lisa has got nice manners, I must say!" she cried, delighted to be able to relieve herself. "Fancy her telling me that I sold nothing but stinking fish! But I gave her as good as she deserved, I can tell you! A nice den they keep, with their tainted pig-meat which poisons all their customers!"

"But what had you been saying to her?" asked the old maid, quite frisky with excitement, and delighted to hear that the two women had quarrelled.

"I! I'd said just nothing at all—no, not that! I just went into the shop and told her very civilly that I'd buy some black puddings tomorrow evening, and then she overwhelmed me with abuse. A dirty hypocrite she is, with her saint-like airs! But she'll pay more dearly for this than she fancies!"

The three women felt that La Normande was not telling them the truth, but this did not prevent them from taking her part with a rush of bad language. They turned towards the Rue Rambuteau with insulting mien, inventing all sorts of stories about the uncleanliness of the cookery at the

Quenu's shop, and making the most extraordinary accusations. If the Quenus had been detected selling human flesh the women could not have displayed more violent and threatening anger. The fish-girl was obliged to tell her story three times over.

"And what did the cousin say?" asked Mademoiselle Saget, with wicked intent.

"The cousin!" repeated La Normande, in a shrill voice. "Do you really believe that he's a cousin? He's some lover or other, I'll wager, the great booby!"

The three others protested against this. Lisa's honorableness was an article of faith in the neighborhood.

"Stuff and nonsense!" retorted La Normande. "You can never be sure about those smug, sleek hypocrites."

Mademoiselle Saget nodded her head as if to say that she was not very far from sharing La Normande's opinion. And she softly added: "Especially as this cousin has sprung from no one knows where; for it's a very doubtful sort of account that the Quenus give of him."

"Oh, he's the fat woman's sweetheart, I tell you!" reaffirmed the fish-girl; "some scamp or vagabond picked up in the streets. It's easy enough to see it."

"She has given him a complete outfit," remarked Madame Lecœur. "He must be costing her a pretty penny."

"Yes, yes," muttered the old maid; "perhaps you are right. I must really get to know something about him."

Then they all promised to keep one another thoroughly informed of whatever might take place in the Quenu-Gradelle establishment. The butter-dealer pretended that she wished to open her brother-in-law's eyes as to the sort of places he frequented. However, La Normande's anger had by this time toned down, and, a good sort of girl at heart, she went off, weary of having talked so much on the matter.

"I'm sure that La Normande said something or other insolent," remarked Madame Lecœur knowingly, when the fish-girl had left them. "It is just her way; and it scarcely becomes a creature like her to talk as she did of Lisa."

The three women looked at each other and smiled. Then, when Madame Lecœur also had gone off, La Sarriette remarked to Mademoiselle Saget: "It is foolish of my aunt to worry herself so much about all these affairs. It's that which makes her so thin. Ah! she'd have willingly taken Gavard for a husband if she could only have got him. Yet she used to beat me if ever a young man looked my way."

Mademoiselle Saget smiled once more. And when she found herself alone, and went back towards the Rue Pirouette, she reflected that those three cackling hussies were not worth a rope to hang them. She was, indeed, a little afraid that she might have been seen with them, and the idea some what troubled her, for she realized that it would be bad policy to fall out with the Quenu-Gradelles, who, after all, were well-to-do folks and much esteemed. So she went a little out of her way on purpose to call at Taboureau the baker's, in the Rue Turbigo—the finest baker's shop in the whole neighborhood. Madame Taboureau was not only an intimate friend of Lisa's, but an accepted authority on every subject. When it was remarked that "Madame Taboureau had said this," or "Madame Taboureau had said that," there was no more to be urged. So the old maid, calling at the baker's under pretense of inquiring at what time the oven would be hot, as she wished to bring a dish of pears to be baked, took the opportunity to eulogize Lisa, and lavish praise upon the sweetness and excellence of her black-puddings.

Then, well pleased at having prepared this moral alibi and delighted at having done what she could to fan the flames of a quarrel without involving herself in it, she briskly returned home, feeling much easier in her mind, but still striving to recall where she had previously seen Madame Quenu's so-called cousin.

That same evening, after dinner, Florent went out and

strolled for some time in one of the covered ways of the markets. A fine mist was rising, and a gray sadness, which the gas lights studded as with yellow tears, hung over the deserted pavilions. For the first time Florent began to feel that he was in the way and to recognize the unmannerly fashion in which he, thin and artless, had tumbled into this world of fat people; and he frankly admitted to himself that his presence was disturbing the whole neighborhood, and that he was a source of discomfort to the Quenus—a spurious cousin of far too compromising appearance. These reflections made him very sad; not, indeed, that he had noticed the slightest harshness on the part of his brother or Lisa: it was their very kindness, rather, that was troubling him, and he accused himself of a lack of delicacy in quartering himself upon them. He was beginning to doubt the propriety of his conduct. The recollection of the conversation in the shop during the afternoon caused him a vague disquietude. The odor of the viands on Lisa's counter seemed to penetrate him; he felt himself gliding into nerveless, satiated cowardice. Perhaps he had acted wrongly in refusing the inspectorship offered him. This reflection gave birth to a stormy struggle in his mind, and he was obliged to brace and shake himself before he could recover his wonted rigidity of principles. However, a moist breeze had risen, and was blowing along the covered way, and he regained some degree of calmness and resolution on being obliged to button up his coat. The wind seemingly swept from his clothes all the greasy odor of the pork-shop, which had made him feel so languid.

He was returning home when he met Claude Lantier. The artist, hidden in the folds of his greenish overcoat, spoke in a hollow voice full of suppressed anger. He was in a passion with painting, declared that it was a dog's trade, and swore that he would not take up a brush again as long as he lived. That very afternoon he had thrust his foot through a study which he had been making of the head of that hussy Cadine.

Claude was subject to these outbursts, the fruit of his inability to execute the lasting, living works which he dreamed of. And at such times life became an utter blank to him, and he wandered about the streets, wrapped in the gloomiest thoughts, and waiting for the morning as for a sort of resurrection. He used to say that he felt bright and cheerful in the morning, and horribly miserable in the evening. Each of his days was a long effort ending in disappointment. Florent scarcely recognized in him the careless night-wanderer of the markets. They had already met again at the pork-shop, and Claude, who knew the fugitive's story, had grasped his hand and told him that he was a sterling fellow. It was very seldom, however, that the artist went to the Quenus'.

"Are you still at my aunt's?" he asked. "I can't imagine how you manage to exist amidst all that cookery. The place reeks with the smell of meat. When I've been there for an hour I feel as though I shouldn't want anything to eat for another three days. I ought not to have gone there this morning; it was that which made me make a mess of my work."

Then, after he and Florent had taken a few steps in silence, he resumed:

"Ah! the good people! They quite grieve me with their fine health. I had thought of painting their portraits, but I've never been able to succeed with such round faces, in which there is never a bone. Ah! You wouldn't find my aunt Lisa kicking her foot through her pans! I was an idiot to have destroyed Cadine's head! Now that I come to think of it, it wasn't so very bad, perhaps, after all."

Then they began to talk about Aunt Lisa. Claude said that his mother had not seen anything of her for a long time, and he hinted that the pork butcher's wife was somewhat ashamed of her sister having married a common working man; moreover, she wasn't at all fond of unfortunate folks. Speaking of himself, he told Florent that a benevolent gentleman had sent him to college, being very pleased with the donkeys and old women that he had managed to draw when only eight years old; but the good soul had died, leaving him an income of a thousand francs, which just saved him from perishing of hunger.

"All the same, I would rather have been a working man," continued Claude. "Look at the carpenters, for instance. They are very happy folks, the carpenters. They have a table to make, say; well, they make it and then go off to bed, happy at having finished the table and perfectly satisfied with themselves. Now I, on the other hand, scarcely get any sleep at night. All those confounded pictures which I can't finish go flying about my brain. I never get anything finished and done with—never, never!"

His voice almost broke into a sob. Then he attempted to laugh; and afterwards began to swear and pour forth coarse expressions, with the cold rage of one who, endowed with a delicate, sensitive mind, doubts his own powers and dreams of wallowing in the mire. He ended by squatting down before one of the gratings which admit air into the cellars beneath the markets—cellars where the gas is continually kept burning. And in the depths below he pointed out Marjolin and Cadine tranquilly eating their supper, while seated on one of the stone blocks used for killing the poultry. The two young vagabonds had discovered a means of hiding themselves and making themselves at home in the cellars after the doors had been closed.

"What a magnificent animal he is, eh!" exclaimed Claude, with envious admiration, speaking of Marjolin. "He and Cadine are happy, at all events! All they care for is eating and kissing. They haven't a care in the world. Ah, you do quite right, after all, to remain at the pork shop; perhaps you'll grow sleek and plump there."

Then he suddenly went off. Florent climbed up to his garret, disturbed by Claude's nervous restlessness, which revived his own uncertainty. The next day, he avoided the pork shop all the morning and went for a long walk on the quays. When he returned to lunch, however, he was struck by Lisa's kindliness. Without any undue insistence she again spoke to him about the inspectorship, as of something which was well worth his consideration. As he listened to her, with a full plate in front of him, he was affected, in spite of himself, by the prim comfort of his surroundings. The matting beneath his feet seemed very soft; the gleams of the brass hanging lamp, the soft, yellow tint of the wall paper, and the bright oak of the furniture filled him with appreciation of a life spent in comfort, which disturbed his notions of right and wrong. He still, however, had sufficient strength to persist in his refusal and repeated his reasons; albeit conscious of the bad taste he was showing in thus ostentatiously parading his animosity and obstinacy in such a place. Lisa showed no signs of vexation; on the contrary, she smiled, and the sweetness of her smile embarrassed Florent far more than her suppressed irritation of the previous evening. At dinner the subject was not renewed; they talked solely of the great winter saltings, which would keep the whole staff of the establishment busily employed.

The evenings were growing cold, and as soon as they had dined they retired into the kitchen, where it was very warm. The room was so large, too, that several people could sit comfortably at the square central table, without in any way impeding the work that was going on. Lighted by gas, the walls were coated with white and blue tiles to a height of some five or six feet from the floor. On the left was a great iron stove, in the three apertures of which were set three large round pots, their bottoms black with soot. At the end was a small range, which, fitted with an oven and a smoking-place, served for the broiling; and up above, over the skimming-spoons, ladles, and long-handled forks were several numbered drawers, containing rasped bread, both fine and coarse, toasted crumbs, spices, cloves, nutmegs, and pepper. On the right, leaning heavily against the wall, was the chopping-block, a huge mass of oak, slashed and scored all over. Attached to it were several appliances, an injecting-pump, a forcing-machine, and a mechanical mincer, which, with their wheels and cranks, imparted to the place an uncanny and mysterious aspect, suggesting some kitchen of the infernal regions.

Then, all round the walls upon shelves, and even under the tables, were iron pots, earthenware pans, dishes, pails, various kinds of tin utensils, a perfect battery of deep copper saucepans, and swelling funnels, racks of knives and choppers, rows of larding-pins and needles—a perfect world of greasy things. In spite of the extreme cleanliness, grease was paramount; it oozed forth from between the blue and white tiles on the wall, glistened on the red tiles of the flooring, gave a grayish glitter to the stove, and polished the edges of the chopping-block with the transparent sheen of varnished oak. And, indeed, amidst the ever-rising steam, the continuous evaporation from the three big pots, in which pork was boiling and melting, there was not a single nail from ceiling to floor from which grease did not exude.

The Quenu-Gradelles prepared nearly all their stock themselves. All that they procured from outside were the potted meats of celebrated firms, with jars of pickles and preserves, sardines, cheeses, and edible snails. They consequently became very busy after September in filling the cellars which had been emptied during the summer. They continued working even after the shop had been closed for the night. Assisted by Auguste and Léon, Quenu would stuff sausage-skins, prepare hams, melt down lard, and salt the different sorts of bacon. There was a tremendous noise of caldrons and cleavers, and the odor of cooking spread through the whole house. And all this was quite independent of the daily business in fresh pork, *pâté de foie gras*, hare patty, galantine, saveloys, and black puddings.

That evening, at about eleven o'clock, Quenu, after placing a couple of pots on the fire in order to melt down some lard, began to prepare the black-puddings. Auguste assisted him. At one corner of the square table Lisa and Augustine sat mending linen, while opposite to them, on the other side, with his face turned towards the fireplace, was Florent, smiling at little Pauline, who had installed herself on his feet and wished him to make her spring into the air. Behind Florent, Léon was mincing some sausage meat on the oak block in a slow, rhythmical fashion.

Auguste first of all went out into the yard to fetch a couple of jug-like cans full of pigs' blood. It was he who stuck the animals in the slaughter house. He himself would carry away the blood and interior portions of the pigs, leaving the men who scalded the carcasses to bring them home completely dressed in their carts. Quenu asserted that no assistant in all Paris was Auguste's equal as a pig-sticker. The truth was that Auguste was a wonderfully keen judge of the quality of the blood; and the black pudding proved good every time that he said such would be the case.

"Well, will the black pudding be good this time?" asked Lisa.

Auguste put down the two cans and slowly answered: "I believe so, Madame Quenu; yes, I believe so. I tell it at first by the way the blood flows. If it spurts out very gently when I pull out the knife, that's a bad sign, and shows that the blood is poor."

"But doesn't that depend on how far the knife has been stuck in?" asked Quenu.

A smile came over Auguste's pale face. "No," he replied; "I always let four digits of the blade go in; that's the right measure. But the best sign of all is when the blood runs out and I beat it with my hand when it pours into the pail; it ought to be of a good warmth, and creamy, without being too thick."

Augustine had put down her needle and with her eyes raised was now gazing at Auguste. On her ruddy face, crowned by wiry chestnut hair, there was an expression of profound attention. Lisa and even little Pauline were also listening with deep interest.

"Well, I beat it, and beat it, and beat it," continued the young man, whisking his hand about as though he were whipping cream. "And then, when I take my hand out and look at it, it ought to be greased, as it were, by the blood and equally coated all over. And if that's the case, anyone can say without fear of mistake that the black puddings will be good."

He remained for a moment in an easy attitude, complacently holding his hand in the air. This hand, which spent so much of its time in pails of blood, had brightly gleaming nails and looked very rosy above his white sleeve. Quenu had nodded his head in approbation, and an interval of silence followed. Léon was still mincing. Pauline, however, after remaining thoughtful for a little while, mounted upon Florent's feet again, and in her clear voice exclaimed: "Cousin, tell me the story of the gentleman who was eaten by the wild beasts!"

It was probably the mention of the pig's blood which

had aroused in the child's mind the recollection of "the gentleman who had been eaten by the wild beasts." Florent did not at first understand what she referred to and asked her what gentleman she meant. Lisa began to smile.

"She wants you to tell her," she said, "the story of that unfortunate man—you know whom I mean—which you told to Gavard one evening. She must have heard you."

At this Florent grew very grave. The little girl got up, and taking the big cat in her arms, placed it on his knees, saying that Mouton also would like to hear the story. Mouton, however, leapt on to the table, where, with rounded back, he remained contemplating the tall, scraggy individual who for the last fortnight had apparently afforded him matter for deep reflection. Pauline meantime began to grow impatient, stamping her feet and insisting on hearing the story.

"Oh, tell her what she wants," said Lisa, as the child persisted and became quite unbearable; "she'll leave us in peace then."

Florent remained silent for a moment longer, with his eyes turned towards the floor. Then slowly raising his head he let his gaze rest first on the two women who were plying their needles, and next on Quenu and Auguste, who were preparing the pot for the black puddings. The gas was burning quietly, the stove diffused a gentle warmth, and all the grease of the kitchen glistened in an atmosphere of comfort such as attends good digestion.

Then taking little Pauline upon his knee and smiling a sad smile, Florent addressed himself to the child as follows:—

"Once upon a time there was a poor man who was sent away, a long, long way off, right across the sea. On the ship which carried him were four hundred convicts, and he was thrown among them. He was forced to live for five weeks amidst all those scoundrels, dressed like them in coarse canvas, and feeding at their mess. Foul insects preyed on him, and terrible sweats robbed him of all his strength. The kitchen, the bakehouse, and the engine room made the orlop deck so terribly hot that ten of the convicts died from it. In the daytime they were sent up in batches of fifty to get a little fresh air from the sea; and as the crew of the ship feared them, a couple of cannons were pointed at the little bit of deck where they took exercise. The poor fellow was very glad indeed when his turn to go up came. His terrible perspiration then abated somewhat; still, he could not eat and felt very ill. During the night, when he was manacled again, and the rolling of the ship in the rough sea kept knocking him against his companions, he quite broke down, and began to cry, glad to be able to do so without being seen."

Pauline was listening with dilated eyes, and her little hands crossed primly in front of her.

"But this isn't the story of the gentleman who was eaten by the wild beasts," she interrupted. "This is quite a different story; isn't it now, cousin?"

"Wait a bit, and you'll see," replied Florent gently. "I shall come to the gentleman presently. I'm telling you the whole story from the beginning."

"Oh, thank you," murmured the child, with a delighted expression. However, she remained thoughtful, evidently struggling with some great difficulty to which she could find no explanation. At last she spoke.

"But what had the poor man done," she asked, "that he was sent away and put in the ship?"

Lisa and Augustine smiled. They were quite charmed with the child's intelligence; and Lisa, without giving the little one a direct reply, took advantage of the opportunity to teach her a lesson by telling her that naughty children were also sent away in boats like that.

"Oh, then," remarked Pauline judiciously, "perhaps it served my cousin's poor man quite right if he cried all night long."

Lisa resumed her sewing, bending over her work. Quenu had not listened. He had been cutting some little rounds of onion over a pot placed on the fire; and almost at once the onions began to crackle, raising a clear shrill chirrup like that of grasshoppers basking in the heat. They gave out a pleasant odor too, and when Quenu plunged his great wooden spoon into the pot the chirruping became yet louder, and the whole kitchen was filled with the penetrating perfume of the onions. Auguste meantime was preparing some bacon fat in a dish, and Léon's chopper fell faster and faster, and every now and then scraped the block so as to gather together the sausage meat, now almost a paste.

"When they got across the sea," Florent continued, "they took the man to an island called the Devil's Island, where he found himself amongst others who had been carried away from their own country. They were all very unhappy. At first they were kept to hard labor, just like convicts. The gendarme who had charge of them counted them three times every day, so as to be sure that none was missing. Later on, they were left free to do as they liked, being merely locked up at night in a big wooden hut, where they slept in hammocks stretched between two bars. At the end of the year they went about barefooted, as their boots were quite worn out, and their clothes had become so ragged that their flesh showed through them. They had built themselves some huts with trunks of trees as a shelter against the sun, which is terribly hot in those parts; but these huts did not shield them against the mosquitoes, which covered them with pimples and swellings during the night. Many of them died, and the others turned quite yellow, so shrunken and wretched, with their long, unkempt beards, that one could not look at them without pity."

"Auguste, give me the fat," cried Quenu; and when the apprentice had handed him the dish he let the pieces of bacon fat slide gently into the pot, and then stirred them with his spoon. A yet denser steam now rose from the fireplace.

"What did they give them to eat?" asked little Pauline, who seemed deeply interested.

"They gave them maggoty rice and foul meat," answered Florent, whose voice grew lower as he spoke. "The rice could scarcely be eaten. When the meat was roasted and very well done it was just possible to swallow it; but if it was boiled, it smelt so dreadfully that the men had nausea and stomach-ache."

"I'd rather have lived upon dry bread," said the child, after thinking the matter carefully over.

Léon, having finished the mincing, now placed the sausage meat upon the square table in a dish. Mouton, who had remained seated with his eyes fixed upon Florent, as though filled with amazement by his story, was obliged to retreat a few steps, which he did with a very bad grace. Then he rolled himself up, with his nose close to the sausage meat, and began to purr.

Lisa was unable to conceal her disgust and amazement. That foul rice, that evil-smelling meat, seemed to her to be scarcely credible abominations, which disgraced those who had eaten them as much as it did those who had provided them; and her calm, handsome face and round neck quivered with vague fear of the man who had lived upon such horrid food.

"No, indeed, it was not a land of delights," Florent resumed, forgetting all about little Pauline, and fixing his dreamy eyes upon the steaming pot. "Every day brought fresh annoyances—perpetual grinding tyranny, the violator of every principle of justice, contempt for all human charity which exasperated the prisoners and slowly consumed them with a fever of sickly rancor. They lived like wild beasts,

with the lash ceaselessly raised over their backs. Those tor-
turers would have liked to kill the poor ma— Oh, no; it can
never be forgotten; it is impossible! Such sufferings will some
day claim vengeance."

His voice had fallen, and the pieces of fat hissing merrily
in the pot drowned it with the sound of their boiling. Lisa,
however, heard him and was frightened by the implacable
expression which had suddenly come over his face; and, recollecting the gentle look which he habitually wore, she judged
him to be a hypocrite.

Florent's hollow voice had brought Pauline's interest and
delight to the highest pitch, and she fidgeted with pleasure
on his knee.

"But the man?" she exclaimed. "Go on about the man!"

Florent looked at her, and then appeared to remember,
and smiled his sad smile again.

"The man," he continued, "was weary of remaining on
the island and had but one thought—that of making his escape by crossing the sea and reaching the mainland, whose
white coast-line could be seen on the horizon in clear weather.
But it was no easy matter to escape. It was necessary that a
raft should be built, and as several of the prisoners had already made their escape, all the trees on the island had been
felled to prevent the others from obtaining timber. The island was, indeed, so bare and naked, so scorched by the
blazing sun, that life on it had become yet more perilous
and terrible. However, it occurred to the man and two of his
companions to employ the timbers of which their huts were
built; and one evening they put out to sea on some rotten
beams, which they had fastened together with dry branches.
The wind carried them towards the coast. Just as daylight
was about to appear, the raft struck on a sandbank with
such violence that the beams were severed from their lash-
ings and carried out to sea. The three poor fellows were

almost engulfed in the sand. Two of them sank in it to their waists, while the third disappeared up to his chin, and his companions were obliged to pull him out. At last they reached a rock, so small that there was scarcely room for them to sit down upon it. When the sun rose they could see the coast in front of them, a bar of grey cliffs stretching all along the horizon. Two, who knew how to swim, determined to reach those cliffs. They preferred to run the risk of being drowned at once to that of slowly starving on the rock. But they promised their companion that they would return for him when they had reached land and had been able to procure a boat."

"Ah, I know now!" cried little Pauline, clapping her hands with glee. "It's the story of the gentleman who was eaten by the crabs!"

"They succeeded in reaching the coast," continued Florent, "but it was quite deserted; and it was only at the end of four days that they were able to get a boat. When they returned to the rock, they found their companion lying on his back, his hands and feet eaten away, his face gnawed, and his stomach full of a swarming mass of crabs that were shaking the poor dead man's sides, as though the half-eaten but still uncorrupt corpse were being torn by a terrible death agony."

A murmur of disgust escaped Lisa and Augustine, and a horrified grimace passed over the face of Léon, who was preparing the skins for the black puddings. Quenu stopped in the midst of his work and looked at Auguste, who seemed to have turned faint. Only little Pauline was smiling. In imagination the others could picture those swarming, ravenous crabs crawling all over the kitchen and mingling gruesome odors with the aroma of the bacon fat and onions.

"Give me the blood," cried Quenu, who had not been following the story.

Auguste came up to him with the two cans, from which he slowly poured the blood, while Quenu, as it fell, vigorously stirred the now thickening contents of the pot. When the cans were emptied, Quenu reached up to one of the drawers above the range and took out some pinches of spice. Then he added a plentiful seasoning of pepper.

"They left him there, didn't they," Lisa now asked of Florent, "and returned themselves in safety?"

"As they were going back," continued Florent, "the wind changed, and they were driven out into the open sea. A wave carried away one of their oars, and the water swept so furiously into the boat that their whole time was taken up in baling it out with their hands. They tossed about in this way in sight of the coast, carried away by squalls and then brought back again by the tide, without a mouthful of bread to eat, for their scanty stock of provisions had been consumed. This went on for three days."

"Three days!" cried Lisa in stupefaction; "three days without food!"

"Yes, three days without food. When the east wind at last brought them to shore, one of them was so weak that he lay on the beach the whole day. In the evening he died. His companion had vainly attempted to get him to chew some leaves which he gathered from the trees."

At this point Augustine broke into a slight laugh. Then, ashamed at having done so and not wishing to be considered heartless, she stammered out in confusion: "Oh! I wasn't laughing at that. It was Mouton. Do just look at Mouton, madame."

Then Lisa in her turn began to smile. Mouton, who had been lying all this time with his nose close to the dish of sausage meat, had probably begun to feel distressed and disgusted by the presence of all this food, for he had risen and was rapidly scratching the table with his paws as though he wanted to bury the dish and its contents. At last, however, turning his back to it and lying down on his side, he stretched himself out, half-closing his eyes and rubbing his head against the table with languid pleasure. Then they all began to compliment Mouton. He never stole anything, they said, and could be safely left with the meat. Pauline related that he licked her fingers and washed her face after dinner without trying to bite her.

However, Lisa now came back to the question of whether it were possible to live for three days without food. In her opinion it was not. "No," she said, "I can't believe it. No one ever goes three days without food. When people talk of a person dying of hunger, it is a mere expression. They always get something to eat, more or less. It is only the most abandoned wretches, people who are utterly lost—"

She was doubtless going to add, "vagrant rogues," but she stopped short and looked at Florent. The scornful pout of her lips and the expression of her bright eyes plainly signified that in her belief only villains made such prolonged fasts. It seemed to her that a man able to remain without food for three days must necessarily be a very dangerous character. For, indeed, honest folks never placed themselves in such a position.

Florent was now almost stifling. In front of him the stove, into which Leon had just thrown several shovelfuls of coal, was snoring like a lay clerk asleep in the sun; and the heat was very great. Auguste, who had taken charge of the lard melting in the pots, was watching over it in a state of perspiration, and Quenu wiped his brow with his sleeve while waiting for the blood to mix. A drowsiness such as follows gross feeding, an atmosphere heavy with indigestion, pervaded the kitchen.

"When the man had buried his comrade in the sand," Florent continued slowly, "he walked off alone straight in front of him. Dutch Guiana, in which country he now was, is a land of forests intermingled with rivers and swamps. The man walked on for more than a week without coming across a single human dwelling place. All around death seemed to be lurking and lying in wait for him. Though his stomach was racked by hunger, he often did not dare to eat the bright-colored fruits which hung from the trees; he was afraid to touch the glittering berries, fearing they might be poisonous. For whole days he did not see a patch of sky, but tramped on beneath a canopy of branches, amid a greenish gloom that swarmed with horrible living creatures. Great birds flew over his head with a terrible flapping of wings and sudden strange calls resembling death-groans; apes sprang, wild animals rushed through the thickets around him, bending the saplings and bringing down a rain of leaves, as though a gale were passing. But it was particularly the serpents that turned his blood cold when, stepping upon a matting of moving, withered leaves, he caught sight of their slim heads gliding amid a horrid maze of roots. In certain nooks, nooks of dank shadow, swarming colonies of reptiles—some black, some yellow, some purple, some striped, some spotted, and some resembling withered reeds—suddenly awakened into life and wriggled away. At such times the man would stop and look about for a stone on which he might take refuge from the soft yielding ground into which his feet sank; and there he would remain for hours, terror-stricken on spying in some open space nearby a boa, who, with tail coiled and head erect, swayed like the trunk of a big tree splotched with gold.

"At night he used to sleep in the trees, alarmed by the slightest rustling of the branches, and fancying that he could hear endless swarms of serpents gliding through the gloom. He almost stifled beneath the interminable expanse of foliage. The gloomy shade reeked with close, oppressive heat, a clammy dankness and pestilential sweat, impregnated with the coarse aroma of scented wood and malodorous flowers.

"And when at last, after a long weary tramp, the man made his way out of the forest and beheld the sky again, he found himself confronted by wide rivers which barred his way. He skirted their banks, keeping a watchful eye on the gray backs of the alligators and the masses of drifting vegetation, and then, when he came to a less suspicious-looking spot, he swam across. And beyond the rivers the forests began again. At other times there were vast prairie-lands, leagues of thick vegetation, in which, at distant intervals, small lakes gleamed bluely. The man then made a wide detour and sounded the ground beneath him before advancing, having but narrowly escaped from being swallowed up and buried beneath one of those smiling plains which he could hear cracking at each step he took. The giant grass, nourished by all the collected humus, concealed pestiferous marshes, depths of liquid mud; and amongst the expanses of verdure spread over the glaucous immensity to the very horizon there were only narrow stretches of firm ground with which the traveller must be acquainted if he would avoid disappearing for ever. One night the man sank down as far as his waist. At each effort he made to extricate himself the mud threatened to rise to his mouth. Then he remained quite still for nearly a couple of hours; and when the moon rose he was fortunately able to catch hold of a branch of a tree above his head. By the time he reached a human dwelling his hands and feet were bruised and bleeding, swollen with poisonous stings. He presented such a pitiable, famished appearance that those who saw him were afraid of him. They tossed him some food fifty yards away from the house, and the master of it kept guard over his door with a loaded gun."

Florent stopped, his voice choked by emotion, and his eyes gazing blankly before him. For some minutes he had seemed to be speaking to himself alone. Little Pauline, who had grown drowsy, was lying in his arms with her head thrown back, though striving to keep her wondering eyes open. And Quenu, for his part, appeared to be getting impatient.

"Why, you stupid!" he shouted to Léon, "don't you know how to hold a skin yet? What do you stand staring at me for? It's the skin you should look at, not me! There, hold it like that and don't move again!"

With his right hand Léon was raising a long string of sausage skin, at one end of which a very wide funnel was inserted; while with his left hand he coiled the black pudding round a metal bowl as fast as Quenu filled the funnel with big spoonfuls of the meat. The latter, black and steaming, flowed through the funnel, gradually inflating the skin, which fell down again, gorged to repletion and curving languidly. As Quenu had removed the pot from the range both he and Léon stood out prominently, he broad visaged, and the lad slender of profile, in the burning glow which cast over their pale faces and white garments a flood of rosy light.

Lisa and Augustine watched the filling of the skin with great interest, Lisa especially; and she in her turn found fault with Léon because he nipped the skin too tightly with his fingers, which caused knots to form, she said. When the skin was quite full, Quenu let it slip gently into a pot of boiling water; and seemed quite easy in his mind again, for now nothing remained but to leave it to boil.

"And the man—go on about the man!" murmured Pauline, opening her eyes and surprised at no longer hearing the narrative.

Florent rocked her on his knee and resumed his story in a slow, murmuring voice, suggestive of that of a nurse singing an infant to sleep.

"The man," he said, "arrived at a large town. There he was at first taken for an escaped convict and was kept in prison for several months. Then he was released and turned his hand to all sorts of work. He kept accounts and taught children to read, and at one time he was even employed as a laborer in making an embankment. He was continually hoping to return to his own country. He had saved the necessary amount of money when he was attacked by yellow fever. Then, believing him to be dead, those about him divided his clothes amongst themselves; so that when he at last recovered he had not even a shirt left. He had to begin all over again. The man was very weak and was afraid he might have to remain where he was. But at last he was able to get away, and he returned."

His voice had sunk lower and lower and now died away altogether in a final quivering of his lips. The close of the story had lulled little Pauline to sleep, and she was now slumbering with her head on Florent's shoulder. He held her with one arm and still gently rocked her on his knee. No one seemed to pay any further attention to him, so he remained still and quiet where he was, holding the sleeping child.

Now came the tug of war, as Quenu said. He had to remove the black puddings from the pot. In order to avoid breaking them or getting them entangled, he coiled them round a thick wooden pin as he drew them out, and then carried them into the yard and hung them on screens, where they quickly dried. Léon helped him, holding up the drooping ends. And as these reeking festoons of black pudding crossed the kitchen they left behind them a trail of odorous steam, which still further thickened the dense atmosphere.

Auguste, on his side, after giving a hasty glance at the lard moulds, now took the covers off the two pots in which the fat was simmering, and each bursting bubble discharged an acrid vapor into the kitchen. The greasy haze had been gradually rising ever since the beginning of the evening, and now it shrouded the gas lights and pervaded the whole

room, streaming everywhere, and veiling the ruddy whiteness of Quenu and his two assistants. Lisa and Augustine
had risen from their seats; and all were panting as though
they had eaten too much.

Augustine carried the sleeping Pauline upstairs; and
Quenu, who liked to fasten up the kitchen himself, gave
Auguste and Léon leave to go to bed, saying that he would
fetch the black pudding himself. The younger apprentice
stole off with a very red face, having managed to secrete
under his shirt nearly a yard of the pudding, which must
have almost scalded him. Then the Quenus and Florent remained alone, in silence. Lisa stood nibbling a little piece of
the hot pudding, keeping her pretty lips well apart all the
while, for fear of burning them, and gradually the black compound vanished in her rosy mouth.

"Well," said she, "La Normande was foolish in behaving
so rudely; the black pudding is excellent today."

However, there was a knock at the passage door, and
Gavard, who stayed at Monsieur Lebigre's every evening
until midnight, came in. He had called for a definite answer
about the fish inspectorship.

"You must understand," he said, "that Monsieur Verlaque
cannot wait any longer; he is too ill. So Florent must make
up his mind. I have promised to give a positive answer early
tomorrow."

"Well, Florent accepts," Lisa quietly remarked, taking another nibble at some black pudding.

Florent, who had remained in his chair, overcome by a
strange feeling of prostration, vainly endeavored to rise and
protest.

"No, no, say nothing," continued Lisa; "the matter is quite
settled. You have suffered quite enough already, my dear
Florent. What you have just been telling us is enough to
make one shudder. It is time now for you to settle down.

You belong to a respectable family, you received a good education, and it is really not fitting that you should go wandering about the highways like a vagrant. At your age childishness is no longer excusable. You have been foolish; well, all that will be forgotten and forgiven. You will take your place again among those of your own class—the class of respectable folks—and live in future like other people."

Florent listened in astonishment, quite unable to say a word. Lisa was, doubtless, right. She looked so healthy, so serene, that it was impossible to imagine that she desired anything but what was proper. It was he, with his fleshless body and dark, equivocal-looking countenance, who must be in the wrong and indulge in unrighteous dreams. He could, indeed, no longer understand why he had resisted before.

Lisa, however, continued to talk to him with an abundant flow of words, as though he were a little boy found in fault and threatened with the police. She assumed, indeed, a most maternal manner and plied him with the most convincing reasons. And at last, as a final argument, she said:

"Do it for us, Florent. We occupy a fair position in the neighborhood which obliges us to use a certain amount of circumspection; and, to tell you the truth, between ourselves, I'm afraid that people will begin to talk. This inspectorship will set everything right; you will be somebody; you will even be an honor to us."

Her manner had become caressingly persuasive, and Florent was penetrated by all the surrounding plenteousness, all the aroma filling the kitchen, where he fed, as it were, on the nourishment floating in the atmosphere. He sank into blissful meanness, born of all the copious feeding that went on in the sphere of plenty in which he had been living during the last fortnight. He felt, as it were, the titillation of forming fat which spread slowly all over his body. He experienced the languid beatitude of shopkeepers, whose chief concern is to fill their bellies. At this late hour of night, in the warm atmosphere of the kitchen, all his acerbity and determination melted away. That peaceable evening, with the odor of the black pudding and the lard, and the sight of plump little Pauline slumbering on his knee, had so enervated him that he found himself wishing for a succession of such evenings—endless ones which would make him fat.

However, it was the sight of Mouton that chiefly decided him. Mouton was sound asleep, with his stomach turned upwards, one of his paws resting on his nose, and his tail twisted over his side, as though to keep him warm; and he was slumbering with such an expression of feline happiness that Florent, as he gazed at him, murmured: "No, it would be too foolish! I accept the berth. Say that I accept it, Gavard."

Then Lisa finished eating her black pudding and wiped her fingers on the edge of her apron. And next she got her brother-in-law's candle ready for him, while Gavard and Quenu congratulated him on his decision. It was always necessary for a man to settle down, said they; the breakneck freaks of politics did not provide one with food. And, meantime, Lisa, standing there with the lighted candle in her hand, looked at him with an expression of satisfaction resting on her handsome face, placid like that of some sacred cow.

Chapter 3

THREE DAYS LATER the necessary formalities were gone
through, and without demur the police authorities at
the Préfecture accepted Florent on Monsieur Verlaque's rec-
ommendation as his substitute. Gavard, by the way, had made
it a point to accompany them. When he again found himself
alone with Florent he kept nudging his ribs with his elbow
as they walked along together, and laughed, without saying
anything, while winking his eyes in a jeering way. He seemed
to find something very ridiculous in the appearance of the
police officers whom he met on the Quai de l'Horloge, for, as
he passed them, he slightly shrugged his shoulders and made
the grimace of a man seeking to restrain himself from laughing in people's faces.

On the following morning Monsieur Verlaque began to
initiate the new inspector into the duties of his office. It had
been arranged that during the next few days he should make
him acquainted with the turbulent sphere which he would
have to supervise. Poor Verlaque, as Gavard called him, was
a pale little man, swathed in flannels, handkerchiefs, and
mufflers. Constantly coughing, he made his way through the
cool, moist atmosphere and running waters of the fish-market,
on a pair of scraggy legs like those of a sickly child.

When Florent made his appearance on the first morning,
at seven o'clock, he felt quite distracted; his eyes were dazed,
his head ached with all the noise and riot. Retail dealers
were already prowling about the auction pavilion; clerks were

arriving with their ledgers, and consigners' agents, with leather bags slung over their shoulders, sat on overturned chairs by the salesmen's desks, waiting to receive their cash. Fish was being unloaded and unpacked not only in the enclosure, but even on the footways. All along the latter were piles of small baskets, an endless arrival of cases and hampers, and sacks of mussels, from which streamlets of water trickled. The auctioneers' assistants, all looking very busy, sprang over the heaps, tore away the straw at the tops of the baskets, emptied the latter, and tossed them aside. They then speedily transferred their contents in lots to huge wickerwork trays, arranging them with a turn of the hand so that they might show to the best advantage. And when the large tray-like baskets were all set out, Florent could almost fancy that a whole shoal of fish had got stranded there, still quivering with life, and gleaming with rosy nacre, scarlet coral, and milky pearl, all the soft, pale, sheeny hues of the ocean.

The deep-lying forests of seaweed, in which the mysterious life of the ocean slumbers, seemed at one haul of the nets to have yielded up all they contained. There were cod, keeling, whiting, flounders, plaice, dabs, and other sorts of common fish of a dingy gray with whitish splotches; there were conger eels, huge serpent-like creatures, with small black eyes and muddy, bluish skins, so slimy that they still seemed to be gliding along, yet alive. There were broad flat skate with pale undersides edged with a soft red, and superb backs bumpy with vertebrae, and marbled down to the tautly stretched ribs of their fins with splotches of cinnabar, intersected by streaks of the tint of Florentine bronze—a dark medley of color suggestive of the hues of a toad or some poisonous flower. Then, too, there were hideous dogfish, with round heads, widely-gaping mouths like those of Chinese idols, and short fins like bats' wings; fit monsters to keep yelping guard over the treasures of the ocean grottoes. And next came the finer fish, displayed singly on the wicker trays; salmon that gleamed like chased silver, every scale seemingly outlined by an engraving tool on a polished metal surface; mullet with larger scales and coarser markings; huge turbot and huge brill with firm flesh white like curdled milk; tuna fish, smooth and glossy, like bags of blackish leather; and rounded bass, with widely-gaping mouths which a soul too large for the body seemed to have rent asunder as it forced its way out amidst the stupefaction of death. And on all sides there were soles, brown and gray, in pairs; sand eels, slim and stiff, like shavings of pewter; herrings, slightly twisted, with bleeding gills showing on their silver-worked skins; fat dories tinged with just a suspicion of carmine; burnished mackerel with green-streaked backs and sides gleaming with ever changing iridescence; and rosy gurnets with white bellies, their heads towards the center of the baskets and their tails radiating all around, so that they simulated some strange florescence splotched with pearly white and brilliant vermilion. There were rock mullet, too, with delicious flesh, flushed with the pinky tinge peculiar to the Cyprinus family; boxes of whiting with opaline reflections; and baskets of smelts—neat little baskets, pretty as those used for strawberries and exhaling a strong scent of violets. And meantime the tiny black eyes of the shrimps dotted as with beads of jet their soft-toned mass of pink and gray; and spiny crawfish and lobsters striped with black, all still alive, raised a grating sound as they tried to crawl along with their broken claws.

Florent gave but indifferent attention to Monsieur Verlaque's explanations. A flood of sunshine suddenly streamed through the lofty glass roof of the covered way, lighting up all these precious colors, toned and softened by the waves—the iridescent flesh-tints of the shell fish, the opal of the whiting, the pearly nacre of the mackerel, the ruddy gold of the mullets, the plated skins of the herrings, and massive silver of the salmon. It was as though the jewel cases of some sea nymph had been emptied there—a mass of fantastical, undreamt-of ornaments, a streaming and heaping of necklaces, monstrous bracelets, gigantic brooches, barbaric gems and jewels, the use of which could not be divined. On the backs of the skate and the dog fish you saw, as it were, big dull green and purple stones set in dark metal, while the slender forms of the sand eels and the tails and fins of the smelts displayed all the delicacy of finely wrought silverwork.

And meantime Florent's face was fanned by a fresh breeze, a sharp, salt breeze redolent of the sea. It reminded him of the coasts of Guiana and his voyages. He half fancied that he was gazing at some bay left dry by the receding tide, with the seaweed steaming in the sun, the bare rocks drying, and the beach smelling strongly of the brine. All around him the fish in their perfect freshness exhaled a pleasant perfume, that slightly sharp, irritating perfume which depraves the appetite.

Monsieur Verlaque coughed. The dampness was affecting him, and he wrapped his muffler more closely about his neck.

"Now," said he, "we will pass on to the fresh-water fish."

This was in a pavilion beside the fruit market, the last one, indeed, in the direction of the Rue Rambuteau. On either side of the space reserved for the auctions were large circular stone basins, divided into separate compartments by iron gratings. Slender streams of water flowed from brass jets shaped like swans' necks; and the compartments were filled with swarming colonies of crawfish, black-backed carp ever on the move, and mazy tangles of eels, incessantly knotting and unknotting themselves. Again was Monsieur Verlaque attacked by an obstinate fit of coughing. The moisture of the atmosphere was more insipid here than amongst the sea-water fish: there was a river-side scent, as of sun-warmed water slumbering on a bed of sand.

A great number of crawfishes had arrived from Germany that morning in cases and hampers, and the market was also crowded with river fish from Holland and England. Several men were unpacking shiny carp from the Rhine, lustrous with ruddy metallic hues, their scales resembling bronze *cloisonné* enamel; and others were busy with huge pike, the cruel iron-gray brigands of the waters, who ravenously protruded their savage jaws; or with magnificent dark-hued tench, that looked like so much dull-red copper spotted with verdigris. And amidst these suggestions of copper, iron, and bronze, the gudgeon and perch, the trout, the bleak, and the flat fish taken in sweep nets showed brightly white, the steel-blue tints of their backs gradually toning down to the soft transparency of their bellies. However, it was the fat snowy-white barbel that supplied the liveliest brightness in this gigantic collection of still life.

Bags of young carp were being gently emptied into the basins. The fish spun round, then remained motionless for a moment, and at last shot away and disappeared. Little eels were turned out of their hampers in a mass and fell to the bottom of the compartments like tangled knots of snakes; while the larger ones—those whose bodies were about as thick as a child's arm—raised their heads and slipped of their own accord into the water with the supple motion of serpents gliding into the concealment of a thicket. And meantime the other fish, whose death agony had been lasting all the morning as they lay on the soiled wicker of the basket-trays, slowly expired amidst all the uproar of the auctions, opening their mouths as though to inhale the moisture of the air, with great silent gasps, renewed every few seconds.

However, Monsieur Verlaque brought Florent back to the

salt-water fish. He took him all over the place and gave him the minutest particulars about everything. Round the nine salesmen's desks ranged along three sides of the pavilion there was now a dense crowd of surging, swaying heads, above which appeared the clerks, perched upon high chairs and making entries in their ledgers.

"Are all these clerks employed by the salesmen?" asked Florent.

By way of reply Monsieur Verlaque made a detour along the outside footway, led him into the enclosure of one of the auctions, and then explained the working of the various departments of the big yellow office, which smelt strongly of fish and was stained all over by drippings and splashings from the hampers. In a little glazed compartment up above, the collector of the municipal dues took note of the prices realized by the different lots of fish. Lower down, seated upon high chairs and with their wrists resting upon little desks, were two female clerks, who kept account of the business on behalf of the salesmen. At each end of the stone table in front of the office was a crier who brought the basket trays forward in turn and in a bawling voice announced what each lot consisted of; while above him the female clerk, pen in hand, waited to register the price at which the lots were knocked down. And outside the enclosure, shut up in another little office of yellow wood, Monsieur Verlaque showed Florent the cashier, a fat old woman, who was ranging sous and five-franc pieces in piles.

"There is a double control, you see," said Monsieur Verlaque; "the control of the Préfecture of the Seine and that of the Préfecture of Police. The latter, which licenses the salesmen, claims to have the right of supervision over them; and the municipality asserts its right to be represented at the transactions as they are subject to taxation."

He went on expatiating at length in his faint cold voice

respecting the rival claims of the two Préfectures. Florent, however, was paying but little heed, his attention being concentrated on a female clerk sitting on one of the high chairs just in front of him. She was a tall, dark woman of thirty, with big black eyes and an easy calmness of manner, and she wrote with outstretched fingers like a girl who had been taught the regulation method of the art.

However, Florent's attention was diverted by the yelping of the crier, who was just offering a magnificent turbot for sale.

"I've a bid of thirty francs! Thirty francs, now; thirty francs!"

He repeated these words in all sorts of keys, running up and down a strange scale of notes full of sudden changes. Hump-backed and with his face twisted askew, and his hair rough and disorderly, he wore a great blue apron with a bib; and with flaming eyes and outstretched arms he cried vociferously: "Thirty-one! thirty-two! thirty-three! Thirty-three francs fifty centimes! thirty-three fifty!"

Then he paused to take breath, turning the basket-tray and pushing it farther upon the table. The fishwives bent forward and gently touched the turbot with their fingertips. Then the crier began again with renewed energy, hurling his figures towards the buyers with a wave of the hand and catching the slightest indication of a fresh bid—the raising of a finger, a twist of the eyebrows, a pouting of the lips, a wink, and all with such rapidity and such a ceaseless jumble of words that Florent, utterly unable to follow him, felt quite disconcerted when, in a sing-song voice like that of a priest intoning the final words of a versicle, he chanted: "Forty-two! forty-two! The turbot goes for forty-two francs!"

It was the beautiful Norman who had made the last bid. Florent recognized her as she stood in the line of fishwives crowding against the iron rails which surrounded the enclosure. The morning was fresh and sharp, and there was a row of tippets above the display of big white aprons, covering the prominent bosoms and stomachs and sturdy shoulders. With high-set chignon set off with curls, and white and dainty skin, the beautiful Norman flaunted her lace bow amidst tangled shocks of hair covered with dirty kerchiefs, red noses eloquent of drink, sneering mouths, and battered faces suggestive of old pots. And she also recognized Madame Quenu's cousin and was so surprised to see him there that she began gossiping to her neighbors about him.

The uproar of voices had become so great that Monsieur Verlaque renounced all further attempt to explain matters to Florent. On the footway close by, men were calling out the larger fish with prolonged shouts, which sounded as though they came from gigantic speaking-trumpets; and there was one individual who roared "Mussels! mussels!" in such a hoarse, cracked, clamorous voice that the very roofs of the market shook. Some sacks of mussels were turned upside down, and their contents poured into hampers, while others were emptied with shovels. And there was a ceaseless procession of basket-trays containing skate, soles, mackerel, conger eels, and salmon, carried backward and forward amid the ever-increasing cackle and pushing of the fish-women as they crowded against the iron rails which creaked with their pressure. The hump-backed crier, now fairly on the job, waved his skinny arms in the air and protruded his jaws. Presently, seemingly lashed into a state of frenzy by the flood of figures that spurted from his lips, he sprang upon a stool, where, with his mouth twisted spasmodically and his hair streaming behind him, he could force nothing more than unintelligible hisses from his parched throat. And in the meantime, up above, the collector of the municipal dues, a little old man, muffled in a collar of imitation astrakhan, remained with nothing but his nose showing under his black velvet skullcap. And the tall, dark-complexioned female clerk, with eyes shining calmly in her face, which had been slightly reddened by the cold, sat on her high wooden chair, quietly writing, apparently unruffled by the continuous rattle which came from the hunchback below her.

"That fellow Logre is wonderful," muttered Monsieur Verlaque with a smile. "He is the best crier in the markets. I believe he could make people buy boot soles in the belief they were fish!"

Then he and Florent went back into the pavilion. As they again passed the spot where the fresh-water fish was being sold by auction, and where the bidding seemed much quieter, Monsieur Verlaque explained that French river fishing was in a bad way. The crier here, a fair, sorry-looking fellow, who scarcely moved his arms, was disposing of some lots of eels and crawfish in a monotonous voice, while the assistants fished fresh supplies out of the stone basins with their short-handled nets.

However, the crowd round the salesmen's desks was still increasing. Monsieur Verlaque played his part as Florent's instructor in the most conscientious manner, clearing the way by means of his elbows, and guiding his successor through the busiest parts. The upper-class retail dealers were there, quietly waiting for some of the finer fish, or loading the porters with their purchases of turbot, tuna, and salmon. The street-hawkers who had clubbed together to buy lots of herrings and small flatfish were dividing them on the pavement. There were also some people of the smaller middle class, from distant parts of the city, who had come down at four o'clock in the morning to buy a really fresh fish, and had ended by allowing some enormous lot, costing from forty to fifty francs, to be knocked down to them, with the result that they would be obliged to spend the whole day in getting their friends and acquaintances to take the surplus off their hands. Every now and then some violent pushing would force a gap through part of the crowd. A fishwife, who had got tightly jammed, freed herself, shaking her fists and pouring out a torrent of abuse. Then a compact mass of people again collected, and Florent, almost suffocated, declared that he had seen quite enough and understood all that was necessary.

As Monsieur Verlaque was helping him to extricate himself from the crowd, they found themselves face to face with the handsome Norman. She remained stock-still in front of them and with her queenly air inquired:

"Well, is it quite settled? You are going to desert us, Monsieur Verlaque?"

"Yes, yes," replied the little man; "I am going to take a rest in the country, at Clamart. The smell of the fish is bad for me, it seems. Here, this is the gentleman who is going to take my place."

So speaking he turned round to introduce Florent to her. The handsome Norman almost choked; however, as Florent went off, he fancied he could hear her whisper to her neighbors, with a laugh: "Well, we shall have some fine fun now, see if we don't!"

The fishwives had begun to set out their stalls. From all the taps at the corners of the marble slabs water was gushing freely; and there was a rustling sound all round, like the plashing of rain, a streaming of stiff jets of water hissing and spurting. And then, from the lower side of the sloping slabs, great drops fell with a softened murmur, splashing on the flagstones where a maze of tiny streams flowed along here and there, turning holes and depressions into miniature lakes, and afterwards gliding in a thousand rills down the slope towards the Rue Rambuteau. A moist haze ascended, a sort of rainy dust, bringing fresh whiffs of air to Florent's face, whiffs of that salt, pungent sea breeze which he remembered so well; while in such fish as was already laid out he once more beheld the rosy nacres, gleaming corals, and milky pearls, all the rippling color and glaucous pallidity of the ocean world.

That first morning left him much in doubt; indeed, he regretted that he had yielded to Lisa's insistence. Ever since his escape from the greasy drowsiness of the kitchen he had been accusing himself of base weakness with such violence that tears had almost risen in his eyes. But he did not dare to go back on his word. He was a little afraid of Lisa and could see the curl of her lips and the look of mute reproach upon her handsome face. He felt that she was too serious a woman to be trifled with. However, Gavard happily inspired him with a consoling thought. On the evening of the day on which Monsieur Verlaque had conducted him through the auction sales, Gavard took him aside and told him, with a good deal of hesitation, that "the poor devil" was not at all well off. And after various remarks about the scoundrelly Government which ground the life out of its servants without allowing them even the means to die in comfort, he ended by hinting that it would be charitable on Florent's part to surrender a part of his salary to the old inspector. Florent welcomed the suggestion with delight. It was only right, he considered, for he looked upon himself simply as Monsieur Verlaque's temporary substitute; and besides, he himself really required nothing, as he boarded and lodged with his brother. Gavard added that he thought if Florent gave up fifty francs out of the hundred and fifty which he would receive monthly, the arrangement would be everything that could be desired; and, lowering his voice, he added that it would not be for long, for the poor fellow was consumptive to his very bones. Finally it was settled that Florent should see Monsieur Verlaque's wife and arrange matters with her, to avoid any possibility of hurting the old man's feelings.

The thought of this kindly action afforded Florent great

relief, and he now accepted his duties with the object of doing good, thus continuing to play the part which he had been fulfilling all his life. However, he made the poultry dealer promise that he would not speak of the matter to anyone; and as Gavard also felt a vague fear of Lisa, he kept the secret, which was really very meritorious in him.

And now the whole pork shop seemed happy. Handsome Lisa manifested the greatest friendliness towards her brother-in-law. She took care that he went to bed early, so as to be able to rise in good time; she kept his breakfast hot for him; and she no longer felt ashamed at being seen talking to him on the footway, now that he wore a laced cap. Quenu, quite delighted by all these good signs, sat down to table in the evening between his wife and brother with a lighter heart than ever. They often lingered over dinner till nine o'clock, leaving the shop in Augustine's charge, and indulging in a leisurely digestion interspersed with gossip about the neighborhood, and the dogmatic opinions of Lisa on political topics; Florent also had to relate how matters had gone in the fish market that day. He gradually grew less frigid and began to taste the happiness of a well-regulated existence. There was a well-to-do comfort and trimness about the light yellowish dining room which had a softening influence upon him as soon as he crossed its threshold. Handsome Lisa's kindly attentions wrapped him, as it were, in cotton wool; and mutual esteem and concord reigned paramount.

Gavard, however, considered the Quenu-Gradelles' home to be too drowsy. He forgave Lisa her weakness for the Emperor, because, he said, one ought never to discuss politics with women, and beautiful Madame Quenu was, after all, a very worthy person, who managed her business admirably. Nevertheless, he much preferred to spend his evenings at Monsieur Lebigre's, where he met a group of friends who shared his own opinions. Thus when Florent was appointed to the inspectorship of the fish market, Gavard began to lead him astray, taking him off for hours, and prompting him to lead a bachelor's life now that he had obtained a berth.

Monsieur Lebigre was the proprietor of a very fine establishment, fitted up in the modern luxurious style. Occupying the right-hand corner of the Rue Pirouette, and looking on to the Rue Rambuteau, it formed, with its four small Norwegian pines in green-painted tubs flanking the doorway, a worthy pendant to the big pork shop of the Quenu-Gradelles. Through the clear glass windows you could see the interior, which was decorated with festoons of foliage, vine branches, and grapes, painted on a soft green ground. The floor was tiled with large black and white squares. At the far end was the yawning cellar entrance, above which rose a spiral staircase hung with red drapery, and leading to the billiard room on the first floor. The counter or "bar" on the right looked especially rich and glittered like polished silver. Its zinc-work, hanging with a broad bulging border over the substructure of white and red marble, edged it with a rippling sheet of metal as if it were some high altar laden with embroidery. At one end, over a gas stove, stood porcelain pots, decorated with circles of brass, and containing punch and hot wine. At the other extremity was a tall and richly sculptured marble fountain, from which a fine stream of water, so steady and continuous that it looked as though it were motionless, flowed into a basin. In the center, edged on three sides by the sloping zinc surface of the counter, was a second basin for rinsing and cooling purposes, where quart bottles of draught wine, partially empty, reared their greenish necks. Then on the counter, to the right and left of this central basin, were batches of glasses symmetrically arranged: little glasses for brandy, thick tumblers for draught wine, cup glasses for brandied fruits, glasses for absinthe, glass mugs for beer, and tall goblets, all turned upside down and reflecting the glitter of the counter. On the left, moreover, was a metal urn, serving as a receptacle for gratuities; while a similar one on the right bristled with a fan-like arrangement of coffee spoons.

Monsieur Lebigre was generally to be found enthroned behind his counter upon a seat covered with buttoned crimson leather. Within easy reach of his hand were the liqueurs in cut-glass decanters protruding from the compartments of a stand. His round back rested against a huge mirror which completely filled the panel behind him; across it ran two glass shelves supporting an array of jars and bottles. Upon one of them the glass jars of preserved fruits, cherries, plums, and peaches, stood out darkly; while on the other, between symmetrically arranged packets of finger biscuits, were bright flasks of soft green and red and yellow glass, suggesting strange mysterious liqueurs, or floral extracts of exquisite limpidity. Standing on the glass shelf in the white glow of the mirror, these flasks, flashing as if on fire, seemed to be suspended in the air.

To give his premises the appearance of a café, Monsieur Lebigre had placed two small tables of bronzed iron and four chairs against the wall, in front of the counter. A chandelier with five lights and frosted globes hung down from the ceiling. On the left was a round gilt timepiece, above a revolving stand fixed to the wall. Then at the far end came the private "cabinet," a corner of the shop shut off by a partition glazed with frosted glass of a small square pattern. In the daytime this little room received a dim light from a window that looked on to the Rue Pirouette; and in the evening a gas jet burnt over the two tables painted to resemble marble. It was there that Gavard and his political friends met each evening after dinner. They looked upon themselves as being quite at home there and had prevailed on the landlord to reserve the place for them. When Monsieur Lebigre had closed the door of the glazed partition, they knew themselves to be so safely screened from intrusion that they spoke quite unreservedly of the great "sweep out" which they were fond of discussing. No unprivileged customer would have dared to enter.

On the first day that Gavard took Florent off he gave him some particulars of Monsieur Lebigre. He was a good fellow, he said, who sometimes came to drink his coffee with them; and, as he had said one day that he had fought in '48, no one felt the least constraint in his presence. He spoke but little and seemed rather thick-headed. As the gentlemen passed him on their way to the private room they grasped his hand in silence across the glasses and bottles. By his side on the crimson leather seat behind the counter there was generally a fair little woman, whom he had engaged as counter assistant in addition to the white-aproned waiter who attended to the tables and the billiard room. The young woman's name was Rose, and she seemed a very gentle and submissive being. Gavard, with a wink of his eye, told Florent that he fancied Lebigre had a weakness for her. It was she, by the way, who waited upon the friends in the private room, coming and going, with her happy, humble air, amidst the stormiest political discussions.

Upon the day on which the poultry dealer took Florent to Lebigre's to present him to his friends, the only person whom the pair found in the little room when they entered it was a man of some fifty years of age, of a mild and thoughtful appearance. He wore a rather shabby-looking hat and a long chestnut-colored overcoat, and sat, with his chin resting on the ivory knob of a thick cane, in front of a glass mug full of beer. His mouth was so completely concealed by a vigorous growth of beard that his face had a dumb, lipless appearance.

"How are you, Robine?" exclaimed Gavard.

Robine silently thrust out his hand, without making any reply, though his eyes softened into a slight smile of welcome. Then he let his chin drop on to the knob of his cane again and looked at Florent over his beer. Florent had made Gavard swear to keep his story a secret for fear of some dangerous indiscretion; and he was not displeased to observe a touch of distrust in the discreet demeanor of the gentleman with the heavy beard. However, he was really mistaken in this, for Robine never talked more than he did now. He was always the first to arrive, just as the clock struck eight; and he always sat in the same corner, never letting go his hold of his cane, and never taking off either his hat or his overcoat. No one had ever seen him without his hat upon his head. He remained there listening to the talk of the others till midnight, taking four hours to empty his mug of beer, and gazing successively at the different speakers as though he heard them with his eyes. When Florent afterwards questioned Gavard about Robine, the poultry dealer spoke of the latter as though he held him in high esteem. Robine, he asserted, was an extremely clever and able man, and, though he was unable to say exactly where he had given proof of his hostility to the established order of things, he declared that he was one of the most dreaded of the Government's opponents. He lived in the Rue Saint Denis, in rooms to which no one as a rule could gain admission. The poultry dealer, however, asserted that he himself had once been in them. The wax floors, he said, were protected by strips of green linen; and there were covers over the furniture, and an alabaster timepiece with columns. He had caught a glimpse of the back of a lady, who was just disappearing through one doorway as he was entering by another, and had taken her to be Madame Robine. She appeared to be an old lady of very genteel appearance, with her hair arranged in corkscrew curls; but of this he could not be quite certain. No one knew why they had taken up their abode amidst all the uproar of a business neighborhood; for the husband did nothing at all, spending his days no one knew how and living on no one knew what, though he made his appearance every evening as though he were tired but delighted with some excursion into the highest regions of politics.

"Well, have you read the speech from the throne?" asked Gavard, taking up a newspaper that was lying on the table.

Robine shrugged his shoulders. Just at that moment, however, the door of the glazed partition clattered noisily, and a hunchback made his appearance. Florent at once recognized the deformed crier of the fish market, though his hands were now washed and he was neatly dressed, with his neck encircled by a great red muffler, one end of which hung down over his hump like the skirt of a Venetian cloak.

"Ah, here's Logre!" exclaimed the poultry dealer. "Now we shall hear what he thinks about the speech from the throne."

Logre, however, was apparently furious. To begin with he almost broke the pegs off in hanging up his hat and muffler. Then he threw himself violently into a chair and brought his fist down on the table, while tossing away the newspaper.

"Do you think I read their fearful lies?" he cried.

Then he gave vent to the anger raging within him. "Did ever anyone hear," he cried, "of masters making such fools of their people? For two whole hours I've been waiting for my pay! There were ten of us in the office kicking our heels there. Then at last Monsieur Manoury arrived in a cab. Where he had come from I don't know, and don't care, but I'm quite sure it wasn't any respectable place. Those salesmen are all a parcel of thieves and libertines! And then, too, the hog actually gave me all my money in small change!"

Robine expressed his sympathy with Logre by a slight movement of his eyelids. But suddenly the hunchback thought of a victim upon whom to pour out his wrath. "Rose! Rose!" he cried, stretching his head out of the little room.

The young woman quickly responded to the call, trembling all over.

"Well," shouted Logre, "what do you stand staring at me like that for? Much good that'll do! You saw me come in, didn't you? Why haven't you brought me my glass of black coffee, then?"

Gavard ordered two similar glasses, and Rose made all haste to bring what was required, while Logre glared sternly at the glasses and little sugar trays as if studying them. When he had taken a drink he seemed to grow somewhat calmer.

"But it's Charvet who must be getting bored," he said presently. "He is waiting outside on the pavement for Clémence."

Charvet, however, now made his appearance, followed by Clémence. He was a tall, scraggy young man, carefully shaved, with a skinny nose and thin lips. He lived in the Rue Vavin, behind the Luxembourg, and called himself a professor. In politics he was a disciple of Hébert. He wore his hair very long, and the collar and lapels of his threadbare frock coat were broadly turned back. Affecting the manner and speech of a member of the National Convention, he would pour out such a flood of bitter words and make such a haughty display of pedantic learning that he generally crushed his adversaries. Gavard was afraid of him, though he would not confess it; still, in Charvet's absence he would say that he really went too far. Robine, for his part, expressed approval of everything with his eyes. Logre sometimes opposed Charvet on the question of salaries; but the other was really the autocrat of the coterie, having the greatest fund of information and the most overbearing manner. For more than ten years he and Clémence had lived together as man and wife, in accordance with a previously arranged contract, the terms of which were strictly observed by both parties to it. Florent looked at the young woman with some little surprise, but at last he recollected where he had previously seen her. This was at the fish auction. She was, indeed, none other than the tall dark female clerk whom he had observed writing with outstretched fingers, after the manner of one who had been carefully instructed in the art of holding a pen.

Rose made her appearance at the heels of the two newcomers. Without saying a word she placed a mug of beer before Charvet and a tray before Clémence, who in a leisurely way began to compound a glass of "grog," pouring some hot water over a slice of lemon, which she crushed with her spoon, and glancing carefully at the decanter as she poured out some rum, so as not to add more of it than a small liqueur glass could contain.

Gavard now presented Florent to the company, but more especially to Charvet. He introduced them to one another as professors and very able men, who would be sure to get on well together. But it was probable that he had already been guilty of some indiscretion, for all the men at once shook hands with a tight and somewhat masonic squeeze of each other's fingers. Charvet, for his part, showed himself almost amiable; and whether he and the others knew anything of Florent's antecedents, they at all events indulged in no embarrassing allusions.

"Did Manoury pay you in small change?" Logre asked Clémence.

She answered affirmatively, and produced a roll of francs, and another of two-franc pieces, and unwrapped them. Charvet watched her, and his eyes followed the rolls as she replaced them in her pocket, after counting their contents and satisfying herself that they were correct.

"We have our accounts to settle," he said in a low voice.

"Yes, we'll settle up tonight," the young woman replied. "But we are about even, I should think. I've breakfasted with you four times, haven't I? But I lent you a hundred sous last week, you know."

Florent, surprised at hearing this, discreetly turned his head away. Then Clémence slipped the last roll of silver into her pocket, drank a little of her grog, and, leaning against the glazed partition, quietly settled herself down to listen to the men talking politics. Gavard had taken up the newspaper again and, in tones which he strove to render comic, was reading out some passages of the speech from the throne which had been delivered that morning at the opening of the Chambers. Charvet made fine sport of the official phraseology; there was not a single line of it which he did not tear to pieces. One sentence afforded special amusement to them all. It was this: "We are confident, gentlemen, that, leaning on your lights and the conservative sentiments of the country, we shall succeed in increasing the national prosperity day by day."

Logre rose up and repeated this sentence and by speaking through his nose succeeded fairly well in mimicking the Emperor's drawling voice.

"It's lovely, that prosperity of his; why, everyone's dying of hunger!" said Charvet.

"Trade is shocking," asserted Gavard.

"And what in the name of goodness is the meaning of anybody 'leaning on lights'?" continued Clémence, who prided herself upon literary culture.

Robine himself even allowed a faint laugh to escape from the depths of his beard. The discussion began to grow warm. The party fell foul of the Corps Législatif, and spoke of it with great severity. Logre did not cease ranting, and Florent found him the same as when he cried the fish at the auctions—protruding his jaws and hurling his words forward with a wave of the arm, while retaining the crouching attitude of a snarling dog. Indeed, he talked politics in just the same furious manner as he offered a tray full of soles for sale.

Charvet, on the other hand, became quieter and colder amidst the smoke of the pipes and the fumes of the gas which were now filling the little den; and his voice assumed a dry incisive tone, sharp like a guillotine blade, while Robine gently wagged his head without once removing his chin from the ivory knob of his cane. However, some remark of Gavard's led the conversation to the subject of women.

"Woman," declared Charvet drily, "is the equal of man; and, that being so, she ought not to inconvenience him in the management of his life. Marriage is a partnership, in which everything should be halved. Isn't that so, Clémence?"

"Clearly so," replied the young woman, leaning back with her head against the wall and gazing into the air.

However, Florent now saw Lacaille, the hawker, and Alexandre, the porter, Claude Lantier's friend, come into the little room. In the past these two had long remained at the other table in the sanctum; they did not belong to the same class as the others. By the help of politics, however, their chairs had drawn nearer, and they had ended by forming part of the circle. Charvet, in whose eyes they represented "the people," did his best to indoctrinate them with his advanced political theories, while Gavard played the part of the shopkeeper free from all social prejudices by clinking glasses with them. Alexandre was a cheerful, good-humored giant, with the manner of a big merry lad. Lacaille, on the other hand, was embittered; his hair was already grizzling; and, bent and wearied by his ceaseless perambulations through the streets of Paris, he would at times glance loweringly at the placid figure of Robine and his sound boots and heavy coat.

That evening both Lacaille and Alexandre called for a liqueur glass of brandy, and then the conversation was renewed with increased warmth and excitement, the party being now quite complete. A little later, while the door of the cabinet was left ajar, Florent caught sight of Mademoiselle Saget standing in front of the counter. She had taken a bottle from under her apron and was watching Rose as the latter poured into it a large measureful of black-currant syrup and a smaller one of brandy. Then the bottle disappeared under the apron again, and Mademoiselle Saget, with her hands out of sight, remained talking in the bright glow of the counter, face to face with the big mirror, in which the flasks and bottles of liqueurs were reflected like rows of Venetian lanterns. In the evening all the metal and glass of the establishment helped to illuminate it with wonderful brilliancy. The old maid, standing there in her black skirts, looked almost like some big strange insect amidst all the crude brightness. Florent noticed that she was trying to inveigle Rose into a conversation and shrewdly suspected that she had caught sight of him through the half-open doorway. Since he had been on duty at the markets he had met her at almost every step, loitering in one or another of the covered ways, and generally in the company of Madame Lecœur and La Sarriette. He had noticed also that the three women stealthily examined him and seemed lost in amazement at seeing him installed in the position of inspector. That evening, however, Rose was no doubt loath to enter into conversation with the old maid, for the latter at last turned round, apparently with the intention of approaching Monsieur Lebigre, who was playing piquet with a customer at one of the bronzed tables. Creeping quietly along, Mademoiselle Saget had at last managed to install herself beside the partition of the cabinet, when she was observed by Gavard, who detested her.

"Shut the door, Florent!" he cried unceremoniously. "We can't even be by ourselves, it seems!"

When midnight came and Lacaille went away he exchanged a few whispered words with Monsieur Lebigre, and as the latter shook hands with him he slipped four five-franc pieces into his palm, without anyone noticing it. "That'll make twenty-two francs that you'll have to pay tomorrow, remember," he whispered in his ear. "The person who lends the money won't do it for less in future. Don't forget, too, that you owe three days' truck hire. You must pay everything off."

Then Monsieur Lebigre wished the friends good night. He was very sleepy and should sleep well, he said, with a yawn which revealed his big teeth, while Rose gazed at him with an air of submissive humility. However, he gave her a push and told her to go and turn out the gas in the little room.

On reaching the pavement, Gavard stumbled and nearly fell. And being in a humorous vein, he thereupon exclaimed: "Confound it all! At any rate, I don't seem to be leaning on anybody's lights."

This remark seemed to amuse the others, and the party broke up. A little later Florent returned to Lebigre's, and indeed he became quite attached to the "cabinet," finding a seductive charm in Robine's contemplative silence, Logre's fiery outbursts, and Charvet's cool venom. When he went home, he did not at once retire to bed. He had grown very fond of his attic, that girlish bedroom, where Augustine had left scraps of ribbon, souvenirs, and other feminine trifles lying about. There still remained some hair-pins on the mantelpiece, with gilt cardboard boxes of buttons and lozenges, cut-out pictures, and empty pomade pots that retained an odor of jasmine. Then there were some reels of thread, needles, and a missal lying by the side of a soiled Dream-book in the drawer of the rickety deal table. A white summer-dress with yellow spots hung forgotten from a nail; while upon the board which served as a toilet-table a big stain behind the water jug showed where a bottle of bandoline had been overturned. The little chamber, with its narrow iron bed, its two rush-bottomed chairs, and its faded gray wallpaper, was instinct with innocent simplicity. The plain white curtains, the childishness suggested by the cardboard boxes and the Dream-book, and the clumsy coquetry which had stained the walls, all charmed Florent and brought him back to dreams of youth. He would have preferred not to have known that plain, wiry-haired Augustine, but to have been able to imagine that he was occupying the room of a sister, some bright sweet girl of whose budding womanhood every trifle around him spoke.

Yet another pleasure which he took was to lean out of the garret window at night time. In front of it was a narrow ledge of roof, enclosed by an iron railing, and forming a sort of balcony, on which Augustine had grown a pomegranate in a box. Since the nights had turned cold, Florent had brought the pomegranate indoors and kept it by the foot of his bed till morning. He would linger for a few minutes by the open window, inhaling deep draughts of the sharp fresh air which was wafted up from the Seine, over the housetops of the Rue de Rivoli. Below him the roofs of the markets spread confusedly in a gray expanse, like slumbering lakes on whose surface the furtive reflection of a pane of glass gleamed every now and then like a silvery ripple. Farther away the roofs of the meat and poultry pavilions lay in deeper gloom, and became mere masses of shadow barring the horizon. Florent delighted in the great stretch of open sky in front of him, in that spreading expanse of the markets which amidst all the narrow city streets brought him a dim vision of some strip of sea coast, of the still gray waters of a bay scarce quivering from the roll of the distant billows. He used to lose himself in dreams as he stood there; each night he conjured up the vision of some fresh coast line. To return in mind to the eight years of despair which he had spent away from France rendered him both very sad and very happy. Then at last, shivering all over, he would close the window. Often, as he stood in front of the fireplace taking off his collar, the photograph of Auguste and Augustine would fill him with a vague disquietude. They seemed to be watching him as they stood there, hand in hand, smiling faintly.

Florent's first few weeks at the fish market were very painful to him. The Méhudins treated him with open hostility, which infected the whole market with a spirit of opposition. The beautiful Norman intended to revenge herself on the handsome Lisa, and the latter's cousin seemed a victim ready to hand.

The Méhudins came from Rouen. Louise's mother still related how she had first arrived in Paris with a basket of eels. She had ever afterwards remained in the fish trade. She had married a man employed in the Octroi service, who had died leaving her with two little girls. It was she who by her full figure and glowing freshness had won for herself in earlier days the nickname of "the beautiful Norman," which her eldest daughter had inherited. Now sixty-five years of age, Madame Méhudin had become flabby and shapeless, and the damp air of the fish market had rendered her voice rough and hoarse and given a bluish tinge to her skin. Sedentary life had made her extremely bulky, and her head was thrown backwards by the exuberance of her bosom. She had never been willing to renounce the fashions of her younger days, but still wore the flowered gown, the yellow kerchief, and turban-like head-gear of the classic fish wife, besides retaining the latter's loud voice and rapidity of gesture as she stood with her hands on her hips, shouting out the whole abusive vocabulary of her calling.

She looked back regretfully to the old Marché des Inno-cents, which the new central markets had supplanted. She would talk of the ancient rights of the market "ladies," and mingle stories of fistfights with the police with reminiscences of the visits she had paid to Court in the time of Charles x and Louis Philippe, dressed in silk, and carrying a bouquet of flowers in her hand. Old Mother Méhudin, as she was now generally called, had for a long time been the banner-bearer of the Sisterhood of the Virgin at St. Leu. She would relate that in the processions in the church there she had worn a dress and cap of tulle trimmed with satin ribbons, while holding aloft in her puffy fingers the gilded staff of the richly-fringed silk standard on which the figure of the Holy Mother was embroidered.

According to the gossip of the neighborhood, the old woman had made a fairly substantial fortune, though the only signs of it were the massive gold ornaments with which she loaded her neck and arms and bosom on important oc-casions. Her two daughters got on badly together as they grew up. The younger one, Claire, an idle, fair-complexioned girl, complained of the ill-treatment which she received from her sister Louise, protesting, in her languid voice, that she could never submit to be the other's servant. As they would certainly have ended by coming to blows, their mother sepa-rated them. She gave her stall in the fish market to Louise, while Claire, whom the smell of the skate and the herrings affected in the lungs, installed herself among the fresh-water fish. And from that time the old mother, although she pre-tended to have retired from business altogether, would flit from one stall to the other, still interfering in the selling of the fish, and causing her daughters continual annoyance by the foul insolence with which she would at times speak to customers.

Claire was a fantastical creature, very gentle in her manner, and yet continually at loggerheads with others. People said that she invariably followed her own whimsical inclinations. In spite of her dreamy, girlish face she was imbued with a nature of silent firmness, a spirit of independence which prompted her to live apart; she never took things as other people did, but would one day evince perfect fairness, and the next day arrant injustice. She would sometimes throw the market into confusion by suddenly increasing or lowering the prices at her stall, without anyone being able to guess her reason for doing so. She herself would refuse to explain her motive. By the time she reached her thirtieth year, her delicate physique and fine skin, which the water of the tanks seemed to keep continually fresh and soft, her small, faintly-marked face and lissome limbs would probably become heavy, coarse, and flabby, till she would look like some faded saint that had stepped from a stained-glass window into the degrading sphere of the markets. At twenty-two, however, Claire, in the midst of her carp and eels, was, to use Claude Lantier's expression, a Murillo. A Murillo, that is, whose hair was often in disorder, who wore heavy shoes and clumsily cut dresses, which left her without any figure. But she was free from all coquetry, and she assumed an air of scornful contempt when Louise, displaying her bows and ribbons, teased her about her clumsily knotted neckerchiefs. Moreover, she was virtuous; it was said that the son of a rich shopkeeper in the neighborhood had gone abroad in despair at having failed to induce her to listen to his suit.

Louise, the beautiful Norman, was of a different nature. She had been engaged to be married to a clerk in the cornmarket; but a sack of flour falling upon the young man had broken his back and killed him. Not very long afterwards Louise had given birth to a boy. In the Méhudins' circle of acquaintance she was looked upon as a widow; and the old fish wife in conversation would occasionally refer to the time when her son-in-law was alive.

The Méhudins were a power in the markets. When Monsieur Verlaque had finished instructing Florent in his new duties, he advised him to conciliate certain of the stallholders, if he wished his life to be endurable; and he even carried his sympathy so far as to put him in possession of the little secrets of the office, such as the various little breaches of rule that it was necessary to wink at, and those at which he would have to feign stern displeasure; and also the circumstances under which he might accept a small present. A market inspector is at once a constable and a magistrate; he has to maintain proper order and cleanliness, and settle in a conciliatory spirit all disputes between buyers and sellers. Florent, who was of a weak disposition, put on an artificial sternness when he was obliged to exercise his authority and generally over-acted his part. Moreover, his gloomy, pariahlike face and bitterness of spirit, the result of long suffering, were against him.

The beautiful Norman's idea was to involve him in some quarrel or other. She had sworn that he would not keep his berth a fortnight. "That fat Lisa's much mistaken," said she one morning on meeting Madame Lecœur, "if she thinks that she's going to put people over us. We don't want such ugly wretches here. That sweetheart of hers is a perfect fright!"

After the auctions, when Florent commenced his round of inspection, strolling slowly through the dripping alleys, he could plainly see the beautiful Norman watching him with an impudent smile on her face. Her stall, which was in the second row on the left, near the fresh-water fish department, faced the Rue Rambuteau. She would turn round, however, and never take her eyes off her victim while making fun of him with her neighbors. And when he passed in front of her, slowly examining the slabs, she feigned hilarious merriment, slapped her fish with her hand, and turned her jets of water on at full stream, flooding the pathway. Nevertheless Florent remained perfectly calm.

At last, one morning, as was bound to happen, war broke out. As Florent reached La Normande's stall that day an unbearable stench assailed his nostrils. On the marble slab, in addition to part of a magnificent salmon, showing its soft roseate flesh, there lay some turbots of creamy whiteness, a few conger eels pierced with black pins to mark their divisions, several pairs of soles, and some bass and red mullet—in fact, quite a display of fresh fish. But in the midst of it, amongst all these fish whose eyes still gleamed and whose gills were of a bright crimson, there lay a huge skate of a ruddy tinge, splotched with dark stains—superb, indeed, with all its strange colorings. Unfortunately, it was rotten; its tail was falling off and the ribs of its fins were breaking through the skin.

"You must throw that skate away," said Florent as he came up.

The beautiful Norman broke into a slight laugh. Florent raised his eyes and saw her standing before him, with her back against the bronze lamppost which lighted the stalls in her division. She had mounted upon a box to keep her feet out of the damp and appeared very tall as he glanced at her. She looked also handsomer than usual, with her hair arranged in little curls, her sly face slightly bent, her lips compressed, and her hands showing somewhat too rosily against her big white apron. Florent had never before seen her decked with so much jewelry. She had long pendants in her ears, a chain round her neck, a brooch in her dress body, and quite a collection of rings on two fingers of her left hand and one of her right.

As she still continued to look slyly at Florent, without making any reply, the latter continued: "Do you hear ? You must remove that skate."

He had not yet noticed the presence of old Madame Méhudin, who sat in a heap on a chair in a corner. She now got up, however, and, with her fists resting on the marble slab, insolently exclaimed: "Dear me! And why is she to throw her skate away? You won't pay her for it, I'll bet!"

Florent immediately understood the position. The women at the other stalls began to titter, and he felt that he was surrounded by covert rebellion, which a word might cause to blaze forth. He therefore restrained himself and in person drew the refuse pail from under the stall and dropped the skate into it. Old Madame Méhudin had already stuck her hands on her hips, while the beautiful Norman, who had not spoken a word, burst into another malicious laugh as Florent strode sternly away amidst a chorus of jeers, which he pretended not to hear.

Each day now some new trick was played upon him, and he was obliged to walk through the market alleys as warily as though he were in a hostile country. He was splashed with water from the sponges employed to cleanse the slabs; he stumbled and almost fell over slippery refuse intentionally spread in his way; and even the porters contrived to run their baskets against the nape of his neck. One day, moreover, when two of the fish wives were quarrelling, and he hastened up to prevent them from coming to blows, he was obliged to duck in order to escape being slapped on either cheek by a shower of little dabs which passed over his head. There was a general outburst of laughter on this occasion, and Florent always believed that the two fishwives were in league with the Méhudins. However, his old-time experiences as a teacher had endowed him with angelic patience, and he was able to maintain a magisterial coolness of manner even when anger was hotly rising within him, and his whole being quivered with a sense of humiliation. Still, the young scamps of the Rue de l'Estrapade had never manifested the savagery of these fishwives, the cruel tenacity of these huge females, whose massive figures heaved and shook with a giant-like joy whenever he fell into any trap. They stared him out of composure with their red faces; and in the coarse tones of their voices and the impudent gestures of their hands he could read volumes of filthy abuse levelled at himself. Gavard would have been quite in his element amid all these petticoats and would have freely cuffed them all round; but Florent, who had always been afraid of women, gradually felt overwhelmed as by a sort of nightmare in which giant women, buxom beyond all imagination, danced threateningly around him, shouting at him in hoarse voices and brandishing bare arms, as massive as any prizefighter's. Among this horde of females, however, Florent had one friend. Claire unhesitatingly declared that the new inspector was a very good fellow. When he passed in front of her, pursued by the coarse abuse of the others, she gave him a pleasant smile, sitting nonchalantly behind her stall, with unruly errant locks of pale hair straying over her neck and her brow, and the bodice of her dress pinned all askew. He also often saw her dipping her hands into her tanks, transferring the fish from one compartment to another, and amusing herself by turning on the brass taps, shaped like little dolphins with open mouths, from which the water poured in streamlets. Amidst the rustling sound of the water she had some of the quivering grace of a girl who has just been bathing and has hurriedly slipped on her clothes.

One morning she was particularly amiable. She called the inspector to her to show him a huge eel which had been the wonder of the market when exhibited at the auction. She opened the grating, which she had previously closed over the basin in whose depths the eel seemed to be lying sound asleep.

"Wait a moment," she said, "and I'll show it to you."

Then she gently slipped her bare arm into the water; it was not a very plump arm, and its veins showed softly blue beneath its satiny skin. As soon as the eel felt her touch, it rapidly twisted round and seemed to fill the narrow trough with its glistening greenish coils. And directly it had settled down to rest again Claire once more stirred it with her fingertips.

"It is an enormous creature," Florent felt bound to say. "I have rarely seen such a fine one."

Claire then confessed to him that she had at first been frightened of eels; but now she had learned how to tighten her grip so that they could not slip away. From another compartment she took a smaller one, which began to wriggle both with head and tail, as she held it about the middle in her closed fist. This made her laugh. She let it go, then seized another and another, scouring the basin and stirring up the whole heap of snaky-looking creatures with her slim fingers.

Afterwards she began to speak of the slackness of trade. The hawkers on the foot-pavement of the covered way did the regular saleswomen a great deal of injury, she said. Meantime her bare arm, which she had not wiped, was glistening and dripping with water. Big drops trickled from each finger.

"Oh," she exclaimed suddenly, "I must show you my carp, too!"

She now removed another grating and, using both hands, lifted out a large carp, which began to flap its tail and gasp. It was too big to be held conveniently, so she sought another one. This was smaller, and she could hold it with one hand, but the latter was forced slightly open by the panting of the sides each time that the fish gasped. To amuse herself it occurred to Claire to pop the tip of her thumb into the carp's mouth while it was dilated. "It won't bite," said she with her gentle laugh; "it's not spiteful. No more are the crawfishes; I'm not the least afraid of them."

She plunged her arm into the water again and from a compartment full of a confused crawling mass brought up a crawfish that had caught her little finger in its claws. She gave the creature a shake, but it no doubt gripped her too tightly, for she turned very red and snapped off its claw with a quick, angry gesture, though still continuing to smile.

"By the way," she continued quickly, to conceal her emotion, "I wouldn't trust myself with a pike; he'd cut off my fingers like a knife."

She then showed him some big pike arranged in order of size upon clean scoured shelves, beside some bronze-hued tench and little heaps of gudgeon. Her hands were now quite slimy with handling the carp, and as she stood there in the dampness rising from the tanks, she held them stretched over the dripping fish on the stall. She seemed enveloped by an odor of spawn, that heavy scent which rises from among the reeds and water lilies when the fish, languid in the sunlight, discharge their eggs. Then she wiped her hands on her apron, still smiling the placid smile of a girl who knew nothing of passion in that quivering atmosphere of the frigid loves of the river.

The kindliness which Claire showed to Florent was but slight consolation to him. By stopping to talk to the girl he only drew upon himself still coarser jeers from the other stallkeepers. Claire shrugged her shoulders and said that her mother was an old jade and her sister a worthless creature. The injustice of the market folk towards the new inspector filled her with indignation. The war between them, however, grew more bitter every day. Florent had serious thoughts of resigning his post; indeed, he would not have retained it for another twenty-four hours if he had not been afraid that Lisa might imagine him to be a coward. He was frightened of what she might say and what she might think. She was naturally well aware of the great contest which was going on between the fish wives and their inspector; for the whole echoing market resounded with it, and the entire neighborhood discussed each fresh incident with endless comments.

"Ah, well," Lisa would often say in the evening, after dinner, "I'd soon bring them to reason if I had anything to do with them! Why, they are a lot of dirty jades that I wouldn't touch with the tip of my finger! That Normande is the lowest of the low! I'd soon crush her, that I would! You should really use your authority, Florent. You are wrong to behave as you do. Put your foot down, and they'll come to their senses very quickly, you'll see."

A terrible climax was presently reached. One morning the servant of Madame Taboureau, the baker, came to the market to buy a brill; and the beautiful Norman, having noticed her lingering near her stall for several minutes, began to make overtures to her in a coaxing way: "Come and see me; I'll suit you," she said. "Would you like a pair of soles, or a fine turbot?"

Then as the servant at last came up and sniffed at a brill with that dissatisfied pout which buyers assume in the hope of getting what they want at a lower price, La Normande continued:

"Just feel the weight of that, now," and so saying she laid the brill, wrapped in a sheet of thick yellow paper, on the woman's open palm.

The servant, a mournful little woman from Auvergne, felt the weight of the brill and examined its gills, still pouting, and saying not a word.

"And how much do you want for it?" she asked presently, in a reluctant tone.

"Fifteen francs," replied La Normande.

At this the servant hastily laid the brill on the stall again and seemed anxious to hurry away, but the other detained her. "Wait a moment," said she. "What do you offer?"

"No, no, I can't take it. It is much too dear."

"Come, now, make me an offer."

"Well, will you take eight francs?"

Old Madame Méhudin, who was there, suddenly seemed to wake up and broke out into a contemptuous laugh. Did people think that she and her daughter stole the fish they sold? "Eight francs for a brill of that size!" she exclaimed. "You'll be wanting one for nothing next, to use as a cooling plaster!"

Meantime La Normande turned her head away, as though greatly offended. However, the servant came back twice and offered nine francs; and finally she increased her bid to ten.

"All right, come on, give me your money!" cried the fishgirl, seeing that the woman was now really going away.

The servant took her stand in front of the stall and entered into a friendly gossip with old Madame Méhudin. Madame Taboureau, she said, was so exacting! She had got some people coming to dinner that evening, some cousins from Blois, a notary and his wife. Madame Taboureau's family, she added, was a very respectable one, and she herself, although only a baker, had received an excellent education.

"You'll clean it nicely for me, won't you?" added the woman, pausing in her chatter.

With a jerk of her finger La Normande had removed the fish's entrails and tossed them into a pail. Then she slipped a corner of her apron under its gills to wipe away a few grains of sand. "There, my dear," she said, putting the fish into the servant's basket, "you'll come back to thank me."

Certainly the servant did come back a quarter of an hour afterwards, but it was with a flushed, red face. She had been crying, and her little body was trembling all over with anger. Tossing the brill onto the marble slab, she pointed to a broad gash in its belly that reached the bone. Then a flood of broken words burst from her throat, which was still contracted by sobbing: "Madame Taboureau won't have it. She says she couldn't put it on her table. She told me, too, that I was an idiot and let myself be cheated by anyone. You can see for yourself that the fish is spoilt. I never thought of turning it round; I quite trusted you. Give me my ten francs back."

"You should look at what you buy," the handsome Norman calmly observed.

And then, as the servant was just raising her voice again, old Madame Méhudin got up. "Just you shut up!" she cried. "We're not going to take back a fish that's been knocking about in other people's houses. How do we know that you didn't let it fall and damage it yourself?"

"I! I damage it!" The little servant was choking with indignation. "Ah! you're a couple of thieves!" she cried, sobbing bitterly. "Yes, a couple of thieves! Madame Taboureau herself told me so!"

Matters then became uproarious. Boiling over with rage and brandishing their fists, both mother and daughter fairly exploded; while the poor little servant, quite bewildered by their voices, the one hoarse and the other shrill, which belabored her with insults as though they were battledores and she a shuttlecock, sobbed on more bitterly than ever.

"Be off with you! Your Madame Taboureau would like to be half as fresh as that fish is! She'd like us to sew it up for her, no doubt!"

"A whole fish for ten francs! What'll she want next!"

Then came coarse words and foul accusations. Had the servant been the most worthless of her sex she could not have been more bitterly upbraided.

Florent, whom the market keeper had gone to fetch, made his appearance when the quarrel was at its hottest. The whole pavilion seemed to be in a state of insurrection. The fish-wives, who manifest the keenest jealousy of each other when the sale of a ten cent herring is in question, display a united front when a quarrel arises with a buyer. They sang the popular old ditty, "The baker's wife has heaps of crowns, which cost her precious little"; they stamped their feet, and goaded the Méhudins as though the latter were dogs which they were urging on to bite and devour. And there were even some, having stalls at the other end of the alley, who rushed up wildly, as though they meant to spring at the chignon of the poor little woman, she meantime being quite submerged by the flood of insulting abuse poured upon her.

"Return mademoiselle her ten francs," said Florent sternly, when he had learned what had taken place.

But old Madame Méhudin had her blood up. "As for you, my little man," said she, "go to blazes! Here, that's how I'll return the ten francs!"

As she spoke, she flung the brill with all her force at the head of Madame Taboureau's servant, who received it full in the face. The blood spurted from her nose, and the brill, after adhering for a moment to her cheeks, fell to the ground and burst with a flop like that of a wet clout. This brutal act threw Florent into a fury. The beautiful Norman felt frightened and recoiled, as he cried out: "I suspend you for a week, and I will have your license withdrawn. You hear me?"

Then, as the other fishwives were still jeering behind him, he turned round with such a threatening air that they quailed like wild beasts mastered by the tamer and tried to assume an expression of innocence. When the Méhudins had returned the ten francs, Florent peremptorily ordered them to cease selling at once. The old woman was choking with rage, while the daughter kept silent, but turned very white. She, the beautiful Norman, to be driven out of her stall!

Claire said in her quiet voice that it served her mother and sister right, a remark which nearly resulted in the two girls tearing each other's hair out that evening when they returned home to the Rue Pirouette. However, when the Méhudins came back to the market at the week's end, they remained very quiet, reserved, and curt of speech, though full of a cold-blooded wrath. Moreover, they found the pavilion quite calm and restored to order again. From that day forward the beautiful Norman must have harbored the thought of some terrible vengeance. She felt that she really had Lisa to thank for what had happened. She had met her, the day after the battle, carrying her head so high, that she had sworn she would make her pay dearly for her glance of triumph. She held interminable confabulations with Mademoiselle Saget, Madame Lecœur, and La Sarriette, in quiet corners of the market; however, all their chatter about the shameless conduct which they slanderously ascribed to Lisa and her cousin, and about the hairs which they declared were found in Quenu's chitterlings, brought La Normande little consolation. She was trying to think of some very malicious plan of vengeance, which would strike her rival to the heart.

Her child was growing up in the fish market in all freedom and neglect. When but three years old the youngster had been brought there, and day by day remained squatting on some rag amid the fish. He would fall asleep beside the big tunas as though he were one of them, and awake among the mackerel and whiting. The little rascal smelt of fish as strongly as though he were some big fish's offspring. For a long time his favorite pastime, whenever his mother's back was turned, was to build walls and houses of herrings; and he would also play at soldiers on the marble slab, arranging the red gurnets in confronting lines, pushing them against each other, and battering their heads, while imitating the sound of drum and trumpet with his lips; after which he would throw them all into a heap again and exclaim that they were dead. When he grew older he would prowl about his aunt Claire's stall to get hold of the bladders of the carp and pike which she gutted. He placed them on the ground and made them burst, an amusement which afforded him vast delight. When he was seven he rushed about the alleys, crawled under the stalls, ferreted amongst the zinc bound fish-boxes, and became the spoiled pet of all the women. Whenever they showed him something fresh which pleased him, he would clasp his hands and exclaim in ecstasy, "Oh, isn't it stunning!" *Muche* was the exact word which he used; *muche* being the equivalent of "stunning" in the lingo of the markets; and he used the expression so often that it clung to him as a nickname. He became known all over the place as "Muche." It was Muche here, there, and everywhere; no one called him anything else. He was to be met with in every nook; in out-of-the-way corners of the offices in the auction pavilion; among the piles of oyster baskets, and betwixt the buckets where the refuse was thrown. With a pinky fairness of skin, he was like a young barbel frisking and gliding about in deep water. He was as fond of running, streaming water as any young fry. He was always dabbling in the pools in the alleys. He wetted himself with the drippings from the tables and when no one was looking often slyly turned on the taps, rejoicing in the bursting gush of water. But it was especially beside the fountains near the cellar steps that his mother went to seek him in the evening, and she would bring him from there with his hands quite blue, and his shoes, and even his pockets, full of water.

At seven years old Muche was as pretty as an angel and as coarse in his manners as any carter. He had curly chestnut hair, beautiful soft eyes, and an innocent-looking mouth which gave vent to language that even a gendarme would have hesitated to use. Brought up amidst all the ribaldry and profanity of the markets, he had the whole vocabulary of the place on the tip of his tongue. With his hands on his hips he often mimicked Grandmother Méhudin in her anger, and at these times the coarsest and vilest expressions would stream from his lips in a voice of crystalline purity that might have belonged to some little chorister chanting the *Ave Maria*. He would even try to assume a hoarse roughness of tone, seek to degrade and taint that exquisite freshness of childhood which made him resemble a *bambino* on the Madonna's knees. The fishwives laughed at him till they cried; and he, encouraged, could scarcely say a couple of words without rapping out an oath. But in spite of all this he still remained charming, understanding nothing of the dirt amidst which he lived, kept in vigorous health by the fresh breezes and sharp odors of the fish market, and reciting his vocabulary of coarse indecencies with as pure a face as though he were saying his prayers.

The winter was approaching, and Muche seemed very sensitive to the cold. As soon as the chilly weather set in he manifested a strong predilection for the inspector's office. This was situated in the left-hand corner of the pavilion, on the side of the Rue Rambuteau. The furniture consisted of a table, a stack of drawers, an easy chair, two other chairs, and a stove. It was this stove which attracted Muche. Florent quite worshipped children, and when he saw the little fellow, with his dripping legs, gazing wistfully through the window, he made him come inside. His first conversation with the lad caused him profound amazement. Muche sat down in front of the stove, and in his quiet voice exclaimed: "I'll just toast my toes, do you see? It's damned cold this morning." Then he broke into a rippling laugh and added: "Aunt Claire looks awfully blue this morning. Is it true, sir, that you are sweet on her?"

Amazed though he was, Florent felt quite interested in the odd little fellow. The handsome Norman retained her surly bearing, but allowed her son to frequent the inspector's office without a word of objection. Florent consequently concluded that he had the mother's permission to receive the

boy, and every afternoon he asked him in; by degrees forming the idea of turning him into a steady, respectable young
fellow. He could almost fancy that his brother Quenu had
grown little again and that they were both in the big room
in the Rue Royer Collard once more. The life which his
self-sacrificing nature pictured to him as perfect happiness
was a life spent with some young being who would never
grow up, whom he could go on teaching for ever, and in
whose innocence he might still love his fellow-men. On the
third day of his acquaintance with Muche he brought an
alphabet to the office, and the lad delighted him by the intelligence he manifested. He learned his letters with all the
sharp precocity which marks the Parisian street urchin, and
derived great amusement from the woodcuts illustrating the
alphabet.

He found opportunities, too, for plenty of fine fun in the
little office, where the stove still remained the chief attraction and a source of endless enjoyment. At first he cooked
potatoes and chestnuts at it, but presently these seemed insipid, and he thereupon stole some gudgeons from his aunt
Claire, roasted them one by one, suspended from a string in
front of the glowing fire, and then devoured them with gusto,
though he had no bread. One day he even brought a carp
with him; but it was impossible to roast it sufficiently, and it
made such a smell in the office that both window and door
had to be thrown open. Sometimes, when the odor of all
these culinary operations became too strong, Florent would
throw the fish into the street, but as a rule he only laughed.
By the end of a couple of months Muche was able to read
fairly well, and his copy-books did him credit.

Meantime, every evening the lad wearied his mother with
his talk about his good friend Florent. His good friend Florent
had drawn him pictures of trees and of men in huts, said he.
His good friend Florent waved his arm and said that men

would be far better if they all knew how to read. And at last La Normande heard so much about Florent that she seemed to be almost intimate with this man against whom she harbored so much rancor. One day she shut Muche up at home to prevent him from going to the inspector's, but he cried so bitterly that she gave him his liberty again on the following morning. There was very little determination about her, in spite of her broad shoulders and bold looks. When the lad told her how nice and warm he had been in the office, and came back to her with his clothes quite dry, she felt a sort of vague gratitude, a pleasure in knowing that he had found a shelter-place where he could sit with his feet in front of a fire. Later on, she was quite touched when he read her some words from a scrap of soiled newspaper wrapped round a slice of conger eel. By degrees, indeed, she began to think, though without admitting it, that Florent could not really be a bad sort of fellow. She felt respect for his knowledge, mingled with an increasing curiosity to see more of him and learn something of his life. Then, all at once, she found an excuse for gratifying this inquisitiveness. She would use it as a means of vengeance. It would be fine fun to make friends with Florent and embroil him with that great fat Lisa.

"Does your good friend Florent ever speak to you about me?" she asked Muche one morning as she was dressing him.

"Oh, no," replied the boy. "We enjoy ourselves."

"Well, you can tell him that I've quite forgiven him, and that I'm much obliged to him for having taught you to read."

From then on the child was entrusted with some message every day. He went backwards and forwards from his mother to the inspector, and from the inspector to his mother, charged with kindly words and questions and answers, which he repeated mechanically without knowing their meaning. He might, indeed, have been safely trusted with the most compromising communications. However, the beautiful Norman felt afraid of appearing timid, and so one day she herself went to the inspector's office and sat down on the second chair, while Muche was having his writing lesson. She proved very suave and complimentary, and Florent was by far the more embarrassed of the two. They only spoke of the lad; and when Florent expressed a fear that he might not be able to continue the lessons in the office, La Normande invited him to come to their home in the evening. She spoke also of payment; but at this he blushed, and said that he certainly would not come if any mention were made of money. Thereupon the young woman determined in her own mind that she would recompense him with presents of choice fish.

Peace was thus made between them; the beautiful Norman even took Florent under her protection. Apart from this, however, the whole market was becoming reconciled to the new inspector, the fishwives arriving at the conclusion that he was really a better fellow than Monsieur Verlaque, notwithstanding his strange eyes. It was only old Madame Méhudin who still shrugged her shoulders, full of rancor as she was against the "long lanky-guts," as she contemptuously called him. And then, too, a strange thing happened. One morning, when Florent stopped with a smile before Claire's tanks, the girl dropped an eel which she was holding and angrily turned her back upon him, her cheeks quite swollen and reddened by temper. The inspector was so much astonished that he spoke to La Normande about it.

"Oh, never mind her," said the young woman; "she's cracked. She makes a point of always differing from everybody else. She only behaved like that to annoy me."

La Normande was now triumphant—she strutted about her stall and became more coquettish than ever, arranging her hair in the most elaborate manner. Meeting the handsome Lisa one day she returned her look of scorn and even burst out laughing in her face. The certainty she felt of driving the mistress of the pork shop to despair by winning her cousin from her endowed her with a gay, sonorous laugh, which rolled up from her chest and rippled her white plump neck. She now had the whim of dressing Muche very show-ily in a little Highland costume and velvet bonnet. The lad had never previously worn anything but a tattered blouse. It unfortunately happened, however, that just about this time he again became very fond of the water. The ice had melted and the weather was mild, so he gave his Scotch jacket a bath, turning the fountain tap on at full flow and letting the water pour down his arm from his elbow to his hand. He called this "playing at gutters." Then a little later, when his mother came up and caught him, she found him with two other young scamps watching a couple of little fishes swim-ming about in his velvet cap, which he had filled with water.

For nearly eight months Florent lived in the markets, feel-ing continual drowsiness. After his seven years of suffering he had lighted upon such calm quietude, such unbroken regularity of life, that he was scarcely conscious of existing. He gave himself up to this jog trot peacefulness with a dazed sort of feeling, continually experiencing surprise at finding himself each morning in the same armchair in the little office. This office with its bare hut-like appearance had a charm for him. He here found a quiet and secluded refuge amidst that ceaseless roar of the markets which made him dream of some surging sea spreading around him and isolating him from the world. Gradually, however, a vague nervousness began to prey upon him; he became discontented, accused himself of faults which he could not define, and began to rebel against the emptiness which he experienced more and more acutely in mind and body. Then, too, the evil smells of the fish mar-ket brought him nausea. By degrees he became unhinged, his vague boredom developing into restless, nervous excite-ment.

All his days were precisely alike, spent among the same

sounds and the same odors. In the mornings the noisy buzzing of the auction sales resounded in his ears like a distant
echo of bells; and sometimes, when there was a delay in the
arrival of the fish, the auctions continued till very late. Upon
these occasions he remained in the pavilion till noon, disturbed at every moment by quarrels and disputes, which he
endeavored to settle with scrupulous justice. Hours elapsed
before he could get free of some miserable matter or other
which was exciting the market. He paced up and down amidst
the crush and uproar of the sales, slowly perambulating the
alleys and occasionally stopping in front of the stalls which
fringed the Rue Rambuteau, and where lay rosy heaps of
prawns and baskets of boiled lobsters with tails tied backwards, while live ones were gradually dying as they sprawled
over the marble slabs. And then he would watch gentlemen
in silk hats and black gloves bargaining with the fishwives,
and finally going off with boiled lobsters wrapped in paper
in the pockets of their frock coats. Farther away, at the temporary stalls, where the commoner sorts of fish were sold, he
would recognize the bareheaded women of the neighborhood, who always came at the same hour to make their purchases.

At times he took an interest in some well-dressed lady
trailing her lace petticoats over the damp stones and escorted
by a servant in a white apron; and he would follow her at a
little distance on noticing how the fishwives shrugged their
shoulders at sight of her air of disgust. The medley of hampers and baskets and bags, the crowd of skirts flitting along
the damp alleys, occupied his attention until lunchtime. He
took a delight in the dripping water and the fresh breeze as
he passed from the acrid smell of the shellfish to the pungent odor of the salted fish. It was always with the latter that
he brought his official round of inspection to a close. The
cases of red herrings, the Nantes sardines on their layers of

leaves, and the rolled cod, exposed for sale under the eyes of stout, faded fishwives, brought him thoughts of a voyage necessitating a vast supply of salted provisions.

In the afternoon the markets became quieter, grew drowsy; and Florent then shut himself up in his office, made out his reports, and enjoyed the happiest hours of his day. If he happened to go out and cross the fish market, he found it almost deserted. There was no longer the crushing and pushing and uproar of ten o'clock in the morning. The fishwives, seated behind their stalls, leant back knitting, while a few belated purchasers prowled about casting sidelong glances at the remaining fish, with the thoughtful eyes and compressed lips of women closely calculating the price of their dinner. At last the twilight fell, there was a noise of boxes being moved, and the fish was laid for the night on beds of ice; and then, after witnessing the closing of the gates, Florent went off, seemingly carrying the fish market along with him in his clothes and his beard and his hair.

For the first few months this penetrating odor caused him no great discomfort. The winter was a severe one, the frosts converted the alleys into slippery mirrors, and the fountains and marble slabs were fringed with a lacework of ice. In the mornings it was necessary to place little braziers underneath the taps before a drop of water could be drawn. The frozen fish had twisted tails; and, dull of hue and hard to the touch like unpolished metal, gave out a ringing sound like that of pale cast iron when it snaps. Until February the pavilion presented a most mournful appearance: it was deserted and wrapped in a bristling shroud of ice. But with March came a thaw, with mild weather and fogs and rain. Then the fish became soft again, and unpleasant odors mingled with the smell of the mud wafted from the neighboring streets. These odors were as yet vague, tempered by the moisture which clung to the ground. But in the blazing June afternoons a reeking stench arose, and the atmosphere became heavy with a pestilential haze. The upper windows were then opened, and huge blinds of gray canvas were drawn beneath the burning sky. Nevertheless, a fiery rain seemed to be pouring down, heating the market as though it were a big stove, and there was not a breath of air to waft away the noxious emanations from the fish. A visible steam went up from all the stalls.

The masses of food amongst which Florent lived now began to cause him the greatest discomfort. The disgust with which the pork shop had filled him came back in a still more intolerable fashion. He almost sickened as he passed these masses of fish, which, despite all the water lavished upon them, turned bad under a sudden whiff of hot air. Even when he shut himself up in his office his discomfort continued, for the abominable odor forced its way through the chinks in the woodwork of the window and door. When the sky was gray and leaden, the little room remained quite dark; and then the day was like a long twilight in the depths of some fetid marsh. He was often attacked by fits of nervous excitement and felt a craving desire to walk; and he would then descend into the cellars by the broad staircase opening in the middle of the pavilion. In the pent-up air down below, in the dim light of the occasional gas jets, he once more found the refreshing coolness diffused by pure cold water. He would stand in front of the big tank where the reserve stock of live fish was kept and listen to the ceaseless murmur of the four streamlets of water falling from the four corners of the central urn, and then spreading into a broad stream and gliding beneath the locked gratings of the basins with a gentle and continuous flow. This subterranean spring, this stream murmuring in the gloom, had a tranquillizing effect upon him. Of an evening, too, he delighted in the fine sunsets which threw the delicate lacework of the market buildings blackly against the red glow of the heavens. The dancing dust of the last sun rays streamed through every opening, through every chink of the Venetian shutters, and the whole was like some luminous transparency on which the slender shafts of the columns, the elegant curves of the girders, and the geometrical tracery of the roofs were minutely outlined. Florent feasted his eyes on this mighty diagram washed in with Indian ink on phosphorescent vellum, and his mind reverted to his old fancy of a colossal machine with wheels and levers and beams spied in the crimson glow of the fires blazing beneath its boilers. At each consecutive hour of the day the changing play of the light—from the bluish haze of early morning and the black shadows of noon to the flaring of the sinking sun and the paling of its fires in the ashy gray of the twilight—revealed the markets under a new aspect; but on the flaming evenings, when the foul smells arose and forced their way across the broad yellow beams like hot puffs of steam, Florent again experienced discomfort, and his dream changed, and he imagined himself in some gigantic knacker's boiling-house where the fat of a whole people was being melted down.

The coarseness of the market people, whose words and gestures seemed to be infected with the evil smell of the place, also made him suffer. He was very tolerant, and showed no mock modesty; still, these impudent women often embarrassed him. Madame François, whom he had again met, was the only one with whom he felt at ease. She showed such pleasure on learning he had found a berth and was comfortable and out of worry, as she put it, that he was quite touched. The laughter of Lisa, the handsome Norman, and the others disquieted him; but of Madame François he would willingly have made a confidante. She never laughed mockingly at him; when she did laugh, it was like a woman rejoicing at another's happiness. She was a brave, plucky creature, too; hers was a hard business in winter, during the frosts, and the rainy weather was still more trying. On some mornings Florent saw her arrive in a pouring deluge which had been slowly, coldly falling ever since the previous night. Between Nanterre and Paris the wheels of her cart had sunk up to the axles in mud, and Balthazar was caked with mire to his belly. His mistress would pity him and sympathize with him as she wiped him down with some old aprons.

"The poor creatures are very sensitive," said she; "a mere nothing gives them a cold. Ah, my poor old Balthazar! I really thought that we had tumbled into the Seine as we crossed the Neuilly bridge, the rain came down in such a deluge!"

While Balthazar was housed in the inn stable his mistress remained in the pouring rain to sell her vegetables. The footway was transformed into a lake of liquid mud. The cabbages, carrots, and turnips were pelted by the gray water, quite drowned by the muddy torrent that rushed along the pavement. There was no longer any of that glorious greenery so apparent on bright mornings. The market gardeners, cowering in their heavy cloaks beneath the downpour, swore at the municipality which, after due inquiry, had declared that rain was in no way injurious to vegetables, and that there was accordingly no necessity to erect any shelters.

Those rainy mornings greatly worried Florent, who thought about Madame François. He always managed to slip away and get a word with her. But he never found her at all low-spirited. She shook herself like a poodle, saying that she was quite used to such weather, and was not made of sugar, to melt away beneath a few drops of rain. However, he made her seek refuge for a few minutes in one of the covered ways and frequently even took her to Monsieur Lebigre's, where they had some hot wine together. While she with her peaceful face beamed on him in all friendliness, he felt quite delighted with the healthy odor of the fields which she brought into the midst of the foul market atmosphere. She exhaled a scent of earth, hay, fresh air, and open skies.

"You must come to Nanterre, my lad," she said to him, "and look at my kitchen garden. I have put borders of thyme everywhere. How bad your villainous Paris does smell!"

Then she went off, dripping. Florent, on his side, felt quite reinvigorated when he parted from her. He tried, too, the effect of work upon the nervous depression from which he suffered. He was a man of a very methodical temperament and sometimes carried out his plans for the allotment of his time with a strictness that bordered on mania. He shut himself up two evenings a week in order to write an exhaustive work on Cayenne. His modest bedroom was excellently adapted, he thought, to calm his mind and incline him to work. He lighted his fire, saw that the pomegranate at the foot of the bed was looking all right, and then seated himself at the little table, and remained working till midnight. He had pushed the missal and Dream-book back in the drawer, which was now filling with notes, memoranda, manuscripts of all kinds. The work on Cayenne made but slow progress, however, as it was constantly being interrupted by other projects, plans for enormous undertakings which he sketched out in a few words. He successively drafted an outline of a complete reform of the administrative system of the markets, a scheme for transforming the city dues, levied on produce as it entered Paris, into taxes levied upon the sales, a new system of victualling the poorer neighborhoods, and, lastly, a somewhat vague socialist enactment for the storing in common warehouses of all the provisions brought to the markets and the ensuring of a minimum daily supply to each household in Paris. As he sat there, with his head bent over his table, and his mind absorbed in thoughts of all these weighty matters, his gloomy figure cast a great black shadow on the soft peacefulness of the garret. Sometimes a chaffinch which he had picked up one snowy day in the market would mistake the lamplight for the day and break the silence, which only the scratching of Florent's pen on his paper disturbed, by a cry.

Florent was fated to revert to politics. He had suffered too much through them not to make them the dearest occupation of his life. Under other conditions he might have become a good provincial schoolmaster, happy in the peaceful life of some little town. But he had been treated as though he were a wolf and felt as though he had been marked out by exile for some great combative task. His nervous discomfort was the outcome of his long reveries at Cayenne, the brooding bitterness he had felt at his unmerited sufferings, and the vows he had secretly sworn to avenge humanity and justice—the former scouted with a whip, and the latter trodden under foot. Those colossal markets and their teeming odoriferous masses of food had hastened the crisis. To Florent they appeared symbolical of some glutted, digesting beast, of Paris, wallowing in its fat and silently upholding the Empire. He seemed to be encircled by swelling forms and sleek, fat faces, which over and over protested against his own martyr-like scragginess and sallow, discontented visage. To him the markets were like the stomach of the shopkeeping classes, the stomach of all the folks of average rectitude puffing itself out, rejoicing, glistening in the sunshine, and declaring that everything was for the best, since peaceable people had never before grown so beautifully fat. As these thoughts passed through his mind Florent clenched his fists and felt ready for a struggle, more irritated now by the thought of his exile than he had been when he first returned to France. Hatred resumed entire possession of him. He often let his pen drop and became absorbed in dreams. The dying fire cast a bright glow upon his face; the lamp burned smokily, and the chaffinch fell asleep again on one leg, with its head tucked under its wing.

Sometimes Auguste, on coming upstairs at eleven o'clock and seeing the light shining under the door, would knock, before going to bed. Florent admitted him with some impatience. The assistant sat down in front of the fire, speaking but little, and never saying why he had come. His eyes would all the time remain fixed upon the photograph of himself and Augustine in their Sunday finery. Florent came to the conclusion that the young man took a pleasure in visiting the room for the simple reason that it had been occupied by his sweetheart; and one evening he asked him with a smile if he had guessed rightly.

"Well, perhaps it is so," replied Auguste, very much surprised at the discovery which he himself now made of the reasons which actuated him. "I'd really never thought of that before. I came to see you without knowing why. But if I were to tell Augustine, how she'd laugh!"

Whenever he showed himself at all loquacious, his one eternal theme was the pork shop which he was going to set up with Augustine at Plaisance. He seemed so perfectly assured of arranging his life in accordance with his desires, that Florent grew to feel a sort of respect for him, mingled with irritation. After all, the young fellow was very resolute and energetic, in spite of his seeming stupidity. He made straight for the goal he had in view and would doubtless reach it in perfect assurance and happiness. On the evenings of these visits from the apprentice, Florent could not settle down to work again; he went off to bed in a discontented mood, and did not recover his equilibrium until the thought passed through his mind, "Why, that Auguste is a perfect animal!"

Every month he went to Clamart to see Monsieur Verlaque. These visits were almost a delight to him. The poor man still lingered on, to the great astonishment of Gavard, who had not expected him to last for more than six months. Every time that Florent went to see him Verlaque would declare that he was feeling better and was most anxious to resume his work again. But the days glided by, and he had serious relapses. Florent would sit by his bedside, chat about the fish market, and do what he could to enliven him. He deposited on the pedestal table the fifty francs which he surrendered to him each month; and the old inspector, though the payment had been agreed upon, invariably protested, and seemed disinclined to take the money. Then they would begin to speak of something else, and the coins remained lying on the table. When Florent went away, Madame Verlaque always accompanied him to the street door. She was a gentle little woman, of a very tearful disposition. Her one topic of conversation was the expense necessitated by her husband's illness, the costliness of chicken broth, butcher's meat, Bordeaux wine, medicine, and doctors' fees. Her doleful conversation greatly embarrassed Florent, and on the first few occasions he did not understand the drift of it. But at last, as the poor woman seemed always in a state of tears, and kept saying how happy and comfortable they had been when they had enjoyed the full salary of eighteen hundred francs a year, he timidly offered to make her a private allowance, to be kept secret from her husband. This offer, however, she declined, inconsistently declaring that the fifty francs were sufficient. But in the course of the month she frequently wrote to Florent, calling him their savior. Her handwriting was small and fine, yet she would contrive to fill three pages of letter-paper with humble, flowing sentences entreating the loan of ten francs; and this she at last did so regularly that nearly the whole of Florent's hundred and fifty francs found its way to the Verlaques. The husband was probably unaware of it; however, the wife gratefully kissed Florent's hands. This charity afforded him the greatest pleasure, and he concealed it as though it were some forbidden selfish indulgence.

"That rascal Verlaque is making a fool of you," Gavard would sometimes say. "He's coddling himself up finely now that you are doing the work and paying him an income."

At last one day Florent replied:

"Oh, we've arranged matters together. I'm only to give him twenty-five francs a month in future."

As a matter of fact, Florent had but little need of money. The Quenus continued to provide him with board and lodging; and the few francs which he kept by him sufficed to pay for the refreshment he took in the evening at Monsieur Lebigre's. His life had gradually assumed all the regularity of clockwork. He worked in his bedroom, continued to teach little Muche twice a week from eight to nine o'clock, devoted an evening to Lisa, to avoid offending her, and spent the rest of his spare time in the little "cabinet" with Gavard and his friends.

When he went to the Méhudins' there was a touch of tutorial stiffness in his gentle demeanor. He was pleased with the old house in the Rue Pirouette. On the ground floor he passed through the faint odors pervading the premises of the purveyor of cooked vegetables. Big pans of boiled spinach and sorrel stood cooling in the little backyard. Then he ascended the winding staircase, greasy and dark, with worn and bulging steps which sloped in a disquieting manner. The Méhudins occupied the whole of the second floor. Even when they had attained comfortable circumstances the old mother had always declined to move into fresh quarters, despite all the supplications of her daughters, who dreamt of living in a new house in a fine broad street. But on this point the old woman was not to be moved; she had lived there, she said, and meant to die there. She contented herself, moreover, with a dark little closet, leaving the larger rooms to Claire and La Normande. The latter, with the authority of the elder born, had taken possession of the room that overlooked the street; it was the best and largest of the suite. Claire was so much annoyed at her sister's action in the matter that she refused to occupy the adjoining room, whose window overlooked the yard, and obstinately insisted on sleeping on the other side of the landing, in a sort of garret, which she did not even have whitewashed. However, she had her own key and so was independent; whenever anything happened to displease her she locked herself up in her own quarters.

As a rule, when Florent arrived the Méhudins were just finishing their dinner. Muche sprang to his neck, and for a moment the young man remained seated with the lad chattering between his legs. Then, when the oilcloth cover had been wiped, the lesson began on a corner of the table. The beautiful Norman gave Florent a cordial welcome. She generally began to knit or mend some linen, and would draw her chair up to the table and work by the light of the same lamp as the others; and she frequently put down her needle to listen to the lesson, which filled her with surprise. She soon began to feel warm esteem for this man who seemed so clever, who, in speaking to the little one, showed himself as gentle as a woman and manifested angelic patience in again and again repeating the same instructions. She no longer considered him at all plain, but even felt somewhat jealous of beautiful Lisa. And then she drew her chair still nearer and gazed at Florent with an embarrassing smile.

"But you are jogging my elbow, mother, and I can't write," Muche exclaimed angrily. "There! see what a blot you've made me make! Get further away, do!"

La Normande now gradually began to say a good many unpleasant things about beautiful Lisa. She pretended that the latter concealed her real age, that she laced her stays so tightly that she nearly suffocated herself, and that if she came down of a morning looking so trim and neat, without a single hair out of place, it must be because she looked perfectly

hideous when in dishabille. Then La Normande would raise
her arm a little, and say that there was no need for her to
wear any stays to cramp and deform her figure. At these
times the lessons would be interrupted, and Muche gazed
with interest at his mother as she raised her arms. Florent
listened to her, and even laughed, thinking to himself that
women were very odd creatures. The rivalry between the
beautiful Norman and beautiful Lisa amused him.

Muche, however, managed to finish his page of writing.
Florent, who was a good penman, set him copies in large
hand and round hand on slips of paper. The words he chose
were very long and took up the whole line, and he evinced a
marked partiality for such expressions as "tyrannically,"
"liberticide," "unconstitutional," and "revolutionary. At times
also he made the boy copy such sentences as these: "The
day of justice will surely come"; "The suffering of the just
man is the condemnation of the oppressor"; "When the hour
strikes, the guilty shall fall." In preparing these copy slips he
was, indeed, influenced by the ideas which haunted his brain;
he would for the time become quite oblivious of Muche, the
beautiful Norman, and all his surroundings. The lad would
have copied Rousseau's "Contrat Social" had he been told
to do so; and thus, drawing each letter in turn, he filled page
after page with lines of "tyrannically" and "unconstitutional."

As long as the tutor remained there, old Madame Méhudin
kept fidgeting round the table, muttering to herself. She still
harbored terrible rancor against Florent; and asserted that it
was folly to make the lad work in that way at a time when
children ought to be in bed. She would certainly have turned
that "spindle-shanks" out of the house, if the beautiful
Norman, after a stormy scene, had not bluntly told her that
she would go to live elsewhere if she were not allowed to
receive whom she chose. However, the pair began quarrelling again on the subject every evening.

"You may say what you like," exclaimed the old woman;

"but he's got treacherous eyes. And, besides, I'm always suspicious of those skinny people. A skinny man's capable of anything. I've never come across a decent one yet. That one's as flat as a board. And he's got such an ugly face, too! Though I'm sixty-five and more, I'd precious soon send him about his business if he came a-courting of me!"

She said this because she had a shrewd idea of how matters were likely to turn out. And then she went on to speak in laudatory terms of Monsieur Lebigre, who, indeed, paid the greatest attention to the beautiful Norman. Apart from the handsome dowry which he imagined she would bring with her, he considered that she would be a magnificent acquisition to his counter. The old woman never missed an opportunity to sound his praises; there was no lankiness, at any rate, about him, said she; he was stout and strong, with a pair of calves which would have done honor even to one of the Emperor's footmen.

However, La Normande shrugged her shoulders and snappishly replied: "What do I care whether he's stout or not? I don't want him or anybody. And besides, I shall do as I please."

Then, if the old woman became too pointed in her remarks, the other added: "It's no business of yours, and, besides, it isn't true. Hold your tongue and don't worry me." She would then go off into her room, banging the door behind her. Florent, however, had a yet more bitter enemy than Madame Méhudin in the house. As soon as he arrived there, Claire would get up without a word, take a candle, and go off to her own room on the other side of the landing; and she could be heard locking her door in a burst of sullen anger. One evening when her sister asked the tutor to dinner, she prepared her own food on the landing and ate it in her bedroom; and now and again she secluded herself so closely that nothing was seen of her for a week at a time.

She usually retained her appearance of soft lissomeness, but periodically had a fit of iron rigidity, when her eyes blazed from under her pale tawny locks like those of a distrustful wild animal. Old Mother Méhudin, fancying that she might relieve herself in her company, only made her furious by speaking to her of Florent; and thereupon the old woman, in her exasperation, told everyone that she would have gone off and left her daughters to themselves had she not been afraid of their devouring each other if they remained alone together.

As Florent went away one evening, he passed in front of Claire's door, which was standing wide open. He saw the girl look at him and turn very red. Her hostile demeanor annoyed him; and it was only the timidity which he felt in the presence of women that restrained him from seeking an explanation of her conduct. On this particular evening he would certainly have addressed her if he had not detected Mademoiselle Saget's pale face peering over the balustrade of the upper landing. So he went his way, but had not taken a dozen steps before Claire's door was closed behind him with such violence as to shake the whole staircase. It was after this that Mademoiselle Saget, eager to propagate slander, went about repeating everywhere that Madame Quenu's cousin was "carrying on" most dreadfully with both the Méhudin girls.

Florent, however, gave very little thought to these two handsome young women. His usual manner towards them was that of a man who has but little success with the sex. Certainly he had come to entertain a feeling of genuine friendship for La Normande, who really displayed a very good heart when her impetuous temper did not run away with her. But he never went any further than this. Moreover, the queenly proportions of her robust figure filled him with a kind of alarm; and of an evening, whenever she drew her chair up to the lamp and bent forward as though to look at Muche's copy book, he drew in his own sharp bony elbows and shrunken shoulders as if realizing what a pitiful specimen of humanity he was by the side of that buxom, hardy creature so full of the life of ripe womanhood. Moreover, there was another reason why he recoiled from her. The smells of the markets distressed him; on finishing his duties of an evening he would have liked to escape from the fishy odor amid which his days were spent; but, unfortunately, beautiful though La Normande was, this odor seemed to adhere to her silky skin. She had tried every sort of aromatic oil, and bathed freely; but as soon as the freshening influence of the bath was over, her blood again impregnated her skin with the faint odor of salmon, the musky perfume of smelts, and the pungent scent of herrings and skate. Her skirts, too, as she moved about, exhaled these fishy smells, and she walked as though amidst an atmosphere redolent of slimy seaweed. With her tall, goddess-like figure, her purity of form, and transparency of complexion she resembled some lovely antique marble that had rolled about in the depths of the sea and had been brought to land in some fisherman's net.

Mademoiselle Saget, however, swore by all her gods that Florent was the young woman's lover. According to her account, indeed, he courted both the sisters. She had quarrelled with the beautiful Norman about a ten-sou dab; and ever since this falling-out she had manifested warm friendship for handsome Lisa. By this means she hoped the sooner to arrive at a solution of what she called the Quenus' mystery. Florent still continued to elude her curiosity, and she told her friends that she felt like a body without a soul, though she was careful not to reveal what was troubling her so grievously. A young girl infatuated with a hopeless passion could not have been in more distress than this terrible old woman at finding herself unable to solve the mystery of the Quenus' cousin. She was constantly playing the spy on Florent, following him about, and watching him, in a burning rage at her failure to satisfy her rampant curiosity. Now that he had begun to visit the Méhudins she was forever haunting the stairs and landings. She soon discovered that handsome Lisa was much annoyed at Florent visiting "those women," and accordingly she called at the pork shop every morning with a budget of information. She went in shrivelled and shrunk by the frosty air, and, resting her hands on the heating pan to warm them, remained in front of the counter buying nothing, but repeating in her shrill voice: "He was with them again yesterday; he seems to live there now. I heard La Normande call him 'my dear' on the staircase."

She indulged like this in all sorts of lies in order to remain in the shop and continue warming her hands for a little longer. On the morning after the evening when she had heard Claire close her door behind Florent, she spun out her story for a good half-hour, inventing all sorts of mendacious and abominable particulars.

Lisa, who had assumed a look of contemptuous scorn, said but little, simply encouraging Mademoiselle Saget's gossip by her silence. At last, however, she interrupted her. "No, no," she said; "I can't really listen to all that. Is it possible that there can be such women?"

Thereupon Mademoiselle Saget told Lisa that unfortunately all women were not so well conducted as herself. And then she pretended to find all sorts of excuses for Florent: it wasn't his fault; he was no doubt a bachelor; these women had very likely inveigled him in their snares. In this way she hinted questions without openly asking them. But Lisa preserved silence with respect to her cousin, merely shrugging her shoulders and compressing her lips. When Mademoiselle Saget at last went away, the mistress of the shop glanced with disgust at the cover of the heating pan, the glistening metal of which had been tarnished by the impression of the old woman's little hands.

"Augustine," she cried, "bring a duster and wipe the cover of the heating pan. It's quite filthy!"

The rivalry between the beautiful Lisa and the beautiful Norman now became formidable. The beautiful Norman flattered herself that she had carried a lover off from her enemy; and the beautiful Lisa was indignant with the hussy who, by luring the sly cousin to her home, would surely end by compromising them all. The natural temperament of each woman manifested itself in the hostilities which ensued. The one remained calm and scornful, like a lady who holds up her skirts to keep them from being soiled by the mud; while the other, much less subject to shame, displayed insolent gaiety and swaggered along the footways with the airs of a duelist seeking a cause of quarrel. Each of their skirmishes would be the talk of the fish market for the whole day. When the beautiful Norman saw the beautiful Lisa standing at the door of her shop, she would go out of her way in order to pass her, and brush against her with her apron; and then the angry glances of the two rivals crossed like rapiers, with the rapid flash and thrust of pointed steel. When the beautiful Lisa, on the other hand, went to the fish market, she assumed an expression of disgust on approaching the beautiful Norman's stall. And then she proceeded to purchase some big fish—a turbot or a salmon—of a neighboring dealer, spreading her money out on the marble slab as she did so, for she had noticed that this seemed to have a painful effect upon the "hussy," who ceased laughing at the sight. To hear the two rivals speak, anyone would have supposed that the fish and pork they sold were quite unfit for food. However, their principal engagements took place when the beautiful Norman was seated at her stall and the beautiful Lisa at her counter, and they glowered blackly at each other across the Rue Rambuteau. They sat in state in their big white aprons, decked out with showy toilets and jewels, and the battle between them would commence early in the morning.

"Hallo, the fat woman's got up!" the beautiful Norman would exclaim. "She ties herself up as tightly as her sausages! Ah, she's got Saturday's collar on again, and she's still wearing that poplin dress!"

At the same moment, on the opposite side of the street, beautiful Lisa was saying to her shop girl: "Just look at that creature staring at us over there, Augustine! She's getting quite deformed by the life she leads. Do you see her earrings? She's wearing those big drops of hers, isn't she? It makes one feel ashamed to see a girl like that with brilliants."

All complaisance, Augustine echoed her mistress's words.

When either of them was able to display a new ornament it was like scoring a victory—the other one almost choked with spleen. Every day they would scrutinize and count each other's customers, and manifest the greatest annoyance if they thought that the "big thing over the way" was doing the better business. Then they spied out what each had for lunch. Each knew what the other ate and even watched to see how she digested it. In the afternoon, while the one sat amid her cooked meats and the other amid her fish, they posed and gave themselves airs, as though they were queens of beauty. It was then that the victory of the day was decided. The beautiful Norman embroidered, selecting the most delicate and difficult work, and this aroused Lisa's exasperation.

"Ah!" she said, speaking of her rival, "she had far better mend her boy's stockings. He's running about quite barefooted. Just look at that fine lady, with her red hands stinking of fish!"

For her part, Lisa usually knitted.

"She's still at that same sock," La Normande would say, as she watched her. "She eats so much that she goes to sleep over her work. I pity her poor husband if he's waiting for those socks to keep his feet warm!"

They would sit glowering at each other with this implacable hostility until evening, taking note of every customer, and displaying such keen eyesight that they detected the smallest details of each other's dress and person when other women declared that they could see nothing at such a distance. Mademoiselle Saget expressed the highest admiration for Madame Quenu's wonderful sight when she one day detected a scratch on the fishgirl's left cheek. With eyes like those, said the old maid, one might even see through a door. However, the victory often remained undecided when night fell; sometimes one or other of the rivals was temporarily crushed, but she took her revenge the next day. Several people of the neighborhood actually laid wagers on these contests, some backing the beautiful Lisa and others the beautiful Norman.

At last they ended by forbidding their children to speak to one another. Pauline and Muche had formerly been good friends, notwithstanding the girl's stiff petticoats and lady-like demeanor, and the lad's tattered appearance, coarse language, and rough manners. They had at times played together at horses on the broad footway in front of the fish market, Pauline always being the horse and Muche the driver. One day, however, when the boy came in all simplicity to seek his playmate, Lisa turned him out of the house, declaring that he was a dirty little street urchin.

"One can't tell what may happen with children who have been so shockingly brought up," she observed.

"Yes, indeed; you are quite right," replied Mademoiselle Saget, who happened to be present.

When Muche, who was barely seven years old, came in tears to his mother to tell her of what had happened, La Normande broke out into a terrible passion. At the first moment she felt a strong inclination to rush over to the Quenu-Gradelles' and smash everything in their shop. But eventually she contented herself with giving Muche a whipping.

"If ever I catch you going there again," she cried, boiling over with anger, "you'll get it hot from me, I can tell you!"

Florent, however, was the real victim of the two women. It was he, in truth, who had set them by the ears, and it was on his account that they were fighting each other. Ever since he had appeared upon the scene things had been going from bad to worse. He compromised and disturbed and embittered all these people, who had previously lived in such sleek peace and harmony. The beautiful Norman felt inclined to claw him when he lingered too long with the Quenus, and it was chiefly from an impulse of hostile rivalry that she desired to win him to herself. The beautiful Lisa, on her side, maintained a cold judicial bearing, and although extremely annoyed, forced herself to silence whenever she saw Florent leaving the pork shop to go to the Rue Pirouette.

Still, there was now much less cordiality than formerly round the Quenus' dinner table in the evening. The clean, prim dining room seemed to have assumed an aspect of chilling severity. Florent divined a reproach, a sort of condemnation in the bright oak, the polished lamp, and the new matting. He scarcely dared to eat for fear of letting crumbs fall on the floor or soiling his plate. There was a guileless simplicity about him which prevented him from seeing how the land really lay. He still praised Lisa's affectionate kindliness on all sides; and outwardly, indeed, she did continue to treat him with all gentleness.

"It is very strange," she said to him one day with a smile,

as though she were joking; "although you don't eat at all badly now, you don't get fatter. Your food doesn't seem to do you any good."

At this Quenu laughed aloud, and tapping his brother's stomach, protested that the whole contents of the pork shop might pass through it without depositing a layer of fat as thick as a two-sou piece. However, Lisa's insistence on this particular subject was instinct with that same suspicious dislike for fleshless men which Madame Méhudin manifested more outspokenly; and behind it all there was likewise a veiled allusion to the disorderly life which she imagined Florent was leading. She never, however, spoke a word to him about La Normande. Quenu had attempted a joke on the subject one evening, but Lisa had received it so icily that the good man had not ventured to refer to the matter again. They would remain seated at table for a few moments after dessert, and Florent, who had noticed his sister-in-law's vexation if he ever went off too soon, tried to find something to talk about. On these occasions Lisa would be near him, and certainly he did not suffer in her presence from that fishy smell which assailed him when he was in the company of La Normande. The mistress of the pork shop, on the contrary, exhaled an odor of fat and rich meats. Moreover, not a thrill of life stirred her tight-fitting bodice; she was all massiveness and all sedateness. Gavard once said to Florent in confidence that Madame Quenu was no doubt handsome, but that for his own part he did not admire such armor-plated women.

Lisa avoided talking to Quenu of Florent. She habitually prided herself on her patience and considered, too, that it would not be proper to cause any unpleasantness between the brothers, unless some peremptory reason for her interference should arise. As she said, she could put up with a good deal, but, of course, she must not be tried too far. She had now reached the period of courteous tolerance, wearing an expressionless face, affecting perfect indifference and strict politeness, and carefully avoiding everything which might seem to hint that Florent was boarding and lodging with them without their receiving the slightest payment from him. Not, indeed, that she would have accepted any payment from him, she was above all that; still he might, at any rate, she thought, have lunched away from the house.

"We never seem to be alone now," she remarked to Quenu one day. "If there is anything we want to say to one another we have to wait till we go upstairs at night."

And then, one night when they were in bed, she said to him: "Your brother earns a hundred and fifty francs a month, doesn't he? Well, it's strange he can't put a trifle by to buy himself some more linen. I've been obliged to give him three more of your old shirts."

"Oh, that doesn't matter," Quenu replied. "Florent's not hard to please; and we must let him keep his money for himself."

"Oh, yes, of course," said Lisa, without pressing the matter further. "I didn't mention it for that reason. Whether he spends his money well or ill, it isn't our business."

In her own mind she felt quite sure that he wasted his salary at the Méhudins'.

Only on one occasion did she break through her habitual calmness of demeanor, the quiet reserve which was the result of both natural temperament and preconceived design. The beautiful Norman had made Florent a present of a magnificent salmon. Feeling very much embarrassed with the fish, and not daring to refuse it, he brought it to Lisa.

"You can make a pâté of it," he said ingenuously.

Lisa looked at him sternly with whitening lips. Then, striving to restrain her anger, she exclaimed: "Do you think that we are short of food? Thank God, we've got quite enough to eat here! Take it back!"

"Well, at any rate, cook it for me," replied Florent, amazed by her anger; "I'll eat it myself."

At this she burst out furiously.

"The house isn't an inn! Tell those who gave you the fish to cook it for you! I won't have my pans tainted and infected! Take it back again! Do you hear?"

If he had not gone away with it, she would certainly have seized it and hurled it into the street. Florent took it to Monsieur Lebigre's, where Rose was ordered to make a pâté of it; and one evening the pâté was eaten in the little "cabinet," Gavard, who was present, treating some oysters for the occasion. Florent now gradually came more and more frequently to Monsieur Lebigre's, till at last he was constantly to be met in the little private room. He there found an atmosphere of heated excitement in which his political feverishness could pulsate freely. At times, now, when he shut himself up in his garret to work, the quiet simplicity of the little room irritated him, his theoretical search for liberty proved quite insufficient, and it became necessary that he should go downstairs and seek satisfaction in the trenchant axioms of Charvet and the wild outbursts of Logre. During the first few evenings the clamor and chatter had made him feel ill at ease; he was then still quite conscious of their utter emptiness, but he felt a need of drowning his thoughts, of goading himself on to some extreme resolution which might calm his mental disquietude. The atmosphere of the little room, reeking with the odor of spirits and warm with tobacco smoke, intoxicated him and filled him with peculiar beatitude, prompting a kind of self-surrender which made him willing to acquiesce in the wildest ideas. He grew attached to those he met there, and looked for them and awaited their coming with a pleasure which increased with habit. Robine's mild, bearded countenance, Clémence's serious profile, Charvet's fleshless pallor, Logre's hump, Gavard, Alexandre, and

Lacaille, all entered into his life and assumed a larger and larger place in it. He took quite a sensual enjoyment in these meetings. When his fingers closed round the brass knob on the door of the little cabinet it seemed to be animated with life, to warm him, and turn of its own accord. Had he grasped the supple wrist of a woman he could not have felt a more thrilling emotion.

To tell the truth, very serious things took place in that little room. One evening, Logre, after indulging in wilder outbursts than usual, banged his fist upon the table, declaring that if they were men they would make a clean sweep of the Government. And he added that it was necessary they should come to an understanding without further delay, if they desired to be fully prepared when the time for action arrived. Then they all bent their heads together, discussed the matter in lower tones, and decided to form a little "group," which should be ready for whatever might happen. From that day forward Gavard flattered himself that he was a member of a secret society and was engaged in a conspiracy. The little circle received no new members, but Logre promised to put it into communication with other associations with which he was acquainted; and then, as soon as they held all Paris in their grasp, they would rise and make the Tuileries' people dance. A series of endless discussions, renewed during several months, then began—discussions on questions of organization, on questions of ways and means, on questions of strategy, and of the form of the future Government. As soon as Rose had brought Clémence's grog, Charvet's and Robine's beer, the coffee for Logre, Gavard, and Florent, and the liqueur glasses of brandy for Lacaille and Alexandre, the door of the cabinet was carefully fastened, and the debate began.

Charvet and Florent were naturally those whose utterances were listened to with the greatest attention. Gavard had not been able to keep his tongue from wagging, but had gradually related the whole story of Cayenne; and Florent found himself surrounded by a halo of martyrdom. His words were received as though they were the expression of indisputable dogmas. One evening the poultry dealer, vexed at hearing his friend, who happened to be absent, attacked, exclaimed: "Don't say anything against Florent; he's been to Cayenne!"

Charvet was rather annoyed by the advantage which this circumstance gave to Florent. "Cayenne, Cayenne," he muttered between his teeth. "Ah, well, they were not so badly off there, after all!"

Then he attempted to prove that exile was a mere nothing, and that real suffering consisted in remaining in one's oppressed country, gagged in presence of triumphant despotism. And besides, he urged, it wasn't his fault that he hadn't been arrested on the Second of December. Next, however, he hinted that those who had allowed themselves to be captured were imbeciles. His secret jealousy made him a systematic opponent of Florent; and the general discussions always ended in a duel between these two, who, while their companions listened in silence, would speak against one another for hours at a time, without either of them allowing that he was beaten.

One of the favorite subjects of discussion was that of the reorganization of the country which would have to be effected immediately following their victory.

"We are the conquerors, are we not?" began Gavard.

And, triumph being taken for granted, everyone offered his opinion. There were two rival parties. Charvet, who was a disciple of Hébert, was supported by Logre and Robine; while Florent, who was always absorbed in humanitarian dreams, and called himself a Socialist, was backed by Alexandre and Lacaille. As for Gavard, he felt no repugnance for violent action; but, as he was often twitted about his fortune with no end of sarcastic witticisms which annoyed him, he declared himself a Communist.

"We must make a clean sweep of everything," Charvet would curtly say, as though he were delivering a blow with a cleaver. "The trunk is rotten, and it must come down."

"Yes! yes!" cried Logre, standing up that he might look taller, and making the partition shake with the excited motion of his hump. "Everything will be levelled to the ground; take my word for it. After that we shall see what to do."

Robine signified approval by wagging his beard. His silence seemed implicit with delight whenever violent revolutionary propositions were made. His eyes assumed a soft ecstatic expression at the mention of the guillotine. He half closed them, as though he could see the machine, and was filled with pleasant emotion at the sight; and next he would gently rub his chin against the knob of his stick, with a subdued purr of satisfaction.

"All the same," said Florent, in whose voice a vague touch of sadness lingered, "if you cut down the tree it will be necessary to preserve some seed. For my part, I think that the tree ought to be preserved, so that we may graft new life on it. The political revolution, you know, has already taken place; today we have got to think of the laborer, the working man. Our movement must be altogether a social one. I defy you to reject the claims of the people. They are weary of waiting and are determined to have their share of happiness."

These words aroused Alexandre's enthusiasm. With a beaming, radiant face he declared that this was quite true, that the people were weary of waiting.

"And we will have our share," added Lacaille, with a more menacing expression. "All the revolutions that have taken place have been for the good of the middle classes. We've had quite enough of that sort of thing, and the next one shall be for our benefit."

From this moment disagreement set in. Gavard offered to make a division of his property, but Logre declined, asserting that he cared nothing for money. Then Charvet gradually overcame the tumult, till at last he alone was heard speaking.

"The selfishness of the different classes does more than anything else to uphold tyranny," said he. "It is wrong of the people to display egotism. If they assist us they shall have their share. But why should I fight for the working man if the working man won't fight for me? Moreover, that is not the question at present. Ten years of revolutionary dictatorship will be necessary to accustom a nation like France to the fitting enjoyment of liberty."

"All the more so as the working man is not ripe for it and requires to be directed," said Clémence bluntly.

She but seldom spoke. This tall, serious-looking girl, alone among so many men, listened to all the political chatter with a learnedly critical air. She leaned back against the partition, and every now and then sipped her grog while gazing at the speakers with frowning brows or inflated nostrils, thus silently signifying her approval or disapproval, and making it quite clear that she held decided opinions upon the most complicated matters. At times she would roll a cigarette and puff slender whiffs of smoke from the corners of her mouth, while lending increased attention to what was being debated. It was as though she were presiding over the discussion and would award the prize to the victor when it was finished. She certainly considered that it became her, as a woman, to display some reserve in her opinions and to remain calm while the men grew more and more excited. Now and then, however, in the heat of the debate, she would let a word or a phrase escape her and even "shut Charvet's mouth," as Gavard said. In her heart she believed herself the superior of all these fellows. The only one of them for whom she felt any respect was Robine, and she would thoughtfully contemplate his silent bearing.

Neither Florent nor any of the others paid any special attention to Clémence. They treated her just as though she were a man, shaking hands with her so roughly as almost to dislocate her arms. One evening Florent witnessed the periodical settlement of accounts between her and Charvet. She had just received her pay, and Charvet wanted to borrow ten francs from her; but she first of all insisted that they must reckon up how matters stood between them. They lived together in a voluntary partnership, each having complete control of his or her earnings, and strictly paying his or her expenses. By so doing, they said, they were under no obligations to one another, but retained entire freedom. Rent, food, washing, and amusements, were all noted down and added up. That evening, when the accounts had been verified, Clémence proved to Charvet that he already owed her five francs. Then she handed him the other ten which he wished to borrow and exclaimed: "Recollect that you now owe me fifteen. I shall expect you to repay me on the fifth, when you get paid for teaching little Léhudier."

When Rose was summoned to receive payment for the drinks, each produced the few sous required to discharge his or her liability. Charvet laughingly called Clémence an aristocrat because she drank grog. She wanted to humiliate him, said he, and make him feel that he earned less than she did, which, as it happened, was the fact. Beneath his laugh, however, there was a feeling of bitterness that the girl should be better circumstanced than himself, for, in spite of his theory of the equality of the sexes, this lowered him.

Although the discussions in the little room had virtually no result, they served to exercise the speakers' lungs. A tremendous hubbub proceeded from the sanctum, and the panes of frosted glass vibrated like drum-skins. Sometimes the uproar became so great that Rose, while languidly serving some blouse-wearing customer in the shop, would turn her head uneasily.

"Why, they're surely fighting together in there," the customer would say, as he put his glass down on the zinc-covered counter, and wiped his mouth with the back of his hand.

"Oh, there's no fear of that," Monsieur Lebigre tranquilly replied. "It's only some gentlemen talking together."

Monsieur Lebigre, indeed, although very strict with his other customers, allowed the politicians to shout as loudly as they pleased, and never made the least remark on the subject. He would sit for hours together on the bench behind the counter, with his big head lolling drowsily against the mirror, while he watched Rose uncorking the bottles and giving a wipe here and there with her duster. And in spite of the somniferous effects of the wine fumes and the warm streaming gaslight, he would keep his ears open to the sounds proceeding from the little room. At times, when the voices grew noisier than usual, he got up from his seat and went to lean against the partition; and occasionally he even pushed the door open and went inside and sat down there for a few minutes, giving Gavard a friendly slap on the thigh. And then he would nod approval of everything that was said. The poultry dealer asserted that although friend Lebigre hadn't the stuff of an orator in him, they might safely reckon on him when the "rumpus" came.

One morning, however, at the markets, when a tremendous row broke out between Rose and one of the fishwives, through the former accidentally knocking over a basket of herrings, Florent heard Rose's employer spoken of as a "dirty spy" in the pay of the police. And after he had succeeded in restoring peace, all sorts of stories about Monsieur Lebigre were poured into his ears. Yes, the wine seller was in the pay of the police, the fishwives said; all the neighborhood knew it. Before Mademoiselle Saget had begun to deal with him she had once met him entering the Préfecture to make his report. It was asserted, too, that he was a money-monger, a usurer, and lent petty sums by the day to hawkers, and let out barrows to them, exacting a scandalous rate of interest in return. Florent was greatly disturbed by all this and felt it his duty to repeat it that evening to his fellow-politicians. The latter, however, only shrugged their shoulders and laughed at his uneasiness.

"Poor Florent!" Charvet exclaimed sarcastically; "he imagines that the whole police force is on his track, just because he happens to have been sent to Cayenne!"

Gavard gave his word of honor that Lebigre was perfectly staunch and true, while Logre, for his part, manifested extreme irritation. He fumed and declared that it would be quite impossible for them to get on if everyone was to be accused of being a police spy; for his own part, he would rather stay at home and have nothing more to do with politics. Why, hadn't people even dared to say that he, Logre himself, who had fought in '48 and '51, and had twice narrowly escaped transportation, was a spy as well? As he shouted that out, he thrust his jaws forward and glared at the others as though he would have liked to ram the conviction that he had nothing to do with the police down their throats. At the sight of his furious glances his companions made gestures of protestation. However, Lacaille, on hearing Monsieur Lebigre accused of usury, silently lowered his head.

The incident was forgotten in the discussions which ensued. Since Logre had suggested a conspiracy, Monsieur Lebigre had grasped the hands of the frequenters of the little room with more vigor than ever. Their custom, to tell the truth, was of but small value to him, for they never ordered more than one drink apiece. They drained the last drops just as they rose to leave, having been careful to allow a little to remain in their glasses, even during their most heated arguments. In this way the one round lasted throughout the evening. They shivered as they turned out into the cold dampness of the night and for a moment or two remained standing on the footway with dazzled eyes and buzzing ears, as though surprised by the dark silence of the street. Rose, meanwhile, fastened the shutters behind them. Then, quite exhausted, at a loss for another word, they shook hands, separated, and went their different ways, still mentally continuing the discussion of the evening, and regretting that they could not ram their particular theories down each other's throats. Robine walked away, with his bent back bobbing up and down, in the direction of the Rue Rambuteau; while Charvet and Clémence went off through the markets on their return to the Luxembourg quarter, their heels sounding on the flag-stones in military fashion, while they still discussed some question of politics or philosophy, walking along side by side, but never arm-in-arm.

The conspiracy ripened very slowly. At the commencement of the summer the plotters had got no further than agreeing that it was necessary a stroke should be attempted. Florent, who had at first looked upon the whole business with a kind of distrust, had now, however, come to believe in the possibility of a revolutionary movement. He took up the matter seriously; making notes, and preparing plans in writing, while the others still did nothing but talk. For his part, he began to concentrate his whole life in the one persistent idea which made his brain throb night after night; and this to such a degree that he at last took his brother Quenu with him to Monsieur Lebigre's, as though such a course were quite natural. Certainly he had no thought of doing anything improper. He still looked upon Quenu as in some degree his pupil and may even have considered it his duty to start him on the proper path. Quenu was an absolute novice in politics, but after spending five or six evenings in the little room he found himself quite in accord with the others. When Lisa was not present he manifested much docility, a sort of respect for his brother's opinions. But the greatest charm of the affair for him was really the mild dissipation of leaving his shop and shutting himself up in the little room where the others shouted so loudly, and where Clémence's presence, in his opinion, gave a tinge of rakishness and romance to the proceedings. He now made all haste with his chitterlings in order that he might get away as early as possible, anxious to lose not a single word of the discussions, which seemed to him to be very brilliant, though he was not always able to follow them. The beautiful Lisa did not fail to notice his hurry to be gone, but as yet she refrained from saying anything. When Florent took him off, she simply went to the door-step, and watched them enter Monsieur Lebigre's, her face paling somewhat, and a severe expression coming into her eyes.

One evening, as Mademoiselle Saget was peering out of her garret casement, she recognized Quenu's shadow on the frosted glass of the "cabinet" window facing the Rue Pirouette. She had found her casement an excellent post of observation, as it overlooked that milky transparency, on which the gaslight threw silhouettes of the politicians, with noses suddenly appearing and disappearing, gaping jaws abruptly springing into sight and then vanishing, and huge arms, apparently destitute of bodies, waving back and forth. This extraordinary jumble of detached limbs, these silent but frantic profiles, bore witness to the heated discussions that went on in the little room and kept the old maid peering from behind her muslin curtains until the transparency turned black. She shrewdly suspected some "bit of trickery," as she phrased it. By continual watching she had come to recognize the different shadows by their hands and hair and clothes. As she gazed upon the chaos of clenched fists, angry heads, and swaying shoulders, which seemed to have become detached from their trunks and to roll about one atop of the other, she would exclaim unhesitatingly, "Ah, there's that big booby of a cousin; there's that miserly old Gavard; and there's the hunchback; and there's that maypole of a Clémence!" Then, when the action of the shadow-play became more pronounced, and they all seemed to have lost control over themselves, she felt an irresistible impulse to go downstairs to try to find out what was happening. Thus she now made a point of buying her black-currant syrup at nights, pretending that she felt out-of-sorts in the morning and was obliged to take a sip as soon as she was out of bed. On the evening when she noticed Quenu's massive head shadowed on the transparency in close proximity to Charvet's fist, she made her appearance at Monsieur Lebigre's in a breathless condition. To gain more time, she made Rose rinse out her little bottle for her; however, she was about to return to her room when she heard the pork butcher exclaim with a sort of childish candor:

"No, indeed, we'll stand it no longer! We'll make a clean sweep of all those humbugging Deputies and Ministers! Yes, we'll send the whole lot packing."

Eight o'clock had scarcely struck on the following morning when Mademoiselle Saget was already at the pork shop. She found Madame Lecœur and La Sarriette there, dipping their noses into the heating pan, and buying hot sausages for breakfast. As the old maid had managed to draw them into her quarrel with La Normande with respect to the ten-sou dab, they had at once made friends again with Lisa, and they now had nothing but contempt for the handsome fish girl and assailed her and her sister as good-for-nothing hussies whose only aim was to fleece men of their money. This opinion had been inspired by the assertions of Mademoiselle Saget, who had declared to Madame Lecœur that Florent had induced one of the two girls to coquette with Gavard, and that the four of them had indulged in the wildest dissipation at Barratte's—of course, at the poultry dealer's expense. From the effects of this impudent story Madame Lecœur had not yet recovered; she wore a doleful appearance, and her eyes were quite yellow with spleen.

That morning, however, it was for Madame Quenu that the old maid had a shock in store. She looked round the counter and then in her most gentle voice remarked:

"I saw Monsieur Quenu last night. They seem to enjoy themselves immensely in that little room at Lebigre's, if one may judge from the noise they make."

Lisa had turned her head towards the street, listening very attentively, but apparently unwilling to show it. The old maid paused, hoping that one of the others would question her; and then, in a lower tone, she added: "They had a woman with them. Oh, I don't mean Monsieur Quenu, of course! I didn't say that; I don't know—"

"It must be Clémence," interrupted La Sarriette; "a big scraggy creature who gives herself all sorts of airs just because she went to boarding school. She lives with a threadbare usher. I've seen them together; they always look as though they were taking each other off to the police station."

"Oh, yes; I know," replied the old maid, who, indeed, knew everything about Charvet and Clémence, and whose only purpose was to alarm Lisa.

The mistress of the pork shop, however, never flinched. She seemed to be absorbed in watching something of great interest in the market beyond. Accordingly the old maid had recourse to stronger measures. "I think," said she, addressing herself to Madame Lecœur, "that you ought to advise your brother-in-law to be careful. Last night they were shouting out the most shocking things in that little room. Men really seem to lose their heads over politics. If anyone had heard them, it might have been a very serious matter for them."

"Oh! Gavard will go his own way," sighed Madame Lecœur. "It only wanted this to fill my cup. I shall die of anxiety, I am sure, if he ever gets arrested."

As she spoke, a gleam shot from her dim eyes. La Sarriette, however, laughed and wagged her little face, bright with the freshness of the morning air.

"You should hear what Jules says of those who speak against the Empire," she remarked. "They ought all to be thrown into the Seine, he told me; for it seems there isn't a single respectable person amongst them."

"Oh! there's no harm done, of course, so long as only people like myself hear their foolish talk," resumed Mademoiselle Saget. "I'd rather cut my hand off, you know, than make mischief. Last night now, for instance, Monsieur Quenu was saying—"

She again paused. Lisa had started slightly.

"Monsieur Quenu was saying that the Ministers and Deputies and all who are in power ought to be shot."

At this Lisa turned sharply, her face quite white and her hands clenched beneath her apron.

"Quenu said that?" she curtly asked.

"Yes, indeed, and several other similar things that I can't recollect now. I heard him myself. But don't distress yourself like that, Madame Quenu. You know very well that I won't breathe a word. I'm quite old enough to know what might harm a man if it came out. Oh, no; it will go no further."

Lisa had recovered her equanimity. She took pride in the happy peacefulness of her home; she would not acknowledge that there had ever been the slightest difference between herself and her husband. And so now she shrugged her shoulders and said with a smile: "Oh, it's all a pack of foolish nonsense."

When the three others were in the street together they agreed that handsome Lisa had pulled a very doleful face; and they were unanimously of the opinion that the mysterious goings-on of the cousin, the Méhudins, Gavard, and the Quenus would end in trouble. Madame Lecœur inquired what was done to the people who got arrested "for politics," but on this point Mademoiselle Saget could not enlighten her; she only knew that they were never seen again—no, never. And this induced La Sarriette to suggest that perhaps they were thrown into the Seine, as Jules had said they ought to be.

Lisa avoided all reference to the subject at breakfast and dinner that day; and even in the evening, when Florent and Quenu went off together to Monsieur Lebigre's, there was no unwonted severity in her glance. On that particular evening, however, the question of framing a constitution for the future came under discussion, and it was one o'clock in the morning before the politicians could tear themselves away from the little room. The shutters had already been fastened, and they were obliged to leave by a small door, passing out one at a time with bent backs. Quenu returned home with an uneasy conscience. He opened the three or four doors on his way to bed as gently as possible, walking on tip-toe and stretching out his hands as he passed through the sitting room, to avoid a collision with any of the furniture. The whole house seemed to be asleep. When he reached the bedroom, he was annoyed to find that Lisa had not extinguished the candle, which was burning with a tall, mournful flame in the midst of the deep silence. As Quenu took off his shoes and put them down in a corner, the time-piece struck half-past one with such a clear, ringing sound that he turned in alarm, almost frightened to move, and gazing with an expression of angry reproach at the shining gilded Gutenberg standing there, with his finger on a book. Lisa's head was buried in her pillow, and Quenu could only see her back; but he divined that she was merely feigning sleep, and her conduct in turning her back upon him was so full of reproach that he felt sorely ill at ease. At last he slipped beneath the bed-clothes, blew out the candle, and lay perfectly still. He could have sworn that his wife was awake, though she did not speak to him; and presently he fell asleep, feeling intensely miserable, and lacking the courage to say good night.

He slept till late, and when he awoke he found himself sprawling in the middle of the bed with the eiderdown quilt up to his chin, while Lisa sat in front of the secretaire, arranging some papers. His slumber had been so heavy that he had not heard her rise. However, he now took courage and spoke to her from the depths of the alcove: "Why didn't you wake me? What are you doing there?"

"I'm sorting the papers in these drawers," she replied in her usual tone of voice.

Quenu felt relieved. But Lisa added: "One never knows what may happen. If the police were to come—"

"What! The police?"

"Yes, indeed, the police; for you're mixing yourself up with politics now."

At this Quenu sat up in bed, quite dazed and confounded by such a violent and unexpected attack.

"I mix myself up with politics! I mix myself up with politics!" he repeated. "It's no concern of the police. I've nothing to do with any compromising matters."

"No," replied Lisa, shrugging her shoulders; "you merely talk about shooting everybody."

"I! I!"

"Yes. And you bawl it out in a tavern! Mademoiselle Saget

heard you. All the neighborhood knows by this time that you are a Red Republican!"

Quenu fell back in bed again. He was not perfectly awake as yet. Lisa's words resounded in his ears as though he already heard the heavy tramp of gendarmes at the bedroom door. He looked at her as she sat there, with her hair already arranged, her figure tightly imprisoned in her stays, her whole appearance the same as it was on any other morning; and he felt more astonished than ever that she should be so neat and prim under such extraordinary circumstances.

"I leave you absolutely free, you know," she continued, as she went on arranging the papers. "I don't want to wear the breeches, as the saying goes. You are the master, and you are at liberty to endanger your position, compromise our credit, and ruin our business."

Then, as Quenu tried to protest, she silenced him with a gesture. "No, no; don't say anything," she continued. "This is no quarrel, and I am not even asking an explanation from you. But if you had consulted me, and we had talked the matter over together, I might have intervened. Ah! it's a great mistake to imagine that women understand nothing about politics. Shall I tell you what my politics are?"

She had risen from her seat while speaking and was now walking back and forth between the bed and the window, wiping as she went some specks of dust from the bright mahogany of the mirrored wardrobe and the dressing table.

"My politics are the politics of honest folks," said she. "I'm grateful to the Government when business is prosperous, when I can eat my meals in peace and comfort, and can sleep at nights without being awakened by the firing of guns. There were pretty times in '48, were there not? You remember our uncle Gradelle, the worthy man, showing us his books for that year? He lost more than six thousand francs. Now that we have got the Empire, however, everything prospers.

We sell our goods readily enough. You can't deny it. Well, then, what is it that you want? How will you be better off when you have shot everybody?"

She took her stand in front of the little night table, crossed her arms over her breast, and fixed her eyes upon Quenu, who had shuffled himself beneath the bed-clothes, almost out of sight. He attempted to explain what it was that his friends wanted, but he got quite confused in his endeavors to summarize Florent's and Charvet's political and social systems; and could only talk about the disregard shown to principles, the accession of the democracy to power, and the regeneration of society, in such a strange tangled way that Lisa shrugged her shoulders, quite unable to understand him. At last, however, he extricated himself from his difficulties by declaring that the Empire was the reign of licentiousness, swindling finance, and highway robbery. And, recalling an expression of Logre's, he added: "We are the prey of a band of adventurers, who are pillaging, violating, and assassinating France. We'll have no more of them."

Lisa, however, still shrugged her shoulders.

"Well, and is that all you have got to say?" she asked with perfect coolness. "What has all that got to do with me? Even supposing it were true, what then? Have I ever advised you to practice dishonest courses? Have I ever prompted you to dishonor your acceptances, or cheat your customers, or pile up money by fraudulent practices? Really, you'll end by making me quite angry! We are honest folks, and we don't pillage or assassinate anybody. That's quite sufficient. What other folks do is no concern of ours. If they choose to be rogues it's their affair."

She looked quite majestic and triumphant; and again pacing the room, drawing herself up to her full height, she resumed: "A pretty notion it is that people are to let their business go to rack and ruin just to please those who are penniless. For my part, I'm in favor of making hay while the sun shines and supporting a Government which promotes trade. If it does do dishonorable things, I prefer to know nothing about them. I know that I myself commit none and that no one in the neighborhood can point a finger at me. It's only fools who go tilting at windmills. At the time of the last elections, you remember, Gavard said that the Emperor's candidate had been bankrupt and was mixed up in all sorts of scandalous matters. Well, perhaps that was true, I don't deny it; but all the same, you acted wisely in voting for him, for all that was not in question; you were not asked to lend the man any money or to transact any business with him, but merely to show the Government that you were pleased with the prosperity of the pork trade."

At this moment Quenu called to mind a sentence of Charvet's, asserting that "the bloated bourgeois, the sleek shopkeepers, who backed up that Government of universal gormandizing, ought to be hurled into the sewers before all others, for it was owing to them and their gluttonous egotism that tyranny had succeeded in mastering and preying upon the nation." He was trying to complete this piece of eloquence when Lisa, carried off by her indignation, cut him short.

"Don't talk such stuff! My conscience doesn't reproach me with anything. I don't owe a sou to anybody; I'm not mixed up in any dishonest business; I buy and sell good sound stuff; and I charge no more than others do. What you say may perhaps apply to people like our cousins, the Saccards. They pretend to be even ignorant that I am in Paris; but I am prouder than they are, and I don't care a rap for their millions. It's said that Saccard speculates in condemned buildings and cheats and robs everybody. I'm not surprised to hear it, for he was always that way inclined. He loves money just for the sake of wallowing in it and then tossing it out of his windows, like the imbecile he is. I can understand people attacking men of his stamp, who pile up excessive fortunes. For my part, if you care to know it, I have but a bad opinion of Saccard. But we—we who live so quietly and peaceably, who will need at least fifteen years to put by sufficient money to make ourselves comfortably independent, we who have no reason to meddle in politics, and whose only aim is to bring up our daughter respectably, and to see that our business prospers—why, you must be joking to talk such stuff about us. We are honest folks!"

She came and sat down on the edge of the bed. Quenu was already much shaken in his opinions.

"Listen to me, now," she resumed in a more serious voice. "You surely don't want to see your own shop pillaged, your cellar emptied, and your money taken from you? If these men who meet at Monsieur Lebigre's should prove triumphant, do you think that you would then lie as comfortably in your bed as you do now? And on going down into the kitchen, do you imagine that you would set about making your galantines as peacefully as you will presently? No, no, indeed! So why do you talk about overthrowing a Government which protects you and enables you to put money by? You have a wife and a daughter, and your first duty is toward them. You would be at fault if you imperilled their happiness. It is only those who have neither home nor hearth, who have nothing to lose, who want to be shooting people. Surely you don't want to pull the chestnuts out of the fire for them! So stay quietly at home, you foolish fellow, sleep comfortably, eat well, make money, keep an easy conscience, and leave France to free herself of the Empire if the Empire annoys her. France can get on very well without *you*."

She laughed her bright melodious laugh as she finished; and Quenu was now altogether convinced. Yes, she was right, after all; and she looked so charming, he thought, as she sat there on the edge of the bed, so trim, although it was so early, so bright, and so fresh in the dazzling whiteness of her linen. As he listened to her his eyes fell on their portraits hanging on either side of the fireplace. Yes, they were certainly honest folks; they had such a respectable, well-to-do air in their black clothes and their gilded frames! The bedroom, too, looked as though it belonged to people of some account in the world. The lace squares seemed to give a dignified appearance to the chairs; and the carpet, the curtains, and the vases decorated with painted landscapes—all spoke of their exertions to get on in the world and their taste for comfort. Thereupon he plunged yet further beneath the eiderdown quilt, which kept him in a state of pleasant warmth. He began to feel that he had risked losing all these things at Monsieur Lebigre's—his huge bed, his cozy room, and his business, on which his thoughts now dwelt with tender remorse. And from Lisa, from the furniture, from all his cozy surroundings, he derived a sense of comfort which thrilled him with a delightful, overpowering charm.

"You foolish fellow!" said his wife, seeing that he was now quite conquered. "A pretty business it was that you'd embarked upon; but you'd have had to reckon with Pauline and me, I can tell you! And now don't bother your head any more about the Government. To begin with, all Governments are alike, and if we didn't have this one, we should have another. A Government is necessary. But the one thing is to be able to live on, to spend one's savings in peace and comfort when one grows old, and to know that one has gained one's means honestly."

Quenu nodded his head in acquiescence and tried to commence a justification of his conduct.

"It was Gavard—" he began.

But Lisa's face again assumed a serious expression, and she interrupted him sharply.

"No, it was not Gavard. I know very well who it was; and it would be a great deal better if he would look after his own safety before compromising that of others."

"Is it Florent you mean?" Quenu timidly inquired after a pause.

Lisa did not immediately reply. She got up and went back to the secretaire, as if trying to restrain herself.

"Yes, it is Florent," she said presently, in incisive tones. "You know how patient I am. I would bear almost anything rather than come between you and your brother. The tie of relationship is a sacred thing. But the cup is filled to overflowing now. Since your brother came here things have been constantly getting worse and worse. But no, I won't say anything more; it is better that I shouldn't."

There was another pause. Then, as her husband gazed up at the ceiling with an air of embarrassment, she continued, with increased violence:

"Really, he seems to ignore all that we have done for him. We have put ourselves to great inconvenience for his sake; we have given him Augustine's bedroom, and the poor girl sleeps without a murmur in a stuffy little closet where she can scarcely breathe. We board and lodge him and give him every attention—but no, he takes it all quite as a matter of course. He is earning money, but what he does with it nobody knows; or, rather, one knows only too well."

"But there's his share of the inheritance, you know," Quenu ventured to say, pained at hearing his brother attacked.

Lisa suddenly stiffened herself as though she were stunned, and her anger vanished.

"Yes, you are right; there is his share of the inheritance. Here is the statement of it, in this drawer. But he refused to take it; you remember, you were present and heard him. That only proves that he is a brainless, worthless fellow. If he had had an idea in his head, he would have made something out of that money by now. For my own part, I should be very glad to get rid of it; it would be a relief to us. I have told him so twice, but he won't listen to me. You ought to persuade him to take it. Talk to him about it, will you?"

Quenu growled something in reply; and Lisa refrained from pressing the point further, being of the opinion that she had done all that could be expected of her.

"He is not like other men," she resumed. "He's not a comfortable sort of person to have in the house. I shouldn't have said this if we hadn't got talking on the subject. I don't busy myself about his conduct, though it's setting the whole neighborhood gossiping about us. Let him eat and sleep here and put us about, if he likes; we can get over that; but what I won't tolerate is that he should involve us in his politics. If he tries to lead you off again, or compromises us in the least degree, I shall turn him out of the house without the least hesitation. I warn you, and now you understand!"

Florent was doomed. Lisa was making a great effort to restrain herself, to prevent the animosity which had long been rankling in her heart from flowing forth. But Florent and his ways jarred against her every instinct; he wounded her, frightened her, and made her quite miserable.

"A man who has had such a discreditable career," she murmured, "who has never been able to get a roof of his own over his head! I can very well understand his partiality for bullets! He can go and stand in their way if he chooses; but let him leave honest folks to their families! And then, he isn't pleasant to have about one! He reeks of fish in the evening at dinner! It prevents me from eating. He himself never lets a mouthful go past him, though it's little better he seems to be for it all! He can't even grow decently stout, the wretched fellow, to such a degree do his bad instincts prey on him!"

She had stepped up to the window while speaking and

now saw Florent crossing the Rue Rambuteau on his way to the fish market. There was a very large arrival of fish that morning; the tray-like baskets were covered with rippling silver, and the auction rooms roared with the hubbub of their sales. Lisa kept her eyes on the bony shoulders of her brother-in-law as he made his way into the pungent smells of the market, stooping beneath the sickening sensation which they brought him; and the glance with which she followed his steps was that of a woman bent on combat and resolved to be victorious.

When she turned round again, Quenu was getting up. As he sat on the edge of the bed in his nightshirt, still warm from the pleasant heat of the eiderdown quilt and with his feet resting on the soft fluffy rug below him, he looked quite pale, quite distressed at the misunderstanding between his wife and his brother. Lisa, however, gave him one of her sweetest smiles, and he felt deeply touched when she handed him his sock.

Chapter 4

MARJOLIN HAD BEEN FOUND in a heap of cabbages at the Marché des Innocents. He was sleeping under the shelter of a large white-hearted one, a broad leaf of which concealed his rosy childish face. It was never known what poverty-stricken mother had laid him there. When he was found he was already a fine little fellow of two or three years of age, very plump and merry, but so backward and dense that he could scarcely stammer a few words, and only seemed able to smile. When one of the vegetable saleswomen found him lying under the big white cabbage she raised such a loud cry of surprise that her neighbors rushed up to see what was the matter, while the youngster, still in petticoats, and wrapped in a scrap of old blanket, held out his arms towards her. He could not tell who his mother was, but opened his eyes in wide astonishment as he squeezed against the shoulder of a stout tripe-dealer who eventually took him up. The whole market busied itself about him throughout the day. He soon recovered confidence, ate slices of bread and butter, and smiled at all the women. The stout tripe-dealer kept him for a time, then a neighbor took him; and a month later a third woman gave him shelter. When they asked him where his mother was, he waved his little hand with a pretty gesture which embraced all the women present. He became the adopted child of the place, always clinging to the skirts of one or another of the women, and always finding a corner of a bed and a share of a meal somewhere. Somehow, too, he managed to find clothes, and he even had a couple of sous at the bottom of his ragged pockets. It was a buxom, ruddy girl dealing in medicinal herbs who gave him the name of Marjolin, though no one knew why.

When Marjolin was nearly four years of age, old Mother Chantemesse also happened to find a child, a little girl, lying on the footway of the Rue Saint Denis, near the corner of the market. Judging by the little one's size, she seemed to be a couple of years old, but she could already chatter like a magpie, murdering her words in an incessant childish babble. Old Mother Chantemesse after a time gathered that her name was Cadine and that on the previous evening her mother had left her sitting on a doorstep, with instructions to wait till she returned. The child had fallen asleep there and did not cry. She related that she was beaten at home; and she gladly followed Mother Chantemesse, seemingly quite enchanted with that huge square, where there were so many people and such piles of vegetables. Mother Chantemesse, a retail dealer by trade, was a crusty but very worthy woman, approaching her sixtieth year. She was extremely fond of children and had lost three boys of her own when they were mere babies. She came to the opinion that the chit she had found "was far too wide awake to kick the bucket," and so she adopted her.

One evening, however, as she was going off home with her right hand clasping Cadine's, Marjolin came up and unceremoniously caught hold of her left hand.

"Nay, my lad," said the old woman, stopping, "the place is filled. Have you left your big Thérèse, then? What a fickle little gadabout you are!"

The boy gazed at her with his smiling eyes, without letting go of her hand. He looked so pretty with his curly hair that she could not resist him. "Well, come along, then, you little scamp," said she; "I'll put you to bed as well."

Thus she made her appearance in the Rue au Lard, where she lived, with a child clinging to either hand. Marjolin made himself quite at home there. When the two children proved too noisy the old woman cuffed them, delighted to shout and worry herself, and wash the youngsters, and pack them away beneath the blankets. She had fixed them up a little bed in an old hawker's barrow, the wheels and shafts of which had disappeared. It was like a big cradle, a trifle hard, but retaining a strong scent of the vegetables which it had long kept fresh and cool beneath a covering of damp cloths. And there, when four years old, Cadine and Marjolin slept locked in each other's arms.

They grew up together and were always to be seen with their arms about one another's waist. At nighttime old Mother Chantemesse heard them prattling softly. Cadine's clear treble went chattering on for hours together, while Marjolin listened with occasional expressions of astonishment vented in a deeper tone. The girl was a mischievous young creature and concocted all sorts of stories to frighten her companion; telling him, for instance, that she had one night seen a man, dressed all in white, looking at them and putting out a great red tongue, at the foot of the bed. Marjolin quite perspired with terror and anxiously asked for further particulars; but the girl would then begin to jeer at him and end by calling him a big donkey. At other times they were not so peaceably disposed, but kicked each other beneath the blankets. Cadine would pull up her legs and try to restrain her laughter as Marjolin missed his aim and sent his feet banging against the wall. When this happened, old Madame Chantemesse was obliged to get up to put the bed-clothes straight again; and, by way of sending the children to sleep, she would administer a box on the ear to both of them. For a long time their bed was a sort of playground. They carried their toys into it and munched stolen carrots and turnips as they lay side by side. Every morning their adopted mother was amazed at the strange things she found in the bed—pebbles, leaves, apple cores, and dolls made out of scraps of rags. When the very cold weather came, she went off to her work, leaving them sleeping there, Cadine's black mop mingling with Marjolin's sunny curls, and their mouths so near together that they looked as though they were keeping each other warm with their breath.

The room in the Rue au Lard was a big, dilapidated garret, with a single window, the panes of which were dimmed by the rain. The children would play at hide-and-seek in the tall walnut wardrobe and underneath Mother Chantemesse's colossal bed. There were also two or three tables in the room, and they crawled under these on all fours. They found the place a very charming playground, on account of the dim light and the vegetables scattered about in the dark corners. The street itself, too, narrow and very quiet, with a broad arcade opening into the Rue de la Lingerie, provided them with plenty of entertainment. The door of the house was by the side of the arcade; it was a low door and could only be opened half-way owing to the near proximity of the greasy corkscrew staircase. The house, which had a projecting pent roof and bulging front, dark with damp, and displaying greenish drain-sinks near the windows of each floor, also served as a big toy for the young couple. They spent their mornings below in throwing stones up into the drain-sinks, and the stones then fell down the pipes with a very merry clatter. In thus amusing themselves, however, they managed to break a couple of windows, and filled the drains with stones, so that Mother Chantemesse, who had lived in the house for forty-three years, narrowly escaped being turned out of it.

Cadine and Marjolin then directed their attention to the vans and drays and tumbrels which were drawn up in the quiet street. They clambered onto the wheels, swung from the dangling chains, and larked about amongst the piles of boxes and hampers. Here also were the back premises of the commission agents of the Rue de la Poterie—huge, gloomy warehouses, each day filled and emptied afresh, and affording a constant succession of delightful hiding-places, where the youngsters buried themselves amidst the scent of dried fruits, oranges, and fresh apples. When they got tired of playing in this way, they went off to join old Madame Chantemesse at the Marché des Innocents. They arrived there arm-in-arm, laughing gaily as they crossed the streets with never the slightest fear of being run over by the endless vehicles. They knew the pavement well and plunged their little legs knee-deep in the vegetable refuse without ever slipping. They jeered merrily at any porter in heavy boots who, in stepping over an artichoke stem, fell sprawling full-length upon the ground. They were the rosy-cheeked familiar spirits of those greasy streets. They were to be seen everywhere.

On rainy days they walked gravely beneath the shelter of a ragged old umbrella, with which Mother Chantemesse had protected her stock-in-trade for twenty years, and sticking it up in a corner of the market they called it their house. On sunny days they romped to such a degree that when evening came they were almost too tired to move. They bathed their feet in the fountains, dammed up the gutters, or hid themselves beneath piles of vegetables, and remained there prattling to each other just as they did in bed at night. People passing some huge mountain of romaine or cabbage lettuces often heard a muffled sound of chatter coming from it. And when the green stuff was removed, the two children would be discovered lying side by side on their couch of verdure, their eyes glistening uneasily like those of birds discovered in the depth of a thicket. As time went on, Cadine could not get along without Marjolin, and Marjolin began to cry when he lost Cadine. If they happened to get separated, they sought one another behind the petticoats of every stallkeeper in the markets, amongst the boxes and under the cabbages. It was, indeed, chiefly under the cabbages that they grew up and learned to love each other.

Marjolin was nearly eight years old, and Cadine six, when old Madame Chantemesse began to reproach them for their idleness. She told them that she would interest them in her business and pay them a sou a day to assist her in paring her vegetables. During the first few days the children displayed eager zeal; they squatted down on either side of the big flat basket with little knives in their hands and worked away energetically. Mother Chantemesse made a specialty of pared vegetables; on her stall, covered with a strip of damp black lining, were little lots of potatoes, turnips, carrots, and white onions, arranged in pyramids of four—three at the base and one at the apex, all quite ready to be popped into the pans of dilatory housewives. She also had bundles duly stringed in readiness for the soup pot—four leeks, three carrots, a parsnip, two turnips, and a couple of sprigs of celery. Then there were finely-cut vegetables for julienne soup laid out on squares of paper, cabbages cut into quarters, and little heaps of tomatoes and slices of pumpkin which gleamed like red stars and golden crescents amidst the pale hues of the other vegetables. Cadine evinced much more dexterity than Marjolin, although she was younger. The peelings of the potatoes she pared were so thin that you could see through them; she tied up the bundles for the soup pot so artistically that they looked like bouquets; and she had a way of making the little heaps she set up, though they contained but three carrots or turnips, look like very big ones. The passers-by would stop and smile when she called out in her shrill childish voice: "Madame! madame! come and try me! Each little pile for two sous."

She had her regular customers, and her little piles and

bundles were widely known. Old Mother Chantemesse, seated between the two children, would indulge in a silent laugh which made her bosom rise almost to her chin, at seeing them working away so seriously. She paid them their daily sous most faithfully. But they soon began to weary of the little heaps and bundles; they were growing up and began to dream of some more lucrative business. Marjolin remained very childish for his years, and this irritated Cadine. He had no more brains than a cabbage, she often said. And it was, indeed, quite useless for her to devise any plan for him to make money; he never earned any. He could not even do an errand satisfactorily. The girl, on the other hand, was very shrewd. When but eight years old she obtained employment from one of those women who sit on a bench in the neighborhood of the markets provided with a basket of lemons and employ a troop of children to go about selling them. Carrying the lemons in her hands and offering them at two for three sous, Cadine thrust them under every woman's nose and ran after every passer-by. Her hands empty, she hastened back for a fresh supply. She was paid two sous for every dozen lemons that she sold, and on good days she could earn some five or six sous. During the following year she hawked caps at nine sous apiece, which proved a more profitable business; only she had to keep a sharp look-out, as street trading of this kind is forbidden unless one be licensed. However, she scented a policeman at a distance of a hundred yards; and the caps forthwith disappeared under her skirts, while she began to munch an apple with an air of guileless innocence. Then she took to selling pastry, cakes, cherry tarts, gingerbread, and thick yellow maize biscuits on wicker trays. Marjolin, however, ate up nearly the whole of her stock-in-trade. At last, when she was eleven years old, she succeeded in realizing a grand idea which had long been worrying her. In a couple of months she put by four francs, bought a small carrying basket, and then set up as a dealer in birds' food.

It was a big affair. She got up early in the morning and purchased her stock of groundsel, millet, and bird-cake from the wholesale dealers. Then she set out on her day's work, crossing the river, and perambulating the Latin Quarter from the Rue Saint Jacques to the Rue Dauphine, and even to the Luxembourg. Marjolin used to accompany her, but she would not let him carry the basket. He was only fit to call out, she said; and so, in his thick, drawling voice, he would raise the cry, "Chickweed for the little birds!"

Then Cadine herself, with her flute-like voice, would start on a strange scale of notes ending in a clear, protracted alto, "Chickweed for the little birds!"

They each took one side of the road and looked up in the air as they walked along. In those days Marjolin wore a big scarlet waistcoat which hung down to his knees; it had belonged to the defunct Monsieur Chantemesse, who had been a cabdriver. Cadine for her part wore a white and blue check gown, made out of an old tartan of Madame Chantemesse's. All the canaries in the garrets of the Latin Quarter knew them; and, as they passed along, repeating their cry, each echoing the other's voice, every cage poured out a song.

Cadine sold watercress, too. "Two sous a bunch! two sous a bunch!" And Marjolin went into the shops to offer it for sale. "Fine watercress! health for the body! fine fresh watercress!"

However, the new central markets had just been erected, and the girl would stand gazing in ecstasy at the avenue of flower-stalls which runs through the fruit pavilion. Here on either hand, from end to end, big clumps of flowers bloom as in the borders of a garden-walk. It is a perfect harvest, sweet with perfume, a double hedge of blossoms, between which the girls of the neighborhood love to walk, smiling the while, though almost stifled by the heavy perfume. And on the top tiers of the stalls are artificial flowers, with paper leaves, in which dewdrops are simulated by drops of gum; and memorial wreaths of black and white beads rippling with bluish reflections. Cadine's rosy nostrils would dilate with feline sensuality; she would linger as long as possible in that sweet freshness and carry as much of the perfume away with her as she could. When her hair bobbed under Marjolin's nose he would remark that it smelt of pinks. She said that she had given up using pomade; that it was quite sufficient for her to stroll through the flower walk in order to scent her hair. Next she began to intrigue and scheme with such success that she was engaged by one of the stallkeepers. And then Marjolin declared that she smelt sweet from head to foot. She lived in the midst of roses, lilacs, wallflowers, and lilies of the valley; and Marjolin would play-fully smell at her skirts, feign a momentary hesitation, and then exclaim, "Ah, that's lily of the valley!" Next he would sniff at her waist and bodice: "Ah, that's wallflowers!" And at her sleeves and wrists: "Ah, that's lilac!" And at her neck, and her cheeks and lips: "Ah, but that's roses!" he would cry. Cadine used to laugh at him, and call him a "silly stupid," and tell him to get away, because he was tickling her with the tip of his nose. As she spoke her breath smelt of jasmine. She was truly a bouquet, full of warmth and life.

She now got up at four o'clock every morning to assist her mistress in her purchases. Each day they bought armfuls of flowers from the suburban florists, with bundles of moss, and bundles of fern fronds and periwinkle leaves to garnish the bouquets. Cadine would gaze with amazement at the diamonds and Valenciennes lace worn by the daughters of the great gardeners of Montreuil, who came to the markets amidst their roses.

On the saints' days of popular observance, such as Saint

Mary's, Saint Peter's, and Saint Joseph's days, the sale of flowers began at two o'clock. More than a hundred thousand francs worth of cut flowers would be sold on the footways, and some of the retail dealers would make as much as two hundred francs in a few hours. On days like those only Cadine's curly locks peered over the mounds of pansies, mignonette, and marguerites. She was quite drowned and lost in the flood of flowers. Then she would spend all her time in mounting bouquets on bits of rush. In a few weeks she acquired considerable skillfulness in her business and manifested no little originality. Her bouquets did not always please everybody, however. Sometimes they made one smile, sometimes they alarmed the eyes. Red predominated in them, mottled with violent tints of blue, yellow, and violet of a barbaric charm. On the mornings when she pinched Marjolin, and teased him till she made him cry, she made up fierce-looking bouquets, suggestive of her own bad temper, bouquets with strong rough scents and glaring irritating colors. On other days, however, when she was softened by some thrill of joy or sorrow, her bouquets would assume a tone of silvery gray, very soft and subdued, and delicately perfumed.

Then, too, she would set roses, as sanguineous as open hearts, in lakes of snow-white pinks; arrange bunches of tawny iris that shot up in tufts of flame from foliage that seemed scared by the brilliance of the flowers; work elaborate designs, as complicated as those of Smyrna rugs, adding flower to flower, as on a canvas; and prepare rippling fanlike bouquets spreading out with all the delicacy of lace. Here was a cluster of flowers of delicious purity, there a fat nosegay, whatever one might dream of for the hand of a marchioness or a fishwife; all the charming quaint fancies, in short, which the brain of a sharp-witted child of twelve, budding into womanhood, could devise.

There were only two flowers for which Cadine retained

respect; white lilac, which by the bundle of eight or ten sprays cost from fifteen to twenty francs in the winter time; and camellias, which were still more costly, and arrived in boxes of a dozen, lying on beds of moss, and covered with cotton wool. She handled these as delicately as though they were jewels, holding her breath for fear of dimming their luster, and fastening their short stems to sprigs of cane with the tenderest care. She spoke of them with serious reverence. She told Marjolin one day that a speckless white camellia was a very rare and exceptionally lovely thing, and, as she was making him admire one, he exclaimed: "Yes; it's pretty; but I prefer your neck, you know. It's much more soft and transparent than the camellia, and there are some little blue and pink veins just like the pencillings on a flower." Then, drawing near and sniffing, he murmured: "Ah! you smell of orange blossom today."

Cadine was self-willed, and did not get on well in the position of a servant, so she ended by setting up in business on her own account. As she was only thirteen at the time, and could not hope for a big trade and a stall in the flower avenue, she took to selling one-sou bunches of violets pricked into a bed of moss in an wicker tray which she carried hanging from her neck. All day long she wandered about the markets and their precincts with her little bit of hanging garden. She loved this continual stroll which relieved the numbness of her limbs after long hours spent with bent knees, on a low chair, making bouquets. She fastened her violets together with marvelous deftness as she walked along. She counted out six or eight flowers, according to the season, doubled a sprig of cane in half, added a leaf, twisted some damp thread round the whole, and broke off the thread with her strong young teeth. The little bunches seemed to spring spontaneously from the layer of moss, so rapidly did she stick them into it.

Along the footways, amidst the jostling of the street traffic, her nimble fingers were ever flowering though she gave them not a glance, but boldly scanned the shops and passers-by. Sometimes she would rest in a doorway for a moment; and alongside the gutters, greasy with kitchen slops, she set, as it were, a patch of spring time, a suggestion of green woods and purple blossoms. Her flowers still betokened her frame of mind, her fits of bad temper and her thrills of tenderness. Sometimes they bristled and glowered with anger amidst their crumpled leaves; at other times they spoke only of love and peacefulness as they smiled in their prim collars. As Cadine passed along, she left a sweet perfume behind her; Marjolin followed her devoutly. From head to foot she now exhaled but one scent, and the lad repeated that she was herself a violet, a great big violet.

"Do you remember the day when we went to Romainville together?" he would say; "Romainville, where there are so many violets. The scent was just the same. Oh! don't change again—you smell too sweet."

And she did not change again. This was her last trade. Still, she often neglected her wicker tray to go rambling about the neighborhood. The building of the central markets—as yet incomplete—provided both children with endless opportunities for amusement. They made their way into the midst of the work-yards through some gap or other between the planks; they descended into the foundations and climbed up to the cast-iron pillars. Every nook, every piece of the framework witnessed their games and quarrels; the pavilions grew up under the touch of their little hands. From all this arose the affection which they felt for the great markets, and which the latter seemed to return. They were on familiar terms with that gigantic pile, old friends as they were, who had seen each pin and bolt put into place. They felt no fear of the huge monster; but slapped it with their childish hands, treated it like a good friend, a chum whose presence brought no constraint. And the markets seemed to smile at these two light-hearted children whose love was the song, the idyll of their immensity.

Cadine alone now slept at Mother Chantemesse's. The old woman had packed Marjolin off to a neighbor's. This made the two children very unhappy. Still, they contrived to spend much of their time together. In the daytime they would hide themselves away in the warehouses of the Rue au Lard, behind piles of apples and cases of oranges; and in the evening they would dive into the cellars beneath the poultry market, and secrete themselves among the huge hampers of feathers which stood near the blocks where the poultry was killed. They were quite alone there, amidst the strong smell of the poultry, and with never a sound but the sudden crowing of some rooster to break upon their babble and their laughter. The feathers amidst which they found themselves were of all sorts—turkey's feathers, long and black; goose quills, white and flexible; the downy plumage of ducks, soft like cotton wool; and the ruddy and mottled feathers of fowls, which at the faintest breath flew up in a cloud like a swarm of flies buzzing in the sun. And then in wintertime there was the purple plumage of the pheasants, the ashen gray of the larks, the splotched silk of the partridges, quails, and thrushes. And all these feathers freshly plucked were still warm and odoriferous, seemingly endowed with life. The spot was as cozy as a nest; at times a quiver as of flapping wings sped by, and Marjolin and Cadine, nestling amidst all the plumage, often imagined that they were being carried aloft by one of those huge birds with outspread pinions that one hears of in the fairy tales.

As time went on their childish affection took the inevitable turn. Veritable offsprings of Nature, knowing naught of social conventions and restraints, they loved one another in all innocence and guilelessness. They mated even as the birds of the air mate, even as youth and maid mated in primeval times, because such is Nature's law. At sixteen Cadine was a dusky town gypsy, greedy and sensual, while Marjolin, now eighteen, was a tall, strapping fellow, as handsome a youth as could be met, but still with his mental faculties quite undeveloped. He had lived, indeed, a mere animal life, which had strengthened his frame, but left his intellect in a rudimentary state.

When old Madame Chantemesse realized the turn that things were taking she wrathfully upbraided Cadine and struck out vigorously at her with her broom. But the hussy only laughed and dodged the blows, and then hied off to her lover. And gradually the markets became their home, their manger, their aviary, where they lived and loved amidst the meat, the butter, the vegetables, and the feathers.

They discovered another little paradise in the pavilion where butter, eggs, and cheese were sold wholesale. Enormous walls of empty baskets were here piled up every morning, and amidst these Cadine and Marjolin burrowed and hollowed out a dark lair for themselves. A mere partition of wickerwork separated them from the market crowd, whose loud voices rang out all around them. They often shook with laughter when people, without the least suspicion of their presence, stopped to talk together a few yards away from them. On these occasions they would contrive peepholes and spy through them; and when cherries were in season Cadine tossed the stones in the faces of all the old women who passed along—a pastime which amused them the more as the startled old crones could never make out from where the hail of cherry stones had come. They also prowled about the depths of the cellars, knowing every gloomy corner of them, and contriving to get through the most carefully locked gates. One of their favorite amusements was to visit the track of the subterranean railway, which had been laid under the markets, and which those who planned the latter had intended to connect with the different goods' stations of Paris. Sections of this railway were laid beneath each of the covered ways, between the cellars of each pavilion; the work, indeed, was in such an advanced state that turntables had been put into position at all the points of intersection and were in readiness for use. After much examination, Cadine and Marjolin had at last succeeded in discovering a loose plank in the hoarding which enclosed the track, and they had managed to convert it into a door, by which they could easily gain access to the line. There they were quite shut off from the world, though they could hear the continuous rumbling of the street traffic over their heads.

The line stretched through deserted vaults, here and there illumined by a glimmer of light filtering through iron gratings, while in certain dark corners gas jets were burning. And Cadine and Marjolin rambled about as in the secret recesses of some castle of their own, secure from all interruption, and rejoicing in the buzzy silence, the murky glimmer, and subterranean secrecy, which imparted a touch of melodrama to their experiences. All sorts of smells were wafted through the hoarding from the neighboring cellars; the musty smell of vegetables, the pungency of fish, the overpowering stench of cheese, and the warm reek of poultry.

At other times, on clear nights and fine dawns, they would climb onto the roofs, ascending there by the steep staircases of the turrets at the angles of the pavilions. Up above they found fields of lead roofs, endless promenades and squares, a stretch of undulating country which belonged to them. They rambled round the square roofs of the pavilions, followed the course of the long roofs of the covered ways, climbed and descended the slopes, and lost themselves in endless perambulations of discovery. And when they grew tired of the lower levels they ascended still higher, venturing up the iron ladders, on which Cadine's skirts flapped like flags. Then they ran along the second tier of roofs beneath the open heavens. There was nothing save the stars above them. All sorts of sounds rose up from the echoing markets, a clattering and rumbling, a vague roar as of a distant tempest heard at nighttime. At that height the morning breeze swept away the evil smells, the foul breath of the awaking markets. They would kiss one another at the edge of the gutterings like sparrows frisking on the housetops. The rising fires of the sun illumined their faces with a ruddy glow. Cadine laughed with pleasure at being so high up in the air, and her neck shone with iridescent tints like a dove's; while Marjolin bent down to look at the streets still wrapped in gloom, with his hands clutching hold of the lead edge like the feet of a wood pigeon. When they descended to earth again, joyful from their excursion in the fresh air, they would remark to one another that they were coming back from the country.

It was in the tripe market that they had made the acquaintance of Claude Lantier. They went there every day, impelled to go there by an animal taste for blood, the cruel instinct of urchins who find amusement in the sight of severed heads. A ruddy stream flowed along the gutters round the pavilion; they dipped the tips of their shoes in it and dammed it up with leaves, so as to form large pools of blood. They took a strong interest in the arrival of the loads of offal in carts which always smelt offensively, despite all the drenchings of water they got; they watched the unloading of the bundles of sheep's feet, which were piled up on the ground like filthy paving stones, of the huge stiffened tongues, bleeding at their torn roots, and of the massive bell-shaped bullocks' hearts. But the spectacle which, above all others, made them quiver with delight was that of the big dripping hampers, full of sheep's heads, with greasy horns and black muzzles, and strips of woolly skin dangling from bleeding flesh. The sight of these conjured up in their minds the idea of some guillotine casting into the baskets the heads of countless victims.

They followed the baskets into the depths of the cellar, watching them glide down the rails laid over the steps, and listening to the rasping noise which the casters of these wicker wagons made in their descent. Down below there was a scene of exquisite horror. They entered into a charnel house atmosphere and walked along through murky puddles, amid which every now and then purple eyes seem to be glistening. At times the soles of their boots stuck to the ground, at others they splashed through the horrible mire, anxious and yet delighted. The gas jets burned low, like blinking, bloodshot eyes. Near the water taps, in the pale light falling through the gratings, they came upon the blocks; and there they remained in rapture watching the tripe-men, who, in aprons stiffened by gory splashings, broke the sheep's heads one after another with a blow of their mallets. They lingered there for hours, waiting until all the baskets were empty, fascinated by the crackling of the bones, unable to tear themselves away until all was over. Sometimes an attendant passed behind them, cleansing the cellar with a hose; floods of water rushed out with a sluicelike roar, but although the violence of the discharge actually ate away the surface of the flagstones, it was powerless to remove the ruddy stains and stench of blood.

Cadine and Marjolin were sure of meeting Claude between four and five in the afternoon at the wholesale auction of the bullocks' lungs. He was always there amid the tripe-dealers' carts backed up against the curb stones and the blue-bloused, white-aproned men who jostled him and deafened his ears by their loud bids. But he never felt their elbows; he stood in a sort of ecstatic trance before the huge hanging lungs, and often told Cadine and Marjolin that there was no finer sight to be seen. The lungs were of a soft rosy hue, gradually deepening and turning at the lower edges to a rich carmine; and Claude compared them to watered satin, finding no other term to describe the soft silkiness of those flowing lengths of flesh which drooped in broad folds like ballet dancers' skirts. He thought, too, of gauze and lace allowing a glimpse of pinky skin; and when a ray of sunshine fell upon the lungs and girdled them with gold an expression of languorous rapture came into his eyes, and he felt happier than if he had been privileged to contemplate the Greek goddesses in their sovereign nudity, or the chatelaines of romance in their brocaded robes.

The artist became a great friend of the two young scamps. He loved beautiful animals, and such undoubtedly they were. For a long time he dreamt of a colossal picture which should represent the loves of Cadine and Marjolin in the central markets, amidst the vegetables, the fish, and the meat. He would have depicted them seated on some couch of food, their arms circling each other's waists, and their lips exchanging an idyllic kiss. In this conception he saw a manifesto proclaiming the positivism of art—modern art, experimental and materialistic. And it seemed to him also that it would be a smart satire on the school which wishes every painting to embody an "idea," a slap at the old traditions and all they represented. But during a couple of years he began study after study without succeeding in giving the particular "note" he desired. In this way he spoilt fifteen canvases. His failure filled him with rancor; however, he continued to associate with his two models from a sort of hopeless love for his abortive picture. When he met them prowling about in the afternoon, he often scoured the neighborhood with them, strolling around with big hands in his pockets, and deeply interested in the life of the streets.

They all three trudged along together, dragging their heels over the footways and monopolizing their whole breadth so as to force others to step down into the road. With their noses in the air they sniffed in the odors of Paris and could have recognized every corner blindfolded by the spirituous emanations of the wine shops, the hot puffs that came from the bakehouses and confectioners', and the musty odors wafted from the fruiterers'. They would make the circuit of the whole district. They delighted in passing through the rotunda of the corn market, that huge massive stone cage where sacks of flour were piled up on every side, and where their footsteps echoed in the silence of the resonant roof. They were fond, too, of the little narrow streets in the neighborhood, which had become as deserted, as black, and as mournful as though they formed part of an abandoned city. These were the Rue Babille, the Rue Sauval, the Rue des Deux Ecus, and the Rue de Viarmes, this last pallid from its proximity to the millers' stores, and at four o'clock lively by reason of the corn exchange held there. It was generally from this point that they started on their round. They made their way slowly along the Rue Vauvilliers, glancing as they went at the windows of the low eating houses, and thus reaching the miserably narrow Rue des Prouvaires, where Claude blinked his eyes as he saw one of the covered ways of the market at the far end of which, framed round by this huge iron nave, appeared a side entrance of St. Eustache with its rose and its tiers of arched windows. And then, with an air of defiance, he would remark that all the middle ages and the Renaissance put together were less mighty than the central markets. Afterwards, as they paced the broad new streets, the Rue du Pont Neuf and the Rue des Halles, he explained modern life with its wide footways, its lofty houses, and its luxurious shops, to the two urchins. He predicted, too, the advent of new and truly original art, whose approach he could divine, and despair filled him that its revelation should seemingly be beyond his own powers.

Cadine and Marjolin, however, preferred the provincial quietness of the Rue des Bourdonnais, where one can play at marbles without fear of being run over. The girl perked her head affectedly as she passed the wholesale glove and hosiery stores, at each door of which bareheaded assistants, with their pens stuck in their ears, stood watching her with a weary gaze. And she and her lover had yet a stronger preference for such bits of olden Paris as still existed: the Rue de la Poterie and the Rue de la Lingerie, with their butter and egg and cheese dealers; the Rue de la Ferronerie and the Rue de l'Aiguillerie (the beautiful streets of faraway times), with their dark narrow shops; and especially the Rue Courtalon, a dank, dirty byway running from the Place Sainte Opportune to the Rue Saint Denis, and intersected by foul-smelling alleys where they had romped in their younger days. In the Rue Saint Denis they entered into the land of dainties; and they smiled upon the dried apples, the "Spanishwood," the prunes, and the sugar candy in the windows of the grocers and druggists. Their ramblings always set them dreaming of a feast of good things and inspired them with a desire to glut themselves on the contents of the windows. To them the district seemed like some huge table, always laid with an everlasting dessert into which they longed to plunge their fingers.

They devoted but a moment to visiting the other blocks of tumble-down old houses, the Rue Pirouette, the Rue de Mondétour, the Rue de la Petite Truanderie, and the Rue de la Grande Truanderie, for they took little interest in the shops of the dealers in edible snails, cooked vegetables, tripe, and drink. In the Rue de la Grande Truanderie, however, there was a soap factory, an oasis of sweetness in the midst of all the foul odors, and Marjolin was fond of standing outside it until someone happened to enter or come out, so that the perfume which swept through the doorway might blow full in his face. Then with all speed they returned to the Rue Pierre Lescot and the Rue Rambuteau. Cadine was extremely fond of salted provisions; she stood in admiration before the bundles of red herrings, the barrels of anchovies and capers, and the little casks of gherkins and olives, standing on end with wooden spoons inside them. The smell of the vinegar titillated her throat; the pungent odor of the rolled cod, smoked salmon, bacon and ham, and the sharp acidity of the baskets of lemons, made her mouth water longingly. She was also fond of feasting her eyes on the boxes of sardines piled up in metallic columns amid the cases and sacks. In the Rue Montorgueil and the Rue Montmartre were other tempting-looking groceries and restaurants, from whose basements appetizing odors were wafted, with glorious shows of game and poultry, and preserved provision shops, which last displayed beside their doors open kegs overflowing with yellow sauerkraut suggestive of old lacework. Then they lingered in the Rue Coquillière, inhaling the odor of truffles from the premises of a notable dealer in comestibles, which threw so strong a perfume into the street that Cadine and Marjolin closed their eyes and imagined they were swallowing all kinds of delicious things. These perfumes, however, distressed Claude. They made him realize the emptiness of his stomach, he said; and, leaving the "two animals" to feast on the odor of the truffles—the most penetrating odor to be found in all the neighborhood—he went off again to the corn market by way of the Rue Oblin, studying on his road the old women who sold green stuff in the doorways and the displays of cheap pottery spread out on the foot pavements.

Such were their rambles in common; but when Cadine set out alone with her bunches of violets she often went farther afield, making it a point to visit certain shops for which she had a particular partiality. She had a special weakness for the Taboureau bakery establishment, one of the windows of which was exclusively devoted to pastry. She would follow the Rue Turbigo and retrace her steps a dozen times in order to pass again and again before the almond cakes, the *savarins,* the St. Honoré tarts, the fruit tarts, and the various dishes containing bunlike *babas* redolent of rum, *éclairs* combining the finger biscuit with chocolate, and *choux à la crème,* little rounds of pastry overflowing with whipped white of egg. The glass jars full of dry biscuits, macaroons, and *madeleines* also made her mouth water; and the bright shop with its big mirrors, its marble slabs, its gilding, its bread bins of ornamental ironwork, and its second window in which long glistening loaves were displayed slantwise, with one end resting on a crystal shelf while above they were upheld by a brass rod, was so warm and odoriferous of baked dough that her features expanded with pleasure when, yielding to temptation, she went in to buy a brioche for two sous.

Another shop, one in front of the Square des Innocents, also filled her with gluttonous inquisitiveness, a fever of longing desire. This shop made a specialty of forcemeat pasties. In addition to the ordinary ones there were pasties of pike and pasties of truffled *foie gras;* and the girl would gaze yearningly at them, saying to herself that she would really have to eat one some day.

Cadine also had her moments of vanity and coquetry. When these fits were on her, she bought herself in imagination some of the magnificent dresses displayed in the windows of the "Fabriques de France" which made the Pointe Saint Eustache gaudy with their pieces of bright stuff hanging from the first floor to the footway and flapping in the breeze. Somewhat incommoded by the flat basket hanging before her, amid the crowd of market women in dirty aprons gazing at future Sunday dresses, the girl would feel the woollens, flannels, and cottons to test the texture and suppleness of the material; and she would promise herself a gown of bright-colored flannelling, flowered print, or scarlet poplin. Sometimes even from among the pieces draped and set off to advantage by the window-dressers she would choose some soft sky-blue or apple-green silk and dream of wearing it with pink ribbons. In the evenings she would dazzle herself with the displays in the windows of the big jewellers in the Rue Montmartre. That terrible street deafened her with its ceaseless flow of vehicles, and the streaming crowd never ceased to jostle her; still she did not stir, but remained feasting her eyes on the blazing splendor set out in the light of the reflecting lamps which hung outside the windows. On one side all was white with the bright glitter of silver: watches in rows, chains hanging, spoons and forks laid crossways, cups, snuffboxes, napkin rings, and combs arranged on shelves. The silver thimbles, dotting a porcelain stand covered with a glass shade, had a special attraction for her. Then on the other side the windows glistened with the tawny glow of gold. A cascade of long pendant chains descended from above, rippling with ruddy gleams; small ladies' watches, with the backs of their cases displayed, sparkled like fallen stars; wedding rings clustered round slender rods; bracelets, brooches, and other costly ornaments glittered on the black velvet linings of their cases; jewelled rings set their stands aglow with blue, green, yellow, and violet flamelets; while on every tier of the shelves superposed rows of earrings and crosses and lockets hung against the crystal like the rich fringes of altar cloths. The glow of this gold illumined the street half way across with a sun-like radiance.

And Cadine, as she gazed at it, almost fancied that she was in presence of something holy, or on the threshold of the Emperor's treasure chamber. She would for a long time scrutinize all this show of gaudy jewellery, adapted to the taste of the fishwives, and carefully read the large figures on the tickets affixed to each article; and eventually she would select for herself a pair of earrings—pear-shaped drops of imitation coral hanging from golden roses.

One morning Claude caught her standing in ecstasy before a hairdresser's window in the Rue Saint Honoré. She was gazing at the display of hair with an expression of intense envy. High up in the window was a streaming cascade of long manes, soft wisps, loose tresses, frizzy falls, undulating comb-curls, a perfect cataract of silky and bristling hair, real and artificial, now in coils of a flaming red, now in thick black crops, now in pale golden locks, and even in snowy white ones for the coquette of sixty. In cardboard boxes down below were cleverly arranged fringes, curling side-ringlets, and carefully combed chignons glossy with pomade. And amid this framework, in a sort of shrine beneath the ravelled ends of the hanging locks, there revolved the bust of a woman, arrayed in a wrapper of cherry-colored satin fastened between the breasts with a brass brooch. The figure wore a lofty bridal coiffure picked out with sprigs of orange blossom, and smiled with a dollish smile. Its eyes were pale blue; its eyebrows were very stiff and of exaggerated length; and its waxen cheeks and shoulders bore evident traces of the heat and smoke of the gas. Cadine waited until the revolving figure again displayed its smiling face, and as its profile showed more distinctly and it slowly went round from left to right she felt perfectly happy. Claude, however, was indignant, and, shaking Cadine, he asked her what she was doing in front of "that abomination, that corpse-like hussy picked up at the Morgue!"

He flew into a temper with the dummy's cadaverous face and shoulders, that disfigurement of the beautiful, and remarked that artists painted nothing but that unreal type of woman nowadays. Cadine, however, remained unconvinced by his oratory, and considered the lady extremely beautiful. Then, resisting the attempts of the artist to drag her away by the arm and scratching her black mop in vexation, she pointed to an enormous ruddy tail, severed from the quarters of some vigorous mare, and told him she would have liked to have a crop of hair like that.

During the long rambles when Claude, Cadine, and Marjolin prowled about the neighborhood of the markets, they saw the iron ribs of the giant building at the end of every street. Wherever they turned they caught sudden glimpses of it; the horizon was always bounded by it; merely the aspect under which it was seen varied. Claude was perpetually turning round, and particularly in the Rue Montmartre, after passing the church. From that point the markets, seen obliquely in the distance, filled him with enthusiasm. A huge arcade, a giant, gaping gateway, was open before him; then came the crowding pavilions with their lower and upper roofs, their countless Venetian shutters and endless blinds, a vision, as it were, of superposed houses and palaces; a Babylon of metal, of Hindu delicacy of workmanship, intersected by hanging terraces, aerial galleries, and flying bridges poised over space. The trio always returned to this city round which they strolled, unable to stray more than a hundred yards away. They came back to it during the hot afternoons when the Venetian shutters were closed and the blinds lowered. In the covered ways all seemed to be asleep, the ashy grayness was streaked by yellow bars of sunlight falling through the high windows. Only a subdued murmur broke the silence; the steps of a few hurrying passers-by resounded on the footways; while the badge-wearing porters sat in rows on the stone ledges at the corners of the pavilions, taking off their boots and nursing their aching feet. The quietude was that of a colossus at rest, interrupted at times by some cock-crow rising from the cellars below.

Claude, Cadine, and Marjolin then often went to see the empty hampers piled upon the drays, which came to fetch them every afternoon so that they might be sent back to the consignors. There were mountains of them, labelled with black letters and figures, in front of the salesmen's warehouses in the Rue Berger. The porters arranged them symmetrically, tier by tier, on the vehicles. When the pile rose, however, to the height of a first floor, the porter who stood below balancing the next batch of hampers had to make a spring in order to toss them up to his mate, who was perched aloft with arms extended. Claude, who delighted in feats of strength and dexterity, would stand for hours watching the flight of these masses of wicker, and would burst into a hearty laugh whenever too vigorous a toss sent them flying over the pile into the roadway beyond. He was fond, too, of the footways of the Rue Rambuteau and the Rue du Pont Neuf, near the fruit market, where the retail dealers congregated. The sight of the vegetables displayed in the open air, on trestle-tables covered with damp black rags, was full of charm for him. At four in the afternoon the whole of this nook of greenery was aglow with sunshine; and Claude wandered between the stalls, inspecting the bright-colored heads of the saleswomen with keen artistic relish. The younger ones, with their hair in nets, had already lost all freshness of complexion through the rough life they led; while the older ones were bent and shrivelled, with wrinkled, flaring faces showing under the yellow kerchiefs bound round their heads. Cadine and Marjolin refused to accompany him there, as they could perceive old Mother Chantemesse shaking her fist at them, in her anger at seeing them prowling about together. He joined them again, however, on the opposite footway, where he found a splendid subject for a picture in the stallkeepers squatting under their huge umbrellas of faded red, blue, and violet, which, mounted upon poles, filled the whole marketside with bumps, and showed conspicuously against the fiery glow of the sinking sun, whose rays faded amid the carrots and the turnips. One tattered harridan, a century old, was sheltering three spare-looking lettuces beneath an umbrella of pink silk, shockingly split and stained.

Cadine and Marjolin had struck up an acquaintance with Léon, Quenu's apprentice, one day when he was taking a pie to a house in the neighborhood. They saw him cautiously raise the lid of his pan in a secluded corner of the Rue de Mondétour and delicately take out a ball of forcemeat. They smiled at the sight, which give them a very high opinion of Léon. And the idea came to Cadine that she might at last satisfy one of her most ardent longings. Indeed, the very next time that she met the lad with his basket she made herself very agreeable and induced him to offer her a forcemeat ball. But, although she laughed and licked her fingers, she experienced some disappointment. The forcemeat did not prove nearly so nice as she had anticipated. On the other hand, the lad, with his sly, greedy face and his white garments, which made him look like a girl going to her first communion, somewhat took her fancy.

She invited him to a monster lunch which she gave among the hampers in the auction room at the butter market. The three of them—herself, Marjolin, and Léon—completely secluded themselves from the world within four walls of wicker. The feast was laid out on a large fat basket. There were pears, nuts, cream cheese, shrimps, fried potatoes, and radishes. The cheese came from a fruiterer's in the Rue de la Cossonnerie and was a present; and a "frier" of the Rue de la Grande Truanderie had given Cadine credit for two sous' worth of potatoes. The rest of the feast, the pears, the nuts, the shrimps, and the radishes, had been pilfered from different parts of the market. It was a delicious treat; and Léon, desirous of returning the hospitality, gave a supper in his bedroom at one o'clock in the morning. The bill of fare included cold black pudding, slices of polony, a piece of salt pork, some gherkins, and some goose fat. The Quenu-Gradelles' shop had provided everything. And matters did not stop there. Dainty suppers alternated with delicate luncheons, and invitation followed invitation. Three times a week there were banquets, either amid the hampers or in Léon's garret, where Florent, on the nights when he lay awake, could hear a stifled sound of munching and rippling laughter until day began to break.

The loves of Cadine and Marjolin now took another turn. The youth played the gallant and just as another might entertain his *innamorata* at a champagne supper *en tête à tête* in a private room, he led Cadine into some quiet corner of the market cellars to munch apples or sprigs of celery. One day he stole a red herring, which they devoured with immense enjoyment on the roof of the fish market beside the guttering. There was not a single shady nook in the whole place where they did not indulge in secret feasts. The district, with its rows of open shops full of fruit and cakes and preserves, was no longer a closed paradise, in front of which they prowled with greedy, covetous appetites. As they passed the shops they now extended their hands and pilfered a prune, a few cherries, or a bit of cod. They also provisioned themselves at the markets, keeping a sharp look out as they made their way between the stalls, picking up everything that fell, and often assisting the fall by a push of their shoulders.

In spite, however, of all this marauding, some terrible scores had to be run up with the "frier" of the Rue de la

Grande Truanderie. This "frier," whose shanty leaned against a tumble-down house and was propped up by heavy joists, green with moss, made a display of boiled mussels lying in large earthenware bowls filled to the brim with clear water; of dishes of little yellow dabs stiffened by too thick a coating of paste; of squares of tripe simmering in a pan; and of grilled herrings, black and charred, and so hard that if you tapped them they sounded like wood. On certain weeks Cadine owed the frier as much as twenty sous, a crushing debt, which required the sale of an incalculable number of bunches of violets, for she could count upon no assistance from Marjolin. Moreover, she was bound to return Léon's hospitalities; and she even felt some little shame at never being able to offer him a scrap of meat. He himself had now taken to purloining entire hams. As a rule, he stowed everything away under his shirt; and at night when he reached his bedroom he drew from his bosom hunks of polony, slices of *pâté de foie gras*, and bundles of pork rind. They had to do without bread, and there was nothing to drink; but no matter. One night Marjolin saw Léon kiss Cadine between two mouthfuls; however, he only laughed. He could have smashed the little fellow with a blow from his fist, but he felt no jealousy in respect of Cadine. He treated her simply as a comrade with whom he had chummed for years.

Claude never participated in these feasts. Having caught Cadine one day stealing a beet from a little hamper lined with hay, he had pulled her ears and given her a sound scolding. These thieving propensities made her perfect as a ne'er-do-well. However, in spite of himself, he could not help feeling a sort of admiration for these sensual, pilfering, greedy creatures, who preyed upon everything that lay about, feasting off the crumbs that fell from the giant's table.

At last Marjolin nominally took service under Gavard, happy in having nothing to do except to listen to his master's flow of talk, while Cadine still continued to sell violets quite accustomed by this time to old Mother Chantemesse's complaining. They were still the same children as ever, giving way to their instincts and appetites without the slightest shame—they were the growth of the slimy pavements of the market district, where, even in fine weather, the mud remains black and sticky. However, as Cadine walked along the footways, mechanically twisting her bunches of violets, she was sometimes disturbed by disquieting reveries; and Marjolin, too, suffered from an uneasiness which he could not explain. He would occasionally leave the girl and miss some ramble or feast in order to go and gaze at Madame Quenu through the windows of the pork shop. She was so handsome and plump and round that it did him good to look at her. As he stood gazing at her, he felt full and satisfied, as though he had just eaten or drunk something extremely nice. And when he went off, a sort of hunger and thirst to see her again suddenly came upon him. This had been going on for a couple of months. At first he had looked at her with the respectful glance which he bestowed upon the shop fronts of the grocers and provision dealers; but subsequently, when he and Cadine had taken to general pilfering, he began to regard her smooth cheeks much as he regarded the barrels of olives and boxes of dried apples.

For some time past Marjolin had seen handsome Lisa every day, in the morning. She would pass Gavard's stall and stop for a moment or two to chat with the poultry dealer. She now did her marketing herself, so that she might be cheated as little as possible, she said. The truth, however, was that she wished to make Gavard speak out. In the pork shop he was always distrustful, but at his stall he chatted and talked with the utmost freedom. Now, Lisa had made up her mind to ascertain from him exactly what took place in the little room at Monsieur Lebigre's; for she had no great confidence in her secret police officer, Mademoiselle Saget. In a short time she learnt from the incorrigible chatterbox a lot of vague details which very much alarmed her. Two days after her explanation with Quenu she returned home from the market looking very pale. She beckoned to her husband to follow her into the dining room and having carefully closed the door she said to him: "Is your brother determined to send us to the scaffold, then? Why did you conceal from me what you knew?"

Quenu declared that he knew nothing. He even swore a great oath that he had not returned to Monsieur Lebigre's, and would never go there again.

"You will do well not to do so," replied Lisa, shrugging her shoulders, "unless you want to get yourself into a serious scrape. Florent is up to some evil trick, I'm certain of it! I have just learned quite sufficient to show me where he is going. He's going back to Cayenne, do you hear?"

Then, after a pause, she continued in calmer tones: "Oh, the unhappy man! He had everything here that he could wish for. He might have redeemed his character; he had nothing but good examples before him. But no, it is in his blood! He will come to a violent end with his politics! I insist upon there being an end to all this! You hear me, Quenu? I gave you due warning long ago!"

She spoke the last words very incisively. Quenu bent his head, as if awaiting sentence.

"To begin with," continued Lisa, "he shall cease to take his meals here. It will be quite sufficient if we give him a bed. He is earning money; let him feed himself."

Quenu seemed on the point of protesting, but his wife silenced him by adding energetically:

"Make your choice between him and me. If he remains here, I swear to you that I will go away and take my daughter with me. Do you want me to tell you the whole truth about him? He is a man capable of anything; he has come here to bring discord into our household. But I will set things right, you may depend on it. You have your choice between him and me; you hear me?"

Then, leaving her husband in silent consternation, she returned to the shop, where she served a customer with her usual affable smile. The fact was that after artfully inveigled Gavard into a political discussion, the poultry dealer had told her that she would soon see how the land lay, that they were going to make a clean sweep of everything, and that two determined men like her brother-in-law and himself would suffice to set the fire blazing. This was the evil trick of which she had spoken to Quenu, some conspiracy to which Gavard was always making mysterious allusions with a sniggering grin from which he seemingly desired a great deal to be inferred. And in imagination Lisa already saw the gendarmes invading the pork shop, gagging herself, her husband, and Pauline, and casting them into some underground dungeon.

In the evening, at dinner, she evinced an icy frigidity. She made no offers to serve Florent, but several times remarked: "It's very strange what an amount of bread we've got through lately."

Florent at last understood. He felt that he was being treated like a poor relation who is gradually turned out of doors. For the last two months Lisa had dressed him in Quenu's old trousers and coats; and, as he was as thin as his brother was fat, these ragged garments had a most extraordinary appearance upon him. She also turned her oldest linen over to him: pocket handkerchiefs that had been darned a dozen times, ragged towels, sheets which were only fit to be cut up into dusters and dish cloths, and worn-out shirts, distended by Quenu's corpulent figure, and so short that they would have served Florent as undershirts. Moreover,

he no longer found around him the same good-natured kindliness as in the earlier days. The whole household seemed to
shrug its shoulders after the example set by handsome Lisa.
Auguste and Augustine turned their backs upon him, and
little Pauline, with the cruel frankness of childhood, let fall
some bitter remarks about the stains on his coat and the
holes in his shirt. However, during the last days he suffered
most at table. He scarcely dared to eat, as he saw the mother
and daughter fix their gaze upon him whenever he cut himself a piece of bread. Quenu meantime peered into his plate,
to avoid having to take any part in what went on.

That which most tortured Florent was his inability to invent a reason for leaving the house. During a week he kept
on revolving in his mind a sentence expressing his resolve
to take his meals elsewhere, but could not bring himself to
utter it. Indeed, this man of tender nature lived in such a
world of illusions that he feared he might hurt his brother
and sister-in-law by ceasing to lunch and dine with them. It
had taken him over two months to detect Lisa's latent hostility; and even now he was sometimes inclined to think that
he must be mistaken, and that she was in reality kindly disposed towards him. Unselfishness with him extended to for-
getfulness of his requirements; it was no longer a virtue, but
utter indifference to self, an absolute obliteration of person-
ality. Even when he recognized that he was being gradually
turned out of the house, his mind never for a moment dwelt
upon his share in old Gradelle's fortune, or upon the accounts which Lisa had offered him. He had already planned
out his expenditure for the future; reckoning that with what
Madame Verlaque still allowed him to retain of his salary,
and the thirty francs a month which a pupil, obtained through
La Normande, paid him, he would be able to spend eighteen sous on his breakfast and twenty-six sous on his dinner. This, he thought, would be ample. And so, at last, taking

as his excuse the lessons which he was giving his new pupil, he emboldened himself one morning to pretend that it would be impossible for him in future to come to the house at mealtimes. He blushed as he gave utterance to this laboriously constructed lie, which had given him so much trouble, and continued apologetically:

"You mustn't be offended; the boy only has those hours free. I can easily get something to eat, you know; and I will come and have a chat with you in the evenings."

Beautiful Lisa maintained her icy reserve, and this increased Florent's feeling of trouble. In order to have no cause for self-reproach she had been unwilling to send him about his business, preferring to wait till he should weary of the situation and go of his own accord. Now he was going, and it was a good riddance; and she studiously refrained from all show of kindliness for fear it might induce him to remain. Quenu, however, showed some signs of emotion and exclaimed: "Don't think of putting yourself about; take your meals elsewhere by all means, if it is more convenient. It isn't we who are turning you away; you'll at all events dine with us sometimes on Sundays, eh?"

Florent hurried off. His heart was very heavy. When he had gone, the beautiful Lisa did not venture to reproach her husband for his weakness in giving that invitation for Sundays. She had conquered and again breathed freely among the light oak of her dining room, where she would have liked to burn some sugar to drive away the odor of perverse leanness which seemed to linger about. Moreover, she continued to remain on the defensive; and at the end of another week she felt more alarmed than ever. She only occasionally saw Florent in the evenings, and began to have all sorts of dreadful thoughts, imagining that her brother-in-law was constructing some infernal machine upstairs in Augustine's bedroom, or else making signals which would result in barricades covering the whole neighborhood. Gavard, who had become gloomy, merely nodded or shook his head when she spoke to him and left his stall for days together in Marjolin's charge. The beautiful Lisa, however, determined that she would get to the bottom of affairs. She knew that Florent had obtained a day's leave, and intended to spend it with Claude Lantier, at Madame François's, at Nanterre. As he would start in the morning, and remain away until night, she conceived the idea of inviting Gavard to dinner. He would be sure to talk freely, at table, she thought. But throughout the morning she was unable to meet the poultry dealer, and so in the afternoon she went back again to the markets.

Marjolin was in the stall alone. He used to drowse there for hours, recouping himself from the fatigue of his long rambles. He generally sat upon one chair with his legs resting upon another, and his head leaning against a little dresser. In the wintertime he took a keen delight in lolling there and contemplating the display of game; the bucks hanging head downwards, with their forelegs broken and twisted round their necks; the larks festooning the stall like garlands; the big ruddy hares, the mottled partridges, the waterfowl of a bronze-gray hue, the Russian black cocks and hazel hens, which arrived in a packing of oat straw and charcoal; and the pheasants, the magnificent pheasants, with their scarlet hoods, their stomachers of green satin, their mantles of embossed gold, and their flaming tails, that trailed like the trains of court robes. All this show of plumage reminded Marjolin of his rambles in the cellars with Cadine among the hampers of feathers.

That afternoon the beautiful Lisa found Marjolin in the midst of the poultry. It was warm, and whiffs of hot air passed along the narrow alleys of the pavilion. She was obliged to stoop before she could see him stretched out inside the stall, below the bare flesh of the birds. From the hooked bar up above hung fat geese, the hooks sticking in the bleeding wounds of their long stiffened necks, while their huge bodies bulged out, glowing ruddily beneath their fine down, and, with their snowy tails and wings, suggesting nudity encompassed by fine linen. And also hanging from the bar, with ears thrown back and feet parted as though they were bent on some vigorous leap, were gray rabbits whose turned-up tails gleamed whitely, while their heads, with sharp teeth and dim eyes, laughed with the grin of death. On the counter of the stall plucked fowls showed their strained fleshy breasts; pigeons, crowded on wicker trays, displayed the soft bare skin of innocents; ducks, with skin of rougher texture, exhibited their webbed feet; and three magnificent turkeys, speckled with blue dots, like freshly-shaven chins, slumbered on their backs amid the black fans of their expanded tails. On plates nearby were giblets, livers, gizzards, necks, feet, and wings; while an oval dish contained a skinned and gutted rabbit, with its four legs wide apart, its head bleeding, and its kidneys showing through its gashed belly. A streamlet of dark blood, after trickling along its back to its tail, had fallen drop by drop, staining the whiteness of the dish. Marjolin had not even taken the trouble to wipe the block, near which the rabbit's feet were still lying. He reclined there with his eyes half-closed, encompassed by other piles of dead poultry which crowded the shelves of the stall, poultry in paper wrappers like bouquets, rows upon rows of protuberant breasts and bent legs showing confusedly. And amid all this mass of food, the young fellow's big, fair figure, the flesh of his cheeks, hands, and powerful neck covered with ruddy down seemed as soft as that of the magnificent turkeys and as plump as the breasts of the fat geese.

When he caught sight of Lisa, he at once sprang up, blushing at having been caught sprawling in this way. He always seemed very nervous and ill at ease in Madame Quenu's presence; and when she asked him if Monsieur Gavard was there, he stammered out: "No, I don't think so. He was here a little while ago, but he went away again."

Lisa looked at him, smiling; she had a great liking for him. But feeling something warm brush against her hand, which was hanging by her side, she raised a little shriek. Some live rabbits were thrusting their noses out of a box under the counter of the stall and sniffing at her skirts.

"Oh," she exclaimed with a laugh, "it's your rabbits that are tickling me."

Then she stooped and attempted to stroke a white rabbit, which darted in alarm into a corner of the box.

"Will Monsieur Gavard be back soon, do you think?" she asked, as she again rose erect.

Marjolin once more replied that he did not know; then in a hesitating way he continued: "He's very likely gone down into the cellars. He told me, I think, that he was going there."

"Well, I think I'll wait for him, then," replied Lisa. "Could you let him know that I am here? or I might go down to him, perhaps. Yes, that's a good idea; I've been intending to go and have a look at the cellars for these last five years. You'll take me down, won't you, and explain things to me?"

Marjolin blushed crimson, and, hurrying out of the stall, walked on in front of her, leaving the poultry to look after itself. "Of course I will," said he. "I'll do anything you wish, Madame Lisa."

When they got down below, the beautiful Lisa felt quite suffocated by the dank atmosphere of the cellar. She stood on the bottom step and raised her eyes to look at the vaulted roofing of red and white bricks arching slightly between the iron ribs upheld by small columns. What made her hesitate more than the gloominess of the place was a warm, penetrating odor, the exhalations of large numbers of living creatures, which irritated her nostrils and throat.

"What a nasty smell!" she exclaimed. "It must be very unhealthy down here."

"It never does me any harm," replied Marjolin in astonishment. "There's nothing unpleasant about the smell when you've got accustomed to it; and it's very warm and cosy down here in the wintertime."

As Lisa followed him, however, she declared that the strong scent of the poultry quite turned her stomach, and that she would certainly not be able to eat a fowl for the next two months. All around her the storerooms, the small cabins where the stallkeepers keep their livestock, formed regular streets, intersecting each other at right angles. There were only a few scattered gaslights, and the little alleys seemed wrapped in sleep like the lanes of a village where the inhabitants have all gone to bed. Marjolin made Lisa feel the close-meshed wiring, stretched on a framework of cast iron; and as she made her way along one of the little streets she amused herself by reading the names of the different tenants, which were inscribed on blue labels.

"Monsieur Gavard's place is quite at the far end," said the young man, still walking on.

They turned to the left and found themselves in a sort of blind alley, a dark, gloomy spot where not a ray of light penetrated. Gavard was not there.

"Oh, it makes no difference," said Marjolin. "I can show you our birds just the same. I have a key to the storeroom."

Lisa followed him into the darkness.

"You don't suppose that I can see your birds in this black oven, do you?" she asked, laughing.

Marjolin did not reply at once; but presently he stammered out that there was always a candle in the storeroom. He was fumbling about the lock and seemed quite unable to find the keyhole. As Lisa came up to help him, she felt a hot breath on her neck; and when the young man had at last succeeded in opening the door and lighted the candle, she saw that he was trembling.

"You silly fellow!" she exclaimed, "to get yourself into such a state just because a door won't open! Why, you're no better than a girl, in spite of your big fists!"

She stepped inside the storeroom. Gavard had rented two compartments, which he had thrown into one by removing the partition between them. In the dirt on the floor wallowed the larger birds—the geese, turkeys, and ducks—while up above, on tiers of shelves, were boxes with barred fronts containing fowls and rabbits. The grating of the storeroom was so coated with dust and cobwebs that it looked as though covered with gray blinds. The woodwork down below was rotting, and covered with filth. Lisa, however, not wishing to vex Marjolin, refrained from any further expression of disgust. She pushed her fingers between the bars of the boxes and began to lament the fate of the unhappy fowls, which were so closely huddled together and could not even stand upright. Then she stroked a duck with a broken leg which was squatting in a corner, and the young man told her that it would be killed that very evening, for fear lest it should die during the night.

"But what do they do for food?" asked Lisa.

He then explained to her that poultry would not eat in the dark, and that it was necessary to light a candle and wait there until they had finished their meal.

"It amuses me to watch them," he continued; "I often stay here with a light for hours together. You should see how they peck away; and when I hide the flame of the candle with my hand they all stand stock still with their necks in the air, just as though the sun had set. It is against the rules to leave a lighted candle here and go away. One of the dealers, old Mother Palette—you know her, don't you?—nearly burned the whole place down the other day. A fowl must have knocked the candle over into the straw while she was away."

"A pretty thing, isn't it," said Lisa, "for fowls to insist upon having the chandeliers lighted up every time they take a meal?"

This idea made her laugh. Then she came out of the store-room, wiping her feet, and holding up her skirts to keep them from the filth. Marjolin blew out the candle and locked the door. Lisa felt rather nervous at finding herself in the dark again with this big young fellow, and so she hastened on in front.

"I'm glad I came, all the same," she presently said, as he rejoined her. "There is a great deal more under these markets than I ever imagined. But I must make haste now and get home again. They'll wonder what has become of me at the shop. If Monsieur Gavard comes back, tell him that I want to speak to him immediately."

"I expect he's in the killing room," said Marjolin. "We'll go and see, if you like."

Lisa made no reply. She felt oppressed by the close atmosphere which warmed her face. She was quite flushed, and her bodice, generally so still and lifeless, began to heave. Moreover, the sound of Marjolin's hurrying steps behind her filled her with an uneasy feeling. At last she stepped aside and let him go on in front. The lanes of this underground village were still fast asleep. Lisa noticed that her companion was taking the longest way. When they came out in front of the railway track he told her that he had wished to show it to her; and they stood for a moment or two looking through the chinks in the hoarding of heavy beams. Then Marjolin proposed to take her on to the line; but she refused, saying that it was not worth while, as she could see things well enough where she was.

As they returned to the poultry cellars they found old

Madame Palette in front of her storeroom, removing the cords of a large square hamper, in which a furious fluttering of wings and scraping of feet could be heard. As she unfastened the last knot the lid suddenly flew open, as though shot up by a spring, and some big geese thrust out their heads and necks. Then, in wild alarm, they sprang from their prison and rushed away, craning their necks, and filling the dark cellars with a frightful noise of hissing and clattering of beaks. Lisa could not help laughing, in spite of the lamentations of the old woman, who swore like a carter as she caught hold of two of the absconding birds and dragged them back by the neck. Marjolin, meantime, set off in pursuit of a third. They could hear him running along the narrow alleys, hunting for the runaway, and delighting in the chase. Then, far off in the distance, they heard the sounds of a struggle, and presently Marjolin came back again, bringing the goose with him. Mother Palette, a sallow-faced old woman, took it in her arms and clasped it for a moment to her bosom, in the classic attitude of Leda.

"Well, well, I'm sure I don't know what I should have done if you hadn't been here," said she. "The other day I had a regular fight with one of the brutes; but I had my knife with me, and I cut its throat."

Marjolin was quite out of breath. When they reached the stone blocks where the poultry were killed, and where the gas burnt more brightly, Lisa could see that he was perspiring, and had bold, glistening eyes. She thought he looked very handsome like that, with his broad shoulders, big flushed face, and fair curly hair, and she looked at him so complacently, with that air of admiration which women feel they may safely express for quite young lads, that he relapsed into timid bashfulness again.

"Well, Monsieur Gavard isn't here, you see," she said. "You've only made me waste my time."

Marjolin, however, began rapidly explaining the killing of the poultry to her. Five huge stone slabs stretched out in the direction of the Rue Rambuteau under the yellow light of the gasjets. A woman was killing fowls at one end; and this led him to tell Lisa that the birds were plucked almost before they were dead, the operation thus being much easier. Then he wanted her to feel the feathers which were lying in heaps on the stone slabs; and told her that they were sorted and sold for as much as nine sous the pound, according to their quality. To satisfy him, she was also obliged to plunge her hand into the big hampers full of down. Then he turned the watertaps, of which there was one by every pillar. There was no end to the particulars he gave. The blood, he said, streamed along the stone blocks and collected into pools on the paved door, which attendants sluiced with water every two hours, removing the more recent stains with coarse brushes.

When Lisa stooped over the drain which carries away the swillings, Marjolin found a fresh text for talk. On rainy days, said he, the water sometimes rose through this orifice and flooded the place. It had once risen a foot high; and they had been obliged to transport all the poultry to the other end of the cellar, which is on a higher level. He laughed as he recalled the wild flutter of the terrified creatures. However, he had now finished, and it seemed as though there remained nothing else for him to show, when all at once he recalled the ventilator. Thereupon he took Lisa off to the far end of the cellar and told her to look up; and inside one of the turrets at the corner angles of the pavilion she observed a sort of escape pipe, by which the foul atmosphere of the storerooms ascended into space.

Here, in this corner, reeking with abominable odors, Marjolin's nostrils quivered, and his breath came and went violently. His long stroll with Lisa in these cellars, full of warm animal perfumes, had gradually intoxicated him.

She had again turned towards him. "Well," said she, "it was very kind of you to show me all this, and when you come to the shop I will give you something."

While speaking she took hold of his soft chin, as she often did, without recognizing that he was no longer a child; and perhaps she allowed her hand to linger there a little longer than was her wont. At all events, Marjolin, usually so bashful, was thrilled by the caress, and all at once he impetuously sprang forward, clasped Lisa by the shoulders, and pressed his lips to her soft cheeks. She raised no cry, but turned very pale at this sudden attack, which showed her how imprudent she had been. And then, freeing herself from the embrace, she raised her arm, as she had seen men do in slaughterhouses, clenched her comely fist, and knocked Marjolin down with a single blow, planted straight between his eyes; and as he fell his head came into collision with one of the stone slabs and was split open. Just at that moment the hoarse and prolonged crowing of a cock sounded through the gloom.

Handsome Lisa, however, remained perfectly cool. Her lips were tightly compressed, and her bosom had recovered its usually immobility. Up above she could hear the heavy rumbling of the markets, and through the vent holes alongside the Rue Rambuteau the noise of the street traffic made its way into the oppressive silence of the cellar. Lisa reflected that her own strong arm had saved her; and then, fearing lest someone should come and find her there, she hastened off, without giving a glance at Marjolin. As she climbed the steps, after passing through the grated entrance of the cellars, the daylight brought her great relief.

She returned to the shop, quite calm, and only looking a little pale.

"You've been a long time," Quenu said to her.

"I can't find Gavard. I have looked for him everywhere,"

she quietly replied. "We shall have to eat our leg of mutton without him."

Then she filled the lard pot, which she noticed was empty; and cut some pork chops for her friend Madame Taboureau, who had sent her little servant for them. The blows which she dealt with her cleaver reminded her of Marjolin. She felt that she had nothing to reproach herself with. She had acted like an honest woman. She was not going to disturb her peace of mind; she was too happy to do anything to compromise herself. However, she glanced at Quenu, whose neck was coarse and ruddy, and whose shaven chin looked as rough as knotted wood; whereas Marjolin's chin and neck resembled rosy satin. But then she must not think of him anymore, for he was no longer a child. She regretted it, and could not help thinking that children grew up much too quickly.

A slight flush came back to her cheeks, and Quenu considered that she looked wonderfully blooming. He came and sat down beside her at the counter for a moment or two. "You ought to go out oftener," said he; "it does you good. We'll go to the theater together one of these nights, if you like; to the Gaîté, eh? Madame Taboureau has been to see the piece they are playing there, and she declares it's splendid."

Lisa smiled, and said they would see about it, and then once more she took herself off. Quenu thought that it was too good of her to take so much trouble in running about after that brute Gavard. In point of fact, however, she had simply gone upstairs to Florent's bedroom, the key of which was hanging from a nail in the kitchen. She hoped to find out something or other by an inspection of this room, since the poultry dealer had failed her. She went slowly round it, examining the bed, the mantelpiece, and every corner. The window with the little balcony was open, and the budding pomegranate was steeped in the golden beams of the setting sun. The room looked to her as though Augustine had never left it—had slept there only the night before. There seemed to be nothing masculine about the place. She was quite surprised, for she had expected to find some suspicious-looking chests and coffers with strong locks. She went to feel Augustine's summer gown, which was still hanging against the wall. Then she sat down at the table and began to read an unfinished page of manuscript, in which the word "revolution" occurred twice. This alarmed her, and she opened the drawer, which she saw was full of papers. But her sense of honor awoke within her in presence of the secret which the rickety deal table so badly guarded. She remained bending over the papers, trying to understand them, without touching them, in a state of great emotion, when the shrill song of the chaffinch, on whose cage streamed a ray of sunshine, made her start. She closed the drawer. It was a base thing that she had contemplated, she thought.

Then, as she lingered by the window, reflecting that she ought to go and ask counsel of Abbé Roustan, who was a very sensible man, she saw a crowd of people round a stretcher in the market square below. The night was falling, still she distinctly recognized Cadine weeping in the midst of the crowd; while Florent and Claude, whose boots were white with dust, stood together talking earnestly at the edge of the footway. She hurried downstairs again, surprised to see them back so soon, and scarcely had she reached her counter when Mademoiselle Saget entered the shop.

"They have just found that scamp of a Marjolin in the cellar, with his head split open," exclaimed the old maid. "Won't you come to see him, Madame Quenu?"

Lisa crossed the road to look at him. The young fellow was lying on his back on the stretcher, looking very pale. His eyes were closed, and a stiff wisp of his fair hair was clotted with blood. The bystanders, however, declared that there was no serious harm done, and, besides, the scamp had only himself to blame, for he was always playing all sorts of wild pranks in the cellars. It was generally supposed that he had been trying to jump over one of the stone blocks—one of his favorite amusements—and had fallen with his head against the slab.

"I dare say that hussy there gave him a shove," remarked Mademoiselle Saget, pointing to Cadine, who was weeping. "They are always larking together."

Meantime the fresh air had restored Marjolin to consciousness, and he opened his eyes in wide astonishment. He looked round at everybody, and then, observing Lisa bending over him, he gently smiled at her with an expression of mingled humility and affection. He seemed to have forgotten all that had happened. Lisa, feeling relieved, said that he ought to be taken to the hospital at once, and promised to go and see him there, and take him some oranges and biscuits. However, Marjolin's head had fallen back, and when the stretcher was carried away Cadine followed it, with her flat basket slung round her neck, and her hot tears rolling down upon the bunches of violets in their mossy bed. She certainly had no thoughts for the flowers that she was thus scalding with her bitter grief.

As Lisa went back to her shop, she heard Claude say, as he shook hands with Florent and parted from him: "Ah! the confounded young scamp! He's quite spoiled my day for me! Still, we had a very enjoyable time, didn't we?" Claude and Florent had returned both worried and happy, bringing with them the pleasant freshness of the country air. Madame François had disposed of all her vegetables that morning before daylight; and they had all three gone to the Golden Compasses, in the Rue Montorgueil, to get the cart. Here, in the middle of Paris, they found a foretaste of the country.

Behind the Restaurant Philippe, with its frontage of gilt woodwork rising to the first floor, there was a yard like that of a farm, dirty, teeming with life, reeking with the odor of manure and straw. Bands of fowls were pecking at the soft ground. Sheds and staircases and galleries of greeny wood clung to the old houses around, and at the far end, in a shanty of big beams, was Balthazar, harnessed to the cart and eating the oats in his nosebag. He went down the Rue Montorgueil at a slow trot, seemingly well pleased to return to Nanterre so soon. However, he was not going home without a load. Madame François had a contract with the company which undertook the scavenging of the markets, and twice a week she carried off with her a load of leaves, forked up from the mass of refuse which littered the square. It made excellent manure. In a few minutes the cart was filled to overflowing. Claude and Florent stretched themselves out on the deep bed of greenery; Madame François grasped her reins, and Balthazar went off at his slow, steady pace, his head somewhat bent by reason of there being so many passengers to pull along.

This excursion had been talked of for a long time past. Madame François laughed cheerily. She was partial to the two men, and promised them such an *omelette au lard* as had never been eaten, said she, in "that villainous Paris." Florent and Claude revelled in the thought of this day of lounging idleness which as yet had scarcely begun to dawn. Nanterre seemed to be some distant paradise into which they would presently enter.

"Are you quite comfortable?" Madame François asked as the cart turned into the Rue du Pont Neuf.

Claude declared that their couch was as soft as a bridal bed. Lying on their backs, with their hands crossed under their heads, both men were looking up at the pale sky from which the stars were vanishing. All along the Rue de Rivoli they kept unbroken silence, waiting till they should have got clear of the houses, and listening to the worthy woman as she chattered to Balthazar: "Take your time, old man," she said to him in kindly tones. "We're in no hurry; we shall be sure to get there at last."

On reaching the Champs Elysées, when the artist saw nothing but tree tops on either side of him, and the great green mass of the Tuileries gardens in the distance, he woke up, as it were, and began to talk. When the cart had passed the end of the Rue du Roule he had caught a glimpse of the side entrance of Saint Eustache under the giant roofing of one of the market covered ways. He was constantly referring to this view of the church and tried to give it a symbolical meaning.

"It's an odd mixture," he said, "that bit of a church framed round by an avenue of cast iron. The one will kill the other; the iron will slay the stone, and the time is not very far off. Do you believe in chance, Florent? For my part, I don't think that it was any mere chance of position that set a rose window of Saint Eustache right in the middle of the central markets. No; there's a whole manifesto in it. It is modern art, realism, naturalism—whatever you like to call it—that has grown up and dominates ancient art. Don't you agree with me?"

Then, as Florent still kept silence, Claude continued: "Besides, that church is a piece of bastard architecture, made up of the dying gasp of the middle ages, and the first stammering of the Renaissance. Have you noticed what sort of churches are built nowadays? They resemble all kinds of things—libraries, observatories, pigeon cotes, barracks; and surely no one can imagine that the Deity dwells in such places. The pious old builders are all dead and gone; and it would be better to cease erecting those hideous carcasses of stone, in which we have no belief to enshrine. Since the beginning of the century there has only been one large original pile of buildings erected in Paris—a pile in accordance with modern developments—and that's the central markets. You hear me, Florent? Ah! they are a fine bit of building, though they but faintly indicate what we shall see in the twentieth century! And so, you see, Saint Eustache is done for! It stands there with its rose windows, deserted by worshippers, while the markets spread out by its side and teem with noisy life. Yes! that's how I understand it all, my friend."

"Ah! Monsieur Claude," said Madame François, laughing, "the woman who cut your tongue-string certainly earned her money. Look at Balthazar laying his ears back to listen to you. Come, come, get along, Balthazar!"

The cart was slowly making its way up the incline. At this early hour of the morning the avenue, with its double lines of iron chairs on either pathway, and its lawns, dotted with flower beds and clumps of shrubbery, stretching away under the blue shadows of the trees, was quite deserted; however, at the Rond-Point a lady and gentleman on horseback passed the cart at a gentle trot. Florent, who had made himself a pillow with a bundle of cabbage leaves, was still gazing at the sky, in which a far-stretching rosy glow was appearing. Every now and then he would close his eyes, the better to enjoy the fresh breeze of the morning as it fanned his face. He was so happy to escape from the markets and travel on through the pure air, that he remained speechless, and did not even listen to what was being said around him.

"And then, too, what fine jokers are those fellows who imprison art in a toy box!" resumed Claude, after a pause. "They are always repeating the same idiotic words: 'You can't create art out of science,' says one; 'Mechanical appliances kill poetry,' says another; and a pack of fools wail over the fate of the flowers, as though anybody wished the flowers any harm! I'm sick of all such twaddle; I should like to answer all that snivelling with some work of open defiance. I should take a pleasure in shocking those good people. Shall I tell you what was the finest thing I ever produced since I first began to work, and the one which I recall with the greatest pleasure? It's quite a story. When I was at my Aunt Lisa's on Christmas Eve last year that idiot of an Auguste, the assistant, was setting out the shop window. Well, he quite irritated me by the weak, spiritless way in which he arranged the display; and at last I requested him to take himself off, saying that I would group the things myself in a proper manner. You see, I had plenty of bright colors to work with—the red of the tongues, the yellow of the hams, the blue of the paper shavings, the rosy pink of the things that had been cut into, the green of the sprigs of heath, and the black of the black puddings—ah! a magnificent black, which I have never managed to produce on my palette. And naturally the *crépine*, the small sausages, the chitterlings, and the crumbed trotters provided me with delicate grays and browns. I produced a perfect work of art. I took the dishes, the plates, the pans, and the jars, and arranged the different colors; and I devised a wonderful picture of still life, with subtle scales of tints leading up to brilliant flashes of color. The red tongues seemed to thrust themselves out like greedy flames, and the black puddings, surrounded by pale sausages, suggested a dark night fraught with terrible indigestion. I had produced, you see, a picture symbolical of the gluttony of Christmas Eve, when people meet and sup—the midnight feasting, the ravenous gorging of stomachs void and faint after all the singing of hymns. At the top of everything a huge turkey exhibited its white breast, marbled blackly by the truffles showing through its skin. It was something barbaric and superb, suggesting a paunch amid a halo of glory; but there was such a cutting, sarcastic touch about it all that people crowded to the window, alarmed by the fierce flare of the shop front. When my Aunt Lisa came back from the kitchen she was quite frightened, and thought I'd set the fat in the shop on fire; and she considered the appearance of the turkey so indelicate that she turned me out of the place while Auguste rearranged the window after his own idiotic fashion. Such brutes will never understand the language of a red splotch by the side of a gray one. Ah, well! that was my masterpiece. I have never done anything better."

He relapsed into silence, smiling and dwelling with gratification on this reminiscence. The cart had now reached the Arc de Triomphe, and strong currents of air swept from the avenues across the expanse of open ground. Florent sat up and inhaled with zest the first odors of grass wafted from the fortifications. He turned his back on Paris, anxious to behold the country in the distance. At the corner of the Rue de Longchamp, Madame François pointed out to him the spot where she had picked him up. This rendered him thoughtful, and he gazed at her as she sat there, so healthy-looking and serene, with her arms slightly extended so as to grasp the reins. She looked even handsomer than Lisa, with her neckerchief tied over her head, her robust glow of health, and her brusque, kindly air. When she gave a slight cluck with her tongue, Balthazar pricked up his ears and rattled down the road at a quicker pace.

On arriving at Nanterre, the cart turned to the left into a narrow lane, skirted some blank walls, and finally came to a stand still at the end of a sort of blind alley. It was the end of the world, Madame François used to say. The load of vegetable leaves now had to be discharged. Claude and Florent would not hear of the journeyman gardener, who was planting lettuces, leaving his work, but armed themselves with pitchforks and proceeded to toss the leaves into the manure pit. This occupation afforded them much amusement. Claude had quite a liking for manure, since it symbolizes the world and its life. The strippings and parings of the vegetables, the scourings of the markets, the refuse that fell from that colossal table, remained full of life, and returned to the spot where the vegetables had previously sprouted, to warm and nourish fresh generations of cabbages, turnips, and carrots. They rose again in fertile crops, and once more went to spread themselves out upon the market square. Paris rotted everything and returned everything to the soil, which never wearied of repairing the ravages of death.

"Ah!" exclaimed Claude, as he plied his fork for the last time, "here's a cabbage stalk that I'm sure I recognize. It has grown up at least half a score of times in that corner over by the apricot tree."

This remark made Florent laugh. But he soon became grave again and strolled slowly through the kitchen garden, while Claude made a sketch of the stable, and Madame François got breakfast ready. The kitchen garden was a long strip of ground, divided in the middle by a narrow path; it rose slightly, and at the top end, on raising the head, you could perceive the low barracks of Mont Valérien. Green hedges separated it from other plots of land, and these lofty walls of hawthorn fringed the horizon with a curtain of greenery in such a way that of all the surrounding country Mont Valérien alone seemed to rise inquisitively on tiptoe in order to peer into Madame François's close. Great peacefulness came from the countryside which could not be seen. Along the kitchen garden, between the four hedges, the May sun shone with a languid heat, a silence disturbed only by the buzzing of insects, a somnolence suggestive of painless parturition. Every now and then a faint cracking sound, a soft sigh, made one fancy that one could hear the vegetables sprout into being. The patches of spinach and sorrel, the borders of radishes, carrots, and turnips, the beds of potatoes and cabbages, spread out in even regularity, displaying their dark leaf-mould between their tufts of greenery. Farther away, the trenched lettuces, onions, leeks, and celery, planted by line in long straight rows, looked like soldiers on parade; while the peas and beans were beginning to twine their slender tendrils round a forest of sticks, which, when June came, they would transform into a thick and verdant wood. There was not a weed to be seen. The garden resembled two parallel strips of carpet of a geometrical pattern of green on a reddish ground, which were carefully swept every morning. Borders of thyme grew like grayish fringe along each side of the pathway.

Florent paced backwards and forwards amid the perfume of the thyme, which the sun was warming. He felt profoundly happy in the peacefulness and cleanliness of the garden. For nearly a year past he had only seen vegetables bruised and crushed by the jolting of market carts; vegetables torn up on the previous evening and still bleeding. He rejoiced to find them at home, in peace in the dark mould, and sound in every part. The cabbages had a bulky, prosperous appearance; the carrots looked bright and gay; and the lettuces lounged in line with an air of careless indolence. And as he looked at them all, the markets which he had left behind him that morning seemed to him like a vast mortuary, an abode of death, where only corpses could be found, a charnel house reeking with foul smells and putrefaction. He slackened his steps and rested in that kitchen garden, as after a long perambulation amid deafening noises and repulsive odors. The uproar and the sickening humidity of the fish market had departed from him; and he felt as though he were being born anew in the pure fresh air. Claude was right, he thought. The markets were a sphere of death. The soil was the life, the eternal cradle, the health of the world.

"The omelet's ready!" suddenly cried Madame François.

When they were all three seated round the table in the

kitchen, with the door thrown open to the sunshine, they ate their breakfast with such light-hearted gaiety that Madame François looked at Florent in amazement, repeating between each mouthful: "You're quite altered. You're ten years younger. It is that villainous Paris which makes you seem so gloomy. You've got a little sunshine in your eyes now. Ah! those big towns do one's health no good, you ought to come and live here."

Claude laughed and retorted that Paris was a glorious place. He stuck up for it and all that belonged to it, even to its gutters; though at the same time retaining a keen affection for the country.

In the afternoon Madame François and Florent found themselves alone at the end of the garden, in a corner planted with a few fruit trees. Seated on the ground, they talked somewhat seriously together. The good woman advised Florent with an affectionate and quite maternal kindness. She asked him endless questions about his life, and his intentions for the future, and begged him to remember that he might always count upon her, if ever he thought that she could in the slightest degree contribute to his happiness. Florent was deeply touched. No woman had ever spoken to him in that way before. Madame François seemed to him like some healthy, robust plant that had grown up with the vegetables in the leaf-mould of the garden; while the Lisas, the Normans, and other pretty women of the markets appeared to him like flesh of doubtful freshness decked out for exhibition. He here enjoyed several hours of perfect well-being, delivered from all that reek of food which sickened him in the markets, and reviving to new life amid the fertile atmosphere of the country, like that cabbage stalk which Claude declared he had seen sprout up more than half a score of times. The two men took leave of Madame

François at about five o'clock. They had decided to walk back to Paris; and the market gardener accompanied them into the lane. As she bade good-bye to Florent, she kept his hand in her own for a moment and said gently: "If ever anything happens to trouble you, remember to come to me."

For a quarter of an hour Florent walked on without speaking, already getting gloomy again, and reflecting that he was leaving health behind him. The road to Courbevoie was white with dust. However, both men were fond of long walks and the ringing of stout boots on the hard ground. Little clouds of dust rose up behind their heels at every step, while the rays of the sinking sun darted obliquely over the avenue, lengthening their shadows in such a way that their heads reached the other side of the road and journeyed along the opposite footway.

Claude, swinging his arms, and taking long, regular strides, complacently watched these two shadows, while enjoying the rhythmical cadence of his steps, which he accentuated by a motion of his shoulders. Presently, however, as though just awaking from a dream, he exclaimed: "Do you know the 'Battle of the Fat and the Thin'?"

Florent, surprised by the question, replied in the negative; and thereupon Claude waxed enthusiastic, talking of that series of prints in very eulogical fashion. He mentioned certain incidents: the Fat, so swollen that they almost burst, preparing their evening debauch, while the Thin, bent double by fasting, looked in from the street with the appearance of envious stick figures; and then, again, the Fat, with hanging cheeks, driving off one of the Thin, who had been audacious enough to introduce himself into their midst in lowly humility, and who looked like a ninepin amongst a population of balls.

In these designs Claude detected the entire drama of

human life, and he ended by classifying men into Fat and Thin, two hostile groups, one of which devours the other and grows fat and sleek and enjoys itself.

"Cain," said he, "was certainly one of the Fat, and Abel one of the Thin. Ever since that first murder, there have been rampant appetites which have drained the lifeblood of the small eaters. It's a continual preying of the stronger upon the weaker; each swallowing his neighbor, and then getting swallowed in his turn. Beware of the Fat, my friend."

He relapsed into silence for a moment, still watching their two shadows, which the setting sun elongated more than ever. Then he murmured: "You see, we belong to the Thin—you and I. Those who are no more corpulent than we are don't take up much room in the sunlight, eh?"

Florent glanced at the two shadows and smiled. But Claude waxed angry and exclaimed: "You make a mistake if you think it a laughing matter. For my own part, I greatly suffer from being one of the Thin. If I were one of the Fat, I could paint at my ease; I should have a fine studio and sell my pictures for their weight in gold. But, instead of that, I'm one of the Thin; and I have to grind my life out in producing things which simply make the Fat ones shrug their shoulders. I shall die of it all in the end, I'm sure of it, with my skin clinging to my bones, and so flattened that they will be able to bury me between two leaves of a book. And you, too, you are one of the Thin, a wonderful one, the very king of the Thin, in fact! Do you remember your quarrel with the fishwives? It was magnificent; all those colossal bosoms flying at your scraggy breast! Oh! they were simply acting from natural instinct; they were pursuing one of the Thin just as cats pursue a mouse. The Fat, you know, have an instinctive hatred of the Thin, to such an extent that they must drive the latter from their sight, either by means of their teeth or their feet. And that is why, if I were in your place, I should take my precautions. The Quenus belong to the Fat, and so do the Méhudins; indeed, you have none but Fat ones around you. I should feel uneasy under such circumstances."

"And what about Gavard, and Mademoiselle Saget, and your friend Marjolin?" asked Florent, still smiling.

"Oh, if you like, I will classify all our acquaintances for you," replied Claude. "I've had their heads in a portfolio in my studio for a long time past, with memoranda of the order to which they belong. It's really a complete chapter in natural history. Gavard is one of the Fat, but of the kind which pretends to belong to the Thin. The variety is by no means uncommon. Mademoiselle Saget and Madame Lecœur belong to the Thin, but to a variety which is much to be feared—the Thin ones whom envy drives to despair, and who are capable of anything in their craving to fatten themselves. My friend Marjolin, little Cadine, and La Sarriette are three Fat ones, still innocent, however, and having nothing but the guileless hunger of youth. I may remark that the Fat, so long as they've not grown old, are charming creatures. Monsieur Lebigre is one of the Fat—don't you think so? As for your political friends, Charvet, Clémence, Logre, and Lacaille, they mostly belong to the Thin. I only except that big animal Alexandre, and that prodigy Robine, who has caused me a vast amount of annoyance."

The artist continued to talk in this strain from the Pont de Neuilly to the Arc de Triomphe. He returned to some of those whom he had already mentioned and completed their portraits with a few characteristic touches. Logre, he said, was one of the Thin whose belly had been placed between his shoulders. Beautiful Lisa was all stomach, and the beautiful Norman all bosom. Mademoiselle Saget, in her earlier life, must have certainly lost some opportunity to fatten herself, for she detested the Fat, while, at the same time, she despised the Thin. As for Gavard, he was compromising his position as one of the Fat and would end by becoming as flat as a bug.

"And what about Madame François?" Florent asked.

Claude seemed much embarrassed by this question. He cast about for an answer and at last stammered:

"Madame François, Madame François—well, no, I really don't know; I never thought about classifying her. But she's a dear good soul, and that's quite sufficient. She's neither one of the Fat nor one of the Thin!"

They both laughed. They were now in front of the Arc de Triomphe. The sun, over by the hills of Suresnes, was so low on the horizon that their colossal shadows streaked the whiteness of the great structure even above the huge groups of statuary, like strokes made with a piece of charcoal. This increased Claude's merriment, he waved his arms and bent his body; and then, as he started on his way again, he said: "Did you notice—just as the sun set our two heads shot up to the sky!" But Florent no longer smiled. Paris was grasping him again, that Paris which now frightened him so much, after having cost him so many tears at Cayenne. When he reached the markets night was falling, and there was a suffocating smell. He bent his head as he once more returned to the nightmare of endless food, while preserving the sweet yet sad recollection of that day of bright health odorous with the perfume of thyme.

Chapter 5

A T A B O U T F O U R O ' C L O C K on the afternoon of the following day Lisa took herself to Saint Eustache. For the
short walk across the square she had arrayed herself very
seriously in a black silk gown and thick woollen shawl. The
handsome Norman, who, from her stall in the fish market,
watched her until she vanished into the church porch, was
quite amazed.

"Hallo! so the fat thing's gone in for priests now, has she?"
she exclaimed, with a sneer. "Well, a little holy water may do
her good!"

She was mistaken in her surmises, however, for Lisa was
not a devotée. She did not observe the ordinances of the
Church, but said that she did her best to lead an honest life,
and that this was all that was necessary. At the same time,
however, she disliked to hear religion spoken ill of and often silenced Gavard, who delighted in scandalous stories of
priests and their doings. Talk of that sort seemed to her altogether improper. Everyone, in her opinion, should be allowed to believe as they pleased, and every scruple should
be respected. Besides, the majority of the clergy were most
estimable men. She knew Abbé Roustan, of Saint Eustache—
a distinguished priest, a man of shrewd sense, and one, she
thought, whose friendship might be safely relied upon. And
she would wind up by explaining that religion was absolutely necessary for the people; she looked upon it as a sort
of police force that helped to maintain order, and without

which no government would be possible. When Gavard went too far on this subject and asserted that the priests ought to be turned into the streets and have their shops shut up, Lisa shrugged her shoulders and replied: "A great deal of good that would do! Why, before a month was over the people would be murdering one another in the streets, and you would be compelled to invent another God. That was just what happened in '93. You know very well that I'm not given to mixing with the priests, but for all that I say that they are necessary, as we couldn't do without them."

And so when Lisa happened to enter a church she always manifested the utmost decorum. She had bought a handsome missal, which she never opened, for use when she was invited to a funeral or a wedding. She knelt and rose at the proper times and made a point of conducting herself with all propriety. She assumed, indeed, what she considered a sort of official demeanor, such as all well-to-do folks, tradespeople, and house owners ought to observe with regard to religion.

As she entered Saint Eustache that afternoon she let the double doors, covered with green baize, faded and worn by the frequent touch of pious hands, close gently behind her. Then she dipped her fingers in the holy water and crossed herself in the correct fashion. And afterwards, with hushed footsteps, she made her way to the chapel of Saint Agnes, where two kneeling women with their faces buried in their hands were waiting, while the blue skirts of a third protruded from the confessional. Lisa seemed rather put out by the sight of these women, and, addressing a verger who happened to pass along, wearing a black skullcap and dragging his feet over the slabs, she inquired: "Is this Monsieur l'Abbé Roustan's day for hearing confessions?"

The verger replied that his reverence had only two more penitents waiting, and that they would not detain him long, so that if Lisa would take a chair her turn would speedily come. She thanked him, without telling him that she had not come to confess; and, making up her mind to wait, she began to pace the church, going as far as the chief entrance, from where she gazed at the lofty, severe, bare nave stretching between the brightly colored aisles. Raising her head a little, she examined the high altar, which she considered too plain, having no taste for the cold grandeur of stonework, but preferring the gilding and gaudy coloring of the side chapels. Those on the side of the Rue du Jour looked grayish in the light which filtered through their dusty windows, but on the side of the markets the sunset was lighting up the stained glass with lovely tints, limpid greens and yellows in particular, which reminded Lisa of the bottles of liqueurs in front of Monsieur Lebigre's mirror. She came back by this side, which seemed to be warmed by the glow of light, and took a passing interest in the reliquaries, altar ornaments, and paintings steeped in prismatic reflections. The church was empty, quivering with the silence that fell from its vaulted roofing. Here and there a woman's dress showed like a dark splotch amid the vague yellow of the chairs; and a low buzzing came from the closed confessionals. As Lisa again passed the chapel of Saint Agnes she saw the blue dress still kneeling at Abbé Roustan's feet.

"Why, if I'd wanted to confess I could have said everything in ten seconds," she thought, proud of her irreproachable integrity.

Then she went on to the end of the church. Behind the high altar, in the gloom of a double row of pillars, is the chapel of the Blessed Virgin, damp and dark and silent. The dim stained windows only show the flowing crimson and violet robes of saints, which blaze like flames of mystic love in the solemn, silent adoration of the darkness. It is a weird, mysterious spot, like some crepuscular nook of paradise solely illumined by the gleaming stars of two tapers. The four brass lamps hanging from the roof remain unlighted and are but faintly seen; on spying them you think of the golden censers which the angels swing before the throne of Mary. And kneeling on the chairs between the pillars there are always women surrendering themselves languorously to the dim spot's voluptuous charm.

Lisa stood and gazed tranquilly around her. She did not feel the least emotion, but considered that it was a mistake not to light the lamps. Their brightness would have given the place a more cheerful look. The gloom even struck her as savoring of impropriety. Her face was warmed by the flames of some candles burning in a candelabrum by her side, and an old woman armed with a big knife was scraping off the wax which had trickled down and congealed into pale tears. And amid the quivering silence, the mute ecstasy of adoration prevailing in the chapel, Lisa could distinctly hear the rumbling of the vehicles turning out of the Rue Montmartre, behind the scarlet and purple saints on the windows, while in the distance the markets roared without a moment's pause.

Just as Lisa was leaving the chapel, she saw the younger of the Méhudins, Claire, the dealer in fresh water fish, come in. The girl lighted a taper at the candelabrum, and then went to kneel behind a pillar, her knees pressed upon the hard stones, and her face so pale beneath her loose fair hair that she seemed a corpse. And believing herself to be securely screened from observation, she gave way to violent emotion and wept hot tears with a passionate outpouring of prayer which bent her like a rushing wind. Lisa looked on in amazement, for the Méhudins were not known to be particularly pious; indeed, Claire was accustomed to speak of religion and priests in such terms as to horrify one.

"What's the meaning of this, I wonder?" pondered Lisa, as she again made her way to the chapel of St. Agnes. "The hussy must have been poisoning someone or other."

Abbé Roustan was at last coming out of his confessional. He was a handsome man, of some forty years of age, with a smiling, kindly air. When he recognized Madame Quenu he grasped her hand, called her "dear lady," and conducted her to the vestry, where, taking off his surplice, he told her that he would be entirely at her service in a moment. They returned, the priest in his cassock, bareheaded, and Lisa strutting along in her shawl, and paced up and down in front of the side-chapels adjacent to the Rue du Jour. They conversed together in low tones. The sunlight was departing from the stained windows, the church was growing dark, and the retreating footsteps of the last worshippers sounded but faintly over the flagstones.

Lisa explained her doubts and scruples to Abbé Roustan. There had never been any question of religion between them; she never confessed, but merely consulted him in cases of difficulty, because he was shrewd and discreet, and she preferred him, as she sometimes said, to shady business men redolent of the galleys. The abbé, on his side, manifested inexhaustible complaisance. He looked up points of law for her in the Code, pointed out profitable investments, resolved her moral difficulties with great tact, recommended tradespeople to her, invariably having an answer ready however diverse and complicated her requirements might be. And he supplied all this help in a natural matter-of-fact way without ever introducing the Deity into his talk, or seeking to obtain any advantage either for himself or the cause of religion. A word of thanks and a smile sufficed him. He seemed glad to have an opportunity of obliging that handsome Madame Quenu, of whom his housekeeper often spoke to him in terms of praise, as of a woman who was highly respected in the neighborhood.

Their consultation that afternoon was of a peculiarly delicate nature. Lisa was anxious to know what steps she might legitimately take, as a woman of honor, with respect to her brother-in-law. Had she a right to keep a watch upon him and to do what she could to prevent him from compromising her husband, her daughter, and herself? And then how far might she go in circumstances of pressing danger? She did not bluntly put these questions to the abbé, but asked them with such skillful circumlocutions that he was able to discuss the matter without entering into personalities. He brought forward arguments on both sides of the question, but the conclusion he came to was that a person of integrity was entitled, indeed bound, to prevent evil, and was justified in using whatever means might be necessary to ensure the triumph of that which was right and proper.

"That is my opinion, dear lady," he said in conclusion. "The question of means is always a very grave one. It is a snare in which souls of average virtue often become entangled. But I know your scrupulous conscience. Deliberate carefully over each step you think of taking, and if it contains nothing repugnant to you, go on boldly. Pure natures have the marvelous gift of purifying all that they touch."

Then, changing his tone of voice, he continued: "Pray give my kind regards to Monsieur Quenu. I'll come in to kiss my dear little Pauline some time when I'm passing. And now good-bye, dear lady; remember that I'm always at your service."

Thereupon he returned to the vestry. Lisa, on her way out, was curious to see if Claire was still praying, but the girl had gone back to her eels and carp; and in front of the Ladychapel, which was already shrouded in darkness, there was now but a litter of chairs overturned by the ardent vehemence of the women who had knelt there.

When handsome Lisa again crossed the square, La Normande, who had been watching for her exit from the church, recognized her in the twilight by the rotundity of her skirts.

"Good gracious!" she exclaimed, "she's been more than an hour in there! When the priests set about cleansing her of her sins, the choir boys have to form in line to pass the buckets of filth and empty them in the street!"

The next morning Lisa went straight up to Florent's bedroom and settled herself there with perfect equanimity. She felt certain that she would not be disturbed, and, moreover, she had made up her mind to tell a falsehood and say that she had come to see if the linen was clean should Florent by any chance return. While in the shop, however, she had observed him busily engaged in the fish market. Seating herself in front of the little table, she pulled out the drawer, placed it upon her knees, and began to examine its contents, taking the greatest care to restore them to their original positions.

First of all she came upon the opening chapters of the work on Cayenne; then upon the drafts of Florent's various plans and projects, his schemes for converting the Octroi duties into taxes upon sales, for reforming the administrative system of the markets, and all the others. These pages of small writing, which she set herself to read, bored her extremely, and she was about to restore the drawer to its place, feeling convinced that Florent concealed the proofs of his wicked designs elsewhere, and already contemplating a searching visitation of his mattress, when she discovered a photograph of La Normande in an envelope. The impression was rather dark. La Normande was standing up with her right arm resting on a broken column. Decked out with her jewels, and attired in a new silk dress, the fish girl was smiling impudently, and Lisa, at the sight, forgot all about her brother-in-law, her fears, and the purpose for which she had come into the room. She became quite absorbed in her examination of the portrait, as often happens when one woman scrutinizes the photograph of another at her ease, without fear of being seen. Never before had she had so favorable an opportunity to study her rival. She scrutinized her hair, her nose, her mouth; held the photograph at a distance, and then brought it closer again. And, finally, with compressed lips, she read on the back of it, in a big, ugly scrawl: "Louise, to her friend Florent." This quite scandalized her; to her mind it was a confession, and she felt a strong impulse to take possession of the photograph, and keep it as a weapon against her enemy. However, she slowly replaced it in the envelope on coming to the conclusion that this course would be wrong, and reflecting that she would always know where to find it should she want it again.

Then, as she again began turning over the loose sheets of paper, it occurred to her to look at the back end of the drawer, where Florent had relegated Augustine's needles and thread; and there, between the missal and the Dream-book, she discovered what she sought, some extremely compromising memoranda, simply screened from observation by a wrapper of gray paper.

That idea of an insurrection, of the overthrow of the Empire by means of an armed rising, which Logre had one evening propounded at Monsieur Lebigre's, had slowly ripened in Florent's feverish brain. He soon grew to see a duty, a mission in it. Therein undoubtedly lay the task to which his escape from Cayenne and his return to Paris predestined him.

Believing in a call to avenge his leanness upon the city which wallowed in food while the upholders of right and equity were racked by hunger in exile, he took upon himself the duties of a justiciary, and dreamt of rising up, even in the midst of those markets, to sweep away the reign of gluttony and drunkenness. In a sensitive nature like his, this idea quickly took root. Everything about him assumed exaggerated proportions, the wildest fancies possessed him. He imagined that the markets had been conscious of his arrival, and had seized hold of him that they might enervate him and poison him with their stenches. Then, too, Lisa wanted to cast a spell over him, and for two or three days at a time he would avoid her, as though she were some dissolving agency which would destroy all his power of will should he approach too closely. However, these paroxysms of puerile fear, these wild surgings of his rebellious brain, always ended in thrills of the gentlest tenderness, with yearnings to love and be loved, which he concealed with a boyish shame.

It was more especially in the evening that his mind became blurred by all his wild imaginings. Depressed by his day's work, but shunning sleep from a covert fear—the fear of the annihilation it brought with it—he would remain later than ever at Monsieur Lebigre's, or at the Méhudins'; and on his return home he still refrained from going to bed and sat up writing and preparing for the great insurrection. By slow degrees he devised a complete system of organization. He divided Paris into twenty sections, one for each arrondissement. Each section would have a chief, a sort of general, under whose orders there were to be twenty lieutenants commanding twenty companies of affiliated associates. Every week, among the chiefs, there would be a consultation, which was to be held in a different place each time; and, the better to ensure secrecy and discretion, the associates would only come in contact with their respective lieutenants, these alone communicating with the chiefs of the sections. It also occurred to Florent that it would be as well that the companies of associates should believe themselves charged with imaginary missions, as a means of putting the police upon a wrong scent.

As for the employment of the insurrectionary forces, that would be all simplicity. It would, of course, be necessary to wait till the companies were quite complete, and then advantage would be taken of the first public commotion. They would doubtless only have a certain number of guns used for sporting purposes in their possession, so they would commence by seizing the police stations and guard houses, disarming the police, the Gardes de Paris, the firemen, and the soldiers of the line; resorting to violence as little as possible and inviting the men to make common cause with the people. Afterwards they would march upon the Corps Législatif, and from there proceed to the Hôtel de Ville. This plan, to which Florent returned night after night, as though it were some dramatic scenario which relieved his over-excited nervous system, was as yet simply jotted down on scraps of paper, full of erasures, which showed how the writer had felt his way, and revealed each successive phase of his scientific yet puerile conception. When Lisa had glanced through the notes, without understanding some of them, she remained there trembling with fear; afraid to touch them further lest they should explode in her hands like live shells.

A last memorandum frightened her more than any of the others. It was a half-sheet of paper on which Florent had sketched the distinguishing insignia which the chiefs and the lieutenants were to wear. By the side of these were rough drawings of the standards which the different companies were to carry; and notes in pencil even described what colors the banners should assume. The chiefs were to wear red scarves, and the lieutenants red armlets.

To Lisa this seemed like an immediate realization of the rising; she saw all the men with their red badges marching past the pork shop, firing bullets into her mirrors and marble, and carrying off sausages and chitterlings from the window. The infamous projects of her brother-in-law were surely directed against herself—against her own happiness. She closed the drawer and looked round the room, reflecting that it was she herself who had provided this man with a home—

that he slept between her sheets and used her furniture. And she was especially exasperated at his keeping his abominable infernal machine in that little deal table which she herself had used at Uncle Gradelle's before her marriage—a perfectly innocent, rickety little table.

For a while she stood thinking what she should do. In the first place, it was useless to say anything to Quenu. For a moment it occurred to her to provoke an explanation with Florent, but she dismissed that idea, fearing lest he would only go and perpetrate his crime elsewhere, and maliciously make a point of compromising them. Then gradually growing somewhat calmer, she came to the conclusion that her best plan would be to keep a careful watch over her brother-in-law. It would be time enough to take further steps at the first sign of danger. She already had quite sufficient evidence to send him back to the galleys.

On returning to the shop again, she found Augustine in a state of great excitement. Little Pauline had disappeared more than half an hour before, and to Lisa's anxious questions the young woman could only reply: "I don't know where she can have got to, madame. She was on the pavement there with a little boy. I was watching them, and then I had to cut some ham for a gentleman, and I never saw them again."

"I'll wager it was Muche!" cried Lisa. "Ah, the young scoundrel!"

It was, indeed, Muche who had enticed Pauline away. The little girl, who was wearing a new blue-striped frock that day for the first time, had been anxious to exhibit it, and had accordingly taken her stand outside the shop, manifesting great propriety of bearing, and compressing her lips with the grave expression of a little woman of six who is afraid of soiling her clothes. Her short and stiffly-starched petticoats stood out like the skirts of a ballet girl, allowing a full view of her tightly-stretched white stockings and little sky-blue boots. Her pinafore, which hung low about her neck, was finished off at the shoulders with an edging of embroidery, below which appeared her pretty little arms, bare and rosy. She had small turquoise rings in her ears, a cross at her neck, a blue velvet ribbon in her well-brushed hair; and she displayed all her mother's plumpness and softness—the gracefulness, indeed, of a new doll.

Muche had caught sight of her from the market, where he was amusing himself by dropping little dead fishes into the gutter, following them along the curb as the water carried them away, and declaring that they were swimming. However, the sight of Pauline standing in front of the shop and looking so smart and pretty made him cross over to her, capless as he was, with his blouse ragged, his trousers slipping down, and his whole appearance suggestive of a seven-year-old street urchin. His mother had certainly forbidden him to play any more with "that fat booby of a girl who was stuffed by her parents till she almost burst"; so he stood hesitating for a moment, but at last came up to Pauline, and wanted to feel her pretty striped frock. The little girl, who had at first felt flattered, then put on a prim air and stepped back, exclaiming in a tone of displeasure: "Leave me alone. Mother says I'm not to have anything to do with you."

This brought a laugh to the lips of Muche, who was a wily, enterprising young scamp.

"What a little bore you are!" he retorted. "What does it matter what your mother says? Let's go and play at shoving each other, eh?"

He doubtless nourished some wicked idea of dirtying the neat little girl; but she, on seeing him prepare to give her a push in the back, retreated as though about to return inside the shop. Muche then adopted a flattering tone like a born cajoler.

"You silly! I didn't mean it," said he. "How nice you look like that! Is that little cross your mother's?"

Pauline perked herself up, and replied that it was her own, whereupon Muche gently led her to the corner of the Rue Pirouette, touching her skirts the while and expressing his astonishment at their wonderful stiffness. All this pleased the little girl immensely. She had been very much vexed at not receiving any notice while she was exhibiting herself outside the shop. However, in spite of all Muche's blandishments, she still refused to leave the footway.

"You stupid fatty!" thereupon exclaimed the youngster, relapsing into coarseness. "I'll squat you down in the gutter if you don't look out, Miss Fine-airs!"

The girl was dreadfully alarmed. Muche had caught hold of her by the hand; but, recognizing his mistake in policy, he again put on a wheedling air and began to fumble in his pocket.

"I've got a sou," said he.

The sight of the coin had a soothing effect upon Pauline. The boy held up the sou with the tips of his fingers, and the temptation to follow it proved so great that the girl at last stepped down into the roadway. Muche's diplomacy was eminently successful.

"What do you like best?" he asked.

Pauline gave no immediate answer. She could not make up her mind; there were so many things that she liked. Muche, however, ran over a whole list of dainties—licorice, molasses, gum balls, and powdered sugar. The powdered sugar made the girl ponder. One dipped one's fingers into it and sucked them; it was very nice. For a while she gravely considered the matter. Then, at last making up her mind, she said:

"No, I like the mixed screws the best."

Muche then took hold of her arm, and she unresistingly allowed him to lead her away. They crossed the Rue

Rambuteau, followed the broad footway skirting the markets, and went as far as a grocer's shop in the Rue de la Cossonnerie which was celebrated for its mixed screws. These mixed screws are small screws of paper in which grocers put up all sorts of damaged odds and ends, broken sugarplums, fragments of crystallized chestnuts—all the doubtful residuum of their jars of sweets. Muche showed himself very gallant, allowed Pauline to choose the screw—a blue one—paid his sou, and did not attempt to dispossess her of the sweets. Outside, on the footway, she emptied the miscellaneous collection of scraps into both pockets of her pinafore; and they were such little pockets that they were quite filled. Then in delight she began to munch the fragments one by one, wetting her fingers to catch the fine sugary dust, with such effect that she melted the scraps of sweets, and the pockets of her pinafore soon showed two brownish stains. Muche laughed slyly to himself. He had his arm about the girl's waist and rumpled her frock at his ease while leading her round the corner of the Rue Pierre Lescot, in the direction of the Place des Innocents.

"You'll come and play now, won't you?" he asked. "That's nice what you've got in your pockets, ain't it? You see that I didn't want to do you any harm, you big silly!"

Thereupon he plunged his own fingers into her pockets, and they entered the square together. To this spot, no doubt, he had all along intended to lure his victim. He did the honors of the square as though it were his own private property, and indeed it was a favorite haunt of his, where he often larked about for whole afternoons. Pauline had never before strayed so far from home, and would have wept like an abducted damsel had it not been that her pockets were full of sweets. The fountain in the middle of the flowered lawn was sending sheets of water down its tiers of basins, while, between the pilasters above, Jean Goujon's nymphs, looking very white beside the dingy gray stonework, inclined their urns and displayed their nude graces in the grimy air of the Saint Denis quarter. The two children walked round the fountain, watching the water fall into the basins, and taking an interest in the grass, with thoughts, no doubt, of crossing the central lawn, or gliding into the clumps of holly and rhododendrons that bordered the railings of the square. Little Muche, however, who had now effectually rumpled the back of the pretty frock, said, with his sly smile:

"Let's play at throwing sand at each other, eh?"

Pauline had no will of her own left; and they began to throw the sand at each other, keeping their eyes closed meanwhile. The sand made its way in at the neck of the girl's low bodice, and trickled down into her stockings and boots. Muche was delighted to see the white pinafore become quite yellow. But he doubtless considered that it was still far too clean.

"Let's go and plant trees, shall we?" he exclaimed suddenly. "I know how to make such pretty gardens."

"Really, gardens!" murmured Pauline full of admiration.

Then, as the keeper of the square happened to be absent, Muche told her to make some holes in one of the borders; and dropping on her knees in the middle of the soft mould, and leaning forward till she lay at full length on her stomach, she dug her pretty little arms into the ground. He, meantime, began to hunt for scraps of wood and broke off branches. These were the garden trees which he planted in the holes that Pauline made. He invariably complained, however, that the holes were not deep enough, and rated the girl as though she were an idle workman and he an indignant master. When she at last got up, she was black from head to foot. Her hair was full of mould, her face was smeared with it, she looked such a sight with her arms as black as a coalheaver's that Muche clapped his hands with glee, and exclaimed: "Now we must water the trees. They won't grow, you know, if we don't water them."

That was the finishing stroke. They went outside the square, scooped the gutter water up in the palms of their hands, and then ran back to pour it over the bits of wood. On the way, Pauline, who was so fat that she couldn't run properly, let the water trickle between her fingers on to her frock, so that by the time of her sixth journey she looked as if she had been rolled in the gutter. Muche chuckled with delight on beholding her dreadful condition. He made her sit down beside him under a rhododendron near the garden they had made, and told her that the trees were already beginning to grow. He had taken hold of her hand and called her his little wife.

"You're not sorry now that you came, are you," he asked, "instead of mooning about on the pavement, where there was nothing to do? I know all sorts of fun we can have in the streets; you must come with me again. You will, won't you? But you mustn't say anything to your mother, mind. If you say a word to her, I'll pull your hair the next time I come past your shop."

Pauline consented to everything; and then, as a last attention, Muche filled both pockets of her pinafore with mould. However, all the sweets were finished, and the girl began to get uneasy and ceased playing. Muche then started pinching her, and she burst into tears, sobbing that she wanted to go away. But at this the lad only grinned and played the bully, threatening that he would not take her home at all. Then she grew terribly alarmed and sobbed and gasped like a maiden in the power of a libertine. Muche would certainly have ended by punching her in order to stop her row, had not a shrill voice, the voice of Mademoiselle Saget, exclaimed, close by: "Why, I declare it's Pauline! Leave her alone, you wicked young scoundrel!"

Then the old maid took the girl by the hand, with end-less expressions of amazement at the pitiful condition of her clothes. Muche showed no alarm, but followed them, chuck-ling to himself, and declaring that it was Pauline who had wanted to come with him and had tumbled down.

Mademoiselle Saget was a regular frequenter of the Square des Innocents. Every afternoon she would spend a good hour there to keep herself well posted in the gossip of the common people. On either side there is a long crescent of benches placed end to end; and on these the poor folks who stifle in the hovels of the neighboring narrow streets as-semble in crowds. There are withered, chilly-looking old women in tumbled caps and young ones in loose jackets and carelessly fastened skirts, with bare heads and tired, faded faces, eloquent of the wretchedness of their lives. There are some men also: tidy old men, porters in greasy jackets, and equivocal-looking individuals in black silk hats, while the foot path is overrun by a swarm of youngsters dragging toy carts without wheels about, filling pails with sand, and screaming and fighting; a dreadful crew, with ragged clothes and dirty noses, teeming in the sunshine like vermin.

Mademoiselle Saget was so slight and thin that she al-ways managed to insinuate herself into a place on one of the benches. She listened to what was being said and started a conversation with her neighbor, some sallow-faced workingman's wife, who sat mending linen, from time to time producing handkerchiefs and stockings riddled with holes from a little basket patched up with string. Moreover, Mademoiselle Saget had plenty of acquaintances here. Amid the excruciating squalling of the children and the ceaseless rumble of the traffic in the Rue Saint Denis, she took part in no end of gossip, everlasting tales about the tradesmen of the neighborhood, the grocers, the butchers, and the bak-ers, enough, indeed, to fill the columns of a local paper, and the whole envenomed by refusals of credit and covert envy, such as is always harbored by the poor. From these wretched creatures she also obtained the most disgusting revelations, the gossip of low lodging houses and doorkeepers' hovels, all the filthy scandal of the neighborhood, which tickled her inquisitive appetite like hot spice.

As she sat with her face turned towards the markets, she had immediately in front of her the square and its three blocks of houses, into the windows of which her eyes tried to pry. She seemed to gradually rise and traverse the successive floors right up to the garret skylights. She stared at the curtains; based an entire drama on the appearance of a head between two shutters; and, by simply gazing at the façades, ended by knowing the history of all the dwellers in these houses. The Baratte Restaurant, with its wine shop, its gilt wrought-iron *marquise*, forming a sort of terrace from which peeped the foliage of a few plants in flower-pots, and its four low stories, all painted and decorated, had a special interest for her. She gazed at its yellow columns standing out against a background of tender blue, at the whole of its imitation temple front daubed on the façade of a decrepit, tumble-down house, crowned at the summit by a parapet of painted zinc. Behind the red-striped window blinds she spied visions of nice little lunches, delicate suppers, and uproarious, unlimited orgies. And she did not hesitate to invent lies about the place. It was there, she declared, that Florent came to gorge with those two hussies, the Méhudins, on whom he lavished his money.

However, Pauline cried yet louder than before when the old maid took hold of her hand. Mademoiselle Saget at first led her towards the gate of the square; but before she got there she seemed to change her mind; for she sat down at the end of a bench and tried to pacify the child.

"Come, now, give over crying, or the policeman will lock

you up," she said to Pauline. "I'll take you home safely. You know me, don't you? I'm a good friend. Come, come, let me see how prettily you can smile."

The child, however, was choking with sobs and wanted to go away. Mademoiselle Saget quietly allowed her to continue weeping, reserving further remarks until she should have finished. The poor little creature was shivering all over; her petticoats and stockings were wet through, and as she wiped her tears away with her dirty hands she plastered the whole of her face with earth to the very tips of her ears. When at last she became a little calmer the old maid resumed in a caressing tone: "Your mamma isn't unkind, is she? She's very fond of you, isn't she?"

"Oh, yes, indeed," replied Pauline, still sobbing.

"And your papa, he's good to you, too, isn't he? He doesn't flog you, or quarrel with your mother, does he? What do they talk about when they go to bed?"

"Oh, I don't know. I'm asleep then."

"Do they talk about your cousin Florent?"

"I don't know."

Mademoiselle Saget thereupon assumed a severe expression and got up as if about to go away.

"I'm afraid you are a little story-teller," she said. "Don't you know that it's very wicked to tell stories? I shall go away and leave you, if you tell me lies, and then Muche will come back and pinch you."

Pauline began to cry again at the threat of being abandoned. "Be quiet, be quiet, you wicked little imp!" cried the old maid, shaking her. "There, there, now, I won't go away. I'll buy you a stick of barley-sugar; yes, a stick of barley-sugar! So you don't love your cousin Florent, eh?"

"No, mamma says he isn't good."

"Ah, then, so you see your mother does say something."

"One night when I was in bed with Mouton—I sleep with

Mouton sometimes, you know—I heard her say to father, 'Your brother has only escaped from the galleys to take us all back with him there.'"

Mademoiselle Saget gave vent to a faint cry and sprang to her feet, quivering all over. A ray of light had just broken upon her. Then without a word she caught hold of Pauline's hand and made her run till they reached the pork shop, her lips meanwhile compressed by an inward smile, and her eyes glistening with keen delight. At the corner of the Rue Pirouette, Muche, who had so far followed them, amused at seeing the girl running along in her muddy stockings, prudently disappeared.

Lisa was now in a state of terrible alarm; and when she saw her daughter so bedraggled and limp, her consternation was such that she turned the child round and round, without even thinking of beating her.

"She has been with little Muche," said the old maid, in her malicious voice. "I took her away at once, and I've brought her home. I found them together in the square. I don't know what they've been up to; but that young vagabond is capable of anything."

Lisa could not find a word to say; and she did not know where to take hold of her daughter, so great was her disgust at the sight of the child's muddy boots, soiled stockings, torn skirts, and filthy face and hands. The blue velvet ribbon, the earrings, and the necklace were all concealed beneath a crust of mud. But what put the finishing touch to Lisa's exasperation was the discovery of the two pockets filled with mould. She stooped and emptied them, regardless of the pink and white flooring of the shop. And as she dragged Pauline away, she could only gasp: "Come along, you filthy thing!"

Quite enlivened by this scene, Mademoiselle Saget now hurriedly made her way across the Rue Rambuteau. Her little feet scarcely touched the ground; her joy seemed to carry her along like a breeze which fanned her with a caressing touch. She had at last found out what she had so much wanted to know! For nearly a year she had been consumed by curiosity, and now at a single stroke she had gained complete power over Florent! This was unhoped-for contentment, positive salvation, for she felt that Florent would have brought her to the tomb had she failed much longer in satisfying her curiosity about him. At present she was complete mistress of the whole neighborhood of the markets. There was no longer any gap in her information. She could have narrated the secret history of every street, shop by shop. And thus, as she entered the fruit market, she fairly gasped with delight, in a perfect transport of pleasure.

"Hallo, Mademoiselle Saget," cried La Sarriette from her stall, "what are you smiling to yourself like that about? Have you won the grand prize in the lottery?"

"No, no. Ah, my dear, if you only knew!"

Standing there amid her fruit, La Sarriette, in her picturesque disarray, looked charming. Frizzy hair fell over her brow like vine branches. Her bare arms and neck, indeed all the rosy flesh she showed, bloomed with the freshness of peach and cherry. She had playfully hung some cherries on her ears, black cherries which dangled against her cheeks when she stooped, shaking with merry laughter. She was eating currants, and her merriment arose from the way in which she was smearing her face with them. Her lips were bright red, glistening with the juice of the fruit, as though they had been painted and perfumed with some seraglio face paint. A perfume of plum exhaled from her gown, while from the kerchief carelessly fastened across her breast came an odor of strawberries.

Fruits of all kinds were piled around her in her narrow stall. On the shelves at the back were rows of melons, "cantaloupes" swarming with wart-like knots, "maraîchers" whose skin was covered with gray lacelike netting, and "culs-de-singe" displaying smooth bare bumps. In front was an array of choice fruits, carefully arranged in baskets, and showing like smooth round cheeks seeking to hide themselves, or glimpses of sweet childish faces, half veiled by leaves. Especially was this the case with the peaches, the blushing peaches of Montreuil, with skin as delicate and clear as that of northern maidens, and the yellow, sun-burnt peaches from the south, brown like the damsels of Provence. The apricots, on their beds of moss, gleamed with the hue of amber or with that sunset glow which so warmly colors the necks of brunettes at the nape, just under the little wavy curls which fall below the chignon. The cherries, ranged one by one, resembled the short lips of smiling Chinese girls; the Montmorencies suggested the dumpy mouths of buxom women; the English ones were longer and graver-looking; the common black ones seemed as though they had been bruised and crushed by kisses; while the white-hearts, with their patches of rose and white, appeared to smile with mingled merriment and vexation. Then piles of apples and pears, built up with architectural symmetry, often in pyramids, displayed the ruddy glow of budding breasts and the gleaming sheen of shoulders, quite a show of nudity, lurking modestly behind a screen of fern leaves. There were all sorts of varieties—little red ones so tiny that they seemed to be yet in the cradle, shapeless "rambours" for baking, "calvilles" in light yellow gowns, sanguineous-looking "Canadas," blotched "châtaignier" apples, fair, freckled rennets and dusky russets. Then came the pears—the "blanquettes," the "British queens," the "beurrés," the "messirejeans," and the "duchesses"—some dumpy, some long and tapering, some with slender necks, and others with thick-set shoulders, their green and yellow bellies picked out at times with a splotch of carmine. By the side of these the transparent plums resembled tender, chlorotic virgins; the greengages and the Orleans plums paled as with modest innocence, while the mirabelles lay like the golden beads of a rosary forgotten in a box among sticks of vanilla. And the strawberries exhaled a sweet perfume—a perfume of youth—especially those little ones which are gathered in the woods, and which are far more aromatic than the large ones grown in gardens, for these breathe an insipid odor suggestive of the watering pot. Raspberries added their fragrance to the pure scent. The currants—red, white, and black—smiled with a knowing air; while the heavy clusters of grapes, laden with intoxication, lay languorously at the edges of their wicker baskets, over the sides of which dangled some of the berries, scorched by the hot caresses of the voluptuous sun.

It was there that La Sarriette lived in an orchard, as it were, in an atmosphere of sweet, intoxicating scents. The cheaper fruits—the cherries, plums, and strawberries—were piled up in front of her in paper-lined baskets, and the juice oozing from their bruised ripeness stained the stall front and steamed, with a strong perfume, in the heat. She would feel quite giddy on those blazing July afternoons when the melons enveloped her with a powerful, vaporous odor of musk; and then with her loosened kerchief, fresh as she was with the springtide of life, she brought sudden temptation to all who saw her. It was she—it was her arms and neck which gave that semblance of amorous vitality to her fruit. On the stall next to her an old woman, a hideous old drunkard, displayed nothing but wrinkled apples, pears as flabby as herself, and cadaverous apricots of a witch-like sallowness. La Sarriette's stall, however, spoke of love and passion. The cherries looked like the red kisses of her bright lips; the silky peaches were not more delicate than her neck; to the plums she seemed to have lent the skin from her brow and chin; while some of her own crimson blood coursed through the veins of the currants. All the scents of the avenue of flowers behind her stall were but insipid beside the aroma of vitality which exhaled from her open baskets and falling kerchief.

That day she was quite intoxicated by the scent of a large arrival of mirabelle plums, which filled the market. She could plainly see that Mademoiselle Saget had learnt some great piece of news, and she wished to make her talk. But the old maid stamped impatiently while she repeated: "No, no; I've no time. I'm in a great hurry to see Madame Lecœur. I've just learnt something and no mistake. You can come with me, if you like."

As a matter of fact, she had simply gone through the fruit market for the purpose of enticing La Sarriette to go with her. The girl could not resist the temptation. Monsieur Jules, clean-shaven and as fresh as a cherub, was seated there, swaying to and fro on his chair.

"Just look after the stall for a minute, will you?" La Sarriette said to him. "I'll be back directly."

Jules, however, got up and called after her, in a thick voice: "Not I; no fear! I'm off! I'm not going to wait an hour for you, as I did the other day. And, besides, those cursed plums of yours quite make my head ache."

Then he calmly strolled off, with his hands in his pockets, and the stall was left to look after itself. Mademoiselle Saget went so fast that La Sarriette had to run. In the butter pavilion a neighbor of Madame Lecœur's told them that she was below in the cellar; and so, while La Sarriette went down to find her, the old maid installed herself amid the cheeses.

The cellar under the butter market is a very gloomy spot. The rows of storerooms are protected by a very fine wire meshing, as a safeguard against fire; and the gas jets, which are very few and far between, glimmer like yellow splotches destitute of radiance in the heavy, malodorous atmosphere beneath the low vault. Madame Lecœur, however, was at work on her butter at one of the tables placed parallel with the Rue Berger, and here a pale light filtered through the vent-holes. The tables, which are continually sluiced with a flood of water from the taps, are as white as though they were quite new. With her back turned to the pump in the rear, Madame Lecœur was kneading her butter in a kind of oak box. She took some of different sorts which lay beside her and mixed the varieties together, correcting one by another, just as is done in the blending of wines. Bent almost double, and showing sharp, bony shoulders, and arms bared to the elbows, as scraggy and knotted as pea rods, she dug her fists into the greasy paste in front of her, which was assuming a whitish and chalky appearance. It was trying work, and she heaved a sigh at each fresh effort.

"Mademoiselle Saget wants to speak to you, aunt," said La Sarriette.

Madame Lecœur stopped her work and pulled her cap over her hair with her greasy fingers, seemingly quite careless of staining it. "I've nearly finished. Ask her to wait a moment," she said.

"She's got something very particular to tell you," continued La Sarriette.

"I won't be more than a minute, my dear."

Then she again plunged her arms into the butter, which buried them up to the elbows. Previously softened in warm water, it covered Madame Lecœur's parchment-like skin as with an oily film and threw the big purple veins that streaked her flesh into strong relief. La Sarriette was quite disgusted by the sight of those hideous arms working so frantically amid the melting mass. However, she could recall the time when her own pretty little hands had manipulated the butter for whole afternoons at a time. It had even been a sort of almond paste to her, a cosmetic which had kept her skin white and her nails delicately pink; and even now her slender fingers retained the suppleness it had endowed them with.

"I don't think that butter of yours will be very good, aunt," she continued, after a pause. "Some of the sorts seem much too strong."

"I'm quite aware of that," replied Madame Lecœur, between a couple of groans. "But what can I do? I must use everything up. There are some folks who insist upon having butter cheap, and so cheap butter must be made for them. Oh! it's always quite good enough for those who buy it."

La Sarriette reflected that she would hardly care to eat butter which had been worked by her aunt's arms. Then she glanced at a little jar full of a sort of reddish dye. "Your coloring is too pale," she said.

This coloring-matter—"raucourt," as the Parisians call it— is used to give the butter a fine yellow tint. The butter women imagine that its composition is known only to themselves and keep it very secret. However, it is merely made from anotta; though a composition of carrots and marigolds is at times substituted for it.

"Come, do be quick!" La Sarriette now exclaimed, for she was getting impatient, and was, moreover, no longer accustomed to the malodorous atmosphere of the cellar. "Mademoiselle Saget will be going. I fancy she's got something very important to tell you about my uncle Gavard."

On hearing this, Madame Lecœur abruptly ceased working. She at once abandoned both butter and dye and did not even wait to wipe her arms. With a slight tap of her hand she settled her cap on her head again, and made her way up the steps, at her niece's heels, anxiously repeating: "Do you really think that she'll have gone away?"

She was reassured, however, on catching sight of Mademoiselle Saget amid the cheeses. The old maid had taken good care not to go away before Madame Lecœur's arrival. The three women seated themselves at the far end of the stall, crowding closely together, and their faces almost touching one another. Mademoiselle Saget remained silent for two long minutes, and then, seeing that the others were burning with curiosity, she began, in her shrill voice: "You know that Florent! Well, I can tell you now where he comes from."

For another moment she kept them in suspense; and then, in a deep, melodramatic voice, she said: "He comes from the galleys!"

The cheeses were reeking around the three women. On the two shelves at the far end of the stall were huge masses of butter: Brittany butters overflowing from baskets; Normandy butters, wrapped in canvas, and resembling models of stomachs over which some sculptor had thrown damp cloths to keep them from drying; while other great blocks had been cut into, fashioned into perpendicular rocky masses full of crevasses and valleys, and resembling fallen mountain crests gilded by the pale sun of an autumn evening.

Beneath the stall show table, formed of a slab of red marble veined with gray, baskets of eggs gleamed with a chalky whiteness; while on layers of straw in boxes were Bondons, placed end to end, and Gournays, arranged like medals, forming darker patches tinted with green. But it was upon the table that the cheeses appeared in greatest profusion. Here, by the side of the pound rolls of butter lying on white beet leaves, spread a gigantic Cantal cheese, cloven here and there as by an axe; then came a golden-hued Cheshire, and next a Gruyère, resembling a wheel fallen from some barbarian chariot; while farther on were some Dutch cheeses, suggesting decapitated heads suffused with dry blood, and having all that hardness of skulls which in France has gained them the name of "death's heads." Amid the heavy exhalations of

these, a Parmesan set a spicy aroma. Then there came three
Brie cheeses displayed on round platters and looking like
melancholy extinct moons. Two of them, very dry, were at
the full; the third, in its second quarter, was melting away in
a white cream, which had spread into a pool and flowed
over the little wooden barriers with which an attempt had
been made to arrest its course. Next came some Port Saluts,
similar to antique discs, with exergues bearing their makers'
names in print. A Romantour, in its tinfoil wrapper, suggested
a bar of nougat or some sweet cheese astray amid all these
pungent, fermenting curds. The Roqueforts under their glass
covers also had a princely air, their fat faces marbled with
blue and yellow, as though they were suffering from some
unpleasant malady such as attacks the wealthy gluttons who
eat too many truffles. And on a dish by the side of these, the
hard gray goats' milk cheeses, about the size of a child's fist,
resembled the pebbles which the billy goats send rolling
down the stony paths as they clamber along ahead of their
flocks. Next came the strong-smelling cheeses: the Mont
d'Ors, of a bright yellow hue, and exhaling a comparatively
mild odor; the Troyes, very thick, and bruised at the edges,
and of a far more pungent smell, recalling the dampness of
a cellar; the Camemberts, suggestive of high game; the square
Neufchâtels, Limbourgs, Marolles, and Pont l'Evêques, each
adding its own particular sharp scent to the malodorous bouquet, until it became perfectly pestilential; the Livarots, ruddy
in hue, and as irritating to the throat as sulphur fumes; and,
lastly, stronger than all the others, the Olivets, wrapped in
walnut leaves, like the carrion which peasants cover with
branches as it lies rotting in the hedgerow under the blazing
sun.

The heat of the afternoon had softened the cheeses; the
patches of mould on their crusts were melting and glisten-

ing with tints of ruddy bronze and verdigris. Beneath their cover of leaves, the skins of the Olivets seemed to be heaving as with the slow, deep respiration of a sleeping man. A Livarot was swarming with life; and in a fragile box behind the scales a Géromé flavored with aniseed diffused such a pestilential smell that all around it the very flies had fallen lifeless on the gray-veined slab of ruddy marble.

This Géromé was almost immediately under Mademoiselle Saget's nose; so she drew back and leaned her head against the big sheets of white and yellow paper which were hanging in a corner.

"Yes," she repeated, with an expression of disgust, "he comes from the galleys! Ah, those Quenu-Gradelles have no reason to put on so many airs!"

Madame Lecœur and La Sarriette, however, had burst into exclamations of astonishment: "It wasn't possible, surely! What had he done to be sent to the galleys? Could anyone, now, have ever suspected that Madame Quenu, whose virtue was the pride of the whole neighborhood, would choose a convict for a lover?"

"Ah, but you don't understand it at all!" cried the old maid impatiently. "Just listen, now, while I explain things. I was quite certain that I had seen that great lanky fellow somewhere before."

Then she proceeded to tell them Florent's story. She had recalled to mind a vague report which had circulated of a nephew of old Gradelle being transported to Cayenne for murdering six gendarmes at a barricade. She had even seen this nephew on one occasion in the Rue Pirouette. The pretended cousin was undoubtedly the same man. Then she began to bemoan her waning powers. Her memory was quite going, she said; she would soon be unable to remember anything. And she bewailed her perishing memory as bitterly as any learned man might bewail the loss of his notes representing the work of a lifetime, on seeing them swept away by a gust of wind.

"Six gendarmes!" murmured La Sarriette, admiringly; "he must have a very heavy fist!"

"And he's made away with plenty of others, as well," added Mademoiselle Saget. "I shouldn't advise you to meet him at night!"

"What a villain!" stammered out Madame Lecœur, quite terrified.

The slanting beams of the sinking sun were now enfilading the pavilion, and the odor of the cheeses became stronger than ever. That of the Marolles seemed to predominate, borne this way and that in powerful whiffs. Then, however, the wind appeared to change, and suddenly the emanations of the Limbourgs were wafted towards the three women, pungent and bitter, like the last gasps of a dying man.

"But in that case," resumed Madame Lecœur, "he must be fat Lisa's brother-in-law. And we thought that he was her lover!"

The women exchanged glances. This aspect of the case took them by surprise. They were loth to give up their first theory. However, La Sarriette, turning to Mademoiselle Saget, remarked: "That must have been all wrong. Besides, you yourself say that he's always running after the two Méhudin girls."

"Certainly he is," exclaimed Mademoiselle Saget sharply, fancying that her word was doubted. "He dangles about them every evening. But, after all, it's no concern of ours, is it? We are virtuous women, and what he does makes no difference to us, the horrid scoundrel!"

"No, certainly not," agreed the other two. "He's a consummate villain."

The affair was becoming tragical. Of course beautiful Lisa

was now out of the question, but for this they found ample consolation in prophesying that Florent would bring about some frightful catastrophe. It was quite clear, they said, that he had got some base design in his head. When people like him escaped from jail it was only to burn everything down; and if he had come to the markets it must assuredly be for some abominable purpose. Then they began to indulge in the wildest suppositions. The two dealers declared that they would put additional padlocks to the doors of their store-rooms; and La Sarriette called to mind that a basket of peaches had been stolen from her during the previous week. Mademoiselle Saget, however, quite frightened the two others by informing them that that was not the way in which the Reds behaved; they despised such trifles as baskets of peaches; their plan was to band themselves together in companies of two or three hundred, kill everybody they came across, and then plunder and pillage at their ease. That was "politics," she said, with the superior air of one who knew what she was talking about. Madame Lecœur felt quite ill. She already saw Florent and his accomplices hiding in the cellars, and rushing out during the night to set the markets in flames and sack Paris.

"Ah! by the way," suddenly exclaimed the old maid, "now I think of it, there's all that money of old Gradelle's! Dear me, dear me, those Quenus can't be at all at their ease!"

She now looked quite gay again. The conversation took a fresh turn, and the others fell foul of the Quenus when Mademoiselle Saget had told them the history of the treasure discovered in the salting tub, with every particular of which she was acquainted. She was even able to inform them of the exact amount of the money found—eighty-five thousand francs—though neither Lisa nor Quenu was aware of having revealed this to a living soul. However, it was clear that the Quenus had not given the great lanky fellow his share. He was too shabbily dressed for that. Perhaps he had never even heard of the discovery of the treasure. Plainly enough, they were all thieves in his family. Then the three women bent their heads together and spoke in lower tones. They were unanimously of the opinion that it might perhaps be dangerous to attack the beautiful Lisa, but it was decidedly necessary that they should settle the Red Republican's hash, so that he might no longer prey upon the purse of poor Monsieur Gavard.

At the mention of Gavard there came a pause. The gossips looked at each other with a circumspect air. And then, as they drew breath, they inhaled the odor of the Camemberts, whose gamy scent had overpowered the less penetrating emanations of the Marolles and the Limbourgs, and spread around with remarkable power. Every now and then, however, a slight whiff, a flutelike note, came from the Parmesan while the Bries contributed a soft, musty scent, the gentle, insipid sound, as it were, of damp tambourines. Next followed an overpowering refrain from the Livarots, and afterwards the Géromé, flavored with aniseed, kept up the symphony with a high prolonged note, like that of a vocalist during a pause in the accompaniment.

"I have seen Madame Léonce," Mademoiselle Saget at last continued, with a significant expression.

At this the two others became extremely attentive. Madame Léonce was the doorkeeper of the house where Gavard lived in the Rue de la Cossonnerie. It was an old house standing back, with its ground floor occupied by an importer of oranges and lemons, who had had the frontage colored blue as high as the first floor. Madame Léonce acted as Gavard's housekeeper, kept the keys of his cupboards and closets, and brought him up tisane when he happened to catch cold. She was a severe-looking woman, between fifty and sixty years of age, and spoke slowly, but at endless length.

Mademoiselle Saget, who went to drink coffee with her every Wednesday evening, had cultivated her friendship more closely than ever since the poultry dealer had gone to lodge in the house. They would talk about the worthy man for hours at a time. They both professed the greatest affection for him and a keen desire to ensure his comfort and happiness.

"Yes, I have seen Madame Léonce," repeated the old maid. "We had a cup of coffee together last night. She was greatly worried. It seems that Monsieur Gavard never comes home now before one o'clock in the morning. Last Sunday she took him up some broth, as she thought he looked quite ill."

"Oh, she knows very well what she's about," exclaimed Madame Lecœur, whom these attentions to Gavard somewhat alarmed.

Mademoiselle Saget felt bound to defend her friend. "Oh, really, you are quite mistaken," said she. "Madame Léonce is much above her position; she is quite a lady. If she wanted to enrich herself at Monsieur Gavard's expense, she might easily have done so long ago. It seems that he leaves everything lying about in the most careless fashion. It's about that, indeed, that I want to speak to you. But you'll not repeat anything I say, will you? I am telling it to you in strict confidence."

Both the others swore that they would never breathe a word of what they might hear; and they craned out their necks with eager curiosity, while the old maid solemnly resumed: "Well, then, Monsieur Gavard has been behaving very strangely of late. He has been buying firearms—a great big pistol—one of those which revolve, you know. Madame Léonce says that things are awful, for this pistol is always lying about on the table or the mantelpiece; and she daren't dust anywhere near it. But that isn't all. His money—"

"His money!" echoed Madame Lecœur, with blazing cheeks.

"Well, he's disposed of all his stocks and shares. He's sold everything and keeps a great heap of gold in a cupboard."

"A heap of gold!" exclaimed La Sarriette in ecstasy.

"Yes, a great heap of gold. It covers a whole shelf and is quite dazzling. Madame Léonce told me that one morning Gavard opened the cupboard in her presence and that the money quite blinded her, it shone so."

There was another pause. The eyes of the three women were blinking as though the dazzling pile of gold was before them. Presently La Sarriette began to laugh.

"What a jolly time I would have with Jules if my uncle would give that money to me!" said she.

Madame Lecœur, however, seemed quite overwhelmed by this revelation, crushed beneath the weight of the gold which she could not banish from her sight. Covetous envy thrilled her. But at last, raising her skinny arms and shrivelled hands, her fingernails still stuffed with butter, she stammered in a voice full of bitter distress: "Oh, I mustn't think of it! It's too dreadful!"

"Well, it would all be yours, you know, if anything were to happen to Monsieur Gavard," retorted Mademoiselle Saget. "If I were in your place, I should look after my interests. That revolver means nothing good, you may depend upon it. Monsieur Gavard has got into the hands of evil counsellors and I'm afraid it will all end badly."

Then the conversation again turned upon Florent. The three women assailed him more violently than ever. And afterwards, with perfect composure, they began to discuss what would be the result of all these dark goings-on so far as he and Gavard were concerned; certainly it would be no pleasant one if there was any gossiping. And thereupon they swore that they themselves would never repeat a word of what they knew; not, however, because that scoundrel Florent merited any consideration, but because it was necessary, at all costs, to save that worthy Monsieur Gavard from being compromised. Then they rose from their seats, and Mademoiselle Saget was turning as if to go away when the butter dealer asked her: "All the same, in case of accident, do you think that Madame Léonce can be trusted? I dare say she has the key of the cupboard."

"Well, that's more than I can tell you," replied the old maid. "I believe she's a very honest woman; but, after all, there's no telling. There are circumstances, you know, which tempt the best of people. Anyhow, I've warned you both; and you must do what you think proper."

As the three women stood there, taking leave of each other, the odor of the cheeses seemed to become more pestilential than ever. It was a cacophony of smells, ranging from the heavily oppressive odor of the Dutch cheeses and the Gruyères to the alkaline pungency of the Olivets. From the Cantal, the Cheshire, and the goats' milk cheeses there seemed to come a deep breath like the sound of a bassoon, amid which the sharp, sudden whiffs of the Neufchâtels, the Troyes, and the Mont d'Ors contributed short, detached notes. And then the different odors appeared to mingle one with another, the reek of the Limbourgs, the Port Saluts, the Géromés, the Marolles, the Livarots, and the Pont l'Evêques uniting in one general, overpowering stench sufficient to provoke asphyxia. And yet it almost seemed as though it were not the cheeses but the vile words of Madame Lecœur and Mademoiselle Saget that diffused this awful odor.

"I'm very much obliged to you, indeed I am," said the butter dealer. "If ever I get rich, you shall not find yourself forgotten."

The old maid still lingered in the stall. Taking up a Bondon, she turned it round, and put it down on the slab again. Then she asked its price.

"To me!" she added, with a smile.

"Oh, nothing to you," replied Madame Lecœur. "I'll make you a present of it." And again she exclaimed: "Ah, if I were only rich!"

Mademoiselle Saget then told her that some day or other she would be rich. The Bondon had already disappeared within the old maid's bag. And now the butter dealer returned to the cellar, while Mademoiselle Saget escorted La Sarriette back to her stall. On reaching it they talked for a moment or two about Monsieur Jules. The fruits around them diffused a fresh scent of summer.

"It smells much nicer here than at your aunt's," said the old maid. "I felt quite ill a little time ago. I can't think how she manages to exist there. But here it's very sweet and pleasant. It makes you look quite rosy, my dear."

La Sarriette began to laugh, for she was fond of compliments. Then she served a lady with a pound of mirabelle plums, telling her that they were as sweet as sugar.

"I should like to buy some of those mirabelles too," murmured Mademoiselle Saget, when the lady had gone away; "only I want so few. A lone woman, you know."

"Take a handful of them," exclaimed the pretty brunette. "That won't ruin me. Send Jules back to me if you see him, will you? You'll most likely find him smoking his cigar on the first bench to the right as you turn out of the covered way."

Mademoiselle Saget distended her fingers as widely as possible in order to take a handful of mirabelles, which joined the Bondon in the bag. Then she pretended to leave the market, but in reality made a detour by one of the covered ways, thinking, as she walked slowly along, that the mirabelles and Bondon would not make a very substantial dinner. When she was unable, during her afternoon perambulations, to wheedle the stallkeepers into filling her bag for her, she was reduced to dining off the merest scraps. So she now slyly made her way back to the butter pavilion, where, on the side of the Rue Berger, at the back of the offices of the oyster salesmen, there were some stalls at which cooked meat was sold. Every morning little closed box-like carts, lined with zinc and furnished with ventilators, drew up in front of the larger Parisian kitchens and carried away the leavings of the restaurants, the embassies, and State Ministries. These leavings were conveyed to the market cellars and there sorted. By nine o'clock plates of food were displayed for sale at prices ranging from three to five sous, their contents comprising slices of meat, scraps of game, heads and tails of fishes, bits of galantine, stray vegetables, and, by way of dessert, cakes scarcely cut into, and other confectionery. Poor starving wretches, scantily-paid clerks, and women shivering with fever were to be seen crowding around, and the street lads occasionally amused themselves by hooting at the pale-faced individuals, known to be misers, who only made their purchases after slyly glancing about them to see that they were not observed. Mademoiselle Saget wriggled her way to a stall, the keeper of which boasted that the scraps she sold came exclusively from the Tuileries. One day, indeed, she had induced the old maid to buy a slice of leg of mutton by informing her that it had come from the plate of the Emperor himself; and this slice of mutton, eaten with no little pride, had been a soothing consolation to Mademoiselle Saget's vanity. The wariness of her approach to the stall was, moreover, solely caused by her desire to keep well with the neighboring shop people, whose premises she was eternally haunting without ever buying anything. Her usual tactics were to quarrel with them as soon as she had managed to learn their histories, when she would bestow her patronage upon a fresh set, desert it in due course, and then gradually make friends again with those with whom she had quarrelled. In this way she made the complete circuit of the market neighborhood, ferreting about in every shop and stall.

Anyone would have imagined that she consumed an enormous amount of provisions, whereas, in point of fact, she lived solely upon presents and the few scraps which she was compelled to buy when people were not in the giving vein.

On that particular evening there was only a tall old man standing in front of the stall. He was sniffing at a plate containing a mixture of meat and fish. Mademoiselle Saget, in her turn, began to sniff at a plate of cold fried fish. The price of it was three sous, but, by dint of bargaining, she got it for two. The cold fish then vanished into the bag. Other customers now arrived and with a uniform impulse lowered their noses over the plates. The smell of the stall was very disgusting, suggestive alike of greasy dishes and a dirty sink.

"Come and see me tomorrow," the stallkeeper called out to the old maid, "and I'll put something nice on one side for you. There's going to be a grand dinner at the Tuileries tonight."

Mademoiselle Saget was just promising to come, when, happening to turn round, she discovered Gavard looking at her and listening to what she was saying. She turned very red, and, contracting her skinny shoulders, hurried away, affecting not to recognize him. Gavard, however, followed her for a few yards, shrugging his shoulders and muttering to himself that he was no longer surprised at the old shrew's malice, now he knew that "she poisoned herself with the filth carted away from the Tuileries."

On the very next morning vague rumors began to circulate in the markets. Madame Lecœur and La Sarriette were in their own fashion keeping the oaths of silence they had taken. For her part, Mademoiselle Saget warily held her tongue, leaving the two others to circulate the story of Florent's antecedents. At first only a few meager details were hawked about in low tones; then various versions of the facts got into circulation, incidents were exaggerated, and gradually quite a legend was constructed, in which Florent played the part of a perfect bogey man. He had killed ten gendarmes at the barricade in the Rue Greneta, said some; he had returned to France on a pirate ship whose crew scoured the seas to murder everyone they came across, said others; while a third set declared that ever since his arrival he had been observed prowling about at nighttime with suspicious-looking characters, of whom he was undoubtedly the leader. Soon the imaginative market women indulged in the highest flights of fancy, revelled in the most melodramatic ideas. There was talk of a band of smugglers plying their nefarious calling in the very heart of Paris and of a vast central association formed for systematically robbing the stalls in the markets. Much pity was expressed for the Quenu-Gradelles, mingled with malicious allusions to their uncle's fortune. That fortune was an endless subject of discussion. The general opinion was that Florent had returned to claim his share of the treasure; however, as no good reason was forthcoming to explain why the division had not taken place already, it was asserted that Florent was waiting for some opportunity which might enable him to pocket the whole amount. The Quenu-Gradelles would certainly be found murdered some morning, it was said; and a rumor spread that dreadful quarrels already took place every night between the two brothers and beautiful Lisa.

When these stories reached the ears of the beautiful Norman, she shrugged her shoulders and burst out laughing.

"Get away with you!" she cried; "you don't know him. Why, the dear fellow's as gentle as a lamb."

She had recently refused the hand of Monsieur Lebigre, who had at last ventured upon a formal proposal. For two months past he had given the Méhudins a bottle of some liqueur every Sunday. It was Rose who brought it, and she was always charged with a compliment for La Normande, some pretty speech which she faithfully repeated, without appearing in the slightest degree embarrassed by the peculiar commission. When Monsieur Lebigre was rejected, he did not pine, but to show that he took no offense and was still hopeful, he sent Rose on the following Sunday with two bottles of champagne and a large bunch of flowers. She gave them into the handsome fish girl's own hands, repeating, as she did so, the wine dealer's prose madrigal:

"Monsieur Lebigre begs you to drink this to his health, which has been greatly shaken by you know what. He hopes that you will one day be willing to cure him, by being for him as pretty and as sweet as these flowers."

La Normande was much amused by the servant's delighted air. She kissed her as she spoke to her of her master, and asked her if he wore braces and snored at nights. Then she made her take the champagne and flowers back with her. "Tell Monsieur Lebigre," said she, "that he's not to send you here again. It quite vexes me to see you coming here so meekly, with your bottles under your arms."

"Oh, he wishes me to come," replied Rose, as she went away. "It is wrong of you to distress him. He is a very handsome man."

La Normande, however, was quite conquered by Florent's affectionate nature. She continued to follow Muche's lessons of an evening in the lamplight, indulging the while in a dream of marrying this man who was so kind to children. She would still keep her fish stall, while he would doubtless rise to a position of importance in the administrative staff of the markets. This dream of hers, however, was scarcely furthered by the tutor's respectful bearing towards her. He bowed to her, and kept himself at a distance, when she would have liked to laugh with him, and love him as she knew how to love. But it was just this covert resistance on Florent's part which continually brought her back to the dream of marrying him. She realized that he lived in a loftier sphere than her own; and by becoming his wife she imagined that her vanity would reap no little satisfaction.

She was greatly surprised when she learned the history of the man she loved. He had never mentioned a word of those things to her; and she scolded him about it. His extraordinary adventures only increased her tenderness for him, and for evenings together she made him relate all that had befallen him. She trembled with fear lest the police should discover him; but he reassured her, saying that the matter was now too old for the police to trouble their heads about it. One evening he told her of the woman on the Boulevard Montmartre, the woman in the pink bonnet, whose blood had dyed his hands. He still frequently thought of that poor creature. His anguish-stricken mind had often dwelt upon her during the clear nights he had passed in Cayenne; and he had returned to France with a wild dream of meeting her again on some footway in the bright sunshine, even though he could still feel her corpse-like weight across his legs. And yet, he thought, she might perhaps have recovered. At times he received quite a shock while he was walking through the streets, on fancying that he recognized her; and he followed pink bonnets and shawl-draped shoulders with a wildly beating heart. When he closed his eyes he could see her walking, and advancing towards him; but she let her shawl slip down, showing the two red stains on her chemisette; and then he saw that her face was pale as wax, and that her eyes were blank, and her lips distorted by pain. For a long time he suffered from not knowing her name, from being forced to look upon her as a mere shadow, whose recollection filled him with sorrow. Whenever any idea of woman crossed his mind it was always she that rose up before him, as the one pure, tender wife. He often found himself fancying that she might be looking for him on that boulevard where she had fallen dead, and that if she had met him a few seconds sooner she would have given him a life of joy. And he wished for no other wife; none other existed for him. When he spoke of her, his voice trembled to such a degree that La Normande, her wits quickened by her love, guessed his secret and felt jealous.

"Oh, it's really much better that you shouldn't see her again," she said maliciously. "She can't look particularly nice by this time."

Florent turned pale with horror at the vision which these words evoked. His love was rotting in her grave. He could not forgive La Normande's savage cruelty, which henceforth made him see the grinning jaws and hollow eyes of a skeleton within that lovely pink bonnet. Whenever the fish girl tried to joke with him on the subject he turned quite angry, and silenced her with almost coarse language.

That, however, which especially surprised the beautiful Norman in these revelations was the discovery that she had been quite mistaken in supposing that she was enticing a lover away from handsome Lisa. This so diminished her feeling of triumph, that for a week or so her love for Florent abated. She consoled herself, however, with the story of the inheritance, no longer calling Lisa a strait-laced prude, but a thief who kept back her brother-in-law's money and assumed sanctimonious airs to deceive people. Every evening, while Muche took his writing lesson, the conversation turned upon old Gradelle's treasure.

"Did anyone ever hear of such an idea?" the fish girl would exclaim with a laugh. "Did the old man want to salt his money, since he put it in a salting tub? Eighty-five thousand francs! That's a nice sum of money! And, besides, the Quenus, no doubt, lied about it—there was perhaps two or three times as much. Ah, if I were in your place, I shouldn't lose any time about claiming my share; indeed I shouldn't."

"I've no need of anything," was Florent's invariable answer. "I shouldn't know what to do with the money if I had it."

"Oh, you're no man!" cried La Normande, losing all control over herself. "It's pitiful! Can't you see that the Quenus are laughing at you? That great fat thing passes all her husband's old clothes over to you. I'm not saying this to hurt your feelings, but everybody makes remarks about it. Why, the whole neighborhood has seen the greasy pair of trousers, which you're now wearing, on your brother's legs for three years and more! If I were in your place I'd throw their dirty rags in their faces and insist upon my rights. Your share comes to forty-two thousand five hundred francs, doesn't it? Well, I shouldn't go out of the place until I'd got forty-two thousand five hundred francs."

It was useless for Florent to explain to her that his sister-in-law had offered to pay him his share, that she was taking care of it for him, and that it was he himself who had refused to receive it. He entered into the most minute particulars, seeking to convince her of the Quenus' honesty, but she sarcastically replied: "Oh yes, I dare say! I know all about their honesty. That fat thing folds it up every morning and puts it away in her wardrobe for fear it should get soiled. Really, I quite pity you, my poor friend. It's easy to gull you, for you can't see any further than a child of five. One of these days she'll simply put your money in her pocket, and you'll never look on it again. Shall I go, now, and claim your share for you, just to see what she says? There'd be some fine fun, I can tell you! I'd either have the money, or I'd break everything in the house—I swear I would!"

"No, no; it's no business of yours," Florent replied, quite

alarmed. "I'll see about it; I may possibly be wanting some money soon."

At this La Normande assumed an air of doubt, shrugged her shoulders, and told him that he was really too chicken-hearted. Her one great aim now was to embroil him with the Quenu-Gradelles, and she employed every means she could think of to effect her purpose, both anger and banter, as well as affectionate tenderness. She also cherished another design. When she had succeeded in marrying Florent, she would go and administer a sound cuffing to beautiful Lisa, if the latter did not yield up the money. As she lay awake in her bed at night she pictured every detail of the scene. She saw herself sitting down in the middle of the pork shop in the busiest part of the day and making a terrible fuss. She brooded over this idea to such an extent, it obtained such a hold upon her, that she would have been willing to marry Florent simply in order to be able to go and demand old Gradelle's forty-two thousand five hundred francs.

Old Madame Méhudin, exasperated by La Normande's dismissal of Monsieur Lebigre, proclaimed everywhere that her daughter was mad and that the "long spindle-shanks" must have administered some insidious drug to her. When she learned the Cayenne story, her anger was terrible. She called Florent a convict and murderer and said it was no wonder that his villainy had kept him lank and flat. Her versions of Florent's biography were the most horrible of all that were circulated in the neighborhood. At home she kept a moderately quiet tongue in her head, and restricted herself to muttered indignation, and a show of locking up the drawer where the silver was kept whenever Florent arrived. One day, however, after a quarrel with her elder daughter, she exclaimed:

"Things can't go on much longer like this! It is that vile man who is setting you against me. Take care that you don't try me too far, or I'll go and denounce him to the police. I will, as true as I stand here!"

"You'll denounce him!" echoed La Normande, trembling violently and clenching her fists. "You'd better not! Ah, if you weren't my mother—"

At this, Claire, who was a spectator of the quarrel, began to laugh, with a nervous laughter that seem to rasp her throat. For some time past she had been gloomier and more erratic than ever, invariably showing red eyes and a pale face.

"Well, what would you do?" she asked. "Would you give her a cuffing? Perhaps you'd like to give me, your sister, one as well? I dare say it will end in that. But I'll clear the house of him. I'll go to the police to save mother the trouble."

Then, as La Normande almost choked with the angry threats that rose to her throat, the younger girl added: "I'll spare you the exertion of beating me. I'll throw myself into the river as I come back over the bridge."

Big tears were streaming from her eyes; and she rushed off to her bedroom, banging the doors violently behind her. Old Madame Méhudin said nothing more about denouncing Florent. Muche, however, told La Normande that he met his grandma talking with Monsieur Lebigre in every corner in the neighborhood.

The rivalry between the beautiful Norman and the beautiful Lisa now assumed a less aggressive but more disturbing character. In the afternoon, when the red-striped canvas awning was drawn down in front of the pork shop, the fish girl would remark that the big fat thing felt afraid and was concealing herself. She was also much exasperated by the occasional lowering of the window blind, on which was pictured a hunting breakfast in a forest glade, with ladies and gentlemen in evening dress partaking of a red pasty, as big as themselves, on the yellow grass.

Beautiful Lisa, however, was by no means afraid. As soon

as the sun began to sink she drew up the blind; and, as she sat knitting behind her counter, she serenely scanned the market square, where numerous urchins were poking about in the soil under the gratings which protected the roots of the plane trees, while porters smoked their pipes on the benches along the footway, at either end of which was an advertisement column covered with theatrical posters, alternately green, yellow, red, and blue, like some harlequin's costume. And while pretending to watch the passing vehicles, Lisa would really be scrutinizing the beautiful Norman. She might occasionally be seen bending forward, as though her eyes were following the Bastille and Place Wagram omnibus to the Pointe Saint Eustache, where it always stopped for a time. But this was only a maneuvre to enable her to get a better view of the fish girl, who, as a set-off against the blind, retorted by covering her head and fish with large sheets of brown paper, on the pretext of warding off the rays of the setting sun. The advantage at present was on Lisa's side, for as the time for striking the decisive blow approached she manifested the calmest serenity of bearing, whereas her rival, in spite of all her efforts to attain the same air of distinction, always lapsed into some piece of gross vulgarity, which she afterwards regretted. La Normande's ambition was to look "like a lady." Nothing irritated her more than to hear people extolling the good manners of her rival. This weak point of hers had not escaped old Madame Méhudin's observation, and she now directed all her attacks upon it.

"I saw Madame Quenu standing at her door this evening," she would say sometimes. "It is quite amazing how well she wears. And she's so refined-looking, too; quite the lady, indeed. It's the counter that does it, I'm sure. A fine counter gives a woman such a respectable look."

In this remark there was a veiled allusion to Monsieur Lebigre's proposal. The beautiful Norman would make no reply; but for a moment or two she would seem deep in thought. In her mind's eye she saw herself behind the counter of the wine shop at the other corner of the street, forming a pendent, as it were, to beautiful Lisa. It was this that first shook her love for Florent.

To tell the truth, it was now becoming a very difficult thing to defend Florent. The whole neighborhood was in arms against him; it seemed as though everyone had an immediate interest in exterminating him. Some of the market people swore that he had sold himself to the police; while others asserted that he had been seen in the butter cellar, attempting to make holes in the wire grating, with the intention of tossing lighted matches through them. There was a vast increase of slander, a perfect flood of abuse, the source of which could not be exactly determined. The fish pavilion was the last one to join in the revolt against the inspector. The fishwives liked Florent on account of his gentleness, and for some time they defended him; but, influenced by the stallkeepers of the butter and fruit pavilions, they at last gave way. Then hostilities began afresh between these huge, swelling women and the lean and lank inspector. He was lost in the whirl of the voluminous petticoats and buxom bodices which surged furiously around his scraggy shoulders. However, he understood nothing, but pursued his course towards the realization of his one haunting idea.

At every hour of the day, and in every corner of the market, Mademoiselle Saget's black bonnet was now to be seen in the midst of this outburst of indignation. Her little pale face seemed to multiply. She had sworn a terrible vengeance against the company which assembled in Monsieur Lebigre's little cabinet. She accused them of having circulated the story that she lived on waste scraps of meat. The truth was that Gavard had told the others one evening that the "old nanny-goat" who came to play the spy upon them gorged herself with the filth which the Bonapartist clique tossed away. Clémence felt quite ill on hearing this, and Robine hurriedly gulped down a draught of beer, as though to wash his throat. In Gavard's opinion, the scraps of meat left on the Emperor's plate were so much political ordure, the putrid remnants of all the filth of the reign. Thenceforth the party at Monsieur Lebigre's looked on Mademoiselle Saget as a creature whom no one could touch except with tongs. She was regarded as some unclean animal that battened upon corruption. Clémence and Gavard circulated the story so freely in the markets that the old maid found herself seriously injured in her intercourse with the shopkeepers, who unceremoniously bade her go off to the scrap stalls when she came to haggle and gossip at their establishments without the least intention of buying anything. This cut her off from her sources of information; and sometimes she was altogether ignorant of what was happening. She shed tears of rage, and in one such moment of anger she bluntly said to La Sarriette and Madame Lecœur: "You needn't give me any more hints: I'll settle your Gavard's hash for him now—that I will!"

The two women were rather startled, but refrained from all protestation. The next day, however, Mademoiselle Saget had calmed down, and again expressed much tender-hearted pity for that poor Monsieur Gavard who was so badly advised and was certainly hastening to his ruin.

Gavard was undoubtedly compromising himself. Ever since the conspiracy had begun to ripen he had carried the revolver, which caused Madame Léonce so much alarm, in his pocket wherever he went. It was a big, formidable-looking weapon, which he had bought of the principal gunmaker in Paris. He exhibited it to all the women in the poultry market, like a schoolboy who has got some prohibited novel hidden in his desk. First he would allow the barrel to peer out of his pocket, and call attention to it with a wink. Then he affected a mysterious reticence, indulged in vague hints and insinuations—played, in short, the part of a man who revelled in feigning fear. The possession of this revolver gave him immense importance, placed him definitely among the dangerous characters of Paris. Sometimes, when he was safe inside his stall, he would consent to take it out of his pocket, and exhibit it to two or three of the women. He made them stand before him so as to conceal him with their petticoats, and then he brandished the weapon, cocked the lock, caused the breech to revolve, and took aim at one of the geese or turkeys that were hanging in the stall. He was immensely delighted at the alarm manifested by the women; but eventually reassured them by stating that the revolver was not loaded. However, he carried a supply of cartridges about with him, in a case which he opened with the most elaborate precautions. When he had allowed his friends to feel the weight of the cartridges, he would again place both weapon and ammunition in his pockets. And afterwards, crossing his arms over his breast, he would chatter away jubilantly for hours.

"A man's a man when he's got a weapon like that," he would say with a swaggering air. "I don't care a fig now for the gendarmes. A friend and I went to try it last Sunday on the plain of Saint Denis. Of course, you know, a man doesn't tell everyone that he's got a plaything of that sort. But, ah! my dears, we fired at a tree and hit it every time. Ah, you'll see, you'll see. You'll hear of Anatole one of these days, I can tell you."

He had bestowed the name of Anatole upon the revolver; and he carried things so far that in a week's time both weapon and cartridges were known to all the women in the pavilion. His friendship for Florent seemed to them suspicious; he was too sleek and rich to be visited with the hatred that was manifested towards the inspector; still, he lost the esteem of the shrewder heads among his acquaintances and succeeded in terrifying the timid ones. This delighted him immensely.

"It is very imprudent for a man to carry firearms about with him," said Mademoiselle Saget. "Monsieur Gavard's revolver will end by playing him a nasty trick."

Gavard now showed the most jubilant bearing at Monsieur Lebigre's. Florent, since ceasing to take his meals with the Quenus, had come almost to live in the little "cabinet." He breakfasted, dined, and constantly shut himself up there. In fact he had converted the place almost into a sort of private room of his own, where he left his old coats and books and papers lying about. Monsieur Lebigre had offered no objection to these proceedings; indeed, he had even removed one of the tables to make room for a cushioned bench, on which Florent could have slept had he felt so inclined. When the inspector manifested any scruples about taking advantage of Monsieur Lebigre's kindness, the latter told him to do as he pleased, saying that the whole house was at his service. Logre also manifested great friendship for him, and even constituted himself his lieutenant. He was constantly discussing affairs with him, rendering an account of the steps he was supposed to take, and furnishing the names of newly affiliated associates. Logre, indeed, had now assumed the duties of organizer; on him rested the task of bringing the various plotters together, forming the different sections, and weaving each mesh of the gigantic net into which Paris was to fall at a given signal. Florent meantime remained the leader, the soul of the conspiracy.

However, much as the hunchback seemed to toil, he attained no appreciable result. Although he had loudly asserted that in each district of Paris he knew two or three groups of men as determined and trustworthy as those who met at Monsieur Lebigre's, he had never yet given any precise information about them, but had merely mentioned a name here and there, and recounted stories of endless alleged secret expeditions, and the wonderful enthusiasm that the people manifested for the cause. He made a great point of the hand grasps he had received. So-and-so, whom he thou'd and thee'd, had squeezed his fingers and declared he would join them. At the Gros Caillou a big, burly fellow, who would make a magnificent sectional leader, had almost dislocated his arm in his enthusiasm; while in the Rue Popincourt a whole group of working men had embraced him. He declared that at a day's notice a hundred thousand active supporters could be gathered together. Each time that he made his appearance in the little room, wearing an exhausted air, and dropping with apparent fatigue on the bench, he launched into fresh variations of his usual reports, while Florent duly took notes of what he said, and relied on him to realize his many promises. And soon in Florent's pockets the plot assumed life. The notes were looked upon as realities, as indisputable facts, upon which the entire plan of the rising was constructed. All that now remained to be done was to wait for a favorable opportunity, and Logre asserted with passionate gesticulations that the whole thing would go on wheels.

Florent was at last perfectly happy. His feet no longer seemed to tread the ground—he was borne aloft by his burning desire to pass sentence on all the wickedness he had seen committed. He had all the credulity of a little child, all the confidence of a hero. If Logre had told him that the Genius of Liberty perched on the Colonne de Juillet would come down and set itself at their head, he would hardly have expressed any surprise. In the evenings, at Monsieur Lebigre's, he showed great enthusiasm and spoke effusively of the approaching battle, as though it were a festival to which all good and honest folks would be invited. But although Gavard in his delight began to play with his revolver, Charvet got more snappish than ever and sniggered and shrugged his shoulders. His rival's assumption of the leadership angered him extremely; indeed, quite disgusted him with politics. One evening when, arriving early, he happened to find himself alone with Logre and Lebigre, he frankly unbosomed himself.

"Why," said he, "that fellow Florent hasn't an idea about politics and would have done far better to seek a berth as writing-master in a ladies' school! It would be nothing short of a misfortune if he were to succeed, for, with his visionary social sentimentalities, he would crush us down beneath his confounded working men! It's all that, you know, which ruins the party. We don't need any more tearful sentimentalists, humanitarian poets, people who kiss and slobber over each other for the merest scratch. But he won't succeed! He'll just get locked up, and that will be the end of it."

Logre and the wine dealer made no remark, but allowed Charvet to talk on without interruption.

"And he'd have been locked up long ago," he continued, "if he were anything as dangerous as he fancies he is. The airs he puts on just because he's been to Cayenne are quite sickening. But I'm sure that the police knew of his return the very first day he set foot in Paris, and if they haven't interfered with him it's simply because they hold him in contempt."

At this Logre gave a slight start.

"They've been dogging me for the last fifteen years," resumed the Hébertist, with a touch of pride, "but you don't hear me proclaiming it from the housetops. However, he won't catch me taking part in his riot. I'm not going to let myself be nabbed like a mere fool. I dare say he's already got half-a-dozen spies at his heels, who will take him by the scruff of the neck whenever the authorities give the word."

"Oh, dear, no! What an idea!" exclaimed Monsieur Lebigre, who usually observed complete silence. He was rather pale, and looked at Logre, who was gently rubbing his hump against the partition.

"That's mere imagination," murmured the hunchback.

"Very well; call it imagination, if you like," replied the tutor; "but I know how these things are arranged. At all events, I don't mean to let the cops nab me this time. You others, of course, will please yourselves, but if you take my advice—and you especially, Monsieur Lebigre—you'll take care not to let your establishment be compromised, or the authorities will close it."

At this Logre could not restrain a smile. On several subsequent occasions Charvet plied him and Lebigre with similar arguments, as though he wished to detach them from Florent's project by frightening them; and he was much surprised at the calmness and confidence which they both continued to manifest. For his own part, he still came pretty regularly in the evening with Clémence. The tall brunette was no longer a clerk at the fish auctions—Monsieur Manoury had discharged her.

"Those salesmen are all scoundrels!" Logre growled, when he heard of her dismissal.

Thereupon Clémence, who, lolling back against the partition, was rolling a cigarette between her long, slim fingers, replied in a sharp voice: "Oh, it's fair fighting! We don't hold the same political views, you know. That fellow Manoury, who's making no end of money, would lick the Emperor's boots. For my part, if I were an auctioneer, I wouldn't keep him in my service for an hour."

The truth was that she had been indulging in some clumsy pleasantry, amusing herself one day by inscribing in the salebook, alongside of the dabs and skate and mackerel sold by auction, the names of some of the best-known ladies and gentlemen of the Court. This bestowal of piscine names upon high dignitaries, these entries of the sale of duchesses and baronesses at thirty sous apiece, had caused Monsieur Manoury much alarm. Gavard was still laughing over it.

"Well, never mind!" said he, patting Clémence's arm; "you are every inch a man, you are!"

Clémence had discovered a new method of mixing her grog. She began by filling her glass with hot water; and after adding some sugar she poured the rum drop by drop upon the slice of lemon floating on the surface, in such a way that it did not mix with the water. Then she lighted it and with a grave expression watched it blaze, slowly smoking her cigarette while the flame of the alcohol cast a greenish tinge over her face. Grog, however, was an expensive luxury in which she could not afford to indulge after she had lost her place. Charvet told her, with a strained laugh, that she was no longer a millionaire. She supported herself by giving French lessons, at a very early hour in the morning, to a young lady residing in the Rue de Miromesnil, who was perfecting her education in secrecy, unknown even to her maid. And so now Clémence merely ordered a glass of beer in the evenings, but this she drank, it must be admitted, with the most philosophical composure.

The evenings in the little sanctum were now far less noisy than they had been. Charvet would suddenly lapse into silence, pale with suppressed rage, when the others deserted him to listen to his rival. The thought that he had been the king of the place, had ruled the whole party with despotic power before Florent's appearance there, gnawed at his heart, and he felt all the regretful pangs of a dethroned monarch. If he still came to the meetings, it was only because he could not resist the attraction of the little room where he had spent so many happy hours in tyrannizing over Gavard and Robine.

In those days even Logre's hump had been his property, as well as Alexandre's fleshy arms and Lacaille's gloomy face.

He had done what he liked with them, stuffed his opinions down their throats, belabored their shoulders with his scepter. But now he endured much bitterness of spirit; and ended by quite ceasing to speak, simply shrugging his shoulders and whistling disdainfully, without condescending to combat the absurdities vented in his presence. What exasperated him more than anything else was the gradual way in which he had been ousted from his position of predominance without being conscious of it. He could not see that Florent was in any way his superior, and after hearing the latter speak for hours, in his gentle and somewhat sad voice, he often remarked: "Why, the fellow's a parson! He only wants a cassock!"

The others, however, to all appearance eagerly absorbed whatever the inspector said. When Charvet saw Florent's clothes hanging from every peg, he pretended not to know where he could put his hat so that it would not be soiled. He swept away the papers that lay about the little room, declaring that there was no longer any comfort for anyone in the place since that "gentleman" had taken possession of it. He even complained to the landlord, and asked if the room belonged to a single customer or to the whole company. This invasion of his realm was indeed the last straw. Men were brutes, and he conceived an unspeakable scorn for humanity when he saw Logre and Monsieur Lebigre fixing their eyes on Florent with rapt attention. Gavard with his revolver irritated him, and Robine, who sat silent behind his glass of beer, seemed to him to be the only sensible person in the company, and one who doubtless judged people by their real value, and was not led away by mere words. As for Alexandre and Lacaille, they confirmed him in his belief that "the people" were mere fools, and would require at least ten years of revolutionary dictatorship to learn how to conduct themselves.

Logre, however, declared that the sections would soon

be completely organized; and Florent began to assign the different parts that each would have to play. One evening, after a final discussion in which he again got worsted, Charvet rose up, took his hat, and exclaimed: "Well, I'll wish you all good night. You can get your skulls cracked if it amuses you; but I would have you understand that I won't take any part in the business. I have never abetted anybody's ambition."

Clémence, who had also risen and was putting on her shawl, coldly added: "The plan's absurd."

Then, as Robine sat watching their departure with a gentle glance, Charvet asked him if he were not coming with them; but Robine, having still some beer left in his glass, contented himself with shaking hands. Charvet and Clémence never returned again; and Lacaille one day informed the company that they now frequented a beer-house in the Rue Serpente. He had seen them through the window, gesticulating with great energy, in the midst of an attentive group of very young men.

Florent was never able to enlist Claude among his supporters. He had once entertained the idea of gaining him over to his own political views, of making a disciple of him, an assistant in his revolutionary task; and in order to initiate him he had taken him one evening to Monsieur Lebigre's. Claude, however, spent the whole time in making a sketch of Robine, in his hat and chestnut cloak, and with his beard resting on the knob of his walking stick.

"Really, you know," he said to Florent as they came away, "all that you have been saying inside there doesn't interest me in the least. It may be very clever, but, for my own part, I see nothing in it. Still, you've got a splendid fellow there, that blessed Robine. He's as deep as a well. I'll come with you again some other time, but it won't be for politics. I shall make sketches of Logre and Gavard, so as to put them with Robine in a picture which I was thinking about while you were discussing the question of—what do you call it? eh? Oh! the question of the two Chambers. Just fancy, now, a picture of Gavard and Logre and Robine talking politics, entrenched behind their glasses of beer! It would be the success of the Salon, my dear fellow, an overwhelming success, a genuine modern picture!"

Florent was grieved by the artist's political skepticism; so he took him up to his bedroom and kept him on the narrow balcony in front of the bluish mass of the markets until two o'clock in the morning, lecturing him and telling him that he was no man to show himself so indifferent to the happiness of his country.

"Well, you're perhaps right," replied Claude, shaking his head; "I'm an egotist. I can't even say that I paint for the good of my country; for in the first place, my sketches frighten everybody, and then, when I'm busy painting, I think about nothing but the pleasure I take in it. When I'm painting, it is as though I were tickling myself; it makes me laugh all over my body. Well, I can't help it, you know; it's my nature to be like that; and you can't expect me to go and drown myself in consequence. Besides, France can get on very well without me, as my aunt Lisa says. And—may I be quite frank with you?—if I like you it's because you seem to me to follow politics just as I follow painting. You titillate yourself, my good friend."

Then, as Florent protested, he continued:

"Yes, yes; you are an artist in your own way; you dream of politics, and I'll wager you spend hours here at night gazing at the stars and imagining they are the voting papers of infinity. And then you titillate yourself with your ideas of truth and justice; and this is so evidently the case that those ideas of yours cause just as much alarm to commonplace middle-class folks as my sketches do. Between ourselves, now, do you imagine that if you were Robine I should take any pleasure in your friendship? Ah, no, my friend, you are a great poet!"

Then he began to joke on the subject, saying that politics caused him no trouble, and that he had got accustomed to hear people discussing them in beer shops and studios. This led him to speak of a café in the Rue Vauvilliers; the café on the ground floor of the house where La Sarriette lodged. This smoky place, with its torn, velvet-cushioned seats and marble table tops discolored by the drippings from coffee-cups, was the chief resort of the young people of the markets. Monsieur Jules reigned there over a company of porters, apprentices, and gentlemen in white blouses and velvet caps. Two curls were glued against his temples; and to keep his neck white he had it scraped with a razor every Saturday at a hairdresser's in the Rue des Deux Ecus. At the café he gave the tone to his associates, especially when he played billiards with studied airs and graces, showing off his figure to the best advantage. After the game the company would begin to chat. They were a very reactionary set, taking a delight in the doings of "society." For his part, Monsieur Jules read the lighter boulevardian newspapers, and knew the performers at the smaller theaters, talked familiarly of the celebrities of the day, and could always tell whether the piece first performed the previous evening had been a success or a failure. He had a weakness, however, for politics. His ideal man was Morny, as he curtly called him. He read the reports of the discussions of the Corps Législatif and laughed with glee over the slightest words that fell from Morny's lips. Ah, Morny was the man to sit upon your rascally republicans! And he would assert that only the scum detested the Emperor, for his Majesty desired that all respectable people should have a good time of it.

"I've been to the café occasionally," Claude said to Florent. "The young men there are vastly amusing, with their clay pipes and their talk about the Court balls! To hear them chatter you might almost fancy they were invited to the Tuileries. La Sarriette's young man was making great fun of Gavard the other evening. He called him uncle. When La Sarriette came downstairs to look for him she was obliged to pay his bill. It cost her six francs, for he had lost at billiards, and the drinks they had played for were owing. And now, good night, my friend, and pleasant dreams. If ever you become a Minister, I'll give you some hints on the beautifying of Paris."

Florent was obliged to relinquish the hope of making a docile disciple of Claude. This was a source of grief to him, for, blinded though he was by his fanatical ardor, he at last grew conscious of the ever-increasing hostility which surrounded him. Even at the Méhudins' he now met with a colder reception: the old woman would laugh slyly; Muche no longer obeyed him, and the beautiful Norman cast glances of hasty impatience at him, unable as she was to overcome his coldness. At the Quenus' too he had lost Auguste's friendship. The assistant no longer came to see him in his room on the way to bed, being greatly alarmed by the reports which he heard concerning this man with whom he had previously shut himself up until midnight. Augustine had made her lover swear that he would never again be guilty of such imprudence; however, it was Lisa who turned the young man into Florent's determined enemy by begging him and Augustine to defer their marriage until her cousin should vacate the little bedroom at the top of the house, as she did not want to give that poky dressing room on the first floor to the new shop girl whom she would have to engage. From that time forward Auguste was anxious that the "convict" should be arrested. He had found such a pork shop as he had long dreamed of, not at Plaisance certainly, but at Montrouge, a little farther away. And now trade had much improved, and Augustine, with her silly, overgrown-girl's laugh, said that she was quite ready. So every night, whenever some slight noise awoke him, Auguste was thrilled with delight as he imagined that the police were at last arresting Florent.

Nothing was said at the Quenu-Gradelles' about all the rumors which circulated. There was a tacit understanding among the staff of the pork shop to keep silent respecting them in the presence of Quenu. The latter, somewhat saddened by the falling-out between his brother and his wife, sought consolation in stringing his sausages and salting his pork. Sometimes he would come and stand on his doorstep, with his red face glowing brightly above his white apron, which his increasing corpulence stretched quite taut, and never did he suspect all the gossip which his appearance set on foot in the markets. Some of the women pitied him and thought that he was losing flesh, though he was, indeed, stouter than ever; while others, on the contrary, reproached him for not having grown thin with shame at having such a brother as Florent. He, however, like one of those betrayed husbands who are always the last to know what has befallen them, continued in happy ignorance, displaying a light-heartedness which was quite affecting. He would stop some neighbor's wife on the footway to ask her if she found his brawn or truffled boar's head to her liking, and she would at once assume a sympathetic expression and speak in a condoling way, as though all the pork on his premises had got jaundice.

"What do they all mean by looking at me with such a funereal air?" he asked Lisa one day. "Do you think I'm looking ill?"

Lisa, well aware that he was terribly afraid of illness and groaned and made a dreadful disturbance if he suffered the slightest ailment, reassured him on this point, telling him that he was as blooming as a rose. The fine pork shop, however, was certainly becoming gloomy; the mirrors seemed to pale, the marbles grew frigidly white, and the cooked meats on the counter stagnated in yellow fat or lakes of cloudy jelly. One day, even, Claude came into the shop to tell his aunt that the display in the window looked quite "in the dumps." This was really the truth. The Strasburg tongues on their beds of blue paper-shavings had a melancholy whiteness of hue, like the tongues of invalids; and the once chubby hams seemed to be wasting away beneath their mournful green topknots. Inside the shop, too, when customers asked for a black pudding, or ten sous' worth of bacon, or half a pound of lard, they spoke in subdued, sorrowful voices, as though they were in the bedchamber of a dying man. There were always two or three lachrymose women in front of the chilled heating pan. Beautiful Lisa meantime discharged the duties of chief mourner with silent dignity. Her white apron fell more primly than ever over her black dress. Her hands, scrupulously clean and closely girded at the wrists by long white sleevelets, her face with its becoming air of sadness, plainly told all the neighborhood, all the inquisitive gossips who streamed into the shop from morning to night, that they, the Quenu-Gradelles, were suffering from unmerited misfortune, but that she knew the cause of it, and would triumph over it at last. And sometimes she stooped to look at the two goldfish, who also seemed ill at ease as they swam languidly around the aquarium in the window, and her glance seemed to promise them better days in the future.

Beautiful Lisa now only allowed herself one indulgence. She fearlessly patted Marjolin's satiny chin. The young man had just come out of the hospital. His skull had healed, and he looked as fat and merry as ever; but even the little intelligence he had possessed had left him, he was now quite an idiot. The gash in his skull must have reached his brain, for he had become a mere animal. The mind of a child of five dwelt in his sturdy frame. He laughed and stammered, he could no longer pronounce his words properly, and he was as submissively obedient as a sheep. Cadine took entire possession of him again; surprised, at first, at the alteration in him, and then quite delighted at having this big fellow to do exactly as she liked with. He was her doll, her toy, her slave in all respects but one: she could not prevent him from going off to Madame Quenu's every now and then. She thumped him, but he did not seem to feel her blows; as soon as she had slung her basket round her neck and set off to sell her violets in the Rue du Pont Neuf and the Rue de Turbigo, he went to prowl about in front of the pork shop.

"Come in!" Lisa cried to him.

She generally gave him some gherkins, of which he was extremely fond; and he ate them, laughing in a childish way, while he stood in front of the counter. The sight of the handsome mistress of the shop filled him with rapture; he often clapped his hands with joy and began to jump about and vent little cries of pleasure, like a child delighted at something shown to it. On the first few occasions when he came to see her after leaving the hospital Lisa had feared that he might remember what had happened.

"Does your head still hurt you?" she asked him.

But he swayed about and burst into a merry laugh as he answered no; and then Lisa gently inquired: "You had a fall, hadn't you?"

"Yes, a fall, fall, fall," he sang, in a happy voice, tapping his skull the while.

Then, as though he were in a sort of ecstasy, he continued in lingering notes, as he gazed at Lisa, "Beautiful, beautiful, beautiful!" This quite touched Madame Quenu. She had prevailed upon Gavard to keep him in his service. It was on the occasions when he so humbly vented his admiration that she caressed his chin and told him that he was a good lad. He smiled with childish satisfaction, at times closing his eyes like some domestic pet fondled by its mistress; and Lisa thought to herself that she was making him some compensation for the blow with which she had felled him in the cellar of the poultry market.

However, the Quenus' establishment still remained under a cloud. Florent sometimes ventured to show himself, and shook hands with his brother, while Lisa observed a frigid silence. He even dined with them sometimes on Sundays, at long intervals, and Quenu then made great efforts at gaiety, but could not succeed in imparting any cheerfulness to the meal. He ate badly and ended by feeling altogether put out. One evening, after one of these icy family gatherings, he said to his wife with tears in his eyes:

"What can be the matter with me? Is it true that I'm not ill? Don't you really see anything wrong in my appearance? I feel just as though I'd got a heavy weight somewhere inside me. And I'm so sad and depressed, too, without in the least knowing why. What can it be, do you think?"

"Oh, a little attack of indigestion, I dare say," replied Lisa.

"No, no; it's been going on too long for that; I feel quite crushed down. Yet the business is going on all right; I've no great worries, and I am leading just the same steady life as ever. But you, too, my dear, don't look well; you seem melancholy. If there isn't a change for the better soon, I shall send for the doctor."

Lisa looked at him with a grave expression.

"There's no need of a doctor," she said, "things will soon be all right again. There's something unhealthy in the atmosphere just now. All the neighborhood is unwell." Then, as if yielding to an impulse of anxious affection, she added: "Don't worry yourself, my dear. I can't have you falling ill; that would be the crowning blow."

As a rule she sent him back to the kitchen, knowing that the noise of the choppers, the tuneful simmering of the fat, and the bubbling of the pans had a cheering effect upon him. In this way, too, she kept him at a distance from the indiscreet chatter of Mademoiselle Saget, who now spent whole mornings in the shop. The old maid seemed bent on arousing Lisa's alarm, and thus driving her to some extreme step. She began by trying to obtain her confidence.

"What a lot of mischievous folks there are about!" she exclaimed; "folks who would be much better employed in minding their own business. If you only knew, my dear Madame Quenu—but no, really, I should never dare to repeat such things to you."

And, as Madame Quenu replied that she was quite indifferent to gossip and that it had no effect upon her, the old maid whispered into her ear across the counter: "Well, people say, you know, that Monsieur Florent isn't your cousin at all."

Then she gradually allowed Lisa to see that she knew the whole story; by way of proving that she had her quite at her mercy. When Lisa confessed the truth, equally as a matter of diplomacy, in order that she might have the assistance of someone who would keep her well posted in all the gossip of the neighborhood, the old maid swore that for her own part she would be as mute as a fish and deny the truth of the reports about Florent, even if she were to be led to the stake for it. And afterwards this drama brought her intense enjoyment; every morning she came to the shop with some fresh piece of disturbing news.

"You must be careful," she whispered one day; "I have just heard two women in the tripe market talking about you know what. I can't interrupt people and tell them they are lying, you know. It would look so strange. But the story's got about, and it's spreading farther every day. It can't be stopped now, I fear; the truth will have to come out."

A few days later she returned to the assault in all earnest. She made her appearance looking quite scared and waited impatiently until there was no one in the shop, when she burst out in her sibilant voice:

"Do you know what people are saying now? Well, they say that all those men who meet at Monsieur Lebigre's have got guns and are going to break out again as they did in '48. It's quite distressing to see such a worthy man as Monsieur Gavard—rich, too, and so respectable—leaguing himself with such scoundrels! I was very anxious to let you know, on account of your brother-in-law."

"Oh, it's mere nonsense, I'm sure; it can't be serious," rejoined Lisa, just to incite the old maid to tell her more.

"Not serious, indeed! Why, when one passes along the Rue Pirouette in the evening one can hear them screaming out in the most dreadful way. Oh! they make no mystery of it all. You know yourself how they tried to corrupt your husband. And the cartridges which I have seen them making from my own window, are they mere nonsense? Well, well, I'm only telling you this for your own good."

"Oh! I'm sure of that, and I'm very much obliged to you," replied Lisa; "but people do invent such stories, you know."

"Ah, but this is no invention, unfortunately. The whole neighborhood is talking of it. It is said, too, that if the police discover the matter there will be a great many people compromised—Monsieur Gavard, for instance."

Madame Quenu shrugged her shoulders as though to say that Monsieur Gavard was an old fool, and that it would do him good to be locked up.

"Well, I merely mention Monsieur Gavard as I might mention any of the others, your brother-in-law, for instance," resumed the old maid with a wily glance. "Your brother-in-law is the leader, it seems. That's very annoying for you, and I'm very sorry for you, very sorry indeed; for if the police were to make a descent here they might march Monsieur

Quenu off as well. Two brothers, you know, they're like two fingers of the same hand."

Beautiful Lisa protested against this, but she turned very pale, for Mademoiselle Saget's last thrust had touched a vulnerable point. From that day forward the old maid was always bringing her stories of innocent people who had been thrown into prison for extending hospitality to criminal scoundrels. In the evening, when Mademoiselle Saget went to get her black-currant syrup at the wine dealer's, she prepared her budget for the next morning. Rose was but little given to gossiping, and the old maid reckoned chiefly on her own eyes and ears. She had been struck by Monsieur Lebigre's extremely kind and obliging manner towards Florent, his eagerness to keep him at his establishment, all the polite civilities, for which the little money which the other spent in the house could never recoup him. And this conduct of Monsieur Lebigre's surprised her the more as she was aware of the position in which the two men stood in respect to the beautiful Norman.

"It looks as though Lebigre were fattening him up for sale," she reflected. "Whom can he want to sell him to, I wonder?"

One evening when she was in the bar she saw Logre fling himself on the bench in the sanctum and heard him speak of his perambulations through the faubourgs, with the remark that he was dead beat. She cast a hasty glance at his feet and saw that there was not a speck of dust on his boots. Then she smiled quietly and went off with her black-currant syrup, her lips closely compressed.

She used to complete her budget of information on getting back to her window. It was very high up, commanding a view of all the neighboring houses, and proved a source of endless enjoyment to her. She was constantly installed at it, as though it were an observatory from which she kept watch upon everything that went on in the neighborhood. She was quite familiar with all the rooms opposite her, both on the right and the left, even to the smallest details of their furniture. She could have described, without the least omission, the habits of their tenants, have related if the latter's homes were happy or the contrary, have told when and how they washed themselves, what they had for dinner, and who it was that came to see them. Then she obtained a side view of the markets, and not a woman could walk along the Rue Rambuteau without being seen by her; and she could have correctly stated from where the woman had come and to where she was going, what she had got in her basket, and, in short, every detail about her, her husband, her clothes, her children, and her means. "That's Madame Loret, over there; she's giving her son a fine education; that's Madame Hutin, a poor little woman who's dreadfully neglected by her husband; that's Mademoiselle Cécile, the butcher's daughter, a girl that no one will marry because she's scrofulous." In this way she could have continued jerking out biographical scraps for days together, deriving extraordinary amusement from the most trivial, uninteresting incidents. However, as soon as eight o'clock struck, she only had eyes for the frosted "cabinet" window on which appeared the black shadows of the coterie of politicians. She discovered the secession of Charvet and Clémence by missing their bony silhouettes from the milky transparency. Not an incident occurred in that room but she sooner or later learnt it by some sudden motion of those silent arms and heads. She acquired great skill in interpretation, and could divine the meaning of protruding noses, spreading fingers, gaping mouths, and shrugging shoulders; and in this way she followed the progress of the conspiracy step by step, in such a way that she could have told day by day how matters stood. One evening the terrible outcome of it all was revealed to her. She saw the shadow of

Gavard's revolver, a huge silhouette with pointed muzzle showing very blackly against the glimmering window. It kept appearing and disappearing so rapidly that it seemed as though the room was full of revolvers. Those were the firearms of which Mademoiselle Saget had spoken to Madame Quenu. On another evening she was much puzzled by the sight of endless lengths of some material or other and came to the conclusion that the men must be manufacturing cartridges. The next morning, however, she made her appearance in the wine shop by eleven o'clock on the pretext of asking Rose if she could let her have a candle, and, glancing furtively into the little sanctum, she spied a heap of red material lying on the table. This greatly alarmed her, and her next budget of news was one of decisive gravity.

"I don't want to alarm you, Madame Quenu," she said, "but matters are really looking very serious. Upon my word, I'm quite alarmed. You must on no account repeat what I am going to confide to you. They would murder me if they knew I had told you."

Then, when Lisa had sworn to say nothing that might compromise her, she told her about the red material.

"I can't think what it can be. There was a great heap of it. It looked just like rags soaked in blood. Logre, the hunchback, you know, put one of the pieces over his shoulder. He looked like a headsman. You may be sure this is some fresh trickery or other."

Lisa made no reply, but seemed deep in thought while, with lowered eyes, she handled a fork and mechanically arranged some pieces of salt pork on a dish.

"If I were you," resumed Mademoiselle Saget softly, "I shouldn't be easy in mind; I should want to know the meaning of it all. Why shouldn't you go upstairs and examine your brother-in-law's bedroom?"

At this Lisa gave a slight start, let the fork drop, and

glanced uneasily at the old maid, believing that she had discovered her intentions. But the other continued: "You would certainly be justified in doing so. There's no knowing into what danger your brother-in-law may lead you, if you don't put a check on him. They were talking about you yesterday at Madame Taboureau's. Ah! you have a most devoted friend in her. Madame Taboureau said that you were much too easygoing, and that if she were you she would have put an end to all this long ago."

"Madame Taboureau said that?" murmured Lisa thoughtfully.

"Yes, indeed she did; and Madame Taboureau is a woman whose advice is worth listening to. Try to find out the meaning of all those red bands; and if you do, you'll tell me, won't you?"

Lisa, however, was no longer listening to her. She was gazing abstractedly at the edible snails and Gervais cheeses between the festoons of sausages in the window. She seemed absorbed in a mental conflict, which brought two little furrows to her brow. The old maid, however, poked her nose over the dishes on the counter.

"Ah, some slices of saveloy!" she muttered, as though she were speaking to herself. "They'll get very dry cut up like that. And that black pudding's broken, I see—a fork's been stuck into it, I expect. It ought to be taken away—it's soiling the dish."

Lisa, still absent-minded, gave her the black pudding and slices of saveloy. "You may take them," she said, "if you would care for them."

The black bag swallowed them up. Mademoiselle Saget was so accustomed to receiving presents that she had actually ceased to return thanks for them. Every morning she carried away all the scraps of the pork shop. And now she went off with the intention of obtaining her dessert from La

Sarriette and Madame Lecœur, by gossiping to them about Gavard.

When Lisa was alone again she installed herself on the bench behind the counter, as though she thought she would be able to come to a sounder decision if she were comfortably seated. For the last week she had been very anxious. Florent had asked Quenu for five hundred francs one evening, in the easy, matter-of-course way of a man who had money lying to his credit at the pork shop. Quenu referred him to his wife. This was distasteful to Florent, who felt somewhat uneasy on applying to beautiful Lisa. But she immediately went up to her bedroom, brought the money down and gave it to him without saying a word, or making the least inquiry as to what he intended to do with it. She merely remarked that she had made a note of the payment on the paper containing the particulars of Florent's share of the inheritance. Three days later he took a thousand francs.

"It was scarcely worthwhile trying to make himself out so disinterested," Lisa said to Quenu that night, as they went to bed. "I did quite right, you see, in keeping the account. By the way, I haven't noted down the thousand francs I gave him today."

She sat down at the secrétaire, and glanced over the page of figures. Then she added: "I did well to leave a blank space. I'll put down what I pay him on the margin. You'll see, now, he'll fritter it all away by degrees. That's what I've been expecting for a long time past."

Quenu said nothing, but went to bed feeling very much put out. Every time that his wife opened the secrétaire the drawer gave out a mournful creak which pierced his heart. He even thought of remonstrating with his brother and trying to prevent him from ruining himself with the Méhudins; but when the time came, he did not dare to do it. Two days later Florent asked for another fifteen hundred francs. Logre had said one evening that things would ripen much faster if

they could only get some money. The next day he was enchanted to find these words of his, uttered quite at random,
result in the receipt of a little pile of gold, which he promptly
pocketed, sniggering as he did so, and his hunch fairly shaking with delight. From that time forward money was constantly being needed: one section wished to hire a room
where they could meet, while another was compelled to provide for various needy patriots. Then there were arms and
ammunition to be purchased, men to be enlisted, and private police expenses. Florent would have paid for anything.
He had thought of Uncle Gradelle's treasure and recalled
La Normande's advice. So he made repeated calls upon Lisa's
secrétaire, being merely kept in check by the vague fear with
which his sister-in-law's grave face inspired him. Never,
thought he, could he have spent his money in a holier cause.
Logre now manifested the greatest enthusiasm and wore
the most wonderful rose-colored neckerchiefs and the shini-
est of varnished boots, the sight of which made Lacaille
glower blackly.

"That makes three thousand francs in seven days," Lisa
remarked to Quenu. "What do you think of that? A pretty
state of affairs, isn't it? If he goes on at this rate his fifty
thousand francs will last him barely four months. And yet it
took old Gradelle forty years to put his fortune together!"

"It's all your own fault!" cried Quenu. "There was no occasion for you to say anything to him about the money."

Lisa gave her husband a severe glance. "It is his own,"
she said; "and he is entitled to take it all. It's not the giving
him the money that vexes me, but the knowledge that he
must make a bad use of it. I tell you again, as I have been
telling you for a long time past, all this must come to an
end."

"Do whatever you like; I won't prevent you," at last exclaimed the pork butcher, who was tortured by his cupidity.

He still loved his brother; but the thought of fifty thousand francs squandered in four months was agony to him. As for his wife, after all Mademoiselle Saget's chattering she guessed what became of the money. The old maid having ventured to refer to the inheritance, Lisa had taken advantage of the opportunity to let the neighborhood know that Florent was drawing his share and spending it after his own fashion.

It was on the following day that the story of the strips of red material impelled Lisa to take definite action. For a few moments she remained struggling with herself while gazing at the depressed appearance of the shop. The sides of pork hung all around in a sullen fashion, and Mouton, seated beside a bowl of fat, displayed the ruffled coat and dim eyes of a cat who no longer digests his meals in peace. Thereupon Lisa called to Augustine and told her to attend to the counter, and she herself went up to Florent's room.

When she entered it, she received quite a shock. The bed, before now so spotless, was quite ensanguined by a bundle of long red scarves dangling down to the floor. On the mantelpiece, between the gilt cardboard boxes and the old pomade-pots, were several red armlets and clusters of red cockades, looking like pools of blood. And hanging from every nail and peg against the faded gray wallpaper were pieces of bunting, square flags—yellow, blue, green, and black—in which Lisa recognized the distinguishing banners of the twenty sections. The childish simplicity of the room seemed quite scared by all this revolutionary decoration. The aspect of guileless stupidity which the shop girl had left behind her, the white innocence of the curtains and furniture, now glared as with the reflection of a fire; while the photograph of Auguste and Augustine looked white with terror. Lisa walked round the room, examining the flags, the armlets, and the scarves, without touching any of them, as though she feared that the dreadful things might burn her.

She was reflecting that she had not been mistaken, that it was indeed on these and similar things that Florent's money had been spent. And to her this seemed an utter abomination, an incredibility which set her whole being surging with indignation. To think that her money, that money which had been so honestly earned, was being squandered to organize and defray the expenses of an insurrection!

She stood there, gazing at the expanded blossoms of the pomegranate on the balcony—blossoms which seemed to her like an additional supply of crimson cockades—and listening to the sharp notes of the chaffinch, which resembled the echo of a distant fusillade. And then it struck her that the insurrection might break out the next day, or perhaps that very evening. She fancied she could see the banners streaming in the air and the scarves advancing in line, while a sudden roll of drums broke on her ear. Then she hastily went downstairs again, without even glancing at the papers which were lying on the table. She stopped on the first floor, went into her own room, and dressed herself.

In this critical emergency Lisa arranged her hair with scrupulous care and perfect calmness. She was quite resolute; not a quiver of hesitation disturbed her; but a sterner expression than usual had come into her eyes. As she fastened her black silk dress, straining the waistband with all the strength of her fingers, she recalled Abbé Roustan's words; and she questioned herself, and her conscience answered that she was going to fulfill a duty. By the time she drew her embroidered shawl round her broad shoulders, she felt that she was about to perform a deed of high morality. She put on a pair of dark mauve gloves, secured a thick veil to her bonnet; and before leaving the room she double-locked the secrétaire, with a hopeful expression on her face which seemed to say that that much worried piece of furniture would at last be able to sleep in peace again.

Quenu was exhibiting his white paunch at the shop door when his wife came down. He was surprised to see her going out in full dress at ten o'clock in the morning. "Hallo! where are you off to?" he asked.

She pretended that she was going out with Madame Taboureau and added that she would call at the Gaîté Theater to buy some tickets. Quenu hurried after her to tell her to secure some front seats, so that they might be able to see well. Then, as he returned to the shop, Lisa made her way to the cab-stand opposite St. Eustache, got into a cab, pulled down the blinds, and told the driver to go to the Gaîté Theater. She felt afraid of being followed. When she had booked two seats, however, she directed the cabman to drive her to the Palais de Justice. There, in front of the gate, she discharged him, and then quietly made her way through the halls and corridors to the Préfecture of Police.

She soon lost herself in a noisy crowd of police officers and gentlemen in long frock coats, but at last gave a man half a franc to guide her to the Prefect's rooms. She found, however, that the Prefect only received such persons as came with letters of audience; and she was shown into a small apartment, furnished after the style of a boarding house parlor. A fat, bald-headed official, dressed in black from head to foot, received her there with sullen coldness. What was her business? he inquired. Thereupon she raised her veil, gave her name, and told her story, clearly and distinctly, without a pause. The bald man listened with a weary air.

"You are this man's sister-in-law, are you not?" he inquired, when she had finished.

"Yes," Lisa candidly replied. "We are honest, straightforward people, and I am anxious that my husband should not be compromised."

The official shrugged his shoulders, as though to say that the whole affair was a great nuisance.

"Do you know," he said impatiently, "that I have been pestered with this business for more than a year past? Denunciation after denunciation has been sent to me, and I am being continually goaded and pressed to take action. You will understand that if I haven't done so as yet, it is because I prefer to wait. We have good reasons for our conduct in the matter. Stay, now, here are the papers relating to it. I'll let you see them."

He laid before her an immense collection of papers in a blue wrapper. Lisa turned them over. They were like detached chapters of the story she had just been relating. The commissaires of police at Havre, Rouen, and Vernon notified Florent's arrival within their respective jurisdictions. Then came a report which announced that he had taken up his residence with the Quenu-Gradelles. Next followed his appointment at the markets, an account of his mode of life, the spending of his evenings at Monsieur Lebigre's; not a detail was deficient. Lisa, quite astounded as she was, noticed that the reports were in duplicate, so that they must have emanated from two different sources. And at last she came upon a pile of letters, anonymous letters of every shape, and in every description of handwriting. They brought her amazement to a climax. In one letter she recognized the villainous hand of Mademoiselle Saget, denouncing the people who met in the little sanctum at Lebigre's. On a large piece of greasy paper she identified the heavy pot-hooks of Madame Lecœur; and there was also a sheet of cream-laid note-paper, ornamented with a yellow pansy, and covered with the scrawls of La Sarriette and Monsieur Jules. These two letters warned the Government to beware of Gavard. Farther on Lisa recognized the coarse style of old Madame Méhudin, who in four pages of almost indecipherable scribble repeated all the wild stories about Florent that circulated in the markets. However, what startled her more than anything else was the discovery of a bill-head of her own establishment, with the inscription *Quenu-Gradelle, Pork Butcher*, on its face, while on the back of it Auguste had penned a denunciation of the man whom he looked upon as an obstacle to his marriage.

The official had acted upon a secret idea in placing these papers before her. "You don't recognize any of these handwritings, do you?" he asked.

"No," she stammered, rising from her seat, quite oppressed by what she had just learned; and she hastily pulled down her veil again to conceal the blush of confusion which was rising to her cheeks. Her silk dress rustled, and her dark gloves disappeared beneath her heavy shawl.

"You see, madame," said the bald man with a faint smile, "your information comes a little late. But I promise you that your visit shall not be forgotten. And tell your husband not to stir. It is possible that something may happen soon that—"

He did not complete his sentence, but, half rising from his armchair, made a slight bow to Lisa. It was a dismissal, and she took her leave. In the anteroom she caught sight of Logre and Monsieur Lebigre, who hastily turned their faces away; but she was more disturbed than they were. She went her way through the halls and along the corridors, feeling as if she were in the clutches of this system of police which, it now seemed to her, saw and knew everything. At last she came out upon the Place Dauphine. When she reached the Quai de l'Horloge she slackened her steps and felt refreshed by the cool breeze blowing from the Seine.

She now had a keen perception of the utter uselessness of what she had done. Her husband was in no danger whatever; and this thought, while relieving her, left her a somewhat remorseful feeling. She was exasperated with Auguste and the women who had put her in such a ridiculous position. She walked on yet more slowly, watching the Seine as it flowed past. Barges, black with coal dust, were floating down the greenish water; and all along the bank anglers were casting their lines. After all, it was not she who had betrayed Florent. This reflection suddenly occurred to her and astonished her. Would she have been guilty of a wicked action, then, if she had been his betrayer? She was quite perplexed; surprised at the possibility of her conscience having deceived her. Those anonymous letters seemed extremely base. She herself had gone openly to the authorities, given her name, and saved innocent people from being compromised. Then at the sudden thought of old Gradelle's fortune she again examined herself, and felt ready to throw the money into the river if such a course should be necessary to remove the blight which had fallen on the pork shop. No, she was not avaricious, she was sure she wasn't; it was no thought of money that had prompted her in what she had just done. As she crossed the Pont au Change she grew quite calm again, recovering all her superb equanimity. On the whole, it was much better, she felt, that others should have anticipated her at the Préfecture. She would not have to deceive Quenu, and she would sleep with an easier conscience.

"Have you booked the seats?" Quenu asked her when she returned home.

He wanted to see the tickets, and made Lisa explain to him the exact position the seats occupied in the dress circle. Lisa had imagined that the police would make a descent upon the house immediately after receiving her information, and her proposal to go to the theater had only been a wily scheme for getting Quenu out of the way while the officers were arresting Florent. She had contemplated taking him for an outing in the afternoon—one of those little jaunts which they occasionally allowed themselves. They would then drive in an open cab to the Bois de Boulogne, dine at a restaurant, and amuse themselves for an hour or two at some café concert. But there was no need to go out now, she thought; so she spent the rest of the day behind her counter, with a rosy glow on her face, and seeming brighter and gayer, as though she were recovering from some indisposition.

"You see, I told you it was fresh air you wanted!" exclaimed Quenu. "Your walk this morning has brightened you up wonderfully!"

"No, indeed," she said after a pause, again assuming her look of severity; "the streets of Paris are not at all healthy places."

In the evening they went to the Gaîté to see the performance of "La Grâce de Dieu." Quenu, in a frock coat and drab gloves, with his hair carefully pomaded and combed, was occupied most of the time in hunting for the names of the performers in the program. Lisa looked superb in her low dress as she rested her hands in their tight-fitting white gloves on the crimson velvet balustrade. They were both of them deeply affected by the misfortunes of Marie. The commander, they thought, was certainly a desperate villain; while Pierrot made them laugh from the first moment of his appearance on the stage. But at last Madame Quenu cried. The departure of the child, the prayer in the maiden's chamber, the return of the poor mad creature, moistened her eyes with gentle tears, which she brushed away with her handkerchief.

However, the pleasure which the evening afforded her turned into a feeling of triumph when she caught sight of La Normande and her mother sitting in the upper gallery. She then puffed herself out more than ever, sent Quenu off to the refreshment bar for a box of caramels, and began to play with her fan, a mother-of-pearl fan, elaborately gilt. The fish girl was quite crushed; and bent her head down to listen to her mother, who was whispering to her. When the performance was over and beautiful Lisa and the beautiful Norman met in the vestibule they exchanged a vague smile.

Florent had dined early at Monsieur Lebigre's that day. He was expecting Logre, who had promised to introduce to him a retired sergeant, a capable man, with whom they were to discuss the plan of attack upon the Palais Bourbon and the Hôtel de Ville. The night closed in, and the fine rain, which had begun to fall in the afternoon, shrouded the vast markets in a leaden gloom. They loomed darkly against the copper-tinted sky, while wisps of murky cloud skimmed by almost on a level with the roofs, looking as though they were caught and torn by the points of the lightning conductors. Florent felt depressed by the sight of the muddy streets and the streaming yellowish rain which seemed to sweep the twilight away and extinguish it in the mire. He watched the crowds of people who had taken refuge on the foot-pavements of the covered ways, the umbrellas flitting past in the downpour, and the cabs that dashed with increased clatter and speed along the nearly deserted roads. Presently there was a rift in the clouds; and a red glow arose in the west. Then a whole army of street-sweepers came into sight at the end of the Rue Montmartre, driving a lake of liquid mud before them with their brooms.

Logre did not turn up with the sergeant; Gavard had gone to dine with some friends at Batignolles, and so Florent was reduced to spending the evening alone with Robine. He had all the talking to himself and ended by feeling very low spirited. His companion merely wagged his beard and stretched out his hand every quarter of an hour to raise his glass of beer to his lips. At last Florent grew so bored that he went off to bed. Robine, however, though left to himself, still lingered there, contemplating his glass with an expression of deep thought. Rose and the waiter, who had hoped to shut up early as the coterie of politicians was absent, had to wait a long half-hour before he at last made up his mind to leave.

When Florent got to his room, he felt afraid to go to bed. He was suffering from one of those nervous attacks which sometimes plunged him into horrible nightmares until dawn. On the previous day he had been to Clamart to attend the funeral of Monsieur Verlaque, who had died after terrible sufferings; and he still felt sad at the recollection of the narrow coffin which he had seen lowered into the earth. Nor could he banish from his mind the image of Madame Verlaque, who with a tearful voice, though there was not a tear in her eyes, kept following him and speaking to him about the coffin, which was not paid for, and of the cost of the funeral, which she was quite at a loss about as she had not a sou in the place, for the druggist, on hearing of her husband's death on the previous day, had insisted upon his bill being paid. So Florent had been obliged to advance the money for the coffin and other funeral expenses, and had even given the gratuities to the mutes. Just as he was going away, Madame Verlaque looked at him with such a heartbroken expression that he left her twenty francs.

And now Monsieur Verlaque's death worried him very much. It affected his situation in the markets. He might lose his berth, or perhaps be formally appointed inspector. In either ease he foresaw vexatious complications which might arouse the suspicions of the police. He would have been delighted if the insurrection could have broken out the very next day, so that he might at once have tossed the laced cap of his inspectorship into the streets. With his mind full of harassing thoughts like these, he stepped out upon the balcony, as though soliciting of the warm night some whiff of air to cool his fevered brow. The rain had laid the wind, and a stormy heat still reigned beneath the deep blue, cloudless heavens. The markets, washed by the downpour, spread out below him, similar in hue to the sky, and, like the sky, studded with the yellow stars of their gas lamps.

Leaning on the iron balustrade, Florent reflected that sooner or later he would certainly be punished for having accepted that inspectorship. It seemed to lie like a stain on his life. He had become an official of the Préfecture, forswearing himself, serving the Empire in spite of all the oaths he had taken in his exile. His anxiety to please Lisa, the charitable purpose to which he had devoted the salary he received, the just and scrupulous manner in which he had always struggled to carry out his duties, no longer seemed to him valid excuses for his base abandonment of principle. If he had suffered in the midst of all that sleek fatness, he had deserved to suffer. And before him arose a vision of the evil year which he had just spent, his persecution by the fishwives, the sickening sensations he had felt on close, damp days, the continuous indigestion which had afflicted his delicate stomach, and the latent hostility which was gathering strength against him. All these things he now accepted as chastisement. That dull rumbling of hostility and spite, the cause of which he could not divine, must forebode some coming catastrophe before whose approach he already stooped, with the shame of one who knows there is a transgression that he must expiate. Then he felt furious with himself as he thought of the popular rising he was preparing; and reflected that he was no longer unsullied enough to achieve success.

In how many dreams he had indulged in that lofty little room, with his eyes wandering over the spreading roofs of the market pavilions! They usually appeared to him like gray seas that spoke to him of far-off countries. On moonless nights they would darken and turn into stagnant lakes of black and pestilential water. But on bright nights they became shimmering fountains of light, the moonbeams streaming over both tiers like water, gliding along the huge plates of zinc, and flowing over the edges of the vast superposed basins.

Then frosty weather seemed to turn these roofs into rigid ice, like the Norwegian bays over which skaters skim; while the warm June nights lulled them into deep sleep. One December night, on opening his window, he had seen them white with snow, so lustrously white that they lighted up the coppery sky. Unsullied by a single footstep, they then stretched out like the lonely plains of the Far North, where never a sledge intrudes. Their silence was beautiful, their soft peacefulness suggestive of innocence.

And at each fresh aspect of the ever-changing panorama before him, Florent yielded to dreams which were now sweet, now full of bitter pain. The snow calmed him; the vast sheet of whiteness seemed to him like a veil of purity thrown over the filth of the markets. The bright, clear nights, the shimmering moonbeams, carried him away into the fairyland of storybooks. It was only the dark, black nights, the burning nights of June when he beheld, as it were, a miasmatic marsh, the stagnant water of a dead and accursed sea that filled him with gloom and grief; and then ever the same dreadful visions haunted his brain.

The markets were always there. He could never open the window and rest his elbows on the balustrade without having them before him, filling the horizon. He left the pavilions in the evening only to behold their endless roofs as he went to bed. They shut him off from the rest of Paris, ceaselessly intruded their huge bulk upon him, entered into every hour of his life. That night again horrible fancies came to him, fancies aggravated by the vague forebodings of evil which distressed him. The rain of the afternoon had filled the markets with malodorous dampness, and as they wallowed there in the center of the city, like some drunken man lying, after his last bottle, under the table, they cast all their foul breath into his face. He seemed to see a thick vapor rising up from each pavilion. In the distance the meat and tripe markets reeked with the sickening steam of blood; nearer in, the vegetable and fruit pavilions diffused the odor of pungent cabbages, rotten apples, and decaying leaves; the butter and cheese exhaled a poisonous stench; from the fish market came a sharp, fresh gust; while from the ventilator in the tower of the poultry pavilion just below him, he could see a warm steam issuing, a fetid current rising in coils like the sooty smoke from a factory chimney. And all these exhalations coalesced above the roofs, drifted towards the neighboring houses, and spread themselves out in a heavy cloud which stretched over the whole of Paris. It was as though the markets were bursting within their tight belt of iron, were heating the slumber of the gorged city with the stertorous fumes of their midnight indigestion.

However, on the footway down below Florent presently heard a sound of voices, the laughter of happy folks. Then the door of the passage was closed noisily. It was Quenu and Lisa coming home from the theater. Stupefied and intoxicated, as it were, by the atmosphere he was breathing, Florent thereupon left the balcony, his nerves still painfully excited by the thought of the tempest which he could feel gathering round his head. The source of his misery was yonder, in those markets, heated by the day's excesses. He closed the window with violence, and left them wallowing in the darkness, naked and perspiring beneath the stars.

Chapter 6

A WEEK LATER, Florent thought that he would at last be able to proceed to action. A sufficiently serious outburst of public dissatisfaction furnished an opportunity for launching his insurrectionary forces upon Paris. The Corps Législatif, whose members had lately shown great variance of opinion respecting certain grants to the Imperial family, was now discussing a bill for the imposition of a very unpopular tax, at which the lower orders had already begun to growl. The Ministry, fearing a defeat, was straining every nerve. It was probable, thought Florent, that no better pretext for a rising would for a long time present itself.

One morning, at daybreak, he went to reconnoiter the neighborhood of the Palais Bourbon. He forgot all about his duties as inspector, and lingered there, studying the approaches of the palace, till eight o'clock, without ever thinking that his absence would revolutionize the fish market. He perambulated all the surrounding streets, the Rue de Lille, the Rue de l'Université, the Rue de Bourgogne, the Rue Saint Dominique, and even extended his examination to the Esplanade des Invalides, stopping at certain crossways, and measuring distances as he walked along. Then, on coming back to the Quai d'Orsay, he sat down on the parapet, and determined that the attack should be made simultaneously from all sides. The contingents from the Gros-Caillou district should arrive by way of the Champ de Mars; the sections from the north of Paris should come down by the

Madeleine; while those from the west and the south would follow the quays, or make their way in small detachments through the then narrow streets of the Faubourg Saint Germain. However, the other side of the river, the Champs Elysées with their open avenues caused him some uneasiness; for he foresaw that cannon would be stationed there to sweep the quays. He thereupon modified several details of his plan and marked down in a memorandum-book the different positions which the several sections should occupy during the combat. The chief attack, he concluded, must certainly be made from the Rue de Bourgogne and the Rue de l'Université, while a diversion might be effected on the side of the river.

While he thus pondered over his plans the eight o'clock sun, warming the nape of his neck, shone gaily on the broad footways and gilded the columns of the great structure in front of him. In imagination he already saw the contemplated battle; clusters of men clinging round those columns, the gates burst open, the peristyle invaded; and then scraggy arms suddenly appearing high aloft and planting a banner there.

At last he slowly went his way homewards again with his gaze fixed upon the ground. But all at once a cooing sound made him look up, and he saw that he was passing through the garden of the Tuileries. A number of wood pigeons, bridling their necks, were strutting over a lawn near by. Florent leant for a moment against the tub of an orange tree, and looked at the grass and the pigeons steeped in sunshine. Right ahead under the chestnut trees all was black. The garden was wrapped in a warm silence, broken only by the distant rumbling which came from behind the railings of the Rue de Rivoli. The scent of all the greenery affected Florent, reminding him of Madame François. However, a little girl ran past, trundling a hoop, and alarmed the pigeons.

They flew off, and settled in a row on the arm of a marble statue of an antique wrestler standing in the middle of the lawn, and once more, but with less vivacity, they began to coo and bridle their necks.

As Florent was returning to the markets by way of the Rue Vauvilliers, he heard Claude Lantier calling to him. The artist was going down into the basement of the poultry pavilion. "Come with me!" he cried. "I'm looking for that brute Marjolin." Florent followed, glad to forget his thoughts and to defer his return to the fish market for a little longer. Claude told him that his friend Marjolin now had nothing further to wish for: he had become an utter animal. Claude entertained an idea of making him pose on all fours in future. Whenever he lost his temper over some disappointing sketch he came to spend whole hours in the idiot's company, never speaking, but striving to catch his expression when he laughed.

"He'll be feeding his pigeons, I dare say," he said; "but unfortunately I don't know whereabouts Monsieur Gavard's storeroom is."

They groped about the cellar. In the middle of it some water was trickling from a couple of taps in the dim gloom. The storerooms here are reserved for pigeons exclusively, and all along the trellising they heard faint cooings, like the hushed notes of birds nestling under the leaves when daylight is departing. Claude began to laugh as he heard it.

"It sounds as though all the lovers in Paris were embracing each other inside here, doesn't it?" he exclaimed to his companion.

However, they could not find a single storeroom open and were beginning to think that Marjolin could not be in the cellar, when a sound of loud, smacking kisses made them suddenly halt before a door which stood slightly ajar. Claude pulled it open and beheld Marjolin, whom Cadine was kissing, while he, a mere dummy, offered his face without feeling the slightest thrill at the touch of her lips.

"Oh, so this is your little game, is it?" said Claude with a laugh.

"Oh," replied Cadine, quite unabashed, "he likes being kissed, because he feels afraid now in the dim light. You do feel frightened, don't you?"

Like the idiot he was, Marjolin stroked his face with his hands as though trying to find the kisses which the girl had just printed there. And he was beginning to stammer out that he was afraid, when Cadine continued: "And, besides, I came to help him; I've been feeding the pigeons."

Florent looked at the poor creatures. All along the shelves were rows of lidless boxes, in which pigeons, showing their motley plumage, crowded closely on their stiffened legs. Every now and then a tremor ran along the moving mass; and then the birds settled down again, and nothing was heard but their confused, subdued notes. Cadine had a saucepan near her; she filled her mouth with the water and tares which it contained, and then, taking up the pigeons one by one, shot the food down their throats with amazing rapidity. The poor creatures struggled and nearly choked, and finally fell down in the boxes with swimming eyes, intoxicated, as it were, by all the food which they were thus forced to swallow.

"Poor creatures!" exclaimed Claude.

"Oh, so much the worse for them," said Cadine, who had now finished. "They are much nicer eating when they've been well fed. In a couple of hours or so all those over there will be given a dose of salt water. That makes their flesh white and tender. Then two hours afterwards they'll be killed. If you would like to see the killing, there are some here which are quite ready. Marjolin will settle their account for them in a jiffy."

Marjolin carried away a box containing some fifty pigeons, and Claude and Florent followed him. Squatting upon the ground near one of the water taps, he placed the box by his side. Then he laid a framework of slender wooden bars on the top of a kind of zinc trough and immediately began to kill the pigeons. His knife flashed rapidly in his fingers, as he seized the birds by the wings, stunned them by a blow on the head from the knife handle, and then thrust the point of the blade into their throats. They quivered for an instant, and ruffled their feathers as Marjolin laid them in a row, with their heads between the wooden bars above the zinc trough, into which their blood fell drop by drop. He repeated each different movement with the regularity of clockwork, the blows from the knife handle falling with a monotonous tick-tack as he broke the birds' skulls, and his hand working backwards and forwards like a pendulum as he took up the living pigeons on one side and laid them down dead on the other. Soon, moreover, he worked with increasing rapidity, gloating over the massacre with glistening eyes, squatting there like a huge delighted bull dog enjoying the sight of slaughtered vermin. Presently, too, he burst into a laugh, and began to sing, "Tick-tack! tick-tack!" while his tongue clucked as an accompaniment to the rhythmical movements of his knife. The pigeons hung down like wisps of silken stuff.

"Ah, you enjoy that, don't you, you great stupid?" exclaimed Cadine. "How comical those pigeons look when they bury their heads in their shoulders to hide their necks! They're horrid things, you know, and would give one nasty bites if they got the chance." Then she laughed more loudly at Marjolin's increasing, feverish haste; and added: "I've killed them sometimes myself, but I can't get on as quickly as he does. One day he killed a hundred in ten minutes."

The wooden frame was nearly full; the blood could be heard falling into the zinc trough; and as Claude happened to turn round he saw Florent looking so pale that he hurriedly led him away. When they got above ground again he made him sit down on a step.

"Why, what's the matter with you?" he exclaimed, tapping him on the shoulder. "You're fainting away like a woman!"

"It's the smell of the cellar," murmured Florent, feeling a little ashamed of himself.

The truth was, however, that those pigeons, which were forced to swallow tares and salt water and then had their skulls broken and their throats slit, had reminded him of the wood pigeons of the Tuileries gardens, strutting over the green turf with their satiny plumage flashing iridescently in the sunlight. He again heard them cooing on the arm of the marble wrestler amid the hushed silence of the garden, while children trundled their hoops in the deep gloom of the chestnuts. And then, on seeing that big fair-haired animal massacring his boxful of birds, stunning them with the handle of his knife and driving its point into their throats, in the depths of that foul-smelling cellar, he had felt sick and faint, his legs had almost given way beneath him, while his eyelids quivered tremulously.

"Well, you'd never do for a soldier!" Claude said to him when he recovered from his faintness. "Those who sent you to Cayenne must have been very simple-minded folks to fear such a man as you! Why, my good fellow, if ever you do put yourself at the head of a rising, you won't dare to fire a shot. You'll be too much afraid of killing somebody."

Florent got up without making any reply. He had become very gloomy, his face was furrowed by deep wrinkles; and he walked off, leaving Claude to go back to the cellar alone. As he made his way towards the fish market his thoughts returned to his plan of attack, to the levies of armed men who were to invade the Palais Bourbon. Cannon would roar from the Champs Elysées; the gates would be burst open; blood would stain the steps, and men's brains would bespatter the pillars. A vision of the fight passed rapidly before him; and he beheld himself in the midst of it, deadly pale, and hiding his face in his hands, not daring to look around him.

As he was crossing the Rue du Pont Neuf he fancied that he spied Auguste's pale face peering round the corner of the fruit pavilion. The assistant seemed to be watching for someone, and his eyes were starting from his head with an expression of intense excitement. Suddenly, however, he vanished and hastened back to the pork shop.

"What's the matter with him?" thought Florent. "Is he frightened of me, I wonder?"

Some very serious occurrences had taken place that morning at the Quenu-Gradelles.' Soon after daybreak, Auguste, breathless with excitement, had awakened his mistress to tell her that the police had come to arrest Monsieur Florent. And he added, with stammering incoherence, that the latter had gone out, and that he must have done so with the intention of escaping. Lisa, careless of appearances, at once hurried up to her brother-in-law's room in her dressing wrapper, and took possession of La Normande's photograph, after glancing round to see if there was anything lying about that might compromise herself and Quenu. As she was making her way downstairs again, she met the police agents on the first floor. The commissary requested her to accompany them to Florent's room, where, after speaking to her for a moment in a low tone, he installed himself with his men, bidding her open the shop as usual so as to avoid giving the alarm to anyone. The trap was set.

Lisa's only worry in the matter was the terrible blow that the arrest would prove to poor Quenu. She was much afraid that if he learned that the police were in the house, he would spoil everything by his tears; so she made Auguste swear to observe the most rigid silence on the subject. Then she went back to her room, put on her stays, and concocted some story for the benefit of Quenu, who was still drowsy. Half-an-hour later she was standing at the door of the shop with all her usual neatness of appearance, her hair smooth and glossy, and her face glowing rosily. Auguste was quietly setting out the window. Quenu came for a moment on to the footway, yawning slightly, and ridding himself of all sleepiness in the fresh morning air. There was nothing to indicate the drama that was in preparation upstairs.

The commissary himself, however, gave the alarm to the neighborhood by paying a domiciliary visit to the Méhudins' abode in the Rue Pirouette. He was in possession of the most precise information. In the anonymous letters which had been sent to the Préfecture, all sorts of statements were made respecting Florent's alleged intrigue with the beautiful Norman. Perhaps, thought the commissary, he had now taken refuge with her; and so, accompanied by two of his men, he proceeded to knock at the door in the name of the law. The Méhudins had only just got up. The old woman opened the door in a fury; but suddenly calmed down and began to smile when she learned the business on hand. She seated herself and fastened her clothes, while declaring to the officers: "We are honest folks here, and have nothing to be afraid of. You can search wherever you like." However, as La Normande delayed to open the door of her room, the commissary told his men to break it open. The young woman was scarcely clad when the others entered, and this unceremonious invasion, which she could not understand, fairly exasperated her. She flushed crimson from anger rather than from shame and seemed as though she were about to fly at the officers. The commissary, at the sight, stepped forward to protect his men, repeating in his cold voice: "In the name of the law! In the name of the law!"

At that La Normande threw herself upon a chair and burst into a wild fit of hysterical sobbing at finding herself so powerless. She was quite at a loss to understand what these men wanted with her. The commissary, however, had noticed how scantily she was clad, and taking a shawl from a peg, he flung it over her. Still she did not wrap it round her, but only sobbed the more bitterly as she watched the men roughly searching the apartment.

"But what have I done?" she at last stammered out. "What are you looking for here?"

Thereupon the commissary pronounced the name of Florent; and La Normande, catching sight of the old woman who was standing at the door, cried out: "Oh, the wretch! This is her doing!" and she rushed at her mother.

She would have struck her if she had reached her; but the police agents held her back, and forcibly wrapped her in the shawl. Meanwhile, she struggled violently and exclaimed in a choking voice:

"What do you take me for? That Florent has never been in this room, I tell you. There was nothing at all between us. People are always trying to injure me in the neighborhood; but just let anyone come here and say anything before my face and then you'll see! You'll lock me up afterwards, I dare say, but I don't mind that! Florent, indeed! What a lie! What nonsense!"

This flood of words seemed to calm her; and her anger now turned against Florent, who was the cause of all the trouble. Addressing the commissary, she sought to justify herself. "I did not know his real character, sir," she said. "He had such a mild manner that he deceived us all. I was unwilling to believe all I heard, because I know people are so malicious. He only came here to give lessons to my little boy and went away directly they were over. I gave him a meal here now and again, that's true, and sometimes made him a present of a fine fish. That's all. But this will be a warning to me, and you won't catch me showing the same kindness to anyone again."

"But hasn't he given you any of his papers to take care of?" asked the commissary.

"Oh no, indeed! I swear it. I'd give them up to you at once if he had. I've had quite enough of this, I can tell you! It's no joke to see you tossing all my things about and ferreting everywhere in this way. Oh! you may look; there's nothing."

The officers, who had examined every article of furniture, now wished to enter the little closet where Muche slept. The child had been awakened by the noise, and for the last few moments he had been crying bitterly, as though he imagined that he was going to be murdered.

"This is my boy's room," said La Normande, opening the door.

Muche, quite naked, ran up and threw his arms round his mother's neck. She pacified him and laid him down in her own bed. The officers came out of the little room again almost immediately, and the commissary had just made up his mind to retire, when the child, still in tears, whispered in his mother's ear: "They'll take my copybooks. Don't let them have my copybooks."

"Oh, yes; that's true," cried La Normande; "there are some copybooks. Wait a moment, gentlemen, and I'll give them to you. I want you to see that I'm not hiding anything from you. There, you'll find some of his writing inside these. You're quite at liberty to hang him as far as I'm concerned; you won't find me trying to cut him down."

Thereupon she handed Muche's books and the copies set by Florent to the commissary. But at this the boy sprang angrily out of bed and began to scratch and bite his mother, who put him back again with a box on the ears. Then he began to bellow.

In the midst of the uproar, Mademoiselle Saget appeared on the threshold, craning her neck forward. Finding all the doors open, she had come in to offer her services to old

Madame Méhudin. She spied about and listened, and expressed extreme pity for these poor women, who had no one to defend them. The commissary, however, had begun to read the copies with a grave air. The frequent repetition of such words as "tyrannically," "liberticide," "unconstitutional," and "revolutionary" made him frown; and on reading the sentence, "When the hour strikes, the guilty shall fall," he tapped his fingers on the paper and said: "This is very serious, very serious indeed."

Thereupon he gave the books to one of his men and went off. Claire, who had not shown herself, now opened her door and watched the police officers go down the stairs. And afterwards she came into her sister's bedroom, which she had not entered for a year. Mademoiselle Saget appeared to be on the best of terms with La Normande, and was hanging over her in a caressing way, bringing the shawl forward to cover her the better, and listening to her angry indignation with an expression of the deepest sympathy.

"You wretched coward!" exclaimed Claire, planting herself in front of her sister.

La Normande sprang up, quivering with anger, and let the shawl fall to the floor.

"Ah, you've been playing the spy, have you?" she screamed. "Dare to repeat what you've just said!"

"You wretched coward!" repeated Claire, in still more insulting tones than before.

Thereupon La Normande struck Claire with all her force; and in return Claire, turning terribly pale, sprang upon her sister and dug her nails into her neck. They struggled together for a moment or two, tearing at each other's hair and trying to choke one another. Claire, fragile though she was, pushed La Normande backward with such tremendous violence that they both fell against the wardrobe, smashing the mirror on its front. Muche was roaring, and old Madame

Méhudin called to Mademoiselle Saget to come and help her to separate the sisters. Claire, however, shook herself free.

"Coward! Coward!" she cried; "I'll go and tell the poor fellow that it is you who have betrayed him."

Her mother, however, blocked the doorway, and would not let her pass, while La Normande seized her from behind, and then, Mademoiselle Saget coming to the assistance of the other two, the three of them dragged Claire into her bedroom and locked the door upon her, in spite of all her frantic resistance. In her rage she tried to kick the door down, and smashed everything in the room. Soon afterwards, however, nothing could be heard except a furious scratching, the sound of metal scraping at the plaster. The girl was trying to loosen the door hinges with the points of her scissors.

"She would have murdered me if she had had a knife," said La Normande, looking about for her clothes, in order to dress herself. "She'll be doing something dreadful, you'll see, one of these days, with that jealousy of hers! We mustn't let her get out on any account: she'd bring the whole neighborhood down upon us!"

Mademoiselle Saget went off in all haste. She reached the corner of the Rue Pirouette just as the commissary of police was re-entering the side passage of the Quenu-Gradelles' house. She grasped the situation at once, and entered the shop with such glistening eyes that Lisa enjoined silence by a gesture which called her attention to the presence of Quenu, who was hanging up some pieces of salt pork. As soon as he had returned to the kitchen, the old maid in a low voice described the scenes that had just taken place at the Méhudins.' Lisa, as she bent over the counter, with her hand resting on a dish of larded veal, listened to her with the happy face of one who triumphs. Then, as a customer entered the shop and asked for a couple of pig's trotters, Lisa wrapped them up and handed them over with a thoughtful air.

"For my own part, I bear La Normande no ill will," she said to Mademoiselle Saget, when they were alone again. "I used to be very fond of her and have always been sorry that other people made mischief between us. The proof that I've no animosity against her is here in this photograph, which I saved from falling into the hands of the police, and which I'm quite ready to give her back if she will come and ask me for it herself."

She took the photograph out of her pocket as she spoke. Mademoiselle Saget scrutinized it and sniggered as she read the inscription, "Louise, to her dear friend Florent."

"I'm not sure you'll be acting wisely," she said in her cutting voice. "You'd do better to keep it."

"No, no," replied Lisa; "I'm anxious for all this silly nonsense to come to an end. Today is the day of reconciliation. We've had enough unpleasantness, and the neighborhood's now going to be quiet and peaceful again."

"Well, well, shall I go and tell La Normande that you are expecting her?" asked the old maid.

"Yes; I shall be very glad if you will."

Mademoiselle Saget then made her way back to the Rue Pirouette and greatly frightened the fish girl by telling her that she had just seen her photograph in Lisa's pocket. She could not, however, at once prevail upon her to comply with her rival's terms. La Normande propounded conditions of her own. She would go, but Madame Quenu must come to the door of the shop to receive her. Thus the old maid was obliged to make another couple of journeys between the two rivals before their meeting could be satisfactorily arranged. At last, however, to her great delight, she succeeded in negotiating the peace which was destined to cause so much talk and excitement. As she passed Claire's door for the last time she still heard the sound of the scissors scraping away at the plaster.

When she had at last carried a definite reply to Madame Quenu, Mademoiselle Saget hurried off to find Madame Lecœur and La Sarriette; and all three of them took up their position on the footway at the corner of the fish market, just in front of the pork shop. Here they would be certain to have a good view of every detail of the meeting. They felt extremely impatient and while pretending to chat together kept an anxious lookout in the direction of the Rue Pirouette, along which La Normande must come. The news of the reconciliation was already travelling through the markets, and while some saleswomen stood up behind their stalls trying to get a view of what was taking place, others, still more inquisitive, actually left their places and took up a position in the covered way. Every eye in the markets was directed upon the pork shop; the whole neighborhood was on the tiptoe of expectation.

It was a very solemn affair. When La Normande at last turned the corner of the Rue Pirouette the excitement was so great that the women held their breath.

"She has got her diamonds on," murmured La Sarriette.

"Just look how she stalks along," added Madame Lecœur; "the stuck-up creature!"

The beautiful Norman was, indeed, advancing with the mien of a queen who condescends to make peace. She had made a most careful toilet, frizzing her hair and turning up a corner of her apron to display her cashmere skirt. She had even put on a new and rich lace bow. Conscious that the whole market was staring at her, she assumed a still haughtier air as she approached the pork shop. When she reached the door she stopped.

"Now it's beautiful Lisa's turn," remarked Mademoiselle Saget. "Mind you pay attention."

Beautiful Lisa smilingly quitted her counter. She crossed the shop floor at a leisurely pace and came and offered her hand to the beautiful Norman. She also was smartly dressed, with her dazzling linen and scrupulous neatness. A murmur ran through the crowd of fishwives, all their heads gathered close together, and animated chatter ensued. The two women had gone inside the shop, and the *crépines* in the window prevented them from being clearly seen. However, they seemed to be conversing affectionately, addressing pretty compliments to one another.

"See!" suddenly exclaimed Mademoiselle Saget, "the beautiful Norman's buying something! What is it she's buying? It's a chitterling, I believe! Ah! Look! look! You didn't see it, did you? Well, beautiful Lisa just gave her the photograph; she slipped it into her hand with the chitterling."

Fresh salutations were then seen to pass between the two women; and the beautiful Lisa, exceeding even the courtesies which had been agreed upon, accompanied the beautiful Norman to the footway. There they stood laughing together, exhibiting themselves to the neighborhood like a couple of good friends. The markets were quite delighted; and the saleswomen returned to their stalls, declaring that everything had passed off extremely well.

Mademoiselle Saget, however, detained Madame Lecœur and La Sarriette. The drama was not over yet. All three kept their eyes fixed on the house opposite with such keen curiosity that they seemed trying to penetrate the very walls. To pass the time away they once more began to talk of the beautiful Norman.

"She's without a lover now," remarked Madame Lecœur.

"Oh! she's got Monsieur Lebigre," replied La Sarriette, with a laugh.

"But surely Monsieur Lebigre won't have anything more to say to her."

Mademoiselle Saget shrugged her shoulders. "Ah, you don't know him," she said. "He won't care a straw about all this business. He knows what he's about, and La Normande is rich. They'll come together in a couple of months, you'll see. Old Madame Méhudin's been scheming to bring about their marriage for a long time past."

"Well, anyway," retorted the butter dealer, "the commissary found Florent at her lodgings."

"No, no, indeed; I'm sure I never told you that. The long spindle-shanks had gone away," replied the old maid. She paused to take breath; then resumed in an indignant tone, "What distressed me most was to hear of all the abominable things that the villain had taught little Muche. You'd really never believe it. There was a whole bundle of papers."

"What sort of abominable things?" asked La Sarriette with interest.

"Oh, all kinds of filth. The commissary said there was quite sufficient there to hang him. The fellow's a perfect monster! To go and demoralize a child! Why, it's almost past believing! Little Muche is certainly a scamp, but that's no reason why he should be given over to the Reds, is it?"

"Certainly not," assented the two others.

"However, all these mysterious goings-on will come to an end now. You remember my telling you once that there was some strange goings-on at the Quenus'? Well, you see, I was right in my conclusions, wasn't I? Thank God, however, the neighborhood will now be able to breathe easily. It was high time strong steps were taken, for things had got to such a pitch that one actually felt afraid of being murdered in broad daylight. There was no pleasure in life. All the dreadful stories and reports one heard were enough to worry one to death. And it was all owing to that man, that dreadful Florent. Now beautiful Lisa and the beautiful Norman have sensibly made friends again. It was their duty to do so for the sake of the peace and quietness of us all. Everything will go on sat-isfactorily now, you'll find. Ah, there's poor Monsieur Quenu laughing there!"

Quenu had again come on to the footway and was joking with Madame Taboureau's little servant. He seemed quite gay and skittish that morning. He took hold of the little servant's hands and squeezed her fingers so tightly, in the exuberance of his spirits, that he made her cry out. Lisa had the greatest trouble to get him to go back into the kitchen.

She was impatiently pacing about the shop, fearing lest Florent should make his appearance; and she called to her husband to come away, dreading a meeting between him and his brother.

"She's getting quite vexed," said Mademoiselle Saget. "Poor Monsieur Quenu, you see, knows nothing at all about what's taking place. Just look at him there, laughing like a child! Madame Taboureau, you know, said that she should have nothing more to do with the Quenus if they persisted in bringing themselves into discredit by keeping that Florent with them."

"Well, now, I suppose, they will stick to the fortune," remarked Madame Lecœur.

"Oh no, indeed, my dear. The other one has had his share already."

"Really? How do you know that?"

"Oh, it's clear enough, that is!" replied the old maid after a momentary hesitation, but without giving any proof of her assertions. "He's had even more than his share. The Quenus will be several thousand francs out of pocket. Money flies, you know, when a man has such vices as he has. I dare say you don't know that there was another woman mixed up in it all. Yes, indeed, old Madame Verlaque, the wife of the former inspector; you know the sallow-faced thing well enough."

The others protested that it surely wasn't possible. Why, Madame Verlaque was positively hideous!

"What! Do you think me a liar?" cried Mademoiselle Saget, with angry indignation. "Why, her letters to him have been found, a whole pile of letters, in which she asks for money, ten and twenty francs at a time. There's no doubt at all about it. I'm quite certain in my own mind that they killed the husband between them."

La Sarriette and Madame Lecœur were convinced; but they were beginning to get very impatient. They had been waiting on the footway for more than an hour and feared that somebody might be robbing their stalls during their long absence. So Mademoiselle Saget began to give them some further interesting information to keep them from going off. Florent could not have taken to flight, said she; he was certain to return, and it would be very interesting to see him arrested. Then she went on to describe the trap that had been laid for him, while Madame Lecœur and La Sarriette continued scrutinizing the house from top to bottom, keeping watch upon every opening, and at each moment expecting to see the hats of the detectives appear at one of the doors or windows.

"Who would ever imagine, now, that the place was full of police?" observed the butter dealer.

"Oh! they're in the garret at the top," said the old maid. "They've left the window open, you see, just as they found it. Look! I think I can see one of them hiding behind the pomegranate on the balcony."

The others excitedly craned out their necks, but could see nothing.

"Ah, no, it's only a shadow," continued Mademoiselle Saget. "The little curtains even are perfectly still. The detectives must be sitting down in the room and keeping quiet."

Just at that moment the women caught sight of Gavard

coming out of the fish market with a thoughtful air. They looked at him with glistening eyes, without speaking. They had drawn close to one another and stood there rigid in their drooping skirts. The poultry dealer came up to them.

"Have you seen Florent go by?" he asked.

They replied that they had not.

"I want to speak to him at once," continued Gavard. "He isn't in the fish market. He must have gone up to his room. But you would have seen him, though, if he had."

The two women had turned rather pale. They still kept looking at each other with a knowing expression, their lips twitching slightly every now and then. "We have only been here some five minutes," said Madame Lecœur unblushingly, as her brother-in-law still stood hesitating.

"Well, then, I'll go upstairs and see. I'll risk the five flights," rejoined Gavard with a laugh.

La Sarriette stepped forward as though she wished to detain him, but her aunt took hold of her arm and drew her back.

"Let him alone, you big simpleton!" she whispered. "It's the best thing that can happen to him. It'll teach him to treat us with more respect in future."

"He won't say again that I eat tainted meat," muttered Mademoiselle Saget in a low tone.

They said nothing more. La Sarriette was very red; but the two others still remained quite yellow. But they now averted their heads, feeling confused by each other's looks, and at a loss what to do with their hands, which they buried beneath their aprons. Presently their eyes instinctively came back to the house, penetrating the walls, as it were, following Gavard in his progress up the stairs. When they imagined that he had entered Florent's room they again exchanged furtive glances. La Sarriette laughed nervously. All at once they fancied they could see the window curtains moving, and this led them to believe that a struggle was taking place. But the house front remained as tranquil as ever in the sunshine; and another quarter of an hour of unbroken quietness passed away, during which the three women's nervous excitement became more and more intense. They were beginning to feel quite faint when a man hurriedly came out of the passage and ran off to get a cab. Five minutes later Gavard appeared, followed by two police officers. Lisa, who had stepped out on to the footway on observing the cab, hastily hurried back into the shop.

Gavard was very pale. The police had searched him upstairs, and had discovered the revolver and cartridge case in his possession. Judging by the commissary's stern expression on hearing his name, the poultry dealer deemed himself lost. This was a terrible ending to his plotting that had never entered into his calculations. The Tuileries would never forgive him! His legs gave way beneath him as though the firing party was already awaiting him outside. When he got into the street, however, his vanity lent him sufficient strength to walk erect; and he even managed to force a smile, as he knew the market people were looking at him. They should see him die bravely, he resolved.

However, La Sarriette and Madame Lecœur rushed up to him and anxiously inquired what was the matter; and the butter dealer began to cry, while La Sarriette embraced her uncle, manifesting the deepest emotion. As Gavard held her clasped in his arms, he slipped a key into her hand and whispered in her ear: "Take everything and burn the papers."

Then he got into the cab with the same mien as he would have ascended the scaffold. As the vehicle disappeared round the corner of the Rue Pierre Lescot, Madame Lecœur observed La Sarriette trying to hide the key in her pocket.

"It's of no use you trying that little game on me, my dear," she exclaimed, clenching her teeth; "I saw him slip it into your hand. As true as there's a God in Heaven, I'll go to the jail and tell him everything, if you don't treat me properly."

"Of course I shall treat you properly, aunt, dear," replied La Sarriette, with an embarrassed smile.

"Very well, then, let us go to his rooms at once. It's of no use to give the police time to poke their dirty hands in the cupboards."

Mademoiselle Saget, who had been listening with gleaming eyes, followed them, running along in the rear as quickly as her short legs could carry her. She had no thought, now, of waiting for Florent. From the Rue Rambuteau to the Rue de la Cossonnerie she manifested the most humble obsequiousness, and volunteered to explain matters to Madame Léonce, the doorkeeper.

"We'll see, we'll see," the butter dealer curtly replied.

However, on reaching the house a preliminary parley—as Mademoiselle Saget had opined—proved to be necessary. Madame Léonce refused to allow the women to go up to her tenant's room. She put on an expression of severe austerity and seemed greatly shocked by the sight of La Sarriette's loosely fastened fichu. However, after the old maid had whispered a few words to her and she was shown the key, she gave way. When they got upstairs she surrendered the rooms and furniture to the others article by article, apparently as heartbroken as if she had been compelled to show a party of burglars the place where her own money was secreted.

"There, take everything and have done with it!" she cried at last, throwing herself into an armchair.

La Sarriette was already eagerly trying the key in the locks of the different closets. Madame Lecœur, all suspicion, pressed her so closely that she exclaimed: "Really, aunt, you get in my way. Do leave my arms free, at any rate."

At last they succeeded in opening a wardrobe opposite the window, between the fireplace and the bed. And then all four women broke into exclamations. On the middle shelf lay some ten thousand francs in gold, methodically arranged in little piles. Gavard, who had prudently deposited the bulk of his fortune in the hands of a notary, had kept this sum by him for the purposes of the coming outbreak. He had been wont to say with great solemnity that his contribution to the revolution was quite ready. The fact was that he had sold out certain stock and every night took an intense delight in contemplating those ten thousand francs, gloating over them, and finding something quite roisterous and insurrectional in their appearance. Sometimes when he was in bed he dreamed that a fight was going on in his wardrobe; he could hear guns being fired there, paving stones being torn up and piled into barricades, and voices shouting in clamorous triumph; and he said to himself that it was his money fighting against the Government.

La Sarriette, however, had stretched out her hands with a cry of delight.

"Paws off, little one!" exclaimed Madame Lecœur in a hoarse voice.

As she stood there in the reflection of the gold, she looked yellower than ever—her face discolored by biliousness, her eyes glowing feverishly from the liver complaint which was secretly undermining her. Behind her Mademoiselle Saget on tiptoe was gazing ecstatically into the wardrobe, and Madame Léonce had now risen from her seat and was growling sulkily.

"My uncle said that I was to take everything," declared the girl.

"And am I to have nothing, then; I who have done so much for him?" cried the doorkeeper.

Madame Lecœur was almost choking with excitement. She pushed the others away and clung hold of the wardrobe, screaming: "It all belongs to me! I am his nearest relative. You are a pack of thieves, you are! I'd rather throw it all out of the window than see you have it!"

Then silence fell, and they all four stood glowering at each other. The kerchief that La Sarriette wore over her breast was now altogether unfastened, and she displayed her bosom heaving with warm life, her moist red lips, her rosy nostrils. Madame Lecœur grew still more sour as she saw how lovely the girl looked in the excitement of her longing desire.

"Well," she said in a lower tone, "we won't fight about it. You are his niece, and I'll divide the money with you. We will each take a pile in turn."

They then pushed the other two aside. The butter dealer took the first pile, which at once disappeared within her skirts. Then La Sarriette took a pile. They kept a close watch upon one another, ready to fight at the slightest attempt at cheating. Their fingers were thrust forward in turn, the hideous knotted fingers of the aunt and the white fingers of the niece, soft and supple as silk. Slowly they filled their pockets. When there was only one pile left, La Sarriette objected to her aunt taking it, as she had commenced; and she suddenly divided it between Mademoiselle Saget and Madame Léonce, who had watched them pocket the gold with feverish impatience.

"Much obliged to you!" snarled the doorkeeper. "Fifty francs for having coddled him up with tisane and broth! The old deceiver told me he had no relatives!"

Before locking the wardrobe up again, Madame Lecœur searched it thoroughly from top to bottom. It contained all the political works which were forbidden admission into the country, the pamphlets printed at Brussels, the scandalous histories of the Bonapartes, and the foreign caricatures ridiculing the Emperor. One of Gavard's greatest delights was to shut himself up with a friend and show him all these compromising things.

"He told me that I was to burn all the papers," said La Sarriette.

"Oh, nonsense! we've no fire, and it would take us too long. The police will soon be here! We must get out of this!"

They all four hastened off; but they had not reached the bottom of the stairs before the police met them, and made Madame Léonce return with them upstairs. The three others, making themselves as small as possible, hurriedly escaped into the street. They walked away in single file at a brisk pace; the aunt and niece considerably incommoded by the weight of their drooping pockets. Mademoiselle Saget had kept her fifty francs in her closed fist, and remained deep in thought, brooding over a plan for extracting something more from the heavy pockets in front of her.

"Ah!" she exclaimed, as they reached the corner of the fishmarket, "we've got here at a lucky moment. There's Florent, just going to walk into the trap."

Florent, indeed, was just then returning to the markets after his prolonged perambulation. He went into his office to change his coat, and then set about his daily duties, seeing that the marble slabs were properly washed, and slowly strolling along the alleys. He fancied that the fishwives looked at him in a somewhat strange manner; they chuckled too, and smiled significantly as he passed them. Some new vexation, he thought, was in store for him. For some time past those huge, terrible women had not allowed him a day's peace. However, as he passed the Méhudins' stall he was very much surprised to hear the old woman address him in a honeyed tone: "There's just been a gentleman inquiring for you, Monsieur Florent; a middle-aged gentleman. He's gone to wait for you in your room."

As the old fishwife, who was squatting, all of a heap, on her chair, spoke these words, she felt such a delicious thrill of satisfied vengeance that her huge body fairly quivered. Florent, still doubtful, glanced at the beautiful Norman; but the young woman, now completely reconciled with her mother, turned on her tap and slapped her fish, pretending not to hear what was being said.

"You are quite sure?" said Florent to Mother Méhudin.

"Oh, yes, indeed. Isn't that so, Louise?" said the old woman in a shriller voice.

Florent concluded that it must be someone who wanted to see him about the great business, and he resolved to go up to his room. He was just about to leave the pavilion, when, happening to turn round, he observed the beautiful Norman watching him with a grave expression on her face. Then he passed in front of the three gossips.

"Do you notice that there's no one in the pork shop?" remarked Mademoiselle Saget. "Beautiful Lisa's not the woman to compromise herself." The shop was, indeed, quite empty. The front of the house was still bright with sunshine; the building looked like some honest, prosperous pile guilelessly warming itself in the morning rays. Up above, the pomegranate on the balcony was in full bloom. As Florent crossed the roadway he gave a friendly nod to Logre and Monsieur Lebigre, who appeared to be enjoying the fresh air on the doorstep of the latter's establishment. They returned his greeting with a smile. Florent was then about to enter the side passage, when he fancied he saw Auguste's pale face hastily vanishing from its dark and narrow depths. Thereupon he turned back and glanced into the shop to make sure that the middle-aged gentleman was not waiting for him there. But he saw no one but Mouton, who sat on a block displaying his double chin and bristling whiskers, and gazed at him defiantly with his great yellow eyes. And when he had at last made up his mind to enter the passage, Lisa's face appeared behind the little curtain of a glazed door at the back of the shop.

A hush had fallen over the fish market. All the huge

paunches and bosoms held their breath, waiting until Florent should disappear from sight. Then there was an uproarious outbreak; and the bosoms heaved wildly and the paunches nearly burst with malicious delight. The joke had succeeded. Nothing could be more comical. As old Mother Méhudin vented her merriment she shook and quivered like a wine-skin that is being emptied. Her story of the middle-aged gentleman went the round of the market, and the fishwives found it extremely amusing. At last the long spindle-shanks was collared, and they would no longer always have his miserable face and jailbird's expression before their eyes. They all wished him a pleasant journey, and trusted that they might get a handsome fellow for their next inspector. And in their delight they rushed about from one stall to another, and felt inclined to dance round their marble slabs like a lot of holiday-making schoolgirls. The beautiful Norman, however, watched this outbreak of joy in a rigid attitude, not daring to move for fear she should burst into tears; and she kept her hands pressed upon a big skate to cool her feverish excitement.

"You see how those Méhudins turn their backs upon him now that he's come to grief," said Madame Lecœur.

"Well, and they're quite right too," replied Mademoiselle Saget. "Besides, matters are settled now, my dear, and we're to have no more disputes. You've every reason to be satisfied; leave the others to act as they please."

"It's only the old woman who is laughing," La Sarriette remarked; "La Normande looks anything but happy."

Meantime, upstairs in his bedroom, Florent allowed himself to be taken as unresistingly as a sheep. The police officers sprang roughly upon him, expecting, no doubt, that they would meet with a desperate resistance. He quietly begged them to leave go of him; and then sat down on a chair while they packed up his papers, and the red scarves, armlets, and banners. He did not seem at all surprised at this ending; indeed, it was something of a relief to him, though he would not frankly confess it. But he suffered acutely at thought of the bitter hatred which had sent him into that room; he recalled Auguste's pale face and the sniggering looks of the fishwives; he thought of old Madame Méhudin's words, La Normande's silence, and the empty shop downstairs. The markets were leagued against him, he reflected; the whole neighborhood had conspired to hand him over to the police. The mud of those greasy streets had risen up all around to overwhelm him!

And amid all the round faces which flitted before his mind's eye there suddenly appeared that of Quenu, and a spasm of mortal agony contracted his heart.

"Come, get along downstairs!" exclaimed one of the officers, roughly.

Florent rose and proceeded to go downstairs. When he reached the second floor he asked to be allowed to return; he had forgotten something, he said. But the officers refused to let him go back and began to hustle him forward. Then he besought them to let him return to his room again and even offered them the money he had in his pocket. Two of them at last consented to return with him, threatening to blow his brains out should he attempt to play them any trick; and they drew their revolvers out of their pockets as they spoke. However, on reaching his room once more Florent simply went straight to the chaffinch's cage, took the bird out of it, kissed it between its wings, and set it at liberty. He watched it fly away through the open window, into the sunshine, and alight, as though giddy, on the roof of the fish market. Then it flew off again and disappeared over the markets in the direction of the Square des Innocents. For a moment longer Florent remained face to face with the sky, the free and open sky; and he thought of the wood pigeons cooing in the garden of the Tuileries, and of those other pigeons down in the market cellars with their throats slit by Marjolin's knife. Then he felt quite broken and turned and followed the officers, who were putting their revolvers back into their pockets as they shrugged their shoulders.

On reaching the bottom of the stairs, Florent stopped before the door which led into the kitchen. The commissary, who was waiting for him there, seemed almost touched by his gentle submissiveness, and asked him: "Would you like to say good-bye to your brother?"

For a moment Florent hesitated. He looked at the door. A tremendous noise of cleavers and pans came from the kitchen. Lisa, with the design of keeping her husband occupied, had persuaded him to make the black puddings in the morning instead of in the evening, as was his habit. The onions were simmering on the fire, and over all the noisy uproar Florent could hear Quenu's joyous voice exclaiming, "Ah, dash it all, the pudding will be excellent, that it will! Auguste, hand me the fat!" Florent thanked the commissary, but refused his offer. He was afraid to return any more into that warm kitchen, reeking with the odor of boiling onions, and so he went on past the door, happy in the thought that his brother knew nothing of what had happened to him, and hastening his steps as if to spare the establishment all further worry. However, on emerging into the open sunshine of the street he felt a touch of shame and got into the cab with bent back and ashen face. He was conscious that the fish market was gazing at him in triumph; it seemed to him, indeed, as though the whole neighborhood had gathered there to rejoice at his fall.

"What a villainous expression he's got!" said Mademoiselle Saget.

"Yes, indeed, he looks just like a thief caught with his hand in somebody's till," added Madame Lecœur.

"I once saw a man guillotined who looked exactly like he does," asserted La Sarriette, showing her white teeth.

They stepped forward, lengthened their necks, and tried to see into the cab. Just as it was starting, however, the old maid tugged sharply at the skirts of her companions, and pointed to Claire, who was coming round the corner of the Rue Pirouette, looking like a mad creature, with her hair loose and her nails bleeding. She had at last succeeded in opening her door. When she discovered that she was too late, and that Florent was being taken off, she darted after the cab, but checked herself almost immediately with a gesture of impotent rage, and shook her fists at the receding wheels. Then, with her face quite crimson beneath the fine plaster dust with which she was covered, she ran back again towards the Rue Pirouette.

"Had he promised to marry her, eh?" exclaimed La Sarriette, laughing. "The silly fool must be quite cracked."

Little by little the neighborhood calmed down, though throughout the day groups of people constantly assembled and discussed the events of the morning. The pork shop was the object of much inquisitive curiosity. Lisa avoided appearing there and left the counter in charge of Augustine.

In the afternoon she felt bound to tell Quenu of what had happened, for fear the news might cause him too great a shock should he hear it from some gossiping neighbor. She waited until she was alone with him in the kitchen, knowing that there he was always most cheerful, and would weep less than if he were anywhere else. Moreover, she communicated her tidings with all sorts of motherly precautions. Nevertheless, as soon as he knew the truth he fell on the chopping block, and began to cry like a calf.

"Now, now, my poor dear, don't give way like that; you'll make yourself quite ill," exclaimed Lisa, taking him in her arms.

His tears were inundating his white apron, the whole of his massive, torpid form quivered with grief. He seemed to be sinking, melting away. When he was at last able to speak, he stammered: "Oh, you don't know how good he was to me when we lived together in the Rue Royer Collard! He did everything. He swept the room and cooked the meals. He loved me as though I were his own child; and after his day's work he used to come back splashed with mud, and so tired that he could scarcely move, while I stayed warm and comfortable in the house, and had nothing to do but eat. And now they're going to shoot him!"

At this Lisa protested, saying that he would certainly not be shot. But Quenu only shook his head.

"I haven't loved him half as much as I ought to have done," he continued. "I can see that very well now. I had a wicked heart, and I hesitated about giving him his half of the money."

"Why, I offered it to him a dozen times and more!" Lisa interrupted. "I'm sure we've nothing to reproach ourselves with."

"Oh, yes, I know that you are good, you would have given him everything you had… But I hesitated, I didn't like to part with it; and now it will be a sorrow to me for the rest of my life. I shall always think that if I'd shared the fortune with him he wouldn't have gone wrong a second time. Oh, yes; it's my fault! It is I who have driven him to this."

Then Lisa, expostulating still more gently, assured him that he had nothing to blame himself for and even expressed some pity for Florent. But he was really very culpable, she said, and if he had had more money he would probably have perpetrated greater follies. Gradually she gave her husband to understand that it was impossible matters could have had any other termination, and that now everything would go on much better. Quenu was still weeping, wiping his cheeks with his apron, trying to suppress his sobs to listen to her, and then breaking into a wilder fit of tears than before. His fingers had mechanically sought a heap of sausage meat lying on the block, and he was digging holes in it, and roughly kneading it together. "And how unwell you were feeling, you know," Lisa continued. "It was all because our life had got so shifted out of its usual course. I was very anxious, though I didn't tell you so, at seeing you getting so low."

"Yes, wasn't I?" he murmured, ceasing to sob for a moment.

"And the business has been quite under a cloud this year. It was as though a spell had been cast on it. Come, now, don't take on so; you'll see that everything will look up again now. You must take care of yourself, you know, for my sake and your daughter's. You have duties to us as well as to others, remember."

Quenu was now kneading the sausage meat more gently. Another burst of emotion was thrilling him, but it was a softer emotion, which was already bringing a vague smile to his grief-stricken face. Lisa felt that she had convinced him, and she turned and called to Pauline, who was playing in the shop, and sat her on Quenu's knee.

"Tell your father, Pauline, that he ought not to give way like this. Ask him nicely not to go on distressing us so."

The child did as she was told, and their fat, sleek forms united in a general embrace. They all three looked at one another, already feeling cured of that twelve months' depression from which they had but just emerged. Their big, round faces smiled, and Lisa softly repeated, "And after all, my dear, there are only we three, you know, only we three."

Two months later Florent was again sentenced to transportation. The affair caused a great stir. The newspapers published all possible details, and gave portraits of the accused, sketches of the banners and scarves, and plans of the places where the conspirators had met. For a fortnight nothing but the great plot of the central markets was talked of in Paris. The police kept on launching more and more alarming reports, and it was at last even declared that the whole of the Montmartre Quarter was undermined. The excitement in the Corps Législatif was so intense that the members of the Center and the Right forgot their temporary disagreement over the Imperial Grant Bill and became reconciled. And then by an overwhelming majority they voted the unpopular tax, of which even the lower classes, in the panic which was sweeping over the city, dared no longer complain.

The trial lasted a week. Florent was very much surprised at the number of accomplices with which he found himself credited. Out of the twenty and more who were placed in the dock with him, he knew only some six or seven. After the sentence of the court had been read, he fancied he could see Robine's innocent-looking hat and back going off quietly through the crowd. Logre was acquitted, as was also Lacaille; Alexandre was sentenced to two years' imprisonment for his child-like complicity in the conspiracy; while as for Gavard, he, like Florent, was condemned to transportation. This was a heavy blow, which quite crushed him amid the final enjoyment that he derived from those lengthy proceedings in which he had managed to make himself so conspicuous. He was paying very dearly for the way in which he had vented the spirit of perpetual opposition peculiar to the Paris shopkeeping classes. Two big tears coursed down his scared face—the face of a white-haired child.

And then one morning in August, amid the busy awakening of the markets, Claude Lantier, sauntering about in the thick of the arriving vegetables, with his waist tightly girded by his red sash, came to grasp Madame François's hand close by Saint Eustache. She was sitting on her carrots and turnips, and her long face looked very sad. The artist, too, was gloomy, notwithstanding the bright sun which was already softening the deep-green velvet of the mountains of cabbages.

"Well, it's all over now," he said. "They are sending him back again. He's already on his way to Brest, I believe."

Madame François made a gesture of mute grief. Then she gently waved her hand around and murmured in a low voice: "Ah, it is all Paris's doing, this villainous Paris!"

"No, no, not quite that; but I know whose doing it is, the contemptible creatures!" exclaimed Claude, clenching his fists. "Do you know, Madame François, there was nothing too ridiculous for those fellows in the court to say! Why, they even went ferreting in a child's copybooks! That great idiot of a Public Prosecutor made a tremendous fuss over them, and ranted about the respect due to children, and the wickedness of demagogical education! It makes me quite sick to think of it all!"

A shudder of disgust shook him, and then, burying himself more deeply in his discolored cloak, he resumed: "To think of it! A man who was as gentle as a girl! Why, I saw him turn quite faint at seeing a pigeon killed! I couldn't help smiling with pity when I saw him between two gendarmes. Ah, well, we shall never see him again! He won't come back this time."

"He ought to have listened to me," said Madame François, after a pause, "and have come to live at Nanterre with my fowls and rabbits. I was very fond of him, you see, for I could tell that he was a good-hearted fellow. Ah, we might have been so happy together! It's a sad pity. Well, we must bear it as best we can, Monsieur Claude. Come and see me one of these days. I'll have an omelet ready for you."

Her eyes were dim with tears; but all at once she sprang up like a brave woman who bears her sorrows with fortitude.

"Ah!" she exclaimed, "here's old Mother Chantemesse coming to buy some turnips of me. The fat old lady's as sprightly as ever!"

Claude went off and strolled about the footways. The dawn had risen in a white sheaf of light at the end of the Rue Rambuteau; and the sun, now level with the housetops, was diffusing rosy rays which already fell in warm patches on the pavements. Claude was conscious of a gay awakening in the huge resonant markets—indeed, all over the neighborhood—crowded with piles of food. It was like the joy that comes after cure, the mirth of folks who are at last relieved of a heavy weight which has been pulling them down. He saw La Sarriette displaying a gold chain and singing amid her plums and strawberries, while she playfully pulled the moustaches of Monsieur Jules, who was arrayed in a velvet jacket. He also caught sight of Madame Lecœur and Mademoiselle Saget passing along one of the covered ways, and looking less sallow than usual—indeed, almost rosy—as they laughed like bosom friends over some amusing story. In the fish market, old Madame Méhudin, who had returned to her stall, was slapping her fish, abusing customers, and snubbing the new inspector, a presumptuous young man whom she had sworn to spank; while Claire, seemingly more languid and indolent than ever, extended her hands, blue from immersion in the water of her tanks, to gather together a great heap of edible snails, shimmering with silvery slime. In the tripe market Auguste and Augustine, with the foolish expression of newly-married people, had just been purchasing some pigs' trotters and were starting off in a trap for their pork shop at Montrouge. Then, as it was now eight o'clock and already quite warm, Claude, on again coming to the Rue Rambuteau, perceived Muche and Pauline playing at horses. Muche was crawling along on all fours, while Pauline sat on his back and clung to his hair to keep herself from falling. However, a moving shadow which fell from the eaves of the market roof made Claude look up; and he then spied Cadine and Marjolin aloft, kissing and warming themselves in the sunshine, parading their loves before the whole neighborhood like a pair of light-hearted animals.

Claude shook his fist at them. All this joyousness down below and on high exasperated him. He reviled the Fat; the Fat, he declared, had conquered the Thin. All around him he could see none but the Fat protruding their paunches, bursting with robust health, and greeting with delight another day of gorging and digestion. And a last blow was dealt to him by the spectacle which he perceived on either hand as he halted opposite the Rue Pirouette.

On his right, the beautiful Norman, or the beautiful Madame Lebigre, as she was now called, stood at the door of her shop. Her husband had at length been granted the privilege of adding a State tobacco agency to his wine shop, a long-cherished dream of his which he had finally been able to realize through the great services he had rendered to the authorities. And to Claude the beautiful Madame Lebigre looked superb, with her silk dress and her frizzed hair, quite ready to take her seat behind her counter, to which all the gentlemen in the neighborhood flocked to buy their cigars and packets of tobacco. She had become quite distinguished, quite the lady. The shop behind her had been newly painted, with borders of twining vine-branches showing against a soft background; the zinc-plated wine counter gleamed brightly, and in the tall mirror the flasks of liqueurs set brighter flashes of color than ever. And the mistress of all these things stood smiling radiantly at the bright sunshine.

Then, on Claude's left, the beautiful Lisa blocked up the doorway of her shop as she stood on its threshold. Never before had her linen shone with such dazzling whiteness; never had her serene face and rosy cheeks appeared in a more lustrous setting of glossy locks. She displayed the deep calmness of repletion, a massive tranquillity unruffled even by a smile. She was a picture of absolute quietude, of perfect felicity, not only cloudless but lifeless, the simple felicity of basking in the warm atmosphere. Her tightly-stretched bodice seemed to be still digesting the happiness of yesterday; while her dimpled hands hidden in the folds of her apron, did not even trouble to grasp at the happiness of today, certain as they were that it would come of itself. And the shop window at her side seemed to display the same felicity. It had recovered from its former blight; the tongues lolled out, red and healthy; the hams had regained their old chubbiness of form; the festoons of sausages no longer wore that mournful air which had so greatly distressed Quenu. Hearty laughter, accompanied by a jubilant clattering of pans, sounded from the kitchen in the rear. The whole place again reeked with fat health. The flitches of bacon and the sides of pork that hung against the marble showed roundly like paunches, triumphant paunches, while Lisa, with her imposing breadth of shoulders and dignity of mien, bade the markets good morning with those big eyes of hers which so clearly bespoke a gross feeder.

However, the two women bowed to each other. Beautiful Madame Lebigre and beautiful Madame Quenu exchanged a friendly salute.

And then Claude, who had certainly forgotten to dine on the previous day, was thrilled with anger at seeing them standing there, looking so healthy and well-to-do with their buxom bosoms; and tightening his sash, he growled in a tone of irritation:

"What blackguards respectable people are!"

EMILE ZOLA

Emile Zola was born in Paris in 1840, and was raised at Aix-en-Provence in a poor family whose father died seven years after his birth. Zola was educated at the Collège Bourbon at Aix and at the Lycée Saint-Louis in Paris.

He began working as a clerk upon failing his *baccalauréat* in 1859, but in the mid-1860s he decided to support himself by literature alone. Within the next few years, Zola published several of his great masterworks, including *Thérèse Raquin* (1867) and *Madeleine Férat* (1868). In 1868 Zola also began his incredible series of novels, *Les Rougon-Macquart,* which consists of over twenty fictions intended to reveal, in scientific terms, the effects of heredity and environment on one family. This series, appearing between 1871 and 1893, is one of the chief monuments of the French Naturalist Movement and includes some of Zola's best writing. *The Belly of Paris,* published in 1873, was the third novel of that series.

Upon completion of this series, Zola embarked on a new cycle of novels, *Les Trois Villes: Lourdes, Rome, Paris,* written in 1894, 1896 and 1898. He died in 1902.

SUN & MOON CLASSICS

PIERRE ALFERI [France]
  Natural Gaits 95 (1-55713-231-3, $10.95)
  The Familiar Path of the Fighting Fish [in preparation]

DAVID ANTIN [USA]
  Death in Venice: Three Novellas [in preparation]
  Selected Poems: 1963–1973 10 (1-55713-058-2, $13.95)

ECE AYHAN [Turkey]
  A Blind Cat AND *Orthodoxies* [in preparation]

DJUNA BARNES [USA]
  Ann Portuguise [in preperation]
  The Antiphon [in preparation]
  At the Roots of the Stars: The Short Plays 53 (1-55713-160-0, $12.95)
  Biography of Julie von Bartmann [in preparation]
  The Book of Repulsive Women 59 (1-55713-173-2, $6.95)
  Collected Stories [in preparation]
  Interviews 86 (0-940650-37-1, $12.95)
  New York 5 (0-940650-99-1, $12.95)
  Smoke and Other Early Stories 2 (1-55713-014-0, $9.95)

CHARLES BERNSTEIN [USA]
  Content's Dream: Essays 1975–1984 49 (0-940650-56-8, $14.95)
  Dark City 48 (1-55713-162-7, $11.95)
  Republics of Reality: 1975–1995 [in preparation]
  Rough Trades 14 (1-55713-080-9, $10.95)

JENS BJØRNEBOE [Norway]
  The Bird Lovers 43 (1-55713-146-5, $9.95)
  Semmelweis [in preparation]

ANDRÉ DU BOUCHET [France]
  The Indwelling [in preparation]
  Today the Day [in preparation]
  Where Heat Looms [in preparation]

ANDRÉ BRETON [France]
  Arcanum 17 51 (1-55713-170-8, $12.95)
  Earthlight 26 (1-55713-095-7, $12.95)

HEIMITO VON DODERER [Austria]
The Demons 13 (1-55713-030-2, $29.95)
Every Man a Murderer 66 (1-55713-183-X, $14.95)
The Merovingians [in preparation]

JOSÉ DONOSO [Chile]
Hell Has No Limits 101 (1-55713-187-2, $10.95)

ARKADII DRAGOMOSCHENKO [Russia]
Description 9 (1-55713-075-2, $11.95)
Phosphor [in preparation]
Xenia 29 (1-55713-107-4, $12.95)

JOSÉ MARIA DE EÇA DE QUEIROZ [Portugal]
The City and the Mountains [in preparation]
The Mandarins [in preparation]

LARRY EIGNER [USA]
readiness / enough / depends / on [in preparation]

RAYMOND FEDERMAN [b. France/USA]
Smiles on Washington Square 60 (1-55713-181-3, $10.95)
The Twofold Vibration [in preparation]

RONALD FIRBANK [England]
Santal 58 (1-55713-174-0, $7.95)

DOMINIQUE FOURCADE [France]
Click-Rose [in preparation]
Xbo 35 (1-55713-067-1, $9.95)

SIGMUND FREUD [Austria]
Delusion and Dream in Wilhelm Jensen's GRADIVA 38
  (1-55713-139-2, $11.95)

MAURICE GILLIAMS [Belgium/Flanders]
Elias, or The Struggle with the Nightingales 79 (1-55713-206-2, $12.95)

LILIANE GIRAUDON [France]
Fur 114 (1-55713-222-4, $12.95)
Pallaksch, Pallaksch 61 (1-55713-191-0, $12.95)

ALFREDO GIULIANI [Italy]
Ed. *I Novissimi: Poetry for the Sixties* 55
  (1-55713-137-6, $14.95)
Verse and Nonverse [in preparation]

EMMANUEL HOCQUARD [France]
The Cape of Good Hope [in preparation]

SIGURD HOEL [Norway]
The Road to the World's End 75 (1-55713-210-0, $13.95)

FANNY HOWE [USA]
The Deep North 15 (1-55713-105-8, $9.95)
Radical Love: A Trilogy [in preparation]
Saving History 27 (1-55713-100-7, $12.95)

SUSAN HOWE [USA]
The Europe of Trusts 7 (1-55713-009-4, $10.95)

LAURA (RIDING) JACKSON [USA]
Lives of Wives 71 (1-55713-182-1, $12.95)

HENRY JAMES [USA]
The Awkward Age [in preparation]
What Maisie Knew [in preparation]

LEN JENKIN [USA]
Dark Ride and Other Plays 22 (1-55713-073-6, $13.95)
Careless Love 54 (1-55713-168-6, $9.95)
Pilgrims of the Night: Five Plays [in preparation]

WILHELM JENSEN [Germany]
Gradiva 38 (1-55713-139-2, $13.95)

JEFFREY M. JONES [USA]
The Crazy Plays and Others [in preparation]
J. P. Morgan Saves the Nation 157 (1-55713-256-9, $9.95)
Love Trouble 78 (1-55713-198-8, $9.95)
Night Coil [in preparation]

SEVE KATZ [USA]
Florry of Washington Heights [in preparation]
43 Fictions 18 (1-55713-069-8, $12.95)
Swanny's Ways [in preparation]
Wier & Pouce [in preparation]

ALEXEI KRUCHENYKH [Russia]
Suicide Circus: Selected Poems [in preparation]

THOMAS LA FARGE [USA]
Terror of Earth [in preparation]

JOHN WIENERS [USA]
The Journal of John Wieners / is to be called [in preparation]

ÉMILE ZOLA [France]
The Belly of Paris (1-55713-066-3, $14.95)

*

Individuals order from:
Sun & Moon Press
6026 Wilshire Boulevard
Los Angeles, California 90036
213-857-1115

Libraries and Bookstores in the United States and Canada
should order from:
Consortium Book Sales & Distribution
1045 Westgate Drive, Suite 90
Saint Paul, Minnesota 55114-1065
800-283-3572
FAX 612-221-0124

Libraries and Bookstores in the United Kingdom and on the Continent
should order from:
Password Books Ltd.
23 New Mount Street
Manchester M4 4DE, ENGLAND
0161 953 4009
INTERNATIONAL +44 61 953-4009
0161 953 4090